H·I·D·D·E·N

A Novel

P·L·A·C·E·S

Books by
Lynn Austin
FROM BETHANY HOUSE PUBLISHERS

All She Ever Wanted

Eve's Daughters

Hidden Places

Wings of Refuge

REFINER'S FIRE

Candle in the Darkness

Fire by Night

A Light to My Path

CHRONICLES OF THE KINGS

Gods and Kings

Song of Redemption

The Strength of His Hand

Faith of My Fathers

Among the Gods

-LYNN AUSTIN-

H·I·D·D·E·N

A Novel

P·L·A·C·E·S

BethanyHouse

MINNEAPOLIS, MINNESOTA

Hidden Places
Copyright © 2001
Lynn Austin

Cover design by Lookout Design Group, Inc.

Published by Bethany House Publishers
11400 Hampshire Avenue South
Bloomington, Minnesota 55438

Bethany House Publishers is a division of
Baker Publishing Group, Grand Rapids, Michigan.

Printed in the United States of America

ISBN-13: 978-0-7642-2197-2
ISBN-10: 0-7642-2197-3

Library of Congress Cataloging-in-Publication Data

Austin, Lynn N.
    Hidden places / by Lynn N. Austin.
        p.   cm.
    ISBN 0-7642-2197-3 (pbk.)
    1. Depressions—Fiction. 2. Orchards—Fiction 3. Widows—
Fiction. I. Title.
    PS3551.U839 H54   2001
    813'.54—dc21   2001002252

With heartfelt thanks to my
faithful fellow writers:
Florence Anglin, Joy Bocanegra,
Cleo Lampos, and Jane Rubietta

and to
Charlotte and George Gatchell
Gatchell Apple Farm, St. Joseph, MI

and to
Tom and Laurel McGrath
for introducing me to Winky

"In the life of each of us . . .
there is a place,
remote and islanded,
and given to endless regret
or secret happiness."

—Sarah Orne Jewett

They say everybody has a guardian angel watching out for them, but I'd never needed one half as badly as I did after Frank Wyatt died. Frank was my father-in-law, the last remaining Wyatt man in the whole clan.

My husband's Aunt Betty put the idea of a guardian angel into my head. She said she'd pray for one to come and help me out. The last time I'd given any thought to angels was years earlier in a Sunday school class in one of the many whistle-stop towns my daddy and I passed through in our travels. Daddy always made sure I went to church if we happened upon one on a Sunday morning. That Sunday I was in a Methodist church somewhere in Missouri when the little old white-haired Sunday school teacher said we should always entertain strangers because you never knew if one of them just might be an angel. That's the way she put it—

"entertain" them. She made me think I had to juggle balls or do a high-wire act for them, and I wondered what on earth that little old teacher could possibly do that was entertaining, as bent and wrinkled as she was.

So after we laid Frank Wyatt to rest in the family plot beside his wife and two sons, I began hoping God would answer Aunt Betty's prayers soon and that an angel really would show up to help me out. I'd worry about entertaining him once he got here.

"What are you going to do now, Eliza?"

That's what everybody kept asking me after the funeral, and I hardly knew what to say. What they were really asking was "How's a scrawny young thing like you, with three little kids to raise, ever going to run a big outfit like Wyatt Orchards?" Especially since I never even stepped one foot on a farm until ten years ago. Of course, they didn't know about my past—no one in Deer Springs knew, not even my poor dead husband, Sam. I was too ashamed to tell anybody. But people wondered how I was going to manage, just the same. My neighbor, Alvin Greer, was one of them.

"What're you planning to do, Mrs. Wyatt, now that Frank is dead?"

I filled his coffee cup and handed it to him without answering. Couldn't he see that I'd buried my father-in-law scarcely an hour ago and that my house was still filled with all the neighbors who had come to pay their last respects and that I didn't even have time to think? I guess not, because Mr. Greer wouldn't let up.

"Do you have someone in mind to take over Wyatt Orchards for you, come springtime?" he asked.

I filled another cup and offered it to Reverend Dill, who stood in the serving line behind Mr. Greer. I tried not to let my hands shake too much. I'd learned a long time ago that if you don't answer right away, most people get antsy and begin filling up the silence themselves, usually by offering you a piece of their own advice. This time Reverend Dill spoke up first.

"Do you have family close by we could send for, Mrs. Wyatt? I don't believe I ever heard tell where your people are from, exactly."

"You take cream in that, Reverend?" I asked, offering him the pitcher and ignoring his question.

He shook his head. "No, thanks. I take mine black. You're not from Deer Springs originally, are you?"

"No. I'm not." I made myself busy with straightening a pile of teaspoons and checking to see if the sugar bowl needed filling. It was none of his business who my people were or where I came from. This rambling farmhouse with the well-worn furniture and faded wallpaper was my home now and had been for ten years. My three children and I had a right to live here—with or without Frank Wyatt and his son Sam.

"Of course, there's no chance you could ever sell this place with the country sunk in a depression like it is," the reverend added. "The banks have no money to lend."

"Well, she can't run the orchard by herself!" Mr. Greer sounded huffy.

I took a step back, trying to excuse myself by pretending the coffeepot needed refilling. Let the two of them argue about my future if it interested them so much. But my husband's Aunt Betty blocked my escape. Her fingers clamped onto my arm like they were wired with clothespin springs.

"You're ignoring those busybodies on purpose, aren't you, Toots?" she whispered. "I do the same thing. If you act dumb, then people think you really are dumb, and they leave you alone."

Aunt Betty reminded me of a pet parakeet. Her nose stuck out just like a parakeet's beak and she darted all around like a happy little bird wherever she went. She was tiny and plump. Her fluffy gray head barely reached to my chin, and I was not much taller than a schoolgirl myself. Unlike all the drab old crows in town, Aunt Betty dressed in brightly colored clothing like some rare tropical bird, never caring what the occasion was. Today she wore a flowery summer shift, lacy white gloves, and a broad-brimmed straw hat, as if she were on her way to a Fourth of July picnic, not her brother-in-law's funeral on a raw November day. I've seen her walking her one-eyed dog down the road wearing a bright pink bathrobe and slippers, and I've seen her roaming through the orchard in a man's tweed suit and trousers, too. Sam had always called her "Aunt Batty" behind her back. *"She has a few bats in her belfry,"* he would say, and he'd twirl his finger beside his head like the spring of a cuckoo clock. My father-in-law had given me strict orders to steer clear of her.

"It's nobody's business but yours who you are and where your kin's from," Aunt Betty said as she finally unclasped her fingers from my arm. She had a huge straw purse slung over one arm, and she hummed "Joy to the World" as she picked her way around the dining room table, wrapping a chicken leg, two dill pickles, and a slab of spice cake in paper napkins and stuffing them inside her bag. "For later," she explained with a grin. Grease and pickle juice stained the tips of her white gloves.

Mr. Greer and Reverend Dill finally wandered away from the table, still arguing over what should be done with Wyatt Orchards. I breathed a sigh of relief and went back to serving folks.

"Would you like some coffee, Aunt Betty?" I asked when she finished her tour around the table.

"No thanks, Toots. It would just run out of my purse and onto your nice clean floor." She laughed like a mischievous child, and I couldn't help smiling. "By the way," she added, "no one calls me Betty, don't you know that? They haven't for years. It's *Batty*. My name was changed from Betty to *Batty*. People always get their names changed after they've seen God—Abram became Abra-

ham, Sarai changed to Sarah, Jacob to Israel. . . ." She paused to
sniff a deviled egg before adding it to the collection in her purse.
"I've seen God, too, you know. I knew it was Him by His eyes."
She clutched my arm again and leaned close to whisper, "God has
very kind eyes."

Now, I had always pictured God's eyes as sort of tired-looking
ever since I heard a Baptist preacher in Kentucky say that the eyes
of the Lord ran to and fro throughout the whole earth. But I suppose they could be tired and kind at the same time.

Aunt Batty stood on tiptoes to survey the roomful of people,
then tilted her head toward my parlor where a group of church
women stood in a huddle. "You know what those old hens over
there are whispering about?" she asked. "They're discussing how
shocked they all are to see me at Frank's funeral. He was my beau
first, you know, before my sister, Lydia, married him. They think
I've held a grudge all these years, but you know what? I had a
guardian angel looking out for me. That's how I escaped Frank
Wyatt—a guardian angel." She laughed again and dropped a baking powder biscuit into her bottomless purse. "You married my
nephew Sam, didn't you?"

A lump the size of a peach pit suddenly stuck in my throat. I
had to swallow it down before I could answer. "Yes . . . but he's
dead, Aunt Batty. Sam died a year ago, remember?"

Her eyes filled with tears as she stared into space. "My sister,
Lydia, had three boys—Matthew was the oldest, then Samuel, then
young Willie. Poor little Willie died way back in 1910, wasn't it?
Or maybe it was 1911, my memory never was very good." She
parted the lacy dining room curtains with her gloved hand and
pointed to my three children playing in the backyard. "Seems like
only yesterday Lydia's boys were running all around like those
youngsters."

Jimmy, Luke, and Becky Jean had been fidgeting so badly in

their Sunday clothes that I'd finally turned them loose to play. I didn't care if the church women whispered behind their hands about how improper it was for children to be running wild an hour after their granddaddy was laid to rest.

"Those are my three young ones," I said. "Mine and Sam's."

"Well, you look like a mere child yourself," Batty said, "barely old enough to be a wife, let alone a widow. Poor Sammy. And now his father is gone, too? My, my . . . I guess that makes me your closest kin here in Deer Springs." She shook her head, and the black-mesh mourning veil which she had stuck to her straw hat with a piece of sticky tape came loose and fluttered to the floor. "Some folks say this house is jinxed or under a curse, you know. One tragedy after another, over the years. First little Willie died, then young Matthew left us like he did, then my sister died . . . But none of those were accidents. I don't care what folks tell you, young lady."

"Not . . . accidents?" I didn't want to think about what else they could be.

"No, sir! There's a huge load of grief up in the attic of this house. Have you been up there lately? Probably a big pile of it down in the cellar, too."

I watched my children playing tag beneath the clotheslines, and I wanted to tell Aunt Batty that the grief had long-since overflowed the attic and the basement. It was deep enough and wide enough to fill the entire barn.

Aunt Batty squeezed my shoulder. "If you ever need any help shoveling it all out, you give me a call, all right? I live in the cottage down by the pond. What did they say your name was again?"

"Eliza Rose, ma'am. Eliza Rose Wyatt."

Aunt Batty shook her head. "My! That's too much grief for one house to bear." Her purse bumped against my hip as she circled her arm around my waist. "What you need, Toots, is your own guardian angel to watch out for you. Help you out in your time of need. Tell you what—I'll ask God to send you one the next time I see Him, all right?"

I thought of the words my daddy used to say when he tucked me into bed at night—"May the Lord keep His angels 'round about you"—and I had to swallow another big lump.

"I suppose it wouldn't hurt to ask for one, Aunt Batty," I said.

PART I

Wyatt Orchards

Winter 1931

"Do not forget to entertain strangers: for thereby some have

entertained angels unawares."

HEBREWS 13 : 2

— CHAPTER ONE —

February 1931

I had just stepped out the kitchen door into the frozen February night when the stranger startled me half to death. I hadn't heard any automobiles rattling down the long, deserted lane to my farmhouse, so when a shadow in the darkness suddenly turned into the large form of a man, he scared me so bad I dropped a coal scuttle full of ashes down the porch steps. I had to clutch my heart with both hands to keep it from jumping out of my rib cage.

"Forgive me, ma'am. I never meant to frighten you," the stranger said. Even in the dark I could tell he was truly sorry. He had his arm stretched out, like he would gladly catch me if I dropped dead of fright.

"That's okay," I said. "I didn't hear you drive up, is all."

"I didn't drive. I came on foot." He lowered the burlap sack he carried and bent to scoop the spilled ashes back into the scuttle with his hands.

"Careful, those cinders might still be warm."

"Yes, ma'am. Feels good, though." His hands were bare, and he wore no hat—only layers of ragged clothing against the numbing cold. His overgrown hair and bushy beard hid most of his face from view. But it was his odor, the strong smell of unwashed flesh and wood smoke, that told me plain as day that the stranger was a hobo—one of the many thousands that roamed across America looking for work that winter. He must have tramped through the orchard from the railroad tracks, drawn by the light of my farm-house windows.

"Your house is marked," old Abe Walker told me the last time I paid a visit to his general store in Deer Springs. "That's what them tramps do, you know. Once they learn you're a kindhearted Christian woman, they mark your house for the next fellow. You ought to chase them off, Eliza Rose. 'Tisn't safe to have them hanging around, you being a widow and all."

Abe Walker didn't know that I'd grown up with kinkers and lot-loafers and roustabouts, so I was a pretty good judge of people. I knew who to invite inside and who to send packing.

"May I have a word with your husband, ma'am?" the stranger asked, startling me a second time.

"My . . . my husband?"

"Yes, ma'am. I was wondering if he had some odd jobs I could do in exchange for a meal." The tramp had a gentle voice, soft-spoken, polite. I thought of all the endless chores that needed to be done around here—milk buckets to wash, kindling to split, coal to fetch, animals to feed, fences to mend—and I felt tired clear to my bones.

"Why don't you come inside and have a bite to eat," I said. "It's too cold to stand around out here. Just leave those ashes on the porch." I turned and opened the kitchen door for him, but he didn't move.

"I don't mind eating outside. And I'm willing to do some chores first."

It was hard to tell how old the stranger was in the darkness. His voice was neither young nor old. I felt sorry for him, though. In spite of his many layers of clothing, he stood hunched against the cold, shivering.

"We just finished our supper," I said. "The food is still warm. Please come in."

He slowly followed me inside, then stood close to the kitchen door while I sliced some bread, fetched a clean soup bowl, ladled a helping of leftovers into it, and poured him a cup of coffee. When I turned to ask him to sit, he startled me once more—for a split second he reminded me of my husband. The stranger was nearly as tall and broad-shouldered as Sam had been, and he stood exactly like Sam used to stand with one shoulder hitched a little higher than the other, his head cocked to one side as if listening for a sound in the distance. Then the moment passed, and I saw how very different from Sam he really was—dark-haired while Sam had been fair, brown-eyed while Sam's eyes had been as blue as a summer sky.

"Won't you sit down?" I asked. I set the bowl of stewed chicken, carrots, and dumplings on the table and passed him the bread.

"Thank you, ma'am."

I could have sworn I saw the shine of tears in his eyes as he lowered himself into the chair like a very old man. Then he surprised me by folding his hands and bowing his head to pray, just like Sam and his daddy always used to do before they ate.

Across the table from him, my four-year-old daughter gaped at the stranger through wide gray eyes, her fork hanging in the air as she picked at the remains of her dinner. The bare light bulb above the table lit up her coppery hair like flames.

"Quit staring and finish your dinner, Becky Jean," I said. I didn't mean to sound so cross all the time, but lately my words just seemed to jump out of my mouth that way. I turned back to my sink full of dishes, and when I glimpsed my reflection in the kitchen window, I saw a face that was too harsh, too care-worn for a woman just thirty years old. With all those worry lines and my sandy hair drooping in my eyes, I looked nothing at all like the young girl Sam had once called "pretty as a picture."

"My mama won't let you leave the table till you eat all your carrots," Becky told the stranger. "I don't like carrots, do you?"

"Well, yes, miss. As a matter of fact, I like carrots a lot."

"Want mine?" she asked.

"Oh no, you don't," I said. "You finish your dinner, Becky Jean, and let the man finish his." I planted my hands on my hips, watching Becky like a hawk until she finally bit off a tiny piece of carrot. I could tell by the way the man was shoveling food into his mouth that he hadn't eaten for quite some time. I dished him a second helping.

"Don't you want to take your coat off, mister?" Becky asked him a few minutes later.

"No, thank you. It's hardly worth the bother. I'll be going back outside in just a bit." He spoke softly, as if there were a baby sleeping nearby and he didn't want to wake it. But the mood was broken a moment later by the sound of footsteps thundering down the stairs, jumping from the landing to the hallway floor, then racing into the kitchen. I didn't need to turn around to know that it was my son Jimmy. He was nine years old, and he galloped like a spring colt wherever he went.

"Mama, can you help me with my—" He froze in the doorway when he saw the stranger. Jimmy's light brown hair was too long again, hanging in his eyes like a patch of overgrown weeds. I would have to cut it if I could get him to sit still that long.

"It's not polite to stare, Jimmy," I said. "Can't you say 'good evening' to our guest?"

"Good evening," he said. The stranger was caught with a mouthful of dumplings and could only nod in reply. A moment later, a redheaded shadow appeared in the doorway behind Jimmy—seven-year-old Luke. But I knew it would be useless to ask him to greet the man. Luke was as shy and as easily spooked as a stray cat.

"What did you need help with, Jimmy?" I asked, drying my hands on my apron.

"Spelling words." He skirted the table in a wide arc, as far away from the stranger as he could get, and handed me his notebook. Luke hovered close to his shirttail. The boys' eyes—as blue as their father's had been—never left the stranger. I was trying to decipher Jimmy's smudged writing when the man suddenly let out a yelp. I looked up to see him rubbing the back of his hand.

"Mama!" Jimmy said in amazement, "Becky just hauled off and poked that man with her fork!"

"Poked him?"

"Yeah, for no reason at all!"

"But I did have a reason!" Becky said. "I wanted to see if he was an angel!"

The hobo's dark brows lifted. "A what?"

"An angel," she repeated. She was on the verge of tears. "Mama's always feeding strangers 'cause she says they might be angels. But you wouldn't take your coat off, so I couldn't see if you had wings under there."

I gripped Becky's shoulder, shaking her slightly. "Becky Jean! You say you're sorry right now!" Instead, she covered her face and cried.

"No, no, there's no harm done," the man said. He had a nice smile, his teeth even and white. "I think I know which verse your mother means. It's from the book of Hebrews, isn't it, ma'am? 'Do not forget to entertain strangers: for thereby some have entertained angels unawares.' "

"Yes, that's right." I was so dumbfounded to hear a scruffy old hobo spouting off Scripture like a Sunday preacher that I didn't know what else to say.

Becky wiped her eyes with her fists, then looked up at the man again. "I'm sorry I poked you . . . but *are* you an angel?"

"I'm afraid not. Just an ordinary traveling man." He pushed his chair back from the table and stood. "I'm very grateful for the meal, ma'am," he said, bowing slightly. "It was delicious. Now, if there's something I can do for you in return, I'll be glad to do it."

"There's nothing that can't wait till morning. You're welcome to sleep in my husband's workshop out in the barn. There's a cot and a potbelly stove you can light if you're willing to haul your own firewood. You'll find a lantern and some matches on the shelf inside the doorway."

"Thanks again, ma'am." He lifted his hand as if to tip his hat but his head was already bare. He smiled sheepishly. "Good evening to you, then."

All that evening as I sat at the kitchen table helping Jimmy with his spelling words and arithmetic problems, I heard the hollow *crack* of an ax splitting firewood. Again and again the sound of splintering wood broke the silence, followed by the dull *thunk* of wood dropping to the porch floor as the man stacked it against the house.

"I won't have to chop any wood tomorrow," Jimmy said with a wide grin.

"Sounds like you won't have to chop any wood for a week," I said. "I wonder how he can see what he's doing in the dark."

The stranger didn't stop chopping until after the children were in bed. When I went into the kitchen to adjust the stove damper for the night, I saw his dark outline bending and moving against the white drifts, lifting and flinging the snow high into the air as he shoveled a path to the barn and the chicken coop.

Upstairs in my bedroom, I shivered in the cold as I undressed. I hadn't had much of an appetite since Sam died, and I couldn't seem to keep warm at night unless I wore two pairs of his woolen socks and a sweater over my nightgown. *"You're scrawny as a plucked chicken,"* Sam would probably say if he could see how skinny I'd become.

After switching off the light, I peered outside once more from my bedroom window. A wisp of smoke curled from the stovepipe in the workshop, lantern light glowed from inside the barn. But it was only after I lay curled in the cold, empty bed that I realized that I hadn't even asked the stranger his name.

———

I had grown so used to being alone on the farm that I forgot all about the hobo until I opened the kitchen door the next morning to fetch some firewood and saw the huge stack of it piled on the porch. I nearly tripped over the scuttle, which he had re-filled from the coal bin in the barn and set outside the door. Jimmy and I could walk side-by-side on the path the stranger had shoveled to the barn, and he had even sprinkled it with ashes so we wouldn't slip and fall with the milk buckets. But there was no smoke rising from the chimney in the workshop.

"Looks like our angel flew away again," I said.

"Already?" Jimmy sounded disappointed. "I think he must've been *my* guardian angel, chopping all that wood like he done." I followed my son into the dim, frosty barn, our breath hanging in the air in front of us. When Jimmy stopped suddenly, I nearly ran into him.

"Wow!" he said. "One man did all this? He must've worked all night!"

The stranger had shoveled all the manure from the stalls—a task I had been dreading—and he'd pitched a fresh supply of hay down from the loft and piled it within easy reach. There was a tidiness and an order to the barn that sent a small shiver down my spine. This was the work of a man who took pride in what he did—the way Sam used to keep things—not the make-do job of a weary mother and her young sons.

"Looks like he knew what to do and just did it," I mumbled. My eyes burned suddenly, as if smoke had gotten into them. I gave Jimmy a nudge to get him moving. "Come on, now. Quit your gawking and get to work or you'll be late for school."

When we finished milking the cows and feeding the horses, I sent Jimmy into the workshop to make sure the hobo had put the fire out. "And don't forget to close the flue," I warned him.

I'd no sooner unlatched the door to the chicken coop when I heard Jimmy shouting at me from across the barnyard. "Mama! Mama, come here! Quick!"

"What's wrong?" I hurried to where he stood by the open barn door. His freckles looked gray against his pale face.

"That man is just laying there by the stove," he said breathlessly, "and I can't wake him up!"

A cold chill shuddered through me. *Not again.*

Young Jimmy had been the one who'd found his grandfather lying dead on the barn floor three months ago. I could see the memory of that terrible afternoon in his frightened eyes.

"Oh, that old hobo is probably drunk, that's all," I said with a wave of my hand. "As poor as most tramps are, it seems like they can always get their hands on some liquor if they want to. I'll see to him. You hurry and get ready for school—and make sure Luke doesn't dawdle, either."

I found the stranger huddled on the cot in the workshop, wrapped in a filthy blanket. The slow rise and fall of his chest assured me that he wasn't dead. The room felt cold, the fire long gone out. I glanced around but didn't see any empty liquor bottles. He was probably exhausted from all the work he'd done—work that would have taken the boys and me an entire day to do. I felt a wave of pity for the man and carefully stepped around him to rebuild the fire before returning to my chores. His muscles would ache a lot less if he kept warm.

"Did the angel wake up, Mama?" Becky asked when I returned to the house. She still sat at the kitchen table, poking at her oatmeal in her slow, vexing way. I set the basket of eggs in the sink, then held my hands over the stove for a moment to warm them.

"He's just an ordinary hobo, Becky, not an angel."

"Is he . . . d-dead?" Luke asked.

"Of course not. You saw all the wood he chopped. The man is exhausted, that's all."

"He can have my oatmeal if he's hungry." Becky slid off her chair and picked up the bowl with both hands. "Can I take it out to him?"

"No you may not. He'll want bacon and eggs when he wakes up, and your oatmeal had better be in your tummy by then. I'm getting awfully tired of arguing with you over every meal, Becky Jean, especially when there are plenty of children going hungry in this country."

I sent the boys off to school beneath a dismal gray sky that threatened snow. By the time Becky and I finished washing the breakfast dishes and the milk pails, flurries had begun. I mixed a double batch of bread, thinking the stranger might like a fresh loaf to take with him, but when I had it all kneaded and rising in the warming oven, I still saw no sign of him. Leaving Becky with her paper dolls, I pulled on my boots and coat and hiked through the swirling snowflakes to check on him.

"Mister. . . ?" I said, shaking his shoulder. "Hey, mister . . . you all right?" When he didn't respond, I shook him harder and harder, a sense of panic rising inside me like a flock of frightened birds. "Hey, there! Hey, wake up!" He finally stirred, moaning slightly, and I saw by his glazed eyes and flushed cheeks that it wasn't strong drink or exhaustion that had felled him. It was a fever.

I quickly backed away from him. What if he had something contagious, like polio? My children had been exposed to him last night, Jimmy had been in here this morning, touching him. I quickly tossed a few more logs on the fire, then closed the door of the workshop to let him sleep.

By afternoon the snow was falling thick and heavy. The boys arrived home from school early, stamping the fresh snow from their feet, their cheeks and ears raw from the cold. "The teacher sent us home before the storm gets too bad," Jimmy said.

"And there m-might not be s-school tomorrow," Luke added. The idea must have excited him; it was the longest sentence he'd uttered in a month.

I ruffled his sweaty red hair before hanging his hat and mittens on the drying bar beside the stove. The smell of wet wool began to float through the kitchen, replacing the aroma of fresh bread.

"Good thing that angel chopped all that wood for me," Jimmy said. He wiped steam from the kitchen window with his fist as he peered out at the barn. "Did he leave before the storm started?"

"No, he was still in the workshop last time I looked," I said. "He's sick with a fever, so I don't want you boys going anywhere near him, you hear me? In fact, I'd better go check on him myself. I expect he's hungry by now." I spooned some of the broth from last night's stew into a small milk pail and wrapped a slice of buttered bread in a clean dish towel before bundling up for the trek outside.

The wind had piled the fresh snow into deep mounds, erasing the path to the barn. My feet felt heavy as I plodded through the drifts, and the blowing snow stung as the wind whipped it against my face. The familiar outlines of the farmyard looked like a smudged drawing, while beyond the barn the orchard had vanished in a swirl of gray.

The workshop felt cold again. I knelt beside the stranger's cot and shook him until he finally awoke. His eyes were glazed, feverish, and I could tell by the panicked look in them that he had no idea where he was.

"It's okay . . . you're in my barn. You came to my farmhouse last night, remember?" He moved his lips, as if trying to speak, but all that came out was a moan. I lifted his head and helped him take a few sips of the broth. "Listen, I need to know what's wrong with you, mister. I have three children to think about, and I hear there's all kinds of sickness down in those hobo camps."

"My leg," he whispered.

"Your leg? May I see?" He nodded, closing his eyes again. I laid his head down and set aside the broth.

As soon as I lifted the covers off his feet, I saw where the right leg of his trousers had been torn. The fabric was dark and stiff with dried blood. Underneath, he had tied a rag around his leg. I gently unwound the bloodied cloth and saw a jagged cut that ran down his shin from his knee to his ankle. It was swollen and inflamed, festering. He would have blood poisoning at the very least, and I couldn't bear to imagine the very worst. Once in a lifetime was enough to have witnessed the horror of lockjaw. Angry tears filled my eyes.

"How dare you!" I cried, flinging the blanket over his leg again. "How dare you come crawling to *my* house to die, like some mangy old dog! Haven't we been through enough? Why couldn't you have gone on down the road to the next farm or the next town? Someplace that hasn't had the angel of death camped on their doorstep for as long as I care to recall! How dare you pick *my* house!"

He opened his eyes and looked at me. I couldn't tell if the tears I saw were his or my own. I covered my face in shame, weeping silently.

"Mama?"

I whirled and saw Jimmy in the doorway behind me. Luke stood beside him, looking frightened.

"I thought I told both of you to stay away from here!"

"Is he going to die, too, Mama?" Jimmy asked.

"He might."

I stood, wiping my tears on the sleeve of my coat. The old barn creaked as a gust of wind rocked into the side of it; pellets of snow hissed against the windowpane. "We can't leave him out here," I said. "We can't be running in and out all night to tend to him. Go get your sled and help me bring him inside."

I gripped the man beneath his arms and the boys each took one of his feet as we dragged him through the barn none too gently, then hoisted him onto Luke's sled. The stranger surely weighed more than the three of us put together. It took a great deal of pushing and shoving to pull him through the deep drifts to the house. He gritted his teeth through most of the jostling but finally cried out as we hauled him up the porch steps. The jolt of pain seemed to rouse him momentarily, and he was able to bear some of his own weight on his good leg as we helped him into Grandpa Wyatt's old bed in the spare room off the kitchen. Becky watched, wide-eyed, from the foot of the bed as we settled him into it.

"Is he going to die?" she asked.

I saw the fear on my children's faces and my anger for the intruder returned. "I don't know. He's in the Lord's hands now. We'll do the best we can for him, but whatever happens is up to God."

I hated my helplessness. I didn't have a telephone and I couldn't drive into town to fetch the doctor because of the storm. *It doesn't matter,* I told myself in an attempt to push away my own fear. I didn't even know this man. Besides, it was likely his own foolishness that had gotten him into this mess.

"He stinks," Becky said, pinching her nose shut.

"He does indeed. Fill up the kettle, Becky Jean, and put it on to boil. You boys help me get him out of these . . . these rags he's wearing." We stripped him to his tattered long johns and set his clothes outside on the porch. Then I cleaned the wound on his leg as gently as I could and applied a hot poultice, prepared the way the doctor had shown me when he'd treated Sam's injury. The stranger, only half conscious, seemed barcly aware of what we were doing.

"We'll leave him be for now," I said after I'd finished. "There's no time to fuss over him with chores to do." I made up my mind to tend to him on my own. The less my children were involved with the stranger, the easier it would be for them if he died. Even so, his welfare seemed to fill their thoughts that evening—more than the snowstorm, which still raged outside.

"Please don't let the angel man die," Becky prayed when she said grace at suppertime. Luke surprised me when he whispered, "Amen." As for myself, I had no faith in the power of prayer to heal him. God would do whatever He wanted to do, regardless of our feeble pleading.

By the time we finished the evening chores, I felt more exhausted than usual from the added effort of struggling through snow and wind to do them. I waited until after the children were in bed before going back into the stranger's room with a fresh poultice, dreading what I would find. His eyes were open and I could read the pain in them, even though the only light in the room came from the open door to the kitchen. He shivered in spite of all the quilts we'd heaped on top of him. When I laid the hot cloths on his leg he stiffened, sucking in air through his teeth.

"Sorry. I'm trying to help you, not hurt you."

"I know," he whispered. "Thank you."

"You feeling hungry? I can fetch you something."

He shook his head. "Just water . . . please . . ."

I turned away, suddenly unable to face him. "Listen, I'm sorry for yelling at you like I did out in the barn earlier. It's just that . . ." I squeezed my eyes shut, remembering. "It's just that my husband died from a cut on his foot not even half as bad as yours. The doctor said it was lockjaw. There was nothing I could do but watch him suffer. And . . . and it wasn't an easy death."

"It's not your fault if I die," he said softly.

"I know." I fought back my tears and returned to his bedside, steadying his head while he sipped some water. "What's your name?" I asked. His answer was a weak whisper I couldn't understand.

I soaked a washcloth in the basin of soapy water I'd prepared and washed the grime off his face—something I'd been itching to do since we'd brought him inside. It was hard to tell his age because his shaggy, dark brown hair and beard looked as though they hadn't been cut in a long time. His face was deeply tanned under the layer of dirt, and his eyes, under thick brows, were the color of coffee beans. His calloused hands were large and strong, though warmer to the touch than the bath water. I unfastened the top button of his long johns to sponge his neck and chest and saw a terrible, jagged scar just above his heart. It had long-since healed, but I could tell that he must have dodged the angel of death at least once before.

By the time I finished, the water in the basin had turned black. "I'll let you sleep now," I said before leaving the room.

I carried the basin to the back porch to dump outside and noticed the stranger's burlap sack beside the door. Jimmy had brought it up from the barn and left it there. I lifted it and felt the weight of something heavy on the bottom, then heard the *clank* of metal as I set it on the kitchen table.

I felt like a Peeping Tom as I untied the knot around the mouth of the sack and began digging through his things. But how else was I ever going to find out the stranger's name and where he came from? A pair of mud-caked overalls and a flannel shirt lay on top. I set them aside to wash with his other clothes. Beneath them were a U.S. Army canteen and a well-worn Bible with its front cover torn. Inside a waterproof storm slicker I found a stack of notebooks—the kind Jimmy and Luke carried to school. Penciled writing filled all but one of the notebooks from one marbleized cover to the other. Stuffed inside the last one were three letters from the *Chicago Tribune*, addressed to Mr. Gabriel Harper at a post office box in Chicago. I said the name out loud—Gabriel Harper.

I didn't need to dig any further, but I couldn't resist the temptation to find out what the bulky thing on the very bottom of the sack was, wrapped inside an old blanket. I parted the folds of cloth and stared in surprise.

What an odd thing for a hobo to carry—a typewriter!

— CHAPTER TWO —

I awoke with a crick in my neck and was surprised to discover that I'd fallen asleep at the kitchen table. Outside, the sky was growing light. What on earth was I doing, sleeping downstairs all night? I stumbled to my feet, shivering and confused. Then I saw the notebooks spread out on the table and I remembered.

Simple curiosity had nudged me to open the first notebook and start reading. But in no time at all, the story of Gabriel Harper's travels as a hobo had wrapped me up in some kind of a spell and I couldn't stop. I had added more coal to the fire and kept on reading—devouring four notebooks before finally nodding off. Mr. Harper told tales of hopping boxcars and flatcars, crossing the Mississippi River, chugging over the Rocky Mountains, riding from the Canadian border to the Gulf of Mexico, from the Carolina coast to the forests of Washington State. He'd been chased by railroad guards and sheriffs' dogs; he'd eaten from tin cans and garbage pails; he'd slept in barns and in forests and beneath the Milky Way. He told fascinating stories of the other tramps he'd met—young rascals and old-timers, men and women; people with names like "Loony Lou" and "Boxcar Bertha." Some were down-on-their-luck and looking for work, others were content to live the free-wheeling life of a hobo.

But as interesting as all their stories had been, Gabriel Harper hadn't told his own story, and that's what had kept me reading all night. Who was this stranger who might be dying in my spare room, and what had led him to ride the rails as a hobo? I'd read beautiful descriptions of the many places Mr. Harper had been and the people he'd met, but I'd learned almost nothing about him.

Feeling guilty, I glanced at the door to the room where he slept, embarrassed to think he might have caught me reading his private journals, if that's what they were. I opened the spare room door a crack and looked in on him. When I was satisfied that he was still sound asleep, I quickly gathered up his things to rewrap in the waterproof slicker. The last notebook in the stack—the only one I hadn't read—caught my eye. Unlike the others, this one had a title written on the cover: *Prodigal Son.*

I recalled a sermon I'd heard in a Presbyterian church in Pittsburgh, Pennsylvania, about the prodigal son and how he'd run away and ended up eating with pigs. The story stuck in my mind because of all the P's—Presbyterian and Pittsburgh, Pennsylvania, and prodigal and pigs. That's how my mind remembers things.

Anyway, I couldn't resist opening Mr. Harper's story and seeing if it had any pigs or Presbyterians in it. I started to read:

I hate him. I love him. My only brother.
Simon and I shared the same room, the same childhood, the same father. And while my feelings toward my brother

seem clear to me, contradictory as they are, my feelings toward my father aren't nearly as clear. Do I care enough to hate the man? Is it possible to love someone who offers only disapproval and denunciation in return? Have I waited too long to make amends after parting from him in anger? I've decided to return home to find the answers.

I stand beneath the chestnut tree that I climbed so often as a boy—usually to escape my father's rebuke—and stare across the pasture at the farmhouse. It has changed little in the ten years I've been gone except for a fresh coat of whitewash. I've decided to wait until someone emerges from the house before approaching. Better to watch, to try to gauge my father's mood, before announcing my return after all these years. I was once adept at judging his mood, knowing when it was safe to draw close and when it was wise to steer clear.

But after watching the house for more than an hour, I've seen no sign of life aside from the lazy movements of the hound dog, sprawled in the shade on the back porch. One thing is certain: unlike the biblical tale of the prodigal son, my father isn't watching eagerly for my return. Nor can I imagine him running to me with open arms or killing the fatted calf.

Funny how all those Bible stories I once heard thundered from the church pulpit and proclaimed at the dinner table have stayed planted in my mind all these years. If I lean my head against the chestnut tree and close my eyes, I can clearly recall my disquieting childhood, living beneath my father's iron rule:

I am four years old again, seated at the kitchen table not daring to fidget or squirm, listening to my father's voice as he reads the daily portion from the Holy Scriptures: " 'God is jealous, and the LORD revengeth; the LORD revengeth, and is furious; the LORD will take vengeance on his adversaries, and he reserveth wrath for his enemies . . . the LORD hath his way in the whirlwind and in the storm, and the clouds are the dust of his feet. . . . ' "

"Mama. . . ?"

My son's voice startled me. I closed the notebook, guilt-stricken. "Jimmy! Oh, good, you're up. It's time for chores." I lifted the lid on the cast-iron stove and poked the embers, adding kindling and coal.

"Where did all this stuff come from?" Jimmy asked as he approached the table. "Is it the hobo's?"

"Yes . . . I thought I'd better try and find out who he is and where he comes from. It seems his name is Gabriel Harper."

"Gabriel? Wow, he must really be an angel!" Jimmy picked up the notebook I had been reading, but I snatched it away from him before he could open it.

"I don't think angels are supposed to get sick, Jimmy, and Mr. Harper is very ill." I wrapped the notebooks inside the slicker again and stuffed everything back into the burlap bag.

"Luke thinks the man's gonna die," Jimmy said quietly.

I felt a pang of alarm. "Did he tell you that?"

Jimmy nodded.

"What else did Luke say?"

"Not much," he said with a shrug. "You know Luke."

Sometimes I wondered if I did know Luke. He had been a happy little boy until his father died. Then, for a while, he had looked to his grandfather to take Sam's place. But when Grandpa Wyatt had suddenly died, it seemed as though the little boy in Luke had died along with him.

"Do you think they'll cancel school today?" Jimmy asked, interrupting my thoughts. "It's still snowing."

Outside, the wind still hadn't let up. I could barely see the barn through the gray, swirling flakes. "I don't care if there is school. You're not going any farther than the barn on a day like today."

Jimmy did a little dance of joy as he gathered his hat and

mittens from beside the stove and began bundling up to do his chores. Luke wandered into the kitchen, rubbing the sleep from his eyes.

"Guess what, Luke! No school today!" Jimmy announced.

"Is the m-man dead yet?" Luke asked.

His words felt like a knife in my heart. I looked into my son's hollow eyes. "Listen, Luke—" I began, but Jimmy interrupted me.

"Hey, Luke! You'll never guess what the hobo's name is! *Gabriel* . . . like the angel! And his last name is Harper. Get it? *Harp* . . . the thing the angels play in heaven?"

I hadn't made the connection until Jimmy pointed it out. Now the stranger's name sounded phony to me. Maybe it was a nickname like my aunt "Peanut" whose real name was Cecilia, or my mama who had been called "The Singing Angel." If the hobo was some kind of a writer, maybe Gabriel was his pen name. I shoved my arms into the sleeves of my coat and wrapped a scarf around my head.

"Keep an eye on the fire until we get back, okay, Luke? Throw on more wood if the coal doesn't catch."

I was so tired from reading most of the night that I plodded through my chores as if in a dream, my thoughts on Gabriel Harper's tale of the prodigal son. I wished I'd had time to read more of the story. I could easily picture the prodigal's father reading about the wrath of God at the dinner table. Grandpa Wyatt had always read from the Bible after dinner, too, allowing no one to leave the table until he'd finished an entire chapter. I'd never seen much point in reading a long list that told who begot whom, or a bunch of rules about priests sacrificing animals and sprinkling their blood every whichway, but I hadn't dared to question my father-in-law. Like the father in Harper's story, Grandpa Wyatt was not an easy man to approach. Since his death, the Bible had remained in the bureau drawer in his room. None of my kids had asked me why.

As I trudged out of the barn, lugging a milk pail in each hand, a sudden movement near the back porch caught my eye. Across the wide expanse of white, two dark, hunched forms emerged from the house—one tall, one short. I saw a flash of red—Luke's hair—and realized that Mr. Harper was leaning on Luke, limping across the yard through the snow toward the privy.

The fool! He was in no condition to be wandering outside in a storm! Suppose he slipped and fell? I hurried toward them as quickly as I dared, the milk sloshing in the pails.

"Hey!" I called. "Hey there! What do you think you're doing?"

As I had feared, Mr. Harper's knees suddenly gave out and he crumpled to the ground, pulling Luke down with him. I set the pails down and slogged through the drifts to help. Before I could reach him, Mr. Harper crawled the last few feet to the outhouse on his hands and knees. Luke was up and brushing snow off his clothes by the time I got there.

"Are you all right, Luke?"

"He f-fell."

"I know. It wasn't your fault. He's much too weak to be out of bed in the first place."

"He asked me."

"And it was nice of you to help him, Luke. But you have no business being out here without a hat or mittens. Go back inside now, before you catch your death. I'll help him."

I watched Luke plod back to the house, following his own trail of footprints. A few minutes later, the privy door creaked open. Mr. Harper leaned against the door frame, bundled in Grandpa Wyatt's old coat. My anger boiled over.

"What do you think you're doing running around outside? We

have indoor plumbing upstairs, you know. You *trying* to kill yourself, mister?"

"I needed—"

"If you couldn't manage the stairs, you could have found what you needed under the bed."

"I have no right to ask that of you, ma'am. I'm a stranger to you. I don't have a dime to my name and no way to repay you for what you've already done." His voice was soft, his face very pale. His teeth chattered in spite of the heavy wool coat he wore. He looked so pitiful I quickly swallowed all the harsh words I wanted to shout at him.

"You need to get back inside. Put your arm around my neck and I'll help you."

"Thanks. I'm feeling . . . a little . . . dizzy." He closed his eyes and slowly slid toward the ground, leaning against the doorframe. "I'm . . . sorry . . ." he mumbled.

"Stay put. I'll get the boys to fetch the sled."

It seemed to take forever to load him onto the sled again and haul him the short distance to the house; longer still to wrestle him up the porch steps, through the kitchen, and back into bed. All the while, my anger kept swelling inside me like yeast in a batch of dough. I didn't know why, exactly. I wasn't angry at Gabriel Harper—he hadn't done any harm to me or my kids, only to himself. Why, then, did I feel like throwing things or breaking something? I would have worked out my rage on the woodpile if Mr. Harper hadn't chopped so much wood already.

Instead, I fixed fried potatoes and scrambled eggs for breakfast, then bundled the kids up once they had eaten and sent them outside to play in the snow, since the storm had finally stopped. I wanted to tend to the stranger's leg by myself. While I waited for the water to get hot for a fresh compress, I did something I hadn't done since my husband died—I prayed. Except you couldn't really call it a prayer, I don't think, since most of it was just me yelling at God inside my head.

I had asked for an angel, I told Him, and instead He sent me a dying man! Couldn't He see how upset my kids were by all this dying? It was bad enough that God had taken my husband from me—although I admit I probably deserved to be punished for all the lying I'd done. But what on earth had Jimmy and Luke and Becky Jean ever done to deserve losing their daddy? Or their grandfather? Didn't God care that Jimmy had to do a man's share of the work now, or that little Luke barely said two words anymore, or that Becky didn't eat enough to keep a sparrow alive? Maybe I deserved to be punished, but my three children sure didn't. This farm was their home, and how in heaven's name did God expect me to keep it running until they were old enough to run it themselves if He didn't send me any help?

"And speaking of help," I told God, muttering the words out loud, "you'd better make up your mind to help that poor, raggedy man laid up in that bedroom because I won't have him dying on us! I won't stand for it, I tell you! I'm all through begging and pleading for things because you don't seem to hear me when I ask nice. You've got to make him better, you hear? And if he's your idea of an angel, then you'd better send somebody else, mighty quick!"

I'd been making quite a racket, slamming pots and kettles around as I fixed the poultice and cooked some porridge. And I must have still had an angry look on my face when I carried it all into the stranger's room because he was wide awake and gaping at me as if he was afraid I was going to start throwing things at him.

"I'm so sorry for troubling you, ma'am," he said.

"I'm not vexed with you," I replied, trying to smooth the frown off my face. "But you've got to do your level best to get better, you hear me? That means no more running around out-side. Now, I've brought you some food and you're going to eat it whether you want it or not, because you can't get better unless you eat. Then I'm going to dab some iodine on that cut of yours and it's going to hurt like the dickens, but you're going to grit your teeth and take it because it's the only way that cut will ever heal, understand?"

He smiled faintly. "Yes, ma'am."

"Don't call me that. You make me feel like a schoolmarm." I felt a smile tugging at my mouth, too. "Now, do you think you can eat this porridge by yourself or shall I feed you?"

"Let me try." He reached to take the spoon from me, and his hand felt hot as it brushed against mine. Drops of sweat glistened on his forehead as he struggled to sit up in bed. When he was ready, I laid the tray with the porridge bowl on his lap and turned my attention to doctoring his leg. From the corner of my eye I could see oatmeal dripping as he tried to feed himself with shak-ing hands, but I knew enough about men and their stubborn pride to leave him alone.

"Ready for the iodine?" I asked when he'd spooned the last of the porridge down. He nodded and reached behind his head to grip the brass headboard. I tipped the bottle and, as quickly as I could, poured a thin stream of it down the length of the wound. His body went stiff as he stifled a moan.

"You can yell if you want to, mister."

"It's Gabe," he said through clenched teeth. "My name is Gabe."

"Well, no one will hear you, Gabe. My kids are outside playing in the snow, and my closest neighbor is Aunt Batty, who lives way down by the pond. I'm going to put on a fresh compress now, then I promise I'll leave you alone."

I tried to be gentle, but I could tell by the funny way he was breathing that his leg pained him a lot. Maybe talking would help take his mind off it.

"Care to tell me how you did this?" I asked.

He drew a ragged breath. "I was running to catch a slow-moving flatcar. I've done it a hundred times before, but the railroad guards were after me and I didn't want to end up in jail for vagrancy. I ripped my leg open on a jagged piece of the undercarriage as I jumped. It was dark and I didn't see it sticking out."

"How long ago did it happen?"

"I don't know . . . how long have I been here?"

"You spent a night in my barn and a night in this bed."

He exhaled. "It must have been two or three days before that . . . I'm not sure. I lose all track of time being on the road without a calendar or a clock."

He had a smooth, deep voice that rumbled like the low notes on a church organ. Yet his words seemed to settle in the room as softly as snowflakes falling. I glanced at him, longing to ask why someone who spoke as fine as he did and who could make words come alive when he wrote them down on paper had to ride the rails like a worthless tramp. He was still gripping the headboard, his eyes closed. I quickly finished wrapping his leg.

"There. All done."

When he opened his eyes I handed him a towel so he could wipe off the sweat that ran down his face. He looked as white as flour.

"Need anything else?" I asked as I gathered up my things.

"Yes . . . I need to thank you, Mrs. Wyatt."

"Well, then, you can thank me by getting better."

I was almost through the door when the thought struck me. For the life of me, I couldn't recall telling him my married name. I slowly turned to face him. "How did you know my last name?"

His gaze shifted away and for a split second he wore the same look Jimmy gets when I catch him with his hand in the cookie jar. Then the moment passed and he smiled weakly. "I read the sign outside and I just assumed . . ."

"Oh. Of course."

I knew the sign he meant. A long time ago, in better, happier days, my father-in-law had painted on the side of the barn: *Wyatt Orchards—Frank Wyatt & Sons, Proprietors.* I shuddered to think that Frank Wyatt and his sons were all gone.

"It is Mrs. Wyatt . . . isn't it?" he asked shyly.

"Yes, but you can call me Eliza."

I had just put away the iodine and things, when all of a sudden my three kids came thundering through the back door with their boots on, scattering clumps of snow everywhere.

"Mama! Mama! Come quick! You gotta come!" They all tugged on my skirt and jabbered at me at the same time.

"Stop it! You're getting my floor all wet! Look at this mess!" I tried to herd them back out onto the porch, but they weren't listening to me. From the way they carried on, I began to think something terrible must have happened. "Slow down, one at a time. Let Jimmy tell me what's wrong."

He was breathless from running. "We were sliding down the hill behind Aunt Batty's house when she came outside and asked us to help her shovel snow. She said she would pay us and everything. So we followed her over to her house and she kept calling me Matthew even though I told her my name was Jimmy—"

"Is she a witch?" Becky asked suddenly.

"No, of course not," I said. "Who told you that?"

She looked up at Jimmy.

"It was a joke, " he said, giving Becky a shove. "Anyway, I thought she wanted us to shovel a path to her outhouse or something, but she said no, we had to shovel out the snow that was *inside* her house."

I remembered how my father-in-law used to insist that Aunt Batty was crazy, warning us to stay away from her, and I groped for a way to explain her to my kids. "Listen, you need to understand that Aunt Batty is—"

"But, Mama, she was right! The snow *is* inside her house!"

"*Inside!* How on earth did it get there?"

"I don't know, but you gotta come. There's way too much for me and Luke and Becky to shovel out by ourselves."

As I pulled on my coat and an old pair of Sam's boots, I decided that maybe Aunt Batty's door had blown open during the storm and the snow had drifted inside. But as soon as I reached the top of the rise behind her house I saw that it wasn't the case at all. The entire roof of her kitchen had fallen in from the weight of the snow like the top of an undercooked cake. The kitchen looked like it had been added some years after the original stone cottage was built, and its roof was not as steeply pitched—or as well-made.

We walked around to the front door and Aunt Batty let us in. I had never been inside her cottage in all the years I'd lived up in the big farmhouse, and I stood in her front parlor and stared. It was neat and cozy, with the ruffled curtains and crocheted afghans you'd expect in an old spinster's house. But every inch of wall space in the entire cottage was lined with shelves—and every inch of shelf space was crammed with books. It looked to me like Aunt Batty owned more books than the Deer Springs Library. I even saw a long row of thin yellow spines on a bottom shelf that had to be National Geographic magazines. A rocking chair stood beside the coal stove along with a big console radio with a plant perched on top.

What looked to have once been the dining area now held an enormous wooden desk, the kind you'd see in a fancy bank or a lawyer's office. It even had one of those swivel chairs beside it with a black leather seat. The typewriter sitting on top of the desk was much bigger and fancier than the one in Mr. Harper's burlap sack.

The house was freezing inside, and tiny little Aunt Batty looked as though she had on every sweater and coat she owned. "Did you bring the matches, Toots?" she asked.

I frowned. "Matches. . . ?"

"Yes, I asked young Matthew there to bring me some. I keep mine in the kitchen and I won't be able to get to them until we finish the shoveling. My fire went out, you see, and Winky and the girls don't like it when the house gets this cold."

I figured Winky must be the disagreeable little dog that had been yapping and snarling at us ever since we arrived, scaring poor Becky half to death and making her cling to my leg like a monkey. But I didn't see any "girls." From where I stood, though, I could see into the demolished kitchen and I realized right away that there was no way Aunt Batty could close off that part of the house and keep the heat in the parlor and bedroom. And she certainly wouldn't be able to fix any meals in that kitchen. The plain truth was that her house was uninhabitable.

I knew what had I had to do, and it made me feel as though the roof had just caved in on me. I drew a deep breath and rested my hand on her arm, speaking as slowly and carefully as I could. "Aunt Batty, shoveling out all that snow isn't going to help. Neither are matches. You still won't be able to stay warm or cook your food. Your kitchen roof has caved in. Do you understand that? You can't live in this house until the roof gets fixed."

"The roof? Oh my! I don't believe I own a ladder that'll reach to the roof! I'll have to borrow one—"

"No, listen. You'll have to *hire* someone to repair your roof. It's a huge job, Aunt Batty. I can't do it and neither can you. In the meantime, until it's fixed . . ." I paused, wishing that I wasn't Aunt

Batty's closest kin, wishing that I didn't already have an invalid to take care of, wishing I had never asked God to send me another angel. "In the meantime, you can come and live in the farmhouse with the kids and me."

"My sister Lydia's house?"

"Yes." I lacked the energy to explain to her that Lydia, my mother-in-law, had died like all the rest of them. Besides, Aunt Batty would probably just forget all over again. Added to my worries about Mr. Harper dying, I felt like I had more troubles than Job's wife.

"Oh dear," she moaned. "I can't leave Winky and the girls here all alone."

I gritted my teeth. "Winky can come, too."

"But Frank Wyatt hates dogs. He won't allow one in his house."

"Frank Wyatt is dead. It's my house now." Aunt Batty stared at me as if she had just heard the shocking news for the first time, as if she had never even been to his funeral three months ago. What was the Good Lord trying to do to me?

"Can I help you pack a few things to bring along?" I asked gently.

She smiled. "Why, yes. Thank you, Toots."

We went into her tiny bedroom and I helped her toss some clothes and underthings and toiletries into a scruffy carpetbag that was probably last used during the War Between the States. Aunt Batty added her knitting and an old photograph in a brass frame, then glanced around the room.

"There, now. I guess that's all I need. And you're sure that Winky and the girls are welcome, too?"

I nodded grimly.

"I'll have to wake the girls up. They won't like having their nap disturbed, but it can't be helped."

I still saw no sign of any "girls." I wondered if Aunt Batty had imaginary friends like my Becky Jean did. But then she pulled back the quilt on her bed and I saw that what I had mistaken for lumps in an old feather bed were really two enormous cats that had burrowed down like moles beneath the quilts.

Becky squealed in delight. "Oh, look—kitty cats!" She crawled up on Aunt Batty's bed and pulled off her mittens so she could pet them. "Do they have names?"

"Yes, that one is Queen Esther and that's Arabella."

They were both tiger-striped—Esther in shades of gray and Arabella in orange—with splashes of white on their chests and faces. They stretched and yawned and blinked their yellow eyes sleepily at Aunt Batty.

"Come on, girls. Rise and shine," she said. "I'm afraid we have to move someplace warm for a few days."

I wanted to believe that it would only be for a few days, but I knew in my heart that it would likely be much longer. Even if we could find a carpenter who would come all the way out here in this snow, I doubted if he could get much work done on the house until the weather warmed up. It looked to me like Aunt Batty's entire kitchen would have to be rebuilt.

"Now, then," she said. "Would you children like to help me? We'll let Samuel carry this satchel, and Matthew can—"

"I'm Jimmy," he said. "And he's Luke."

"Oh, that's right. Young Matthew went off to France to fight in that awful war, didn't he?" She gave Luke the carpetbag, then bent to snap a dog leash onto Winky's collar. She held out the other end to Jimmy.

"Does your dog bite?" he asked warily. Winky hadn't stopped snarling since we'd arrived.

"Heavens, no!" She bent over the little dog and said sternly,

"Now, that's quite enough of that, please." Winky whined and lay down on the rag rug with a sigh.

"I'll carry Queen Esther," Aunt Batty continued, "because she can be a bit crotchety after her nap. And your mother can carry Arabella."

"What about me?" Becky asked.

"Oh, you'll have a very important job to do, Toots. You must carry my friend Ivy."

I was afraid to ask who Ivy was, but she turned out to be the sprawling ivy plant on top of the radio in the parlor. Aunt Batty nestled the pot in Becky's arms, draping the trailing vines around her shoulders like a wreath so they wouldn't drag on the ground. "I hope you have a radio. Ivy loves listening to the radio."

"No, ma'am," Jimmy said solemnly. "Grandpa Wyatt wouldn't allow one."

"Well, then, I suppose we'll just have to sing to her instead. Can you children sing?"

"I guess so," Jimmy said with a shrug, though I couldn't recall ever hearing any of my kids sing.

"Splendid!" Aunt Batty replied. She returned to her bedroom and rolled each cat over onto its back, then swaddled it in a blanket like a baby. She handed the orange one to me before picking up the gray one herself. Neither cat protested this undignified treatment—but then, they were both so enormously fat it would have been hard for them to put up much of a fight. Aunt Batty glanced wistfully around the cottage one last time before we all headed out the door.

I can't even imagine what a sight we made, parading single file up the hill through the snow drifts to the farmhouse, all of us bundled to our eyebrows in hats and scarves and carrying a worn-out carpetbag, two lumpy cats, a stubby misshapen dog, and an overgrown ivy plant. As we trudged along, I wondered how to explain the bedraggled-looking man in the spare bedroom to Aunt Batty. In the end I decided to let her think he was whomever she wanted him to be—she could call him President Hoover for all I cared. I would have my hands full reminding her that Luke and Jimmy weren't my dead husband and his older brother. Next she would be calling me Lydia.

As it turned out, Becky pointed to the closed spare room door as soon as we got inside the kitchen and said, "We have to be real quiet because there's an angel sleeping in there. He's sick."

Aunt Batty held a finger to her lips and nodded as if it were the most natural thing in the world for people to have an ailing angel asleep in their house. We unwrapped the two cats and they waddled away like they knew exactly where they were going. Becky and Aunt Batty found a new home for Ivy in the parlor. And as soon as we unleashed Winky he sauntered up to the rug I kept by the kitchen stove, circled it three times, then fell over onto his side in the middle of it as if he'd been shot between the eyes. A minute later he was snoring. I longed to lie down beside him but it was already lunchtime and I still hadn't even washed the breakfast dishes.

"Becky Jean, take Aunt Batty upstairs and show her your room," I said. "She'll have to sleep with you for a couple of nights since my spare room is already occupied—that is, if it's all right with you, Aunt Batty."

"That will be just fine and dandy, Toots," she said with a wave of her hand. "I can sleep just about any old place."

"And you're not *really* a witch, are you?" Becky said, as if to reassure herself.

"I should say not! The Bible says that God hates witches . . . and since God is a good friend of mine, I certainly can't be a witch!"

"Jimmy just made that up to scare me, didn't he?"

"I expect so," Aunt Batty replied as they headed toward the stairs. "I never had a brother myself, but I do know that little boys love to tease little girls."

I threw some food together and called it lunch. Afterward, when I went into Mr. Harper's room to bring him some, I found him moaning and burning up with fever again. I sent Jimmy outside to fill a basin with snow and I soaked washcloths in it to lay on Mr. Harper's face and neck to bring the fever down. I spent most of the afternoon doing that, along with changing the poultices on his leg to draw out the poison and tending the stoves and cleaning up the dishes and boiling some navy beans to make soup for our supper.

I heard the kids bundling themselves up while I tended to Mr. Harper, and they disappeared outside with Aunt Batty for a while. They all came trudging up the hill from her cottage an hour or so later, lugging something on Luke's sled. I didn't give it much thought, worried as I was about Mr. Harper.

Later, as I chopped carrots and onions to add to the navy beans, I heard the kids entertaining Aunt Batty in the parlor—or maybe she was entertaining them, it was hard to tell. The mysterious bundle had turned out to be a pile of books, and the kids paged through them with her, spellbound as they gazed at the colorful pictures.

Meanwhile, Winky woke up from his nap and decided to attach himself to me. Every time I took a step he was tangled underfoot. He had to be the ugliest dog I had ever seen, with stumpy legs and splayed feet and a tail like a stubby thumb. His short, white fur bunched in lumpy rolls in some places and wrinkled like a cheap suit of clothing in others. He had a bulldog's body but his head was all wrong. Instead of a smashed-in face, he had a regular dog's long tapered snout—and his tongue didn't seem to fit inside it so his jaw hung open most of the time, lolling and slobbering.

Or if he did manage to close his snout, the tip of his pink tongue stuck out like a rude child's.

Winky was blind in one eye, and his good eye kept winking all the time, like it had a mind of its own. Every time I took a step, that one-eyed dog stepped with me, grinning foolishly and winking at me as if we'd just shared a private joke.

Next my kitchen towels started disappearing. I always kept one hung on a hook near the sink, but when I reached for it to dry my hands, it was gone. I took out a clean one and hung it there, but by the time I'd finished setting the table for supper, it was missing, too. I found them both behind the stove where the orange cat, Arabella, had dragged them. I watched her for a moment as she pawed and nosed the cloth around until it was just so, and it was clear that she was making a nest for herself back there. I groaned.

"Is there any chance that Arabella might be about to give us a litter of kittens?" I asked Aunt Batty during supper.

"Not a chance, Toots. She just thinks she's going to. I figure it's quite impossible." Aunt Batty blushed so fiercely I decided not to pursue it. I just hoped she was right. Things had turned crazy enough around here without a litter of kittens thrown in.

Afterward, when the boys and I started bundling up to do our chores, their mittens were missing, too. My frustration mounted as we searched and searched. I had neither the time nor the patience for this nonsense.

"You boys know you're supposed to hang your wet mittens here by the stove to dry," I scolded.

"But I *did* hang them there," Jimmy insisted. "Honest, I did."

"Then why aren't they there? Mittens don't just sprout wings and fly away, do they?"

"Here they are!" Luke suddenly shouted. He pointed to Arabella's nest behind the stove and I couldn't believe my eyes. The cat lay sprawled on her side like a nursing mother with the mittens snuggled up against her like babies. I lost my temper.

"You stupid cat!" I yelled. "Those are *mittens*, not *kittens!*"

Aunt Batty patted my shoulder. "You won't convince her, Toots. Arabella is a little hard-of-hearing, you know. The two words sound the same to her."

"Well, she isn't blind! Can't she see they're not kittens?"

Aunt Batty smiled faintly. "We all see what we want to see. And Arabella, bless her soul, longs to be a mother."

When I came back inside after my chores I found the other cat, who was half the size of a lion, all sprawled out on my rocking chair in the parlor, smug as you please, as if she owned it. When I tried to move her so I could sit down for a few minutes' rest, she hissed at me.

"That Queen Esther can be just as mean as a snake sometimes," Aunt Batty explained as she shooed the cat off my chair. She lowered her voice to a stage whisper and added, "It's because she knows Arabella is prettier than she is."

Frankly, I couldn't see much beauty in either one of them, fat as they were. And as I said, Winky was no prize, either. He sat drooling on Aunt Batty's feet all evening, watching her knit.

"Where did you find him?" I finally asked.

"Oh, Winky found me. He arrived at my door early one morning like an angel sent from heaven. I kept a flock of chickens at the time, and I needed a good watchdog to chase away the foxes and the raccoons. We've been good friends ever since."

"What kind of a dog is he?" Jimmy asked.

"Winky is a hunting dog."

I nearly laughed out loud. All the hunting dogs I'd seen were sleek, long-legged, graceful creatures, not fat lumpy things that waddled around on splayed feet with their tongues sticking out. I pictured the deer falling over dead from hysterics at the sight of him.

"That's how he lost his eye," Aunt Batty explained. "In a hunting accident."

"Couldn't you find it again?" Becky asked.

"Oh, it didn't fall out like a marble, Toots. He lost the use of it. He's blind in that eye." She lowered her voice to a whisper. "He doesn't like to talk about it." Winky rested his muzzle on Aunt Batty's foot, as if he understood that we were talking about him. She bent to pat his head. "He's a good dog, my Winky."

"What was his name before the accident?" I asked.

"Oh, he was always called Winky." Aunt Batty got a far-away look on her face. "Sort of prophetic, don't you think?"

I nodded, wondering how long it would be before I was as crazy as she and her pets were.

I got the kids to bed and Aunt Batty settled in Becky's room and the fires dampened for the night before returning to Mr. Harper's room one last time. I admit I felt scared to go in there. He'd been doing so poorly all day I thought he surely must be about to die. It's hard taking care of someone who's gravely ill because your natural instinct is to nurse him back to health, and when he gets worse and dies you feel like it's all your fault. Maybe you should've done something differently, maybe you could've done something more.

I took a deep breath, telling myself not to get too attached to him, then went into his room. He was burning up with fever and so delirious he was out of his mind. I knew he'd reached a crisis point—tonight he would either live or die. I bathed him in cold rags until he shivered, then wrapped a bed sheet tightly around him so he'd stop thrashing. Most of his words made no sense, but when he started crying "Father . . . Father, I'm sorry. . . ." it sent chills up my spine. I didn't know if he was calling for his daddy or for his heavenly Father. It made me think about my own daddy, and I wondered if he ever thought about me.

Then Mr. Harper began to weep, and it was such a broken-down sort of weeping that I sat on the edge of the bed and took him into my arms and held him until he stopped. "Forgive me, Father," he said over and over as he clung to me. "Please, please forgive me. . . ."

That's how it went for most of the night. I changed the dressings on his leg, using up an entire bottle of iodine, and tried to keep him cool. He needed a doctor, no question about it, but I couldn't drive anywhere in all this snow. I felt helpless. It was just like when Sam died all over again, except there hadn't been any snow when Sam had gotten sick and nothing but Frank Wyatt's stubbornness to keep me from driving to town to fetch the doctor. I'd finally walked all the way into Deer Springs to get help for Sam, but it was too late.

I couldn't do anything else for Mr. Harper, either, but I wanted him to know that someone cared, that he wasn't all alone. It must be a terrible thing to die all alone and unloved like my father-in-law had. I pulled a chair close, held Mr. Harper's burning hand, stroked his brow, and dropped water onto his tongue with a spoon. I talked to him about my own life, and I cried for Sam all over again because taking care of Mr. Harper brought it all back—how Sam had suffered so horribly, how he never should have died.

Then a miracle happened. Way past midnight, Mr. Harper's fever finally broke. He stopped moaning and thrashing and fell peacefully asleep. I needed some sleep, too, but as I crawled into my own bed early that morning, I couldn't stop my tears.

I had stepped off the train in Deer Springs ten years ago because I'd wanted to take control of my life, to find the home and the family I'd longed for. But now my life had veered wildly off course like a team of runaway horses, and I no longer held the reins in my hands. I thought about praying, then said aloud, "No. I'm not asking for any more angels. They're too much work!"

I'd been waiting for God to send someone to help me for months now, but I guessed He must be hard-of-hearing. I was all alone, isolated from town, holed up with snow piled to the windowsills—and yet I didn't want the snow to melt because I had no idea in the world how I would run Wyatt Orchards all by myself come springtime. I had a houseful of people to tend—three grieving kids, a dying hobo, and a crazy old lady with her lunatic pets—yet I still felt like I was all alone.

As I lay in the darkness, feeling sorrier and sorrier for myself, wishing I had someone to keep me company, I heard the click of a dog's toenails on the wooden floor. The ticking sound moved up the hallway, into my bedroom, across my floor. I peered over the edge of the bed. Winky stood in a pool of moonlight, slobbering and grinning up at me. It was the last straw.

"You don't belong up here!" I said in an angry whisper. I waved my arms at him. "Go on, go back downstairs!"

I didn't think that fat old thing could jump, but that's exactly what he did—jumped right up onto my bed.

"No! Bad dog! Get off!"

Winky lay down beside me where Sam used to sleep and rested his head on my knee. There was something about the weight of his stubby little body, the warmth of him, that was oddly comforting. I didn't really want him to go.

"All right, then," I said sternly. "But just for tonight."

He lifted his head to look at me and winked.

⟶ CHAPTER THREE ⟶

I woke up the next morning to the aroma of coffee. Sunlight streamed through my bedroom window like it was noon. I leaped out of bed when I realized why—I'd overslept!

How could I have done such a stupid thing? I got dressed as fast as I could. I had kids to tend to, chores to do. I raced past the other bedrooms and saw that my kids were already up and gone. Who knew what mischief they were into by now?

I hurried downstairs, then stopped short in the kitchen doorway. Aunt Batty stood at the stove singing "Amazing Grace" and flipping pancakes. She wore a homemade yellow sweater that was nearly as bright as the sunshine outside. All three kids sat at the table wolfing down pancakes smothered in apple butter as fast as she could flip them. Even Becky was eating, her mouth crammed so full that her cheeks puffed out. The milk pails were full of milk, the egg basket was full of eggs, the coal scuttle was full of coal, and both stoves were fired up and heating the house. I ran my hand through my sleep-tousled hair and sank onto a chair, feeling numb.

"You should have called me. I didn't realize it was so late . . . I must have forgotten to set my alarm."

Aunt Batty grinned. "You didn't forget, Toots. I sneaked in and turned it off. Winky told me you needed your rest."

"But the chores—"

"All done." Aunt Batty set a plate of pancakes in front of me. "I'll get you some coffee to go with those."

"We all helped with the chores, Mama, so you could sleep," Jimmy said. The kids were real proud of the gift they had given me. I felt dizzy with the surprise of it all.

"Thank you. But listen, Aunt Batty, you don't have to do chores—"

"Nonsense! Of course I do. As I explained to Winky and the girls this morning, it shows very poor manners to accept someone's hospitality and not do your fair share of the work."

As if to prove Aunt Batty's words, Queen Esther waddled out of my pantry with a dead mouse dangling from her teeth, its tail trailing across my floor. I'd known for some time that I had a mouse or two living in my pantry, nibbling on anything they pleased, but even though I'd set several traps, I hadn't caught a single one.

Esther crossed the kitchen and dropped her prize at my feet, smirking up at me as if to say, "There. That's how it's done." Then she turned her back, tail in the air, and strode into the parlor to take her morning nap on my chair.

"Thank you," I mumbled.

Seated beside me, Becky took one look at the dead mouse and scrambled to stand on her chair, screaming, "Eeee! A mouse! A mouse!" The boys laughed out loud at her—even Luke laughed—

as she danced from foot to foot, wringing her hands.

Aunt Batty scooped up the mouse with a broom and dustpan, shaking her head in dismay. "That Queen Esther is a good little hunter, but she never cleans up after herself." She carried the dustpan outside and set it on the porch, mouse and all. "Esther will be looking for that, come dinnertime," she said as she closed the door again.

"She eats *mice?*" Becky asked with a shiver.

"Certainly, Toots. All cats do. But Esther eats more than her fair share of them, don't you think? That's why she's so chubby." She helped Becky climb down again and fed her a forkful of pancakes. "I'll bet you can't finish your breakfast before your mother finishes hers."

"Yes, I can!"

I watched in astonishment as Becky ate every scrap of food on her plate in record time. It occurred to me that I must still be dreaming.

I tasted the pancakes and understood right away why the kids wolfed them down. And the coffee was the best I'd tasted since the stock market crashed. It must have come from Aunt Batty's house, since my coffee was mixed with chicory and tasted nowhere near this good.

All the while I ate I kept glancing at the spare room door, wondering what I'd find on the other side. Mr. Harper had seemed fine when I went to bed, but fevers could be tricky. He might be all better or he might be dead. I ate slowly, steeling myself for the worst.

When I finally got up the nerve to peek inside his room I was relieved to hear him snoring. I tiptoed to his bedside and laid my hand on his forehead. It still felt cool. Mr. Harper stirred at my touch, then opened his eyes and looked at me. I felt embarrassed, remembering how freely I'd talked to him last night, holding him in my arms and everything. I hoped he didn't remember.

"Hi," I said shyly. "How you feeling?"

"Better than I have in a long time." When he smiled he was an altogether different man from the sick one I'd been tending. His gaze unnerved me.

"Think you could eat something?" I asked when I found my voice.

"That coffee smells awfully good."

"I'll get you some."

"Mrs. Wyatt, wait—" I paused near the door. "Listen," he said, "I was wondering . . . I know I was out of my head last night. Was I saying things?"

"Don't worry. Nothing made any sense." I breathed a sigh of relief knowing he probably wouldn't remember the things I'd said, either. But when I saw that he still had a worried look on his face, I tried to reassure him. "The only words I understood were when you called for your father. You scared me half to death because I figured you were about to die and you were calling on the heavenly Father, asking Him to forgive you." I waited for him to smile again, but he closed his eyes and turned his head away.

"I'll take that coffee now, ma'am . . . if it's not too much trouble."

I shut his door and returned to the kitchen. Aunt Batty was singing for all she was worth as she washed the breakfast dishes. "How's that angel doing this morning?" she said when she'd finished the chorus.

"He's not an angel." I started to explain, then gave up. "He's much better. He'd like some coffee if there's any left."

"Is he hungry?" she asked. "I can fix him some pancakes, too."

For reasons I couldn't explain, I suddenly felt shy about tending to Mr. Harper now that he was awake and aware of things. I handed the cup and saucer to Aunt Batty. "Why don't you bring this to him and ask him yourself?"

"All right." She dropped her voice to a whisper. "The children told me all about him yesterday. We've been praying for him."

A jolt of alarm rocked me. "I wish you hadn't done that."

"Why not? The Good Book says—"

I grabbed Aunt Batty's arm and hustled her into the pantry so the kids couldn't hear us talking. "Listen," I said in an angry whisper, "our experience with prayer hasn't been very good. We prayed and prayed for their daddy to get better, and he died!"

"Oh, we didn't pray that the angel would get better—only that God's will would be done, and that we could accept it."

"What's the difference?" I said bitterly.

"Oh, there's a big diff—"

I pushed past her into kitchen, not wanting to hear her reasoning. "Becky Jean, come dry these dishes. Boys, get ready for school."

"It's Saturday, Mama," Jimmy said. He and Luke exchanged glances. I *was* losing my mind.

Aunt Batty followed me out of the pantry and opened the door to Mr. Harper's room, coffee cup in hand. She stopped short.

"Goodness, you scared me!" she said. "You look just like a big old woolly bear lying in that bed! Now, why would you want to let your hair and beard get all shaggy like that?"

I hurried into the room behind her, afraid she had offended him. "Mr. Harper has been sick with a fever, Aunt Batty. He can't do much for himself."

"Well, I could clean him up real nice, if you want me to. I took good care of Walter years ago, when he was bedridden. And then poor Papa, of course. Shaved them both clean as a whistle."

Even if I were dying I wouldn't let crazy old Aunt Batty near me with a straight razor, but I didn't know how to warn Mr. Harper. He looked from me to Aunt Batty in confusion, as if things were moving too fast for him to keep up.

"Let's wait until he's feeling better," I said quickly.

"Suit yourself," she said, with a shrug. She handed him the coffee. "Here you go. I'm Aunt Batty, by the way. Who might you be?"

"My name's Gabe . . . Gabriel Harper."

Aunt Batty looked thoughtful. "Gabriel, eh? I once knew another angel by the name of Gabriel. You any relation? You do look kind of familiar. . . ."

He gave a nervous laugh. "I'm really sorry to disappoint everyone but I'm not an angel. Far from it, I'm afraid." He took a sip of coffee. "Mmm! This tastes as good as it smells. Thank you, ma'am."

"Would you like some pancakes to go with that?" Aunt Batty asked. "My pancakes are delicious, I must say. I have a secret ingredient—so secret that even *I* don't know what it is."

He smiled slightly as she howled at her own joke. "Sure . . . thank you very much, ma'am."

His attention seemed drawn to something in the doorway behind me so I turned to look. All three kids were trying to sneak into the room. "Everyone out!" I said. "This isn't a sideshow. Mr. Harper deserves a little privacy." I didn't want them getting friendly and feeling Mr. Harper's loss when he either died or left us again. I tried to herd them out but he overruled me.

"No, it's all right," he said in his deep, soft voice. "I wouldn't mind some company."

I gave up and fled to the kitchen to get his breakfast. The kids had left three pancakes sitting all by themselves on the platter. I put them on a clean plate, dabbed a mound of apple butter on top, and brought them in to Mr. Harper. I was only gone a minute or two, but in that time Winky managed to waddle in to join the crowd and the gray cat decided to sprawl herself across the foot of his bed. Before I had a chance to shoo them out, the orange cat jumped onto the bed, too, carrying Becky's mitten in her mouth as if hauling a kitten around by the scruff of the neck.

"Oh, look," Becky said. "Arabella brought you her kitten."

Gabe stared at the cat, squinting his eyes as if he wasn't sure if he was seeing things or not. Arabella dropped the mitten in his lap then lay down beside him, purring and kneading his leg with her paws.

"That's the sorriest-looking kitten I've ever seen," he said.

"It's really my mitten," Becky said in a loud whisper. "Promise you won't tell her?"

Gabe laughed, and the sound of it reminded me again of the low notes on a church organ—the ones that tug on your heart and punch you in the stomach. The kids all laughed along with him and I knew I'd be fighting a losing battle if I tried to keep them away from him. I gave him his breakfast plate, then slipped from the room to go upstairs and make the beds.

It had turned out to be a beautiful day. The sun was shining, the snow was melting, Aunt Batty had given me a much-needed helping hand, and it looked as though Gabe Harper might live after all. I knew I should feel lighthearted, but try as I might, I couldn't shake the feeling that there was more trouble coming down the road. Maybe that's because trouble had been following me around like Aunt Batty's dog for such a long time that I'd forgotten what it was like to take a step and not have it underfoot.

I smoothed the coverlet on my bed, then stared out the window, listening to the steady sound of water dripping as icicles thawed in the sun. *The snow is melting!* That meant that the snow in Aunt Batty's kitchen would be melting, too! I'd have to figure out a way to protect all her belongings.

As I pondered what to do, I saw Alvin Greer's truck slowly drive down the road beyond the house, heading toward Deer Springs. If the roads were passable, I could drive Mr. Harper into town to see the doctor. But he couldn't very well go in his long johns, and I hadn't washed his clothes yet.

I hesitated, then opened Sam's bureau drawer. My husband's clothes lay neatly folded, as if he'd left them there only yesterday. It was the first time I'd handled Sam's things since he'd died. I picked up one of his work-worn flannel shirts, surprised to find that my grief was gone, leaving a brown empty place, like the spot that's left after you've yanked a flower out by its roots. I held the shirt to my cheek. It still smelled like Sam. But when I tried to picture his face I couldn't recall it. Maybe that was part of my punishment. Maybe all of my troubles were my punishment for lying to Sam like I did.

Even so, I missed him. Not just because the kids needed a daddy or because of all the work I had to do now that he was gone, or even because of all the loneliness he'd left behind. But because Sam had truly loved me. I was always very certain of that. He loved me. And I missed feeling loved.

I chose a clean set of clothes for Mr. Harper to wear and closed the drawer again. On my way past Becky's room I stopped to make up her bed, but it was already made. Aunt Batty's work, no doubt. Then I spied the photograph she'd brought from home sitting on Becky's dresser. I picked up the brass frame and studied the picture.

A pleasant-looking man about thirty-some years old sat slumped on a chair in front of Aunt Batty's cottage with a blanket over his legs. He was an invalid, thin and ill-looking, with dark, mournful eyes behind wire-rimmed glasses. The young woman who stood behind him had rested her hand on his shoulder, and he had lifted his own hand to tenderly cover hers. He wore a wedding ring on his finger. The girl stood in a bashful pose. Her head, which had a circle of flowers on it, was tilted away from the camera, and her round shoulders slouched forward. She was barefooted. I looked at her closely—it was a plump, youthful Aunt Batty.

Hadn't she just told me that she'd once taken care of an invalid, shaving him and all? I looked at their joined hands, then at their faces again, and thought I saw in their expressions much more than a nurse and her patient.

Secrets.

Heaven knows I had plenty of my own. Gabe Harper obviously had his secrets. Why not Aunt Batty, too? I thought of a sermon about secrets I'd once heard in a church in Montgomery, Alabama, and I shuddered. The preacher had scared me half to death with his frightening words: *"You may be sure that your sin will find you out!"* I pictured sin like a long-nosed bloodhound, tracking you wherever you went, sniffing your trail of misdeeds, baying out loud for all the world to hear once it had you up a tree.

I set Aunt Batty's photograph back where I'd found it and went downstairs. Everyone was still crowded in Gabe's room, laughing.

"I hate to break up this party," I said crossly, sticking my head in the door, "but the snow is melting. Aunt Batty, you and the kids had better get down to your cottage and pack up some of your things or they're going to get ruined."

"Oh, we were just talking about my roof," she said as gleefully as a child. "Don't worry, Gabe says he'll fix it for me."

I lost my temper. Was I the only responsible adult around here? "Mr. Harper has just taken one tiny step back from death's door. He isn't about to be climbing up on your roof anytime soon. And even if he could get up there, that roof is going to take a lot more than a day's work to fix."

Gabe looked away. The cheerful smile disappeared from Aunt Batty's face. Even my kids started ducking their heads and shuffling their feet. I felt like the thundercloud that had just poured rain on their picnic.

"Then I guess we'd better get busy," Aunt Batty said quietly. "Come on." She made a sweeping motion with her arm, and the dog, both cats, and all three kids followed her out of the room like she was the Pied Piper. I was left alone with Gabe.

"I know that I'm still not completely well," he said, fingering the mitten Arabella had left behind. "I'm sorry if I misled Aunt Batty about her roof. I didn't mean to."

Something about the easy way he said her name struck me as wrong. It was one thing for her own family to call her "Batty," but it seemed wrong for a stranger to do it. We stared at each other in silence for a moment before I remembered Sam's clothes.

"Here. Speaking of getting better, I think the roads are thawing out, too. If you can get yourself dressed, I'll drive you to Deer Springs to see the doctor."

"No! Thank you, ma'am, but no!" His answer came so swiftly, so forcefully, he startled me. It was like I'd offered to take him to a voodoo witch doctor for treatment. As Aunt Peanut used to say, "something smelled fishy." I waited, my hands on my hips, letting my silence demand an explanation from him.

"I . . . uh . . . I don't have any money," he finally said. "I can't pay for a doctor."

"That doesn't matter. Dr. Gilbert is real nice about letting folks pay any way they can. I could bring him a chicken and some eggs and milk—"

"No! Thank you, but you've done too much for me already. As it stands, I don't know how I'll ever repay you for saving my life."

I gestured impatiently. "Fiddlesticks! I plan to get plenty of work out of you once you're feeling better—like fixing Aunt

Batty's roof, for one thing. I'm just not sure you're out of the woods yet, and I'd rest easier if you'd let a doctor take a look at your leg."

"I'll be fine."

I could see by the way he stuck out his chin and held my eyes with his own that he wasn't going to budge. As I stared back, I couldn't shake the feeling that it was more than the money he was worried about. A funny feeling suddenly shivered through me— what if he really *was* an angel? What if a doctor would be able to tell somehow?

I shook myself to dismiss such a silly thought. There were no such things as angels.

"Listen, if you're sure you don't want to see a doctor, then I'd better go help Aunt Batty for a while. Can I get you anything before I leave?"

"No, thank you." He sank back against the pillows, and I could see that he'd used up all his strength. I put Sam's clothes on the dresser top and left Gabe alone to rest.

I spent most of the day hauling stuff up the hill from Aunt Batty's cottage to my house. I'd loaded my father-in-law's truck with empty apple crates and driven them down there, thinking she could pack up her things and store them in her bedroom where they would stay dry. But Aunt Batty had insisted on bringing all of her most precious books up here. This old farmhouse was already cluttered to the rafters with stuff, since it had been in Sam's family for so many years, but now I had books piled everywhere, too. When we ran out of space in the other rooms, I stacked a load of books in the spare room with Mr. Harper. The commotion woke him up. He stared at the boxes in amazement.

"Where does Aunt Batty live? In the public library?"

"Oh, you don't know the half of it!" I said, leaning against the doorframe to rest. "These are just her *special* books. There are twice as many still down there that she didn't make us bring."

"I guess we won't run out of reading material any time soon." He smiled and acted all polite and friendly, but for some reason I was afraid to be friendly in return. It wasn't that I didn't trust him—my instincts told me that he was perfectly trustworthy. But I found myself getting snappish with him for the same unknown reason that I always barked at my kids when I didn't really mean to.

"Help yourself," I said, turning away. "I certainly don't have time to read."

Toward evening Mr. Harper's fever went back up a little bit, but it wasn't nearly as high as it had been the past few days. "I know just the thing to cool him off," Aunt Batty said after we finished washing the supper dishes. She should have been tuckered out from all the work we'd done that day, but she put on her coat and a pair of boots and disappeared out the back door with a kerosene lantern. She was gone for such a long time that I just about gave her up for lost. But she finally reappeared, all out of breath, lugging a crazy-looking bucket with a crank on top. The kids crowded around to see the mysterious contraption.

"It's an ice-cream churn," she announced. "You kids like ice cream?" They stared at her, all wide-eyed and slack-mouthed as if she'd just offered them a trip to the moon for a slice of green cheese. I don't think they'd eaten ice cream but once or twice in their whole lives, what with Grandpa Wyatt running things the way he did.

Aunt Batty soon had everyone buzzing around like a hive of worker bees with herself as the queen. "You run down to the cellar and fetch me a jar of your mama's canned peaches," she told Luke. "You grab your mittens, boy, and fill this full of snow," she said, handing Jimmy a pail. She turned to Becky and me. "We're going to need some fresh cream, some sugar, and some pickling salt. You have any pickling salt, Toots?"

When she had everything ready, Aunt Batty set the churn right outside Gabe's bedroom, opening the door wide and propping him up in bed so he could watch. The kids squabbled over who was going to crank the handle, so Aunt Batty got the egg timer and made them all take turns. Not one to waste time, she took out her knitting needles and a ball of yarn and began casting-on stitches while they churned.

"Whatcha making?" Becky asked her.

"Well, I thought maybe Gabe could use a new pair of socks, seeing as how his have so many holes in the toes."

"When you finish the socks," Becky asked, "could you knit Arabella some new kittens? Mama took my mittens away from her again, and Arabella wants babies *so* bad."

"What a wonderful idea!" Aunt Batty said. "Why didn't I think of that? I'll start the first kitten right now. What color shall we make him?"

I shook my head as Becky sorted through balls of yarn in Aunt Batty's knitting basket, picking out two brown kittens and a white one. Now my children were losing their minds, too.

When the ice cream was finally ready, the kids started all hollering at once. "Let me taste! No, me first! Let me try it!"

"I think we should let Mr. Harper have the first taste," Aunt Batty decided. "He's our guest, after all, and we're making it to cool his fever, remember?" She scooped some into a bowl and brought it to Gabe. The kids' tongues hung nearly down to the floor as he closed his eyes and savored the first bite.

"Mmm . . . Mmm! I believe I must have died and gone to heaven!" he said. "I've never tasted anything this good here on earth!"

The kids did more hopping around than a flea circus as they waited for Aunt Batty to dish up their portions. I tasted mine and discovered that Gabe was right—it was the most delicious thing I'd eaten in a long, long time.

"Do angels eat ice cream up in heaven, Mr. Harper?" Becky asked after she'd eaten a few bites.

"My daddy's up in heaven and he would really like this," Jimmy added.

What little I could see of Gabe's pale, bearded cheeks flushed bright pink. "I . . . uh . . . I didn't mean it that way. I'm not really—"

"Of course they do," Aunt Batty cut in. "The Bible says that heaven is paradise, and how in the world could any place be paradise without ice cream?"

"Or candy," Jimmy said.

"And kitty cats." Becky bent to let Arabella lick ice cream off her fingers. "Heaven must have kitty cats."

"F-fishing holes."

Luke's voice was so soft I wasn't sure if I'd heard right or not. But then I remembered the lazy summer evenings when Sam had taken his sons fishing. Luke must be remembering them, too.

"Yeah, our daddy liked to go fishing," Jimmy said. "Will they let him go fishing up in heaven?"

"It's paradise!" Aunt Batty exclaimed, her arms spread wide. And that seemed to answer all of their questions. "Who wants more ice cream?"

Between the six of us we finished off the entire batch. Gabe said he felt cured for certain, but I touched his brow and it still felt warmer than it should. Aunt Batty decided to top off the evening by reading us some "literature," as she called it. Now, I'd read the poems of Henry Wadsworth Longfellow before, but I'd never noticed how much dying there was in all of them—the blacksmith's wife in the "The Village Blacksmith," the sea captain's little girl in "The Wreck of the Hesperus." When I'd listened to all I could stand, I chased the kids up to bed, then lit into Aunt Batty like an angry mama bear.

"I don't ever want you reading poems about sadness and dying to my kids again, you hear me? We've seen enough death!" My harsh words bounced right off her like hail off a tin roof.

"Dying is simply part of living, Toots." Her childlike smile never left her face as her knitting needles flew. "Everything in the whole world has to die sometime. That's the way God made things."

"Then I don't think God cares about life very much."

"Oh, that's not true!" Her knitting fell to the floor as she stood and gripped my arm. Concern was written all over her face. "Life is very precious to God. That's why He made it so fragile and so short."

"That makes absolutely no sense."

"Yes, it does. He made it fragile so we would treasure it, just like He does. You're not nearly as careful with your cast-iron frying pans as you are with your good china, are you? God wanted life to be precious to us—so He made it as frail as fine china."

I sat at the kitchen table that night after everyone else had gone to bed, knowing I wouldn't be able to sleep. Aunt Batty's words rankled me, like a sliver that was too deep to dig out. Why hadn't I treasured my husband's life while I had the chance? Why had I taken him for granted and used him like . . . like an old cast-iron frying pan? I didn't have any answers, only regrets, so I finally decided to go up to bed. But when I stood up, the first thing I saw was Gabe Harper's burlap bag and I remembered that I hadn't finished reading that last story of his.

I pulled out the notebook labeled *Prodigal Son* and found the place where I'd left off:

I said that Simon was my only brother, but that's not quite

true. Three of us brothers grew up together on the farm. Johnny was the youngest, I was the oldest, and Simon was in the middle. For reasons I've never understood, Johnny was my father's favorite. Johnny knew it, too, and he lorded it over us.

"I'll tell Pa!" he would threaten when things didn't go his way. It wasn't an idle threat, either. If Johnny complained to my father, Simon and I would pay the consequences with our own hides.

While Johnny was his favorite, my father could barely stand to look at me. I never understood why. Hard as I tried, I could never please him. My youngest brother won his love by doing nothing at all, while I seemed to earn his wrath by simply existing.

The Bible says Joseph was his father's favorite and his brothers hated him so much they couldn't speak a kind word to him. I felt the same way toward Johnny. When the opportunity arose, Joseph's brothers got rid of him for good. I did the same thing. Johnny is dead. And I'm the one who killed him.

It happened on a cold December day just after Thanksgiving. Snow had fallen the night before—about six or seven inches worth—so Simon and I decided to go sledding down the hill near the pond. Of course, Johnny tagged along after us like he always did, spoiling our fun and making us pull him up the hill again each time. After a while Simon got tired of listening to Johnny wheedle and whine, and he headed home. I wanted to go with him, but I knew Johnny would follow me, so I grabbed his sled and gave it a hard shove, sliding it out into the middle of the pond. I figured I could make my getaway while he went after it.

Johnny started bawling. "Go get it for me or I'll tell Pa what you did!"

"Get it yourself."

I knew Johnny was terrified of falling through the ice. He

wouldn't even lace up his skates until Simon and I had skated around the whole pond a couple of times to make sure it was safe. He was afraid of the pond in the summertime, too, because he couldn't swim very well. He never could get up the nerve to jump off the rope swing. Now I saw him looking back and forth from me to his sled and I knew he was scared spitless.

"You're a scaredy-cat!" I taunted. "A lily-livered baby!"

"I am not!" His voice grated on me the way fingernails on a blackboard grate on other people.

"Are too! You've got a yellow stripe down your back a mile wide! You're scared stiff to step one foot out onto that ice and fetch your stupid sled."

"I am not!"

"Then prove it! I dare you!" I crossed my arms and glared at him. "I *double* dare you!" I loved to make Johnny squirm. I watched him walk a few steps out past the shoreline and stop.

"Is it safe?"

The truth was, I didn't know. The weather hadn't turned really cold yet. But hatred makes you say all kinds of things that aren't true. "What do you think, dummy? Your sled didn't sink, did it?"

He took a few more tentative steps. The snow made an odd crunching sound beneath his feet. I laughed cruelly.

"You're such a chicken!"

"I am not!" His voice sounded shaky, like he was riding in the back of a wagon down a bumpy road.

"Then why don't you walk out there and get your sled?" I turned my back and strode away. He would dither around for who knows how long before making up his mind. Meanwhile, I could disappear and be rid of him.

I heard that strange snow-crunching sound behind me as I started up the hill. I didn't know if Johnny was walking farther out onto the pond or retracing his steps. I didn't care.

Suddenly the sound changed. I heard an eerie creaking noise, like an old wooden floor in a haunted house. It was the most horrifying sound I've ever heard. The creaking grew louder and faster, like kindling catching fire. Johnny screamed.

I whirled in time to see the ice give way. Johnny went under, his arms flailing uselessly. Then his scream was extinguished as he vanished beneath the fractured surface, disappearing into the coal black water.

It was the most horrible moment of my life—one I've relived a thousand times since that day. I wished I could go back and do things differently, wished it had been me that had died instead of Johnny.

My father doesn't know the truth about his death. Only one other person knows, and I don't think she'll ever tell. But I've been cursed like Cain—condemned to wander the earth for killing my brother.

I stopped reading as a chill shivered through me. Was this a true story? Was this the reason Gabriel Harper wandered all over the country like a tramp?

I felt guilty for reading his private journal. It seemed like I was reading Gabe's mind and his heart. But I just couldn't help myself. I skipped ahead to another place and continued to read:

My father always held the standards of the Bible over our heads, demanding we live up to them, but he never judged himself in the same light. He was really two different men. To folks in town he was the most successful farmer in the county, a respected elder at our church, a benefactor to missionaries in China and Africa. But to his family he was another man altogether. We felt the flames of his terrible temper, as hot and swift as a brush fire, sweeping down out of nowhere and raging out of control in a flash, reducing what was green and sweet just moments earlier into blackened ash and stubble.

I observed the difference his presence made on my mother. The only time I heard her gentle laughter or saw her beautiful smile was when he wasn't around—then she would sometimes swing me up into her arms and dance with me, humming popular songs as we waltzed around the parlor. But as soon as my father appeared she became wary and furtive, cowering like a beaten dog, though I never saw him lay a hand on her.

When I discovered that my own temper was just as swift and deadly as his, it terrified me. I hated the thought that I was like him in any way. I hated my father, and so I hated myself for being his son.

The night I found out that I wasn't his son, that he wasn't my real father, I felt born again—alive and free, knowing that not one drop of his despised blood flowed in my veins.

But then the truth of what my mother had done slowly sank in. Why had she subjected me to his cruelty all those years if I wasn't his real son? How could she have watched him rage at me, scorn and ridicule me, beat me without mercy, when he had no right? She had assured me of her love and I had believed her. I'd trusted her with childlike faith. Now I felt betrayed by her.

I closed Gabe Harper's notebook with shaking hands. I remembered my own mother's betrayal and it seemed like I could hear her voice just as clear as could be: *"You know I love you more than anything in the whole wide world, don't you, Sugarbaby?"*

I was sorry I had ever opened Gabe's book. He had stripped my heart bare beside his own. Later, as I lay in bed, a storm of feelings howled through me like the wind in the snowstorm, emotions too raw and biting to stand up against. Even with Winky alongside me for company that night, it was a long time before I fell asleep.

— CHAPTER FOUR —

The next day was the Lord's Day. My daddy had always made sure I went to church on the Sabbath if he could find one nearby. And my father-in-law would have made us all walk to church through a blizzard rather than miss a single Sunday. But I didn't live with my daddy anymore, and Frank Wyatt was dead. I had no reason at all to attend church.

I had enjoyed sitting in the pew beside Sam every Sunday morning, just as proud as can be of all the respect people gave the Wyatt family. But after Sam died, the white-washed walls of that little church began to feel like they were closing in on me—like it was Frank Wyatt's church and not God's. No one there knew my father-in-law the way I did. I thought about the words Gabe Harper had written: *My father was two different men.* Gabe might have been describing Frank Wyatt.

Aunt Batty brought her Bible with her to the breakfast table that bright Sunday morning and started leafing through it after we'd finished eating. "We need to read something special this morning in honor of the Lord's Day," she said.

I was about to put a stop to the idea, remembering the poems she'd read the night before and remembering all the stuff Grandpa Wyatt used to read from the Bible about God's vengeance and wrath. But Aunt Batty found her place and started reading before I could stop her.

" 'At that time Jesus answered and said, "Come unto me, all ye that labour and are heavy laden, and I will give you rest. Take my yoke upon you, and learn of me; for I am meek and lowly in heart: and ye shall find rest unto your souls. For my yoke is easy, and my burden is light. . . ." ' "

She closed the book with a smile. "Isn't the Lord's Day wonderful? He gives us a day of rest."

I pushed my chair away from the table and stood. "I have chores to do."

"Well, of course you do, Toots. Chores don't go away on the Sabbath, do they? But once they're done we can all have fun!"

My kids looked horrified and I guess I must have, too. "Grandpa never let us play on the Sabbath," Jimmy said solemnly. "We weren't allowed."

Even on the hottest day of the summer, he would make those poor kids stay indoors in their Sunday clothes rather than go for a swim in the pond.

"Your grandpa was wrong," Aunt Batty declared. She was just a little thing, but she planted her hands on her hips and stuck out her chin like she was David taking on Goliath. "The Bible says Sunday is a day of *rest*. It doesn't say to *stop living!* Come on, now," she told the children, "let's give your mama a hand with those chores, then we'll find a nice, clean patch of snow and make snow angels."

"Is that like making a snowman only with wings?" Jimmy asked.

"Heavens, no!" she cried, her arms flying up in surprise. "You mean to tell me you children never made snow angels before?"

"Never," Becky said.

"Well, let's hop to it then and get our work done so I can teach you how."

As all three kids leaped into action I wondered when, exactly, I had surrendered control to Aunt Batty. Wasn't she *my* house-guest? And what on earth were snow angels?

By the time the boys and I finished the outside chores, Becky had helped wash the dishes and Aunt Batty had stew simmering on the back of the stove for Sunday dinner. "You coming outside to make angels with us, Toots?" she asked me as she and Becky bundled into their coats.

"No, thanks," I said. "I need to tend to Mr. Harper."

When they were gone, I started gathering things to make a fresh poultice. While I waited for the water to boil, my eyes fell on Gabe's bag again. I'd vowed I wouldn't read any more of his story, but now I was worried that I hadn't put everything back just the way he'd had it, and that he would know I'd been snooping. When I recalled seeing a Bible amongst his things it gave me an idea. Maybe he'd want to read from it on the Sabbath. Maybe I could take it to him and admit right off that I'd looked inside his bag. He couldn't get mad at me for doing a good deed, could he?

I found the Bible easily enough, but then my curiosity had me leafing through it to peek at the dedication page—was Gabriel Harper really his given name? He must not have wanted anyone to know because that whole page was torn right out. I leafed through the rest of the book to see what else I might learn about him, but all I found was a tiny bunch of pressed violets in the book of Exodus and an old sepia-toned photograph in the book of Acts.

The woman in the picture was very beautiful, with upswept hair and large, dark eyes that seemed to draw you to her face. Her lips were parted slightly in a faint, seductive smile, as if she'd just stolen a kiss from the photographer. There was no name on the back of the photo, only a date—June 16, 1893. I couldn't really tell how old Gabe was, but I didn't think he was old enough for this woman to be his wife or his girlfriend. Was she his mother? I put the picture back where I found it and brought the Bible to him. I had to work hard not to act too guilty as I lied.

"I was gathering up all your dirty clothes to wash tomorrow and I noticed this in your bag. I thought you might want to read it, seeing as today is the Sabbath."

"Please leave my clothes the way they are," he said. It was impossible to read his expression, hidden behind all that hair, but I could tell by the ice in his voice that he was angry. "I'm sure you have enough to do around here, ma'am, without washing my things."

"You saying you prefer to stay dirty?" I asked, just as coldly.

"I'm saying I can take care of my own things once I'm back on my feet."

"Fiddlesticks! I have a load of washing to do on Monday anyway, so what's a couple more things?"

"Ma'am—"

"Besides, they're stinking up my house."

I turned and left the room before he could argue with me. When I came back with the poultice to tend to his leg, his Bible was laying on the nightstand beside the bed, unopened. Gabe was staring up at the ceiling with his hands clasped behind his head. Neither of us said a word as I folded back the bed sheet and carefully removed the old bandage.

"This isn't healing right," I said when I saw the festering wound. "It needs stitching."

"Go ahead and stitch it, then."

I looked up to see if he was joking but he wasn't.

"Are you crazy? A minute ago you didn't want me washing your clothes and now you're willing to let me sew up your leg like . . . like an old torn shirt?"

"I'd do it myself if I could reach that far. Don't you sew?"

"Of course I sew. But I couldn't . . . I haven't the stomach for something like this."

"Maybe Aunt Batty would—"

"She's a half-crazy old woman. You need a doctor."

"No," he said simply. "I already told you, no doctors."

"Why are you being so stubborn?"

"I already explained that, too."

I felt my anger boiling up like a kettle on a hot stove. "And I already explained that my husband died from a cut that wasn't nearly as bad as yours. Sam might still be alive today if he'd seen a doctor in time."

"I'm very sorry for your loss, ma'am," he said politely, "but this is my decision to make, not yours."

I wanted to yell at him again, tell him to get out of my house then and go on down the road and crawl under a bush to die, but he was just stubborn enough to do it. I put a lid on my anger.

"Well, if you don't get this leg looked at you'll have a nasty scar at the very least," I warned. "Maybe even a limp in your step."

"I can live with that. It'll be a good reminder."

"Of what? Your mule-headed stubbornness?"

A slight smile crossed his lips. "Of the hazards of traveling the rails without a ticket."

"And what does that nasty-looking scar on your chest remind you of?"

The words flew out of my mouth before I even thought about

them. His smile faded as he slipped his hand inside his shirt and fingered the spot as if surprised to still find it there. He stared at me without answering.

"I . . . I'm sorry," I said when I saw the pained look in his eyes. "I shouldn't have—"

"It's all right," he said softly. "That scar reminds me of a good friend."

I pulled my gaze away from his and quickly gathered up all my things. I was almost through the door when he stopped me with his words. "I'm going to pay you back, ma'am. Just as soon as I'm able to climb out of this bed, I promise I'll pay you back. I may not have much, but I always pay my debts."

I slowly turned to face him. "I know you will. I thought we already talked about you fixing Aunt Batty's roof."

"That's the very least I can do. But it's you I owe a debt to, not Aunt Batty."

"She's kin. If you help her out, you'll be helping me."

"I know, I know . . . but you're the one who's been feeding me and changing my bandages and . . . and staying up with me for half the night, worrying. You don't even know me. I'm a stranger to you—one that smells pretty bad, too—yet you brought me into your house . . . and you cared."

I looked away, embarrassed. "I'm just doing my Christian duty, same as anyone else would have done."

"No, ma'am. Most folks would have left a worthless tramp like me out there to die all alone."

I didn't know about most folks, but I did know that Frank Wyatt would have run a raggedy old vagrant like Gabriel Harper off his property in no time flat. Lucky for him Frank was dead.

"Eliza, you need to tell me how I can pay you back."

I was so surprised to hear him say my name in that deep, soft voice of his, that I barely understood his question. Then the thought came to me—maybe he really was an angel sent to help me. Maybe his being sick was some kind of a test and now that I had passed, God would let him stay and help me run the orchard.

"You know anything about farm work and apple trees?" I asked.

"Some."

"Then there'll be plenty of ways you can pay me back come springtime."

I didn't know what to do with myself for the rest of the morning. There were still enough of Frank Wyatt's rules instilled in me after living with him for ten years that I couldn't bring myself to do any work on the Sabbath. But to have fun, like Aunt Batty urged us to do? I could barely remember what the word meant.

When I finished in Mr. Harper's room, I put on my coat and quietly went out on the back porch to take a peek at what making snow angels was all about. Jimmy was busy rolling huge snowballs to build a fort. Becky and Aunt Batty were flopping over backward into a snow drift, then waving their arms and legs all around like they were trying to fly. I spotted Luke out in the yard under the clothesline where the snow was all packed down, playing a game with Winky.

Luke would throw the ball for Winky to fetch, but the plump little dog couldn't seem to run in a straight line to where the ball landed. It took him forever to find it, then every time he headed back toward Luke with it in his mouth, his bad eye would cause him to veer off to one side and he'd end up missing Luke by five or six feet. Poor Winky would stop and look around, bewildered and offended, as if Luke had deliberately moved off to one side to trick him.

Luke laughed so hard he dropped to the ground. Tears came to my eyes as I watched him giggling and rolling in the snow with the little dog licking his face like he was a lollipop. What a glorious sound Luke's laughter was! The child inside my son was re-born, thanks to a silly, rumpled-looking, one-eyed dog. Suddenly Winky was beautiful to me, as sleek and as graceful as a real hunting dog.

I remember thinking, *If only this could last—the ice cream, the snow, the little dog and ridiculous cats, the laughter. If only our lives could stay this way, for my children's sakes.* But even on this day of rest I felt trouble sitting patiently at my feet, waiting for me to move so it could shadow me again. God just didn't seem to want me to be happy. I wasn't allowed to be.

I found out the next day just how right I had been.

———

First thing Monday morning I fired up the stove in the wash-house so Aunt Batty and I could do laundry. The water was getting hot in the copper boiler, and we had just set up the bench wringer and galvanized washtubs when a shiny black car pulled into my driveway. I recognized the driver, Mr. Preston, from Frank Wyatt's church. He was an elder, like Frank had been, and a real bigwig with the Savings and Loan in Deer Springs. Was he going to scold me for not coming to church anymore? I dried my hands on my apron and went out to greet him, feeling cornered.

"May I take your coat and hat, Mr. Preston?" I fussed as I led him into my parlor. "Would you care for a cup of coffee?"

"No, thank you, Mrs. Wyatt. This isn't a social call, I'm afraid." He took a seat on the horsehair sofa, still wearing his overcoat, and pulled an envelope from his inside pocket. His eyes were on his shoes, not my face. "I'm here to talk about your mortgage," he said, handing the envelope to me. "I'm very sorry, but we're going to have to foreclose."

I heard my heart pounding in my ears. "What does that mean?"

"The bank is giving you ninety days to pay this loan in full. The letter explains everything—the terms and the amount owed and so forth."

His words made no sense to me. "I don't understand. This farm has been in my husband's family for years. How could they owe your bank money for it?"

"Your father-in-law borrowed money a while back to make some improvements—plant new trees, purchase a truck, things like that. Farmers do it all the time, borrowing in the spring and paying it off when the fall crops come in. He used this house and land as collateral—that's a typical practice, too. Unfortunately, because of the stock market collapse, Frank didn't get as much for his crops as he'd planned. Nobody did. Then he passed away so suddenly. . . ."

"So you're saying I owe you this money now?"

"You're Frank Wyatt's next of kin."

"How much money?"

"It's all there in the letter. He still owed a little over five hundred dollars when he died."

My mind went flying in a hundred directions like a flock of geese at a shotgun blast. It might as well have been five million dollars. I tried to stay calm and recall what little I knew about business matters. "Will I be able to pay the money back in installments, like a regular loan?"

Mr. Preston coughed, then cleared his throat. "The . . . uh . . . the bank has been forced to dissolve. I'm afraid our creditors will need everything in ninety days."

"Where am I supposed to find that kind of money by then?"

He sighed. "Some folks are holding auctions, trying to sell off some of their equipment. Problem is, everyone around here is in pretty much the same predicament. Most folks owe even more money than Frank Wyatt did. There aren't too many folks in a position to buy right now."

"What happens if I can't raise the money?"

"Then the bank will take legal possession of Wyatt Orchards. They can auction it off to reclaim the debt."

"But that isn't fair," I cried. "This house belongs to my children. They never borrowed a single dime from your bank, and now you're saying the bank has a right to turn them out of their own home? Just like that?"

Mr. Preston stood, shoving his hands deep inside his pockets, as if they were stained with blood and he wanted to hide them. "I'm very sorry, Mrs. Wyatt. There's really nothing I can do. I just have the unfortunate task of serving you notice."

I returned to the washhouse in a daze, as if it had all been a terrible dream. I couldn't think what to do, so I concentrated on scrubbing laundry as if my life depended on it.

"What did he want?" Aunt Batty asked. "He's that hot-shot fellow from the bank, isn't he?"

"He had some business of Frank Wyatt's to discuss," I said numbly.

"I never liked that man," Aunt Batty said. "He reminds me of a mule named Barney that my father once owned. Barney was almost as homely as that fellow and just about as cantankerous. That's why I would never put my money in his bank. I'd sooner keep it in Barney's stall out in the barn than leave it with him. Come to think of it, maybe I did leave some of my money out in the barn. . . ."

Aunt Batty went on and on about Barney the mule and his stubborn ways until Becky got the giggles and couldn't stop. But I barely heard a word Aunt Batty said, troubled as I was about owing the bank all that money.

We'd finished hanging all the wash on the line and had gone

inside for lunch when another car pulled into our driveway, this
one much older than the banker's car and not nearly as shiny.
Alvin Greer and his wife, Bertha, stepped out of it. I recognized
the older couple from church, though I'd never been part of their
social circle. They owned a few dozen acres of land just north of
Wyatt Orchards. I was willing to bet they were bringing me more
trouble.

"I know you!" Aunt Batty exclaimed after I'd invited the
Greers into the house. "You're that little Greer boy, aren't you?
Alfred . . . Albert. . . ?"

"Alvin."

"That's it! I went to grammar school with you and your sister
Adelaide." She grabbed the sleeve of Mr. Greer's coat and examined it closely, then smiled up at him. "I see you finally learned to
use a handkerchief. Good for you! When he was a youngster," she
explained to Mrs. Greer and me, "Alvin always had a runny nose
and he used to wipe it on his coat sleeve until he had a shiny patch
right there."

Mr. Greer's face turned brighter than a ripe apple and I was
afraid he was about to have a fit. But just then Becky skipped into
the kitchen with a ball of gray yarn and a crochet hook. She and
Aunt Batty were getting carried away with making kittens for Arabella, and Becky had gone into the parlor to rummage through
my knitting basket for more yarn.

"I found this color," she said gaily, then stopped when she saw
we had company.

"Becky Jean, say 'how do you do' to Mr. and Mrs. Greer," I
prompted.

"How do you do," she repeated, then started chattering like a
Victrola that had been wound up too tight. "Won't this make a
pretty color for Arabella's new kitten? Aunt Batty is knitting our
cat some babies because she wants to be a mama real bad—the

cat, I mean, not Aunt Batty—and I'm going to make their tails."
She waved the crochet hook. "Aunt Batty is teaching me how."

"That's . . . nice . . ." Mrs. Greer looked as if she didn't know
quite what to make of it all. Arabella rubbed against her leg, purring loudly. Bertha Greer was known to be the biggest gossip in the
entire church so it wouldn't be long before everyone in Deer
Springs heard that the Wyatts had all lost their minds.

"If we could have a few minutes of your time," Alvin Greer
said, "we've come to discuss some very important business, Mrs.
Wyatt."

"Of course. Won't you step into the parlor? Would you care
for some coffee?"

"No, thanks." They sat side by side on the good horsehair sofa
where Mr. Preston had sat just a few hours earlier, looking like
they both had broomsticks up their backs. I pushed Queen Esther
off my rocking chair and sat down facing them.

"We've come to make you an offer, Elise—"

"It's *Eliza*. My name is Eliza."

"Yes . . . of course. We'd like to make you an offer on Wyatt
Orchards, and I think you'll agree that it's a very fair one."

"An offer? But the orchard isn't for sale."

I saw the two exchange glances before Mr. Greer continued.
"We understand you've encountered some . . . uh . . . financial
problems with the Savings and Loan and—"

"I don't see how my finances are any of your affair, Mr. Greer.
And if you heard it from Mr. Preston, then he had no business
telling you."

"Now, Eliza, don't get yourself riled up."

"Everybody in Deer Springs knows the bank is folding," Bertha Greer said. "Each one of us is affected by it one way or another—some lost their savings, some are having their mortgages
foreclosed. If you had been in church yesterday, you would know

that everyone is talking about it."

I let her comment go by, too stunned to speak.

"Everyone knows you can't run this place all by yourself," Mr. Greer continued, "and I certainly don't want to see you and your little ones tossed out in the street if the bank forecloses. So I talked it over with Reverend Dill and some of the elders at church yesterday, and they all agree that I'm offering you a fair deal. A very fair deal. You can ask them yourself."

I didn't trust myself to speak, afraid that my voice would come out all shaky or that I'd burst into tears. When I didn't say anything, Mr. Greer kept on talking.

"I'll scrape up enough cash to settle your loan as a down payment to purchase this property—all the orchards, the apple barn, the equipment, and so forth. I'll give you five thousand dollars for everything, paid to you in yearly installments. You can rent the house and the cow barn and enough land for a vegetable patch from me on a yearly basis—subtracted from the purchase price, of course. That way you'll have a place to live until your children are grown. Now, doesn't that sound like a fair deal?" He grinned and it was so unnatural-looking on his usually sour face that he reminded me of a jack-o'-lantern.

"This orchard is worth a lot more than five thousand dollars," I said.

"Well, no, actually it isn't. At the moment, no one has any money to buy it and the banks have no money to lend."

"Besides," Bertha said with a frown, "Alvin and I ought to get a discount because we'll be keeping the orchard in the family. My maiden name was Wyatt, you know."

"Bertha's father and Frank Wyatt's father were brothers," Alvin explained. "The two brothers grew up in this house and the property should have rightfully been divided up between them when old Isaac Wyatt died. I never did understand how Frank and his father ended up owning all of it."

"Everyone agrees that the orchard should stay in the family instead of going to an outsider," Bertha added.

"I may be an outsider," I said, fighting tears, "but my children aren't. Their father was Samuel Wyatt and this land rightfully belongs to them. I'm not about to just hand it over—"

"How old is your oldest boy? Nine, ten years old?" Alvin Greer was beginning to lose his temper, something he'd probably promised his wife he wouldn't do. "There's a lot of responsibility in running a big place like this, and by the time your boy is old enough to run it the way his grandfather did, this orchard will be in ruins."

"Mrs. Wyatt—Eliza—can't you see that my husband and I are just trying to do our Christian duty and help you out?"

"I'm making you a very fair offer," Mr. Greer added.

I stood up, so angry my knees shook. "I need some time to think this over. I'll let you know when I've decided."

I took their coats off the coat rack and handed them back. They were being dismissed without my signature on the deal, and they weren't very happy about it.

"It's a very fair offer," Greer repeated on his way out the door.

"Good day, Mr. and Mrs. Greer."

After they'd gone, Aunt Batty came to me with a worried look on her face. "Are we hosting an open house today, Toots? Because if we are, I really should give Winky a bath and change my dress."

"No, Aunt Batty. Believe me, none of these *guests* were invited."

"Well, they have a lot of nerve coming over here uninvited, don't they? I never could stomach that snotty-nosed Greer boy. I'm telling you, that sleeve of his would just make you sick to look at it."

"I need to drive into Deer Springs," I said, suddenly deciding what I would do. "Will you watch Becky Jean and Mr. Harper for me while I'm gone? I'll be back before the boys get home from school."

"Sure, Toots. Is the open house tomorrow, then?"

"No. There's no open house." I had to walk away before she had me thoroughly exasperated.

I rummaged through my father-in-law's office and gathered up his lockbox and all his important papers, then drove into town to talk to John Wakefield, the family lawyer. Mr. Wakefield was just about as old as Methuselah and had probably been practicing law when Moses led the Israelites out of Egypt. But Frank Wyatt had trusted him and that said a lot.

Mr. Wakefield's secretary, who was nearly as ancient as he was, led me into his dusty office to see him right away when I told her it was an emergency. We caught the poor old man napping at his desk, so I had to let his secretary bring us a pot of tea—even though I was too upset to drink any—in order to give him time to come fully awake.

"Yes . . . yes . . ." he kept saying, and his head wobbled all around on his scrawny neck like it might come loose. "Yes . . . what can I do for you, Mrs. Wyatt?"

I told him all about the bank foreclosing on me and showed him the letter. Then I explained Alvin Greer's offer. It was hard to keep from bursting into tears because I was still so outraged that he would dare to offer me only five thousand dollars for Wyatt Orchards and then expect me to rent my own house from him.

"I don't know anything at all about my father-in-law's finances, Mr. Wakefield," I finished. "He never confided in me like he did in you. Can you help me figure out how to pay back that bank loan?"

"Give me a few days to look through all these papers," he said. "I'll give you a call when I've got them straightened out."

"I don't have a telephone."

"Yes, yes, that's right. Frank wouldn't own a telephone. Come back in a week, then."

I left Mr. Wakefield's office feeling no comfort at all.

— CHAPTER FIVE —

I 'll bet you're getting tired of laying there flat on your back all day," Aunt Batty told Gabe when she brought in his breakfast the next morning. I had bought some iodine and other medicines at the drugstore in Deer Springs and I was doctoring his leg. He still ran a low-grade fever.

"Don't get any ideas about moving him all around," I said, "or his leg is going to rip wide open again."

"Do you want me to help you sit up," she asked him, "so you can read a book, maybe?"

"I can do it," Gabe said, pulling himself upright. "You don't need to fuss over me, Aunt Batty—though I appreciate your kindness."

"It's no trouble at all. The Bible says that when Elijah was all worn out the angels took care of him, so I figure we can all use an angel now and then, right? Now, what kind of books do you like to read, Gabe?" She started digging through the nearest box. "It looks like these are all adventure stories. Would either one of these interest you?" She pulled out two books and handed them to him. From the look on his face, she might have handed him a king's ransom.

"Wow! *Danger in the Jungle* and *African Treasure*, by Herman Walters!"

"You've heard of him?" she asked.

"Who hasn't heard of him! He's one of the most popular adventure writers of his time. I loved these books when I was a boy! I must have read them a hundred times."

"Oh, then maybe you'll want to read something else." She bent to pull out more books and piled them on the bed beside him.

"These are all by Herman Walters!" Gabe said in surprise. He leaned over to peer into the box. "I can't believe it! How many of these do you have?"

"I own every single book he ever wrote."

"And they're all first editions, too," he said, leafing through several of them. He acted as excited as a kid on Christmas morning. "Look at these—they're in mint condition! Do you have any idea what these would be worth?"

"Let's see. Forty-three—no, forty-four books—at a cover price of seventy-five cents comes to . . ." She started drawing numbers in the air on an invisible chalkboard, trying to do the arithmetic.

"They're worth much more than seventy-five cents apiece to a collector!" Gabe said. "Especially if this is Herman Walters' complete works. Don't ever sell them that cheaply, Aunt Batty. You would be giving them away."

She looked confused and worried. "Oh dear. I'm afraid I've already given them away."

"You did? I don't understand. How is it that you still have them?"

"I gave one set to Matthew and Samuel to read and kept the other set for myself. The boys loved reading them when they were young." She smiled, remembering.

"I did, too," Gabe murmured, still leafing through one of them. "I grew up on these books. They're one of the reasons I decided to make writing my life's work."

"Well, isn't that a coincidence?" Aunt Batty exclaimed. "These are Herman's life's work! You remind me a little bit of him."

"You knew Herman Walters?" he asked in amazement.

"Oh yes. Very well. In fact he wrote every single one of these books in my little stone cottage down by the pond."

I decided it was time I jumped into the discussion. "That's a little hard to believe, Aunt Batty. He was a very famous writer, and—"

"Wow!" Gabe cried, interrupting me. "You have all of Betsy Gibson's books, too?" He had pulled himself over to the edge of the bed and was sorting through a second box of books. "I didn't realize Miss Gibson had written this many!"

"Yes, she wrote sixty-two of them down in my little cottage."

"Don't tell me you knew Betsy Gibson, too?" I said skeptically.

"Yes, she was a very close friend of mine—but you won't tell anyone, will you, Toots? It can be our little secret."

Gabe and I both stared at her, unsure whether to believe her or not. As a girl, I had read every Betsy Gibson book that I could get my hands on. They were wholesome tales of spunky young girls who went looking for adventure and love—and usually learned an important moral lesson along the way. I had convinced myself that I could be as brave as one of her heroines the day I stepped off the train in Deer Springs. But could Aunt Batty really have known the author of all those books? I remembered the desk that took up her whole dining room and the huge typewriter, big as you please, sitting on top of it. I dug into a third box of books.

"What about all these other authors," I said, testing her. "Jack London, Mark Twain, Charles Dickens. Did they write all their books down in your little cottage, too?"

"Don't be silly! I never met *those* people!"

"But you knew Betsy Gibson *and* Herman Walters?" I asked.

"Oh yes. Quite well. But to tell you the truth, I always liked Mr. Walters just a wee bit better. He was the more adventuresome of the two."

Gabe leaned back against the pillows and laughed. "This is unbelievable! Your cottage was a writing haven for Herman Walters? Now I can't wait to repair that roof."

I remembered the information that Gabe had just let slip and saw my chance to learn more about him. "I couldn't help noticing that you carry around a typewriter, Gabe. It seemed like a very unusual thing for a hobo to have. You say writing is your life's work, too?" His grin faded away.

Aunt Batty clapped her hands in delight. "Oh, are you a writer? How wonderful! What kinds of things do you write?"

I could see Gabe was reluctant to answer, but as he gazed from the book in his hand to Aunt Batty in obvious awe, he finally confessed. "I'm a journalist. I do free-lance work for the *Chicago Tribune* and sometimes for the *Saturday Evening Post.*"

"And are you down on your luck at the moment," she asked, "or is this your disguise?"

"I was doing research, Aunt Batty. I'm writing about the hobo life, and all the interesting people I've met who ride the rails."

"I never would have guessed!" she said. "You look just like a real tramp with all that shaggy hair—and you even smell like one!"

"Thank you," he said, smiling slightly. "Actually, I've been on the road for quite a while and my story is nearly finished. I was working my way back to Chicago to submit the piece to my editor when I had this little mishap with my leg."

"Well, as long as you're going to be laid up awhile," Aunt Batty said, "why don't you type up your story and mail it from here? I'll be glad to give you a hand. What do you need, some typing paper? Maybe a little table to set your typewriter on? We can fix everything up for him, can't we, Toots?"

"I guess so," I said. Aunt Batty made it sound like such a simple matter that it was pretty hard for either Gabe or me to turn her down.

She lugged her great big typewriter up the hill to my house that very day, insisting that it was much better than Gabe's little old rickety one, along with a stack of typing paper. Gabe worked on and off all that week, as often as his fever allowed. He still tired very easily, and he would have to stop every so often and sleep, but then I'd hear him typing again, sometimes in the middle of the night.

By the time I drove into town for my appointment with Mr. Wakefield, Gabe's story was all finished. Aunt Batty wrapped it all up in a package and I took it with me to the Deer Springs post office and mailed it off to Chicago.

———

"We have a problem, Eliza." The first words out of the lawyer's mouth sent a shiver through me. I didn't need any more problems. I had more than enough problems as it was. How could God even think about heaping any more on me?

"Are you aware that your father-in-law was speculating rather heavily on the commodities market?" Mr. Wakefield asked.

"I don't know anything about his business dealings. Is that like playing the stock market?"

"It's similar, but it involves speculating on farm commodities rather than on corporate stock. Unfortunately, commodities traders can lose a great deal more money than they've invested—and it seems that Frank lost his entire life's savings."

"So there's no money at all? How will I pay back Mr. Preston at the Savings and Loan?"

Mr. Wakefield's mournful face reminded me of a heavyhearted bloodhound. "I'm sorry, but that money will still have to be paid within ninety days or the bank's creditors will take possession. Some folks are holding auctions and selling off their equipment to raise funds. But I have to warn you, with this economic depression we're in, they're not getting anywhere near what the equipment is worth. That goes for farm acreage, too, I'm afraid."

I was much too shocked and stunned to cry. "So . . . so you're telling me that . . . except for the orchard and all the equipment—I'm broke?"

Mr. Wakefield closed his eyes for a moment before he continued. I wondered if he was praying. "I'm afraid it's even worse than that, Eliza. Now, I know that Sam intended for the farm to go to you and the children, but your husband passed away before his father did, so Frank's will has priority. I'm sorry to tell you this, but Frank willed everything to his elder son, Matthew Wyatt. The estate would pass to his second son, Samuel, and his family only in the event that Matthew died without an heir. Frank's will makes no mention of you or your children. Evidently it was drawn up quite some time ago."

"What are you saying?"

"Matthew Wyatt is the legal owner of Wyatt Orchards, not you. Until Matthew renounces all claims to his inheritance, we can't transfer the title to anyone else."

"Matthew! But he's dead, isn't he?"

"Well, I don't know. It's my understanding that Matthew

enlisted in the Army around 1916 or '17 and fought over in France, but Frank never mentioned anything about him dying. In fact, the memorial plaque at church lists the names of all the local boys who gave their lives, and Matthew Wyatt's name isn't on there. I hoped you knew where he'd settled after the war so I could contact him."

I shook my head. "Neither my husband nor his father would ever talk about him. Not one word. I always figured it was because they were too grief-stricken. I figured Matthew was dead and—" I stopped, remembering how I'd made the same assumption about my mother.

"Perhaps he is dead, Eliza. But according to the law, I'll need to see a death certificate before I can transfer the deed over to you."

"So now what do I do?"

"Well, I suggest you go home and try to locate some family records. See if the army sent a death notice for example, or if there's been any other correspondence with Matthew over the years, perhaps with a return address. In the meantime, I'll write to Washington. Their records will tell us if Matthew was killed in action or if he was discharged."

"How long will that take? The bank wants the money in ninety days."

"I'm sorry, but this may take some time. And I can't move forward with Alvin Greer's offer to purchase since the orchard isn't in your name."

I was relieved to finally hear at least one bit of good news. I didn't want to sell the orchard to Alvin Greer, even if he would let us live there.

"But from what I can tell after looking through Frank's papers," Mr. Wakefield said sadly, "everything belongs to Matthew—

the house, the land, the tractor, and all the other equipment . . .
even the truck."

I'd never hated Frank Wyatt as much as I did at that moment.
He had not only robbed my children of their father, but now he
was robbing them of their inheritance, giving everything that
rightfully belonged to them to an ungrateful son who'd left home
years ago.

"What about all those years that my husband worked for his
father," I cried, "slaving away in all kinds of weather to help him
run that place? What about all the backbreaking work Sam did
while Matthew was who-knows-where? Doesn't that count for anything? My husband *died* working for his father, and you're telling
me his children get *nothing*?"

"I'm sorry, Eliza . . . I understand how you feel. . . ."

"No, you don't! That orchard is my home, my children's
home!" I battled my tears, determined not to cry, but a stray drop
rolled down my cheek in spite of my efforts. Mr. Wakefield's eyes
seemed a little watery, too.

"Once we find Matthew Wyatt," he said, "I'll do my best to
convince him that you and your children deserve fair compensa-
tion for all the work Samuel did. But realistically, Mrs. Wyatt, you
know you would never be able to run Wyatt Orchards by yourself.
Perhaps Frank knew that, too."

The only thing Frank knew was that I was an outsider, and he
hated me for it. This was his way of punishing Sam for not marrying well and adding even more land to his little kingdom. I understood that. But what I couldn't understand was how any man
could disinherit his own grandchildren—his own flesh and blood.

When I reached home I sat out in the driveway in the truck—
Matthew's truck—letting my emotions simmer down before going
inside. I felt like spitting on Frank Wyatt's grave. It was so unfair!
I was more determined than ever to hang on to this land and this

home that were rightfully mine. I had to find out what had happened to Matthew Wyatt. But the way I felt right now, if it turned out Matthew was alive, I was angry enough to murder him myself.

I started off by searching Frank's office. He'd kept careful records of every business transaction, every invoice, every receipt for the past twenty years, it seemed. But there was not so much as a scrap of paper with Matthew's name on it—let alone a letter or a mailing address.

When I finished that search to no avail, I got a stepladder and climbed up to the attic. As I looked around at the piles of discarded furniture, dusty boxes, and old steamer trunks, I couldn't help thinking about the comment Aunt Batty had made at Frank's funeral: *"There's a huge load of grief up in the attic of this house."* She didn't know the half of it.

I dug through a mountain of stuff, searching for old photo albums, letters, or any other memorabilia I could find that might mention Matthew. It was much too cold to stay up there for very long, so I carried any box that looked promising downstairs to the parlor.

"Well, will you look at this," Aunt Batty said, pulling an old beaded purse from one of the boxes. "This belonged to my sister, Lydia. Oh, I can see her now—this purse on one arm and a beau on the other. My, how that girl loved to dance."

"Aunt Batty, will you please look through these pictures with me?" I asked when I unearthed a family photo album. "Maybe you can tell me who all these people are." Some of the pictures had captions below them, written in white ink on the black pages, but most did not. I realized that I not only had never met Matthew Wyatt, I'd never even seen a picture of him.

"Wait, let me get my spectacles first." She retrieved them, then sat beside me on the sofa with Becky perched on her lap. The three of us paged through the album together. "A lot of these are

Frank Wyatt's relations," Aunt Batty said as we studied the first few pages.

"I never knew he had relatives here in Deer Springs until the other day," I said. "Mrs. Greer surprised me when she said she was Frank's cousin."

"Oh, there are still a few of them around. You know Julia Foster, the sheriff's wife? She's another Wyatt cousin."

"Is there a picture of Lydia in here?" I asked, leafing ahead through the book. My mother-in-law was another mystery I'd never understood. Both Sam and his father would clam right up if I tried to ask questions about her. But then, I didn't want to answer any questions about my own past either, so I'd learned to let sleeping dogs lie.

"Let me see. . . . Here, this is my sister, Lydia."

"Oh, she's beautiful!" The woman Aunt Batty pointed to was not at all the sturdy, hard-working farmer's wife I had expected to see. Lydia was so lovely she took my breath away. I stared at my mother-in-law's face for the first time, unable to take my eyes off her. Hers was a delicate kind of beauty that was both innocent and alluring at the same time.

"You would never know we were sisters, would you?" Aunt Batty said, chuckling to herself.

I glanced at Aunt Batty and saw little resemblance except for the sisters' arched eyebrows and delicate bones. I studied Lydia's dark eyes and graceful brows, her irresistible smile, searching for a resemblance between my husband and his mother. But I couldn't find any. Sam had been powerfully built, with his father's chiseled jaw, fair hair, and blue eyes. Yet something about his mother seemed familiar to me, as though I'd seen her before, even though I knew that I hadn't.

I saw Lydia in several of the pictures on the next few pages, usually surrounded by her three sons at various ages. It was hard for me to look at pictures of Sam when he was young and strong and healthy. I couldn't get over how much my Jimmy resembled him. In nearly all the pictures, Sam stood as close as a shadow to his older brother, Matthew—the way Luke always hangs onto Jimmy's shirttail.

I stared and stared at each picture of Matthew Wyatt. He had his mother's dark hair and eyes, and looked as different from Sam as two brothers could look. But then, the youngest brother, Willie, looked altogether different, too. I knew for sure that Willie was dead. I'd seen his grave in the family plot beside Lydia's and Frank's—beside my Sam's. According to the dates on Willie's tombstone, he had died when he was nine—Jimmy's age. Aunt Batty pointed to his picture.

"This must be one of the last pictures they ever took of little Willie," she said sadly.

"How did he die?" I asked. "I've forgotten what Sam told me."

"Poor child. He fell through the ice on the pond one winter and drowned."

I felt my skin tingle at the eerie coincidence, as if I'd just plunged into that icy water myself. It was the same way the youngest brother in Gabe Harper's story had died.

"Were you there when it happened?" I asked.

She stirred uncomfortably on the hard sofa. "Well, the pond is just beyond my house, you know. I hear an awful lot that goes on."

"Did you hear what happened the day Willie drowned?"

Aunt Batty carefully slid Becky off her lap and gave her the beaded purse to play with on the floor by our feet. Then she pulled a flowered handkerchief from the sleeve of her yellow sweater and began kneading it.

"The three boys had been sledding on the hill behind my

house—just like your three young ones do. I heard them whooping and yelling, then it got real quiet. I thought maybe they'd gone home. But when I looked out my window I saw Matthew and Willie standing out by the pond. The boys liked to skate on it once it froze solid. I was afraid they'd try it that day and I knew it was still too early in December for the ice to be safe."

I felt another chill shiver through me as she repeated mirrored details from Gabe's story.

"I tried yelling out the door to them," Aunt Batty continued, "but they didn't hear me. I went to get my coat and boots—and I was always sorry afterward that I took so long bundling up. By the time I got outside, Matthew was hysterical, screaming that Willie had fallen through the ice and crying, 'Save him! Save him!' I had all I could do to keep that boy from jumping in after him. We got help as fast as we could, but it was too late." I heard the tears in Aunt Batty's trembling voice. "That poor child . . . and poor, poor Lydia."

I was sorry I'd dredged up such painful memories, but I needed to know something else. "Was Willie Frank Wyatt's favorite son?" I asked.

"It was shameful the way he favored that boy and heaped abuse on the other two. They were as jealous as sin of him, and I couldn't blame them. Poor Matthew felt so responsible for what happened to little Willie that he kept saying it was all his fault. I told him to hush up! Don't ever say that in front of your father!"

"Was it true? Was the accident Matthew's fault?"

"The truth is that Frank Wyatt killed Willie by playing favorites."

Only one other person knows and I don't think she'll ever tell, Gabe had written. My heart began to gallop like a race horse. What if, beneath all that shaggy hair and overgrown beard—what if Gabe Harper was really Matthew Wyatt?

I remembered the way he had stood in my kitchen that first night, reminding me for all the world of my Sam. He had even bowed his head and prayed before eating like Sam always did. And he'd known just what work needed to be done out in the barn. He'd had a guilty look on his face, too, when I'd asked him how he'd known my last name was Wyatt. I shivered again.

I slowly paged through the photo album, staring at Matthew Wyatt's face in every picture, searching for a resemblance to the bushy-haired man in my spare bedroom. Hadn't Aunt Batty said Gabe looked familiar the first time she saw him? And he called her Aunt Batty much too easily to be a stranger.

Maybe that was why Gabe had refused to see the doctor— maybe he had a scar or a birthmark or something that the family doctor would recognize, maybe even that scar on his chest. And maybe that's why Gabe seemed so put out with me when I told him I'd rummaged through his things. He didn't want me to discover the truth.

But why all this secrecy, especially now that his father and brother were both dead? Why didn't he just step forward and say who he was if it was true? I couldn't very well ask him without admitting that I'd read his private journals. Besides, I had no idea how he would react if he found out that the house and the orchard now belonged to him. Would he take it all away from us? Kick us out in the snow? For all I knew, Gabe—or Matthew, or whatever his name was—had a wife and a family of his own somewhere who were just dying to move right in.

"Aunt Batty, whatever happened to Matthew?" I finally asked.

"Matthew?" She glanced around the room with a worried look on her face as if he'd been here a moment ago and she'd misplaced him. Then she caught herself. "No, that young one is named Jimmy," she said aloud. "Matthew joined the army and went to France to fight in the war."

The war. Gabe carried a U.S. Army canteen in his bag.

Part of me wanted Gabe to be Matthew so he could pay off the mortgage and help me run things, but part of me was afraid that the kids and I would lose our home—and I could never allow that to happen.

"The war ended more than ten years ago, Aunt Batty. What happened to Matthew after that? Do you have any idea? Did he ever come home?"

Aunt Batty squinted in concentration. "Matthew was still over in France when his mother died. I wrote to tell him that she'd passed away. Lydia had given me his address and asked me to write to him before . . . before she left us. . . ." It seemed as though there was more Aunt Batty wanted to say. I waited.

"Matthew wrote back to me just the one time," she continued. "He thanked me for telling him the news and asked me to please take care of Sam. That's all—just that one short letter. I don't think anyone has heard from him since."

"Do you still have that letter? Could I see it?" I already knew what Gabe's handwriting looked like. I could easily compare the two.

"I don't know if I kept that letter or not. I could look for it, I suppose. Is it important?"

"Yes, it's very important." But I knew I was asking the impossible with Aunt Batty's house in the mess it was in. "If Matthew had died over in France," I asked her, "would Frank Wyatt have told you?"

"Never! Frank hasn't spoken to me since the night he burned my father's house down."

"He burned your father's house down?"

"Yes, he certainly did! He wanted to plant peach trees on that plot of land and my house was in his way. Oh, he tried to make everyone think it was an accident but I knew better. I'm telling you, Toots—as sure as apples grow on apple trees, Frank Wyatt started that fire. I've had to live in the little cottage ever since."

She was describing a history I knew nothing about, and I wasn't so sure I wanted to know. I had been afraid of my father-in-law from the very first day I met him. Later I grew to hate him for allowing Sam to die. He had always insisted that Aunt Batty was crazy. Now I wondered who I should believe.

"Come to think of it," she said, "it wouldn't surprise me to learn that Frank Wyatt made my kitchen roof cave in, too."

"But he died last November. How could he—"

"Oh, you don't know him like I did, Toots! He might have sawed through the roof timbers and then waited for it to snow."

I heaved a tired sigh. I had more questions now than before I started looking for answers. How was I ever going to untangle this mess? I turned to the last page in the album and found the very last picture of Matthew. He looked to be about eighteen years old, standing beside his brother Sam. Behind them was the newly painted sign on the side of the barn: *Wyatt Orchards—Frank Wyatt & Sons, Proprietors.* I carefully removed the photo and handed it to Aunt Batty.

"I need to find Matthew, Aunt Batty. Do you have any idea what might have happened to him?"

Aunt Batty didn't answer me. Her mind had drifted off to another place and another time. In the silence, I heard a freight train rumbling past the orchard. The whistle's mournful sound reminded me, as it always did, of all my years of longing for a home. I had criss-crossed the country on trains, gazing at the lights that glowed from the windows of the houses I passed, dreaming of a family and a house like this one. I'd made my decision ten years ago to grab hold of Wyatt Orchards and make it my own, never knowing its hidden secrets and heartaches, unprepared for all I had bargained for.

But now I had three kids to think about—kids I would lay down and die for. I had to find a way to make a living for them, to keep the home that belonged to them. I had to prove that Matthew Wyatt was dead.

"Please, Aunt Batty. If you know anything at all about Matthew, please tell me."

She frowned. "If you want to understand what happened to Matthew, you'd have to understand my sister, Lydia, first."

"Tell me anything you think might help. I don't want to lose this orchard. I want it for my kids. It's their home—my home."

She glanced at me sharply, an angry look suddenly crossing her face. "Are you sure you want to keep this orchard for those young ones? The price is very high, you know."

"I know. The man from the bank wants five hundred dollars, and if I don't pay him in ninety days we'll lose everything."

She turned away. "Oh, it costs much more than that. It has already cost the lives of the people I loved. . . ."

PART II

Lydia's Story

Deer Springs, 1894

"We need to be angels for each other, to give each

other strength and consolation. Because only when we

fully realize that the cup of life is not only a cup of

sorrow but also a cup of joy will we be able to drink it."

HENRI NOUWEN

CHAPTER SIX

My sister, Lydia, was the most beautiful girl in Deer Springs—and I was the homeliest. Lydia could spend hours gazing at herself in the mirror, but I always turned my head away whenever I passed one because I hated what I saw. My face was as round and as plain as a baking powder biscuit, with a nose like a Roman emperor's stuck right in the middle of it. And my body—well, my body certainly should have matured by the time I'd celebrated my twentieth birthday, but I was still as plump and flat-chested as a schoolgirl. My mother nagged me constantly about the way I slouched, warning that I'd surely cripple my spine if I didn't stand up straight. But the taunts of my schoolmates and the nickname "Betty Butterball" rang louder in my ears than any of my mother's warnings. I was short and fat and that was that.

My shoulder-length hair wasn't chestnut like Lydia's, or auburn or mahogany or some other glamorous color like the heroines of all my favorite novels. It was plain old brown, like mouse fur. Its unruly waves frizzed around my face like a bush, refusing to stay neatly piled on my head. My eyes, under thick, heavy brows, weren't dark and mysterious like Lydia's eyes, which had the rich luster of bronze velvet. They weren't even an interesting color like hazel or caramel or sandalwood. They were just plain old brown, the color of dirt. No wonder the only things I knew about love and romance had come from books. No wonder I'd never had a single boyfriend until Frank Wyatt courted me. Lydia was the one who attracted boyfriends like bees to apple blossoms.

Lydia was seventeen months younger than me, and from the time she turned fourteen, her voluptuous figure had more curves than a country lane. If she hadn't been my best friend, I would have hated her for certain. But the two of us were as close as two sisters could be, forced to turn to each other for affection and consolation by our grim, practical-minded parents. They staunchly refused to pet and cuddle us for fear we would grow up pampered and spoiled.

"Children need discipline and order in their lives," my mother believed, "not a bunch of foolish molly-coddling." Her typical answer to all our wounds and heartaches was "Quit your bellyaching."

My father had married my mother, a spinster school mistress, when she was thirty-five and he was forty-two. He'd lost his first wife and two sons to a cholera epidemic and had hoped to produce another son to inherit his land. Instead, he'd been sorely disappointed to find himself stuck with two daughters. And after Lydia's difficult arrival as a breech baby, my mother promptly moved him out of her bedroom, making it very clear that he would father no more children by her.

With tenderness and sympathy so hard to come by in our

household, Lydia and I learned to rely on each other. "I'll be your guardian angel, Betsy," she promised, "and you can be mine." We made a solemn vow to watch out for one another when I was eight and a half and she was seven, and we formalized it with a "pinkie promise." We never let each other down.

That's why I turned to Lydia in utter misery after I'd completed the eighth grade of grammar school and my father informed me what the future course of my life would be. He had called me away from my novel and my rocking chair on the front porch one soft summer day and ordered me into our front parlor. It was a bleak, colorless room with worn rugs on the floor and dreary pictures on the bare plaster walls, a room that felt chilly even in the summertime. We lived in an era of ornate Victorian frills—fringed horsehair sofas in silk tapestry and damask, glass-fronted curio cabinets stuffed with ornaments and gewgaws, flocked wallpaper, crocheted doilies and antimacassars—but our farmhouse was as plain and as cold as my cheerless parents. We didn't own a Gramophone or a stereopticon or a magic lantern—not even a piano or a cottage organ. The sound of the mantel clock ticking out the passing of time accompanied our evenings as we sat on the plain, mismatched furniture that other people had discarded. That's where Father ordered me to sit on that warm afternoon, and coming from him, his plans for my future had the tone of a death knell.

"I have decided that you will continue your education next fall," he announced. "You will be a schoolteacher, like your mother."

"But I don't want to be a teacher!" I cried. In my fertile but naïve imagination, I had daydreamed of moving to New York City to become a newspaper reporter like my idol, Nellie Bly. My horror at the thought of being trapped in a desolate one-room schoolhouse all day with two dozen mulish farm children made me outspoken for the first time in my life.

"Please, Father, don't make me be a schoolteacher. I want to be a newspaper reporter and write for the *New York World* like Nellie Bly."

"Out of the question. That is not a suitable career for a young woman, nor is New York City a suitable place to live. You will be a teacher."

The discussion was over. It was useless to try to argue with him. I would've had better luck trying to fly. He was my father and I had to obey him. Fathers were gods in their own households, determining when their family rose and when we slept, who we saw and who we didn't see, how we thought, how we behaved, how we felt. I could no more decide the course of my life or my future than the cows could decide when they would be milked. To defy my father was unthinkable. I poured out my sorrow and disappointment on Lydia's shoulder later that night.

"Don't cry, Betsy. Going to teachers' school is an honor," she tried to assure me. "Didn't you tell me that Nellie Bly once studied to be a teacher, too?"

"Well . . . yes, until her father died and she ran out of money."

"See? You can still become a newspaper reporter, just like she did."

"So it isn't ho . . . hopeless?" I asked, hiccuping through my tears. I took the handkerchief Lydia offered me and honked my beak of a nose.

We were in our attic bedroom where we shared all our secrets and a double bed, along with an ancient three-drawer dresser and an unfinished closet with mice. We'd moved the bed to the middle of the wall, squeezed between the two dormer windows so we could gaze up at the sky and the stars at night, even though the single-glazed windows were so drafty in the wintertime that frost sometimes formed on the inside of the glass. We had long since learned to sit up carefully in the morning so we wouldn't bump our heads on the slanting ceiling. As cold as it was in winter, the room was stifling in the summer with the sun beating down on the tin roof right above our heads all day. On that hot summer night, as we hugged each other in our cotton nightgowns, our sweaty arms stuck together as if we'd been glued to each other with white paste.

"It's not hopeless at all!" Lydia said. "Father knows you've inherited all the brains in this family so he's making sure you get a good education. Look at me—I'm so dim-witted I'll probably never even make it to the eighth grade. All I'll ever be good for is a wife and a mother. At least being a teacher is glamorous."

"Ha! Then why are the women teachers always old spinsters?"

"You won't be a spinster, Betsy," she said smoothing back my unruly hair. "You'll find a very special man who—"

"I don't want a man! I want to be a newspaper reporter and be daring and brave like Nellie Bly. I want to expose injustice and corruption and change the world like she does."

Nellie Bly was twenty-three and I was fourteen when she pretended to be insane in order to write about life in a notorious women's asylum. Her daring won her a job with *The New York World* and launched her adventurous career as a stunt reporter. I loved reading about all her exploits—posing as an unwed mother to expose the baby-buying trade, pretending to be a thief in order to see inside a New York City jail, and so on. In an age when most women were mere adornments on their husbands' arms, Nellie was an independent woman who dared to enter a man's world and prove she was just as good as they were—maybe even better.

But my dream of becoming a stunt reporter would have to wait. I attended school that fall and studied to be a teacher, as my father had decreed. During my second year there, Nellie Bly had the greatest adventure of her life: She traveled around the world, all alone, in an attempt to beat the hero's record in Jules Verne's novel, *Around the World in Eighty Days*. For two-and-a-half months the whole world followed her progress religiously as she made her way over land and sea, returning to New York in only seventy-two days, six hours, eleven minutes, and fourteen seconds. She was the most famous woman in the world and I wanted to be just like her.

My favorite teacher, Mr. Herman, knew how much I loved reading about Nellie and always gave me his *New York World* as soon as he was finished with it. I made a scrapbook of all her exploits and filled notebook after notebook with imaginary exploits of my own. When I wasn't writing I was reading, devouring books as fast as Mr. Herman loaned them to me.

"You're my best student, Betty," he told me one day after I'd finished reading *Sense and Sensibility*, "but I'm worried about how you will fare as a teacher. To be honest, you're so tiny and soft-spoken that I'm afraid the students will mistake you for one of themselves."

It was his polite way of saying that I was absurdly short and painfully shy—and the rough-and-tumble farmers' children were going to mop the floor with me.

"I really don't want to be a teacher, Mr. Herman," I confessed. "It was my father's idea. What I really want to be is a stunt reporter like Nellie Bly."

He thought for a moment before he replied. "That could be a difficult career, too, for someone as . . . as reserved as you are." He might have added "innocent" or "naïve" or "scared of my own shadow." While I loved reading about Nellie Bly's exploits, the truth was that I would have fainted dead away if adventure had tapped me on the shoulder.

Mr. Herman must have seen my quivering chin and brimming eyes because he quickly added, "Don't get me wrong. You're a very gifted writer, Betty. I enjoy reading everything you write. Your work is head and shoulders above your classmates' work. I'm just not sure that being an investigative reporter is right for you, either."

"Sometimes I write poems," I blurted.

He smiled gently. "Yes, I do see you more as an Elizabeth Barrett Browning than a Nellie Bly."

"Would you like to read some of them?"

"I would be honored."

But I never had a chance to show my poems to him or to finish my studies or to become a teacher—let alone a stunt reporter. Mother took sick the year I turned eighteen, and Father made me quit school to take care of her and run his household. Lydia had a good job by then, working at the Deer Springs Dry Goods store, and Father didn't want to give up the paycheck she brought home to him every week.

I don't think Lydia actually did much work at the store. The owner simply parked her behind the counter and told her to smile, and the competing store across town just about went out of business. Every salesman and farmer's son who walked through the door instantly fell in love with her and would start buying whatever she was selling. Give Lydia two dozen umbrellas on a sunny day and they'd be sold out by noon. She was the store's most valuable asset, and they knew it.

I didn't mind staying home to care for Mother. She liked me to read aloud to her when she was awake and I had time for my own writing projects while she slept—after the cooking and the housework and the laundry were done, of course.

Sometimes I got lonely, but Lydia kept me amused each night with hilarious tales of all the latest gossip in Deer Springs. She could describe selling a yard of cloth to crabby old Myrtle Barstow and have me holding my sides with laughter. Then she would ask, "Did you write any poems today, Betsy? You have to read me one of your poems." Lydia always encouraged me in my writing career.

Most of my poetry described my very limited world—the orchard as it changed with the seasons, the bluebirds and chipmunks feeding on the seeds I scattered for them, the doe and her two fawns drinking from our pond in the evening. But one day Lydia copied two of my poems in her beautiful handwriting and convinced me to mail them to a magazine.

"I swear, if you don't send them, I will!" she said, stomping her foot for emphasis. Lydia worked in the real world every day and had learned to pepper her conversation with scandalous phrases like "I swear" and "holy smokes."

When I finally gave in, she helped me compose a cover letter that sounded as confident and poised as Lydia always did, not meek and apologetic, which was my typical manner. We linked our pinkies for good luck and sent my poems off. Much to my surprise, *Garden Magazine* published one of them and asked me to send more. Lydia and I danced and cried and hugged each other in joy. My payment was only two free copies of the magazine, but I didn't care. It thrilled me just to see my name—my poems!—in print for the first time.

The next day Lydia brought home the weekly *Deer Springs News*. She had smiled at the newsboy and he'd given it to her for free.

"Here, this is for you," she told me. "You *must* write something for the newspaper." I handed it right back to her.

"I can't write anything for the *News*! How can I be an investigative reporter when I'm stuck way out here in a farmhouse all day? I can see the headlines now: 'Scandal Exposed in Fowler's Chicken Coop' or maybe 'Big Brouhaha in Betty's Barn.' "

"Write a letter to the editor, Betsy. Didn't you tell me that's how Nellie Bly got her start?"

Lydia was right. According to the story, Nellie had read a column in the *Pittsburgh Dispatch* stating that women were totally useless for anything outside of marriage. Outraged, Nellie wrote a scathing reply that so amused the *Dispatch*'s editor that he offered her a job.

"There isn't anything in the *Deer Springs News* that's worthy of an outraged response," I sighed after reading it from front to back. "And even if there was, the editor doesn't seem to have much of a sense of humor. I doubt that he would be amused by me."

Against my feeble protests, Lydia chose a short piece I'd written about springtime in an apple orchard and sent it to the editor. We were both thrilled when the newspaper paid me $1.75 for it— my very first paycheck. With our pinkie fingers raised in celebration, I treated Lydia to an ice-cream sundae at the soda fountain in town. Lydia's smile mesmerized the young man behind the counter and he gave us both double scoops for the price of a single.

Mother never recovered from her illness. After lying bedridden for almost two years, she died the year I turned twenty. By then my father's health had also started to decline, and at the age of sixty-three, he found it harder and harder to keep up with the farm work. Faced with his own mortality, he recognized his duty to secure a future for Lydia and me. He came up with a plan that most dime novels would call "nefarious."

I was halfheartedly kneading bread dough in the kitchen with *A Tale of Two Cities* propped against the flour canister one morning in May when Frank Wyatt arrived to see my father. I knew very little about Frank except that he was a deacon at our church, a bachelor, and about eight or nine years older than me. His forefathers had been the community's earliest settlers, farming the land that bordered our acreage on the north side. Frank had inherited his father's entire estate and was slowly buying up all the property he could get his hands on, building Wyatt Orchards into a kingdom with himself as the king.

"Betty, get in here!" my father suddenly called from the parlor. He had a voice that made you drop everything and run, whether you had flour on your hands or not. Frank Wyatt rose from his chair like a gentleman when I entered the room, even though he wore overalls.

"Good morning, Miss Fowler," he said, bowing slightly. Frank was very attractive in a rugged, austere sort of way, with a cleft in his granite chin, hair like pale winter sunshine, and eyes the color of a glacial stream. His movements were stiff, as if he was ill-at-ease in his own broad-shouldered body, and whether sitting or standing, Frank always looked as though he was posing for a photograph. The expression on his stern, unsmiling face when he passed me the collection plate on Sunday always made me feel so miserly I wanted to dump the entire contents of my purse into the basket. But Frank Wyatt had such a spotless reputation in the church and in the community that God might have chiseled him out of the same hunk of stone as the Ten Commandments.

"Bring us some coffee," my father ordered.

"Please don't trouble yourself, Mr. Fowler," Frank said, spreading his massive hands. "I can't stay long. I just dropped by to see how you were doing. The pastor announced in church last Sunday that you were ill again—"

"Not that it's any of *his* business," Father said with a grunt.

"And so I wondered if you could use some help. I have a crew coming to my place later this week and—"

"You don't fool me with your cool manners," Father said, interrupting him. "You've been hovering around here ever since you heard I took sick last winter. You're still looking to get your hands on my property, aren't you?" My father's response to Mr. Wyatt's kind offer was so rude that I turned to escape into the kitchen. "Betty, get back in here and sit down," Father shouted.

"I want you to hear what I have to say, too."

I did as Father commanded. I sat, staring at Frank Wyatt's scuffed work boots, my cheeks burning.

"It's my pond you're after, right?" Father asked him.

"Your pond is the envy of every farmer around here, Mr. Fowler, and—"

"Last winter you offered to buy my land if I ever wanted to sell it, remember?"

"Yes, sir."

"Still interested?"

I glanced up at Frank. He was practically salivating with anticipation. He battled to hide his excitement behind a calm facade. "I feel it's my Christian duty to help others in their time of need. That's the only reason I'm here, sir. Nevertheless, my offer still stands should you decide to sell."

"As a matter of fact I *don't* want to sell. I didn't work hard all these years to build this place up just so I could sell it off to strangers someday. I worked so that my children and grandchildren would have something to inherit when I'm gone. Now, I've put a lot of labor into my land. Unfortunately, the Almighty only saw fit to give me daughters. So here's my decision. I'm deeding everything to my daughter Betty here, for a wedding gift. If you want my land, you'll have to marry her."

I don't know which was greater—my absolute horror or my utter humiliation. How could Father offer his own daughter as part of a package deal, as if I were a prize-winning farm animal or a new plow? How unfair to force Mr. Wyatt to decide if he wanted our land badly enough to marry me as part of the bargain. I knew how Leah, the ugly older sister in the Bible, must have felt listening to scheming Jacob and cheating Laban haggle over her. It took every ounce of willpower I possessed not to burst into tears or to run from the room.

But if my father's blunt offer repulsed Frank, he never showed it. "You're much too generous, Mr. Fowler," he said smoothly. "Any man in Deer Springs would be honored to marry a fine Christian woman like your daughter, even if she had no land at all."

I felt a rush of gratitude toward him for taking some of the sting out of my father's words, even if it was pure poppycock. Every man in Deer Springs longed to marry Lydia, not me.

My father stood, a signal that the bargaining had ended. "Now you know the way it is, Wyatt," he said with a frown. "If you're interested, you can begin with a proper courtship. You have permission to call on my daughter."

"Thank you," Frank said, rising as well. He hesitated a moment, as if mulling something over in his mind. "I believe there is an ice-cream social at church next Saturday afternoon. I would be pleased if you would accompany me, Miss Fowler." I managed to nod but couldn't bring myself to look at him. "Good. I'll stop by for you around two o'clock."

He said good-bye then, leaving me alone with my father. I felt desolate, bereaved. I couldn't seem to move from my chair. "Mr. Wyatt doesn't want to marry me," I whimpered.

"Nonsense. He wants our land. He's a hard-working man. He'll make a good son-in-law." Father had analyzed the situation in terms of himself. He'd never questioned what my wishes or dreams might be. I felt trapped.

"But . . . but what if I don't want to marry him?"

"You'll do as you're told," my father said. "I know what's best for you—understand?" The tears I had struggled to hold back began rolling down my cheeks. Father didn't seem to notice my misery as he savored his triumph. "Young Wyatt has always coveted my property, but what he doesn't realize is that I've coveted Wyatt Orchards just as much. He thinks he's getting my land, but he's forgetting that I'm also getting his. My grandson will own Wyatt Orchards someday. I'll insist that he renames it Wyatt & Fowler Orchards."

"I'm sure Mr. Wyatt would much rather marry Lydia than me," I said, wiping my eyes. "Maybe you should give him a choice, Father."

"Lydia!" he said in surprise. "She won't have any trouble finding a husband or getting on in life. This way I'll make sure that you're married off, too—and married well."

I felt torn between wanting to please my father to finally win his love and approval after all these years and with longing to run away from this terrifying arrangement and applying for a job as a reporter in some big city. In spite of my limited writing success, I had no self-confidence at all. I was terrified of the unknown—of marriage as well as of life alone in a strange city. I poured out all my woe to Lydia in our bedroom that night.

"Jeepers creepers, Betsy, that's wonderful news!" she exclaimed. "Frank Wyatt is a real good-looker."

"Sure—if you like courting a fence post." I marched stiffly across the narrow room in pantomime.

"Maybe he is a bit prim," she said, laughing. "But holy smokes, he's rich! He's one of Deer Springs' most eligible bachelors."

"I don't know how I can even face him under these circumstances," I moaned, flopping backward onto the bed. "Father is practically forcing him to marry me."

"Horse feathers! Mr. Wyatt won't do anything he doesn't want to do, even for land. Besides, if there's going to be a stampede of men trying to marry you to inherit this farm, it's better that Mr. Wyatt gets there first than a lot of other drips I could name."

I covered my face. "He's taking me to the ice-cream social this

Saturday, and I don't know what on earth to say to him all afternoon."

"You want to know what I think? I think Mr. Wyatt is just as shy
as you are. Why else would he remain a bachelor all this time?"
Lydia tugged my hands away, pulling on them until I sat up.
"Come on, I'll teach you a few tricks that drive men crazy."

When it came to men, Lydia was an expert. She secretly led a
wild life, breaking a different boy's heart every week. I helped her
concoct elaborate excuses, saying she was visiting shut-ins or working late at the store doing inventory, and poor Father believed us.
I would hear the fascinating details of her escapades when she
returned home at night—a party at the forbidden dance hall, a
moonlit bonfire at the lake, a secret rendezvous with a traveling
salesman—and I wrote down each installment as if it were the latest chapter in a romance novel.

"First of all," she began, "when Mr. Wyatt helps you up into
his carriage, let your hand linger in his a moment, pressing ever
so slightly—like this."

"You mean I have to take his hand? He's such a statue I'm
afraid his touch will turn me into stone, too!"

"More likely gold. I swear, everything he touches turns to gold,
Betsy, not stone. And make sure you sit close enough for your
thigh to accidentally brush against his—like so."

I shuddered involuntarily. "Oh, Lydia, I couldn't! The very
idea makes my skin crawl."

"Don't be a pantywaist. Now listen, if he says something funny,
even if it really isn't, laugh like this—" she demonstrated with a
happy, tinkling chuckle—"and touch his arm or his chest ever so
briefly, like this, while you do."

"I can't imagine Frank Wyatt cracking jokes."

"You're right," Lydia said with a frown, "me either. Okay then,
tell him how wonderful he is. Flatter him. Men love flattery."

"Ugh! I'd probably throw up."

"Make something up. This is your chance to write fiction, Betsy. Give it a try. And don't back away if he tries to kiss you, either."

"His lips are so thin and tight his kiss would probably bounce right off."

"You're so funny," she said, hugging me tightly. "Just be your wonderful, witty self and I swear he'll fall head over heels in love with you!"

I wasn't so sure.

On the afternoon of the ice-cream social, Lydia fixed my hair and let me borrow her best silk shirtwaist with the leg-of-mutton sleeves to wear with my Sunday skirt. She had brought a brand-new, long-waist, five-hook, bust-perfecto corset home from the dry goods store and crammed me into it, yanking on the laces until the rolls of fat around my middle had no place to go but up, lifting my tiny bosom along with them. I stared in disbelief at my reflection in the mirror. For the first time in my life my waist looked tiny and my bust looked full.

"There! You're gorgeous!" my sister cried.

"Lydia, I can't breathe!" I gasped.

"Then don't."

"But what if I faint? I'm feeling light-headed already and I haven't even tried to walk."

"Good. You're allowed to swoon. That's what smelling salts are for. Mr. Wyatt will think it's your dainty, feminine constitution and it will make him feel manly to catch you in his arms."

"Ha! He's more likely to let me drop to the floor like a log."

Lydia put on all the finishing touches—a dab of rouge on my chubby cheeks, her own beaded comb in my hair, Mother's cameo brooch at my throat. I felt like a schoolgirl playing dress-up. Then

I heard the plod of horses in the lane below our windows. Frank Wyatt had arrived, right on time.

"Get the wash basin, Lydia! I'm going to throw up!"

"No, you're not. Don't be a ninny." She smiled, tucking a springy strand of my hair behind my ear. "What are you so afraid of? He's just an ordinary person—not even half as wonderful as you are. Hold your head up, Betsy. He's lucky to have the privilege of stepping out with you."

"*Stepping out . . .*" I moaned. "I . . . I've never done this before. What on earth will I talk about all afternoon?"

"Listen to me," she said sternly. "Calm down! It's his job to start the conversation, not yours. Just don't stop it dead by giving yes and no answers. Keep it going. Ask him a related question back."

I held my breath as I walked down the stairs. I had no choice—the corset was that tight. If the laces ever snapped I would look like an exploding watermelon. Lydia's shirt buttons would go flying in all directions and my skirt would probably split wide open like a gutted fish. I had half a mind to call the whole thing off—until I glimpsed the expression on my father's face. It was the closest he had ever come to smiling. He was already dreaming of the magnificent orchard he would soon be part-owner of, thanks to me, and I couldn't let him down. I just couldn't.

I tried to smile, to breathe normally, to remember everything Lydia had told me as I said farewell and set off for the ice-cream social. At least I had good posture for the first time in my life, thanks to the corset stays. I couldn't have slouched if I'd tried.

Frank held our front door open for me, then offered me his hand to help me up into his surrey. He looked so cold and formal in his Sunday suit and starched collar that the warmth of his palm took me by surprise and I forgot all about squeezing it until it was too late. When he sat down on the carriage seat beside me he left a discreet space between us and it would have been much too obvious to try to rearrange myself closer so our thighs could "accidentally" brush. Besides, I feared I might get frostbite. He held himself so aloof that I would have needed an ice pick to chip through the invisible shield that surrounded him.

"Are you comfortable, Miss Fowler?" he asked suddenly.

"Yes."

"May I call you Betty?"

"Yes."

Oh no! I was already giving yes and no answers! I nearly smacked my forehead in despair, but I hadn't tested the corset's full range of motion. It would look ridiculous if my arm didn't reach that high and I ended up smacking thin air. Or worse still, what if I smacked too hard and I fell over backward and couldn't right myself again? I'd once seen a box turtle in the same predicament.

We rode in silence for several minutes. I knew it was Frank's job to lead the conversation, but I struggled to think of something to say so I wouldn't disappoint my father. "Um . . . it turned out to be a lovely day for the social, didn't it?" I asked.

"Yes."

I wanted to shout, *Ha! I caught you! That was a yes and no answer!* But I didn't think I could draw a deep enough breath to shout, let alone gloat.

"We've had just the right amount of rainfall this spring, haven't we?" I asked, trying again.

"Yes."

I would have heaved a sigh of frustration if my corset would have allowed it. This ridiculous courtship was a sham, an agonizing means to a mutually beneficial end, and Frank and I both knew it. The drive to church only lasted ten minutes but it seemed like ten years.

Everyone gaped when Frank Wyatt showed up on the church lawn with a woman on his arm—although they might have been gaping because it appeared as though poor Betty Fowler had her head ripped off of her frumpy body and pasted onto someone else's. Either way, we created quite a stir. Every maiden, spinster, and scheming mama in Deer Springs began calculating how they could win Frank Wyatt's attention now that he had finally decided to start courting. But courting Betty Butterball of all people? Who would have ever thought?

We made a ridiculous pair. Even with my astonishing new bosom I looked like a child beside Frank. He was tall and sun-browned and muscular from years of hard work—and the top of my frizzy head didn't even reach his shoulder. I had to take five hurried steps to equal one of his strides, so I must have looked like a little lap dog with my tongue hanging out, trotting to keep up with him.

Although Frank was politely courteous and well-mannered, he never warmed up enough to risk melting the ice cream. He kept my lemonade glass filled and he generously spooned all the toppings onto my ice cream for me at the serving table, but he never asked me a single question about myself in order to become better acquainted. I tried very hard to like him, but the knowledge that he wasn't the least bit interested in me hampered my efforts. Every time Frank looked at me he saw my father's pond.

There were three-legged races for the couples and games like musical chairs, horseshoes, and croquet, but Frank showed no interest in any of them. I was just as glad. I could barely walk, let alone dash, bend, reach, or scramble. As we strolled around the church lawn, Frank occasionally stopped to converse with one of the other men, forcing me to make small-talk with their girl-friends. It was hard work for me to be pleasant for an entire afternoon. I wasn't used to being sociable. Banty hens and books were my usual afternoon companions.

By the time Frank brought me home again I was exhausted. As soon as Lydia loosened my bonds, I breathed an enormous sigh of relief. It was short-lived.

"Did you make a favorable impression?" Father demanded to know at the supper table. It was one of the few times in my life that my father had ever shown an interest in me.

"I tried, Father."

"You *tried?* That's *all?* I certainly expect you to do more than *try* if this merger is ever going to take place. Don't you realize that a man like Wyatt can take his pick of women when it's time for him to choose a wife?"

I recalled the scheming mamas all sizing up Frank Wyatt and stared at my mashed potatoes in misery. "Yes, Father."

"Don't slouch, Betty. Sit up. That's better. Did he ask you out again?"

"He said that he'll be busy with the orchard for a while, but he wondered if I would like to take a drive in the country with him sometime."

"Good. Good. I hope you were encouraging?"

"I told him I would be very pleased to ride with him."

"Good. Pass the green beans."

Father's health had been poor for months, so I was glad that this courtship was putting some life back into him. But I knew that today had been just the prologue. A long series of agonizing afternoons with Frank Wyatt would probably follow until he made up his mind whether or not my father's land was worth the sacrifice of marrying me. But I would persevere. Nellie Bly was indomitable and I would be, too. My overwhelming concern was to not disappoint my father.

Frank courted me all that spring, usually on Sunday afternoons when work wasn't allowed. In June we went for a drive in the country, to a temperance lecture in the next town, and to a special missionary presentation at church.

"Do you belong to our Women's Missionary Guild, Betty?" he asked on the way home.

"No, I—"

"You must join."

I joined. I had taken "the pledge" after the temperance lecture, too. I would have stood on my head and spit wooden nickels if that's what it took to convince him I would make a satisfactory wife.

By July the entire town knew that we were an "item." Frank invited me to sit in the hallowed Wyatt pew with him one Sunday morning. Father was overjoyed.

"Good. You have the fish on the line," he said. "Now reel him in."

Whatever *that* meant. When I asked Lydia, she said it meant I should invite him home for Sunday dinner so he would know that I could cook. She faithfully coached me in the feminine art of courtship, but I seemed to be failing the course. Frank and I had courted for two months and he still hadn't stolen a kiss from me or even tried to hold my hand. The gap between us on the carriage seat was just as wide as it had been on our first date.

I couldn't help but compare Frank with the dashing, amorous heroes of my favorite novels, and he always came up short. I wasn't falling in love with him. In fact, the more time I spent with him the more I hated his cold, overbearing ways. But judging from my own experience and the example of my parents, I decided that love and romance must be the stuff of fiction, not real life. I learned to ignore the feeling of dread that settled in the pit of my stomach every time Frank arrived at my house and to disregard the gnawing unease I felt each moment that I spent with him.

While my courtship with Frank plodded slowly on, Lydia reached a milestone of her own—she dated the same man two weeks in a row, then three! Ted Bartlett was a traveling notions salesman whose route brought him to Deer Springs on the train once a week.

"I'm in love, Betsy! Oh, this time I'm really in *love!*" Lydia exclaimed.

It was mid-July, and we lay crossways on the bed in our stifling room hoping that a breeze might find its way through our dormer windows. So far the only thing that had found its way inside was the mosquito that hummed with delight around my head.

"Tell me everything!" I said, smacking my own cheek as I missed the mosquito.

"Ted is unbelievably handsome! He has dark, wavy hair and a luxurious mustache that tickles when he kisses me."

"You let him kiss you already?"

"Of course, silly. When I'm with Ted I never want him to stop kissing me. He makes me feel so . . . loved! I can't describe how wonderful it is to feel his strong arms around me as he showers me with kisses. Or how glorious it is to rest my head against his broad chest and hear his heart beating beneath me."

Lydia'd had more than her share of romances but I'd never heard her talk this passionately before. She made me feel like I was missing out on something. "Tell me more about him," I begged.

"He's a really sharp dresser, and he wears all the latest in men's fashions. I'm sure he must be very rich. He's from Chicago. That's where we'll live after we're married."

"He asked you to marry him?"

"Well, not yet, but I know that he will soon. He loves me, Betsy. He tells me he does all the time. Maybe Frank will ask you to marry him, too, and we can have a double wedding. Won't it be wonderful?"

"Ouch!" I swatted uselessly at the mosquito again after he took a spiteful bite out of my leg. "A double wedding would be nice," I lied. "I won't be nearly as nervous if we go into this venture together. But to tell you the truth, I can't imagine being married to Frank."

"You mean sharing his bed?"

"Lydia!"

She laughed at my embarrassment. "Sharing a bed is wonderful when it's with someone you really love."

"How do you know?" I teased.

She gave me a playful shove. "Be quiet and go to sleep. I'll dream about Ted and you can dream about Frank."

But as I lay awake scratching mosquito bites, I didn't have the heart to tell my sister that any dream about Frank would have been a nightmare.

— CHAPTER SEVEN —

Lydia had bragged for weeks about Ted Bartlett's wealth, so when a fancy carriage with a liveried driver and a matched team of horses pulled up to our farmhouse one hot July afternoon, I thought for sure they were delivering her beau. Father was working out in his orchard, and I was using my few moments of peace and freedom to sit out on the front porch and write. I planned on writing a romantic novel someday, so I was scribbling down all the romantic things Lydia had told me about Ted before I forgot them. And now here he was in person! I was about to tell the mustached gentleman who stepped down from the carriage that Lydia hadn't returned from work yet, but he spoke first.

"Good afternoon," he said, removing his straw boater hat and bowing slightly. I saw right away that Lydia had exaggerated his dark, wavy hair. If this was Ted, he'd be bald in another five years. "I'm inquiring about the sign I saw posted in the dry goods store in Deer Springs," the gentleman said. "You have a cottage for rent?"

"Oh! Yes! Yes, we do."

"My name is Walter Gibson," he said, handing me a beautifully engraved calling card. "I'm visiting from Chicago."

"Betty . . . Betty Fowler. Nice to meet you."

I was so awed by him and by his aura of fine breeding and wealth that I could barely speak. He had a slight build, well under Frank's height of six feet three inches, but was impeccably dressed in an ash-colored linen suit and waistcoat. A heavy gold pocket watch and chain dangled across the front. Even on this humid July afternoon he seemed comfortably cool—not cold and stiff like Frank, but pleasurably relaxed. His hand rested on a walking cane with a silver handle that was carved like a dog's head, and I noticed he had beautifully manicured nails.

He looked like a photograph from a magazine, and I suddenly realized that I looked like a fright! I wasn't wearing my bust-perfecto corset to help squeeze me into a recognizably feminine shape, and I had wiggled out of my petticoats and dropped them into a sweaty heap on the porch. I had also unbuttoned the top two buttons of my calico shirtwaist in the heat and, worst of all, I was barefoot. With the humidity causing my hair to frizz out around my head, I must have resembled a savage peasant wench.

"So . . . may I see it?" He lifted one eyebrow and one side of his mustache in a half-smile. He struck me as a very kind man. I saw it in his eyes and heard it in his voice.

"Oh! The cottage! Oh, of course."

I had heard all about the summer "cottages" of the very rich overlooking the big lake—they were more like palaces! So I was embarrassed to show him our tiny bungalow.

"It's very plain . . . very rustic," I sputtered. "And I'm afraid that the roof of your carriage will be too high to pass beneath the trees. I'd hate to see it get all scratched up or covered with dust. You would have to walk there." I looked down at his perfectly polished, fine-leather shoes and winced. "Oh dear. They would get very dusty, too."

He glanced down at his own feet, then at my bare ones, and smiled—a full-blown smile that revealed an endearing dimple in his right cheek. "Then perhaps I should join you and remove my shoes, as well?" It surprised me to realize that he wasn't laughing at me but at himself.

"No, no. You'd better keep your shoes on. Listen, I'd hate to have you waste your time walking all the way out there for nothing. The cottage is very rustic and quite isolated."

"It sounds perfect. I'm looking for someplace secluded."

"Thoreau's *Walden Pond*?" I asked without thinking. He looked surprised, then delighted.

"Yes, exactly. How did you know?"

"I guess it was on my mind. I just finished rereading the book a few days ago."

"I've read it several times myself," he said. "My favorite line is: 'Rather than love, than money, than fame, give me truth. I sat at a table where were rich food and wine in abundance . . . but sincerity and truth were not; and I went away hungry from the inhospitable board.' "

Our eyes met and I saw that with one poignant line from Thoreau, this stranger had given me a glimpse of himself. His eyes were as soft and gray as a foggy morning. When he suddenly asked, "What's your favorite line?" I returned the gift without hesitation.

" 'If one advances confidently in the direction of his dreams, and endeavors to live the life which he has imagined, he will meet with a success unexpected in common hours.' "

He nodded thoughtfully, then smiled again. "So . . . will I get

to see this cottage or did Thoreau already rent it before I arrived?"

"I'm sorry, of course," I said, laughing. "It's this way."

I set off down the driveway and was nearly to the barn before
I realized that he wasn't keeping up with me. He was a young
man, in his early thirties, but he walked with the slow, frail hesi-
tancy of someone much older, leaning heavily on his cane. I
thought it might embarrass him if I apologized, so I simply slowed
down to keep pace with him.

"The easiest route is to take this shortcut through the orchard," I explained. "There's a dirt road but it's overgrown with
weeds. Father always planned on putting in a better road—a
gravel one—but he never did."

"I'm glad."

"You are?"

"I'm looking for something secluded, remember?"

"So you said." I smiled. "All right, then, you asked for it! It's
just on the other side of these trees, down near the pond."

"A pond? Really? It's not called Walden Pond by any chance,
is it?"

I found myself laughing again, and it amazed me. The only
other person I'd ever felt this relaxed and content to be with was
Lydia. The stranger's gentle humor reminded me of my beloved
school teacher, Mr. Herman.

"You may name the pond whatever you like," I said, grinning
up at him. "I don't think anyone has ever given it a name. Now, I
should warn you, the cabin is very rustic. . . ."

"I think you already have."

"Oh. Well, now you are doubly warned." But as we came
through the orchard and Mr. Gibson got his first glimpse of the
little stone cottage, surrounded by trees and nestled beneath the
hill, I saw it afresh through his eyes.

"But it's lovely!" he said in surprise. A row of nodding pink hollyhocks by the front porch, with blossoms the size of saucers, waved at us in greeting.

"It was originally a log cabin," I explained. "The stones were added to it later. No one really knows how old it is. It was here when my father bought the land, before the War Between the States. He built our farmhouse after his family outgrew it."

I opened the front door and led Mr. Gibson inside. Father had made Lydia and me scrub the place thoroughly before she posted the sign in the store, so it was spotlessly clean. It smelled of pine logs and freshly ironed linen.

"What a charming place!"

"When my sister and I were children we used it for a playhouse," I told him. "I've always loved it, too. I wish I could live here."

It didn't take long to show him through the tiny rooms, and I was sorry the tour ended so quickly. Something about the stranger made him nice to be around. He smelled good, too—like lemons.

"Yes, I think this will do quite nicely," he said, gazing out at the pond from one of the front windows.

"You seriously want to rent it?" I asked in surprise. "But . . . but it's so small, and . . . and . . ."

"And rustic?" He turned to me and his smile was contagious.

"Yes, it's rustic . . . rude . . . backwoods . . . bucolic! Call it whatever you like, but there's no proper kitchen or running water—only a pump outside. And it's small . . . diminutive . . . lilliputian!" I have no idea what made me suddenly indulge in my love of words, but I could see that he found it amusing.

"I don't mind. I'm seeking simplicity, remember?"

"But surely your wife—?"

"I'll be living here alone. I've been ill for the past few months and the doctor recommended I try some country air." His face was thin and a bit too pale, but if I hadn't observed him walking I wouldn't have thought him ill.

"I'm sorry to hear that you haven't been well," I said. "I hope the country air does the trick."

"Yes, so do I. How much do you want per month?"

I told him Father's price.

"I'll tell you what," he said. "If I could arrange for meals to be brought to me, too, I'll pay twice that."

"Twice!"

"Yes. Would I be able to move in today?"

"Today? All the way from Chicago?"

"No, I'm living in my family's summer home over on the lake, but to tell you the truth, I've grown weary of having servants and nurses constantly hovering around me. They mean well but they're beginning to make me feel like an invalid. I've been craving peace and quiet lately, and your 'rustic, lilliputian cottage' should do quite nicely."

"Then we have a deal, Mr. Gibson," I said, smiling. "You may move in whenever you like—and I promise not to 'hover.' "

His dimple reappeared as he grinned in return. "*Mr. Gibson* is my father. Please call me Walter."

"I'm Betsy." I had no idea why I asked him to use the name my sister always used instead of calling me Betty like my father and Frank Wyatt did. At the time, it just seemed natural. We walked back to his carriage, and after I explained to his driver how to find the dirt road that led to the cottage, they drove away.

Late in the afternoon, I heard the clatter of horses and wagon wheels rattling down the old dirt road to the cottage and I felt absurdly excited. After supper, I arranged generous portions of fried chicken, mashed potatoes, and apple pie on a tray to take down to Walter Gibson.

"Why didn't you invite the man up here to eat?" Father asked when I explained that we now had a boarder. I hesitated, unable to picture Mr. Gibson eating dinner in our stark kitchen with my humorless father. Nor could I imagine him occupying the dining room chair Frank Wyatt always sat in for Sunday dinner. Walter seemed to belong in the cozy, pine-scented cottage by the pond, not up here.

"I'll invite him, but I'm sure he'll refuse," I said. "He came here looking for solitude. Besides, it's very difficult for him to walk."

"What's wrong with him?"

"I didn't ask. But here's his calling card," I said, fishing it from the pocket of my skirt.

"Gibson . . ." Father muttered, reading it aloud. "Chicago . . . You say he's rich? I wonder if he's kin to Howard Gibson, the industrialist."

"I don't know. But he's very nice."

I headed out the back door to bring Walter his supper. This time I made certain I was properly combed, buttoned, and wearing shoes and a petticoat.

"Come on in," Walter called after I'd knocked on the cottage door. I found him reading a book by the window, seated in a beautiful leather armchair the color of red wine. Trunks and boxes were piled everywhere.

"You seem to have an awful lot of belongings for someone seeking the simple life," I teased.

"On the contrary," he said with his wry, lopsided smile. "I brought only the bare necessities." He removed his gold-rimmed spectacles and motioned toward one of the boxes. "Go ahead, open a couple of crates and have a look."

Curious, I set the tray on the table beside his chair and peeked into one of the boxes—then another, and another. They were filled with books! I felt as breathless as I had the day I'd worn my new bust-perfecto corset.

"Oh . . ." I breathed. "Oh my!" Overcome with wonder, I picked up one book after another, scanning the gold-embossed titles, marveling at the rich leather bindings. Without thinking, I opened *A Tale of Two Cities* and lifted it to my nose to inhale. "I'm so sorry!" I cried when I caught myself.

Walter laughed with delight. "Don't apologize. I feel the same way about books. As I said, for me, these are the bare necessities of life."

"Along with food," I said, pointing to the tray. "You should probably eat it before it gets cold."

"Will you stay and keep me company while I do?" he asked.

"All right . . . if you're sure you don't mind me 'hovering.' "

"Not at all," he said, spreading a napkin on his lap, " 'Hovering' is what people do when they ask how you're feeling every two minutes. If you start doing that I'm afraid I will have to boot you out. But in the meantime, I'd love to hear what other books you've read lately besides Thoreau's . . . and if you have any favorites."

"Favorites! I'd be here until breakfast time naming all my favorites!"

"I understand," he said, gesturing to all the boxes with his fork. "These are all my favorites. A better question might be, what qualities do you most enjoy in a book?"

I thought for a moment. "I like a story that takes me to places I've never visited before—one with characters that seem like old friends. But most of all, one that gives me something to think about long after I've finished reading it."

"Ah, then we are very much alike," he said, lifting his coffee cup in salute. "By the way, dinner is delicious. My compliments to the chef."

"Thank you." I felt a surge of pleasure. I couldn't recall Frank Wyatt ever complimenting my cooking.

"Are you really the chef? Your husband is a fortunate man."

"I'm not married. I live with my father and younger sister. You probably met Lydia at the dry goods store where the sign was posted."

"Did I? I can't recall."

For some reason, that pleased me more than anything else he'd said. For the next hour, Walter and I talked about everything from American poets to the Greek classics while he slowly savored his dinner. I was unaware of how much time had passed until I noticed that the room had grown dark enough to need lamps.

"I should go!" I said, jumping to my feet. "If I don't lock up Father's chickens before dark, the foxes will be celebrating Thanksgiving."

"I'm sorry if I've kept you—"

"Oh, don't be. I'm certainly not. Shall I light the lamps for you before I go?"

"Yes, please. And then have a look through those boxes again and see if there's anything you'd like to take along to read."

"Are you serious? You would really let me borrow one of your books?"

"Borrow as many as you'd like, Betsy—but there is one condition. You must sit down and tell me your opinion of each one when you return it."

I floated back to the house carrying *Nicholas Nickelby*. For the next two weeks, bringing Walter his meals was the highlight of my day. I would have gladly walked down to the cottage a dozen times a day if I hadn't feared making a pest of myself. For a man seeking solitude he certainly loved to converse. And I thoroughly enjoyed conversing with him. We didn't always agree on who the best authors were and which plots were too melodramatic or too contrived, but the lively debates we had were great fun.

On the first Sunday in August, Frank Wyatt drove me home from church and stayed for dinner as usual. I paid little attention to the conversation as I bided my time, waiting for Frank to go home so I could bring Walter his lunch and finish discussing Walt Whitman's poetry with him. Suddenly Lydia gave me a hard kick beneath the table. I returned from my reverie in time to hear Frank say, "Then with your permission, Mr. Fowler, Betty and I will be married as soon as the harvest is finished."

I nearly shouted, "No!"—until I saw the broad grin on my father's face.

"Just remember, young man," he said, trying to look stern, "you promised to call our merger Wyatt & Fowler Orchards."

"Yes, sir. I remember." They shook hands. I heard a terrible rushing sound in my ears and for a moment I thought I might faint. Suddenly Lydia was beside me, hugging me.

"Smile, you ninny!" she whispered urgently in my ear. "For pete's sake, smile! You're engaged!"

I was engaged—without a single gesture or token of affection passing between Frank and myself. The smile I quickly manufactured felt more like a grimace of pain.

I heard myself agree to an after-dinner tour of Wyatt Orchards and the house that would soon be mine. I heard my father declining to come along. I heard my sister insisting that I go ahead and leave the dishes to her. But the worst moment came when Lydia took the plate I had fixed for Walter out of the warming oven and disappeared through the back door to take it to him. If I could have stopped her from going, stopped Walter Gibson from ever meeting my beautiful younger sister, I would have gladly sacrificed everything I owned. But as Frank Wyatt escorted me out the front door to his carriage, there wasn't a thing in the world I could do.

Frank did all the talking as he drove his carriage around his property. I listened in numb silence to his grand plans for planting a new section with peaches and experimenting with cherry trees next spring, but all I could think about was Walter's smile and the faint dimple that would crease his cheek when Lydia walked through his door.

I followed Frank inside the Wyatt house for the first time in my life—that beautiful white house on the hill with the dark green shutters and the graceful front porch, the house that would soon be mine—and I found it overburdened with other people's stuff to the point of suffocation. I longed to clear every shelf and dresser and sideboard of all its knickknacks and replace them with books—leather-bound books with gold-embossed titles and sweet-smelling pages. I imagined my sister laughing at something Walter said and lightly touching his arm the way she'd shown me, and I longed to sink down in the middle of Frank's parlor and weep.

That afternoon I saw a clear picture of what my life with Frank Wyatt would be like—everything would revolve around Frank as if he were the great sun in the center of the universe, and I would have to fit myself into his solar system someplace, like all the other possessions in his overstuffed parlor. Even so, I might have been able to tolerate that existence if Walter Gibson hadn't come into my life to talk with me and listen to me and laugh with me and to show me what I was going to miss.

I followed Frank out through the kitchen door in blind misery, walking across the backyard, past the barn, and through the apple orchard. We stopped at the top of the hill overlooking my father's property. The pond and the little stone cottage lay below us, and I wondered if Lydia was still inside talking with Walter, laughing together while he ate his meal.

I turned to the man I was now engaged to marry and said, "I think the pond needs a name, don't you Frank? I think we should name it Walden Pond."

"What? Where did that ridiculous name come from?" He had a way of looking directly at people when he was irritated with them that always made them squirm. I felt like a bug at the mercy of a bully, as though his eyes had me pinned to a piece of cardboard.

"You know, Frank, from the book *Walden Pond* by Henry David Thoreau? He was a disciple of Emerson? It's a famous book."

"I'm not interested."

"Not interested in naming the pond or in Thoreau's book?"

"Either one. Once the pond becomes part of Wyatt Orchards it will probably be called Wyatt's Pond. And as far as books are concerned, they're a waste of valuable time."

My stomach made a slow, sickening turn. "I can understand not having time to read during the summer or at harvest time, but surely during the long winter months—"

"All books, except for the Bible, are frivolous—and most of them are of the devil."

"You're joking. Books are of the *devil*?"

He wasn't joking.

"The Bible calls Satan 'the father of lies' and novels are nothing but lies, created from man's own evil imagination. I won't allow them in my house."

I battled my growing panic. "What about *Pilgrim's Progress* and—"

"A rare exception. Listen, Betty, we need to choose a date."

I stared at him blankly.

"For the wedding," he explained. "Would the first Saturday in October give you enough time to prepare?"

Eternity wouldn't be enough time to prepare for a life without books—nevermind a lifetime with Frank Wyatt. Yet in two short months I would vow to spend my life with this man, to honor him and obey him. I forced myself to remember Father's joy at the dinner table and said, "That date will be fine with me."

"Good. I'll drive you home now."

"I'd much rather walk, Frank," I said quickly. "And thanks for the tour. Good-bye."

I set off the down the hill at a brisk pace, praying that he wouldn't follow. My tears had already begun to fall, and like the stones rolling down the hill beneath my stumbling feet, I knew that I wasn't going to be able to stop them.

———

Walter was sitting outside in his Adirondack chair—another "necessity" he had brought from home—when I arrived with his supper tray that night. He looked up from his book when he heard me approach and smiled.

"There you are, Betsy. I missed you at lunch today."

I collapsed to the ground at his feet and wept, grief and relief all tangled together like a skein of yarn. Walter caught the tray just in time and set it on the grass. "Betsy . . . what's wrong?" he asked gently.

I drew several shaky breaths. "The man who's been courting me . . . asked to marry me."

"I see. Those don't exactly look like tears of joy. Was he upset when you refused him, then?"

"I didn't refuse. I couldn't refuse. My father—" I couldn't finish. Walter pressed his handkerchief into my hand. I lifted it to my face to dry my tears, and when I smelled Walter's clean, lemony scent I cried harder still.

"I'm so sorry, Betsy." He said softly. "I wish I knew what to say."

"Thanks. I'll be all right." I struggled to pull myself together. "I just need time to get used to the idea."

"Do you think love might grow, given time?" he asked.

"I'm sure it will," I lied. But I wondered how I could possibly learn to love a man who hated books. I drew another shaky breath. "Did you love your wife when you first married her?"

He looked at me for a long moment. "I'm not married, Betsy. I'm engaged to be, but the wedding has been indefinitely postponed until I recover my health."

"I'm surprised your fiancée doesn't want to be near you so she can take care of you and help you recuperate faster."

Walter sighed. "Maybe that's the way it works in novels, but seldom in real life. My marriage will be just another one of my father's many business arrangements—a socially significant and financially useful match for his only son and heir. Neither the young woman nor I would dare to argue with Howard Knowles Gibson. I've met her, of course, but we don't know each other very well. My illness has made it difficult to have a proper courtship."

I dared to look up at him for the first time. "Then I'm not the only one being married against my will?"

"It's a small consolation I'm sure, but no, you're not the only one. In the social circles I was born into, most marriages are matters of convenience. Love and romance are seldom involved."

I plucked idly at some blades of grass at his feet, then tossed them away on the wind. "I can learn to live without love I suppose, but I don't know how I will ever live without books. The man I'm going to marry hates them. He says he won't allow any book in his house except the Bible . . . and maybe *Pilgrim's Progress*." I had to smile, in spite of my tears, at the sheer absurdity of Frank's intolerance. Walter smiled in return.

"*Pilgrim's Progress*, eh? I'm quite certain that my fiancée has never even heard of it."

We laughed then, and I felt laughter's healing power salving my wounds. I couldn't recall ever laughing with Frank Wyatt, and it occurred to me that a lifetime without laughter might be even worse than a lifetime without books.

Suddenly, without knowing how or when it had happened, I realized that Walter was holding my hand between his own to comfort me. It seemed like the most natural thing in the world.

"Do you remember the first day we met, Betsy? Remember the line you quoted from Thoreau about pursuing your dreams? I just realized something—I've never asked you what those dreams were."

"Promise you won't laugh?"

He considered it for a minute, then grinned. "No, I can't promise. Suppose you told me you wanted to be a Hindu snake charmer or the captain of a whaling ship—I'm sorry, but I'd have to laugh."

I knew that my dreams were very safe with Walter. I smiled in return and told him. "I want to be a writer. That's what I was doing, in fact, the day we met. I used to dream of being a stunt reporter like Nellie Bly."

"I've met her."

"You haven't!"

"Yes, Nellie Bly sat across from me at a dinner once in New York. My father is a good friend of her boss, Joseph Pulitzer."

"What's she like?"

"Actually . . . very much like you," he said quietly. "Except you're easier to talk to, more thoughtful and articulate." I looked away. He tugged on my hand until I looked back. "Seriously, Betsy. I would be glad to talk to Mr. Pulitzer on your behalf if you want me to. I could help you find an apartment in New York."

I was tempted—oh, so tempted—but I knew that it was impossible. "I can't," I said sorrowfully. "My father has his heart set on this marriage."

Walter closed his eyes for a moment and nodded. "I understand. I really do. My father is Howard Knowles Gibson, remember?"

"Yes." I waited for our eyes to meet, then asked, "What are your dreams, Walter?"

He smiled his lopsided grin. "To be a Hindu snake charmer and the captain of a whaling ship." Eventually his smile faded and he shook his head. "I really don't know. For as far back as I can recall my father has always told me what I would be. I'm his heir, I'll take over for him one day . . . and I've always struggled to face up to that. It's not just the work, it's everything that goes along with it—the extravagant lifestyle, the whole social scene, the politicking and dirty-dealing. I may not know what I want, but I know what I don't want." He sighed and shook his head again.

"After I finished college I begged my father for two months off to travel a bit before taking my place in the company. He reluctantly agreed—and I ran off for three years. I explored the world. The jungles of Borneo, the Ivory Coast of Africa, the rain forests of Brazil . . . I even panned for gold in Alaska. I had to pack a lifetime of living into a very short time, you see."

"That's all the time I have, too—two months."

He released my hand and paged through the book he had been reading when I arrived, searching for something. I saw the title—*Walden Pond.*

"Listen to this, Betsy. Thoreau writes, 'Let everyone mind his own business, and endeavor to be what he was made. Why should we be in such desperate haste to succeed and in such desperate enterprises? If a man does not keep pace with his companions, perhaps it is because he hears a different drummer. Let him step to the music which he hears, however measured or far away.' "

I watched a wild mallard fishing on the pond in the fading light, his head dipping down suddenly, his tail feathers pointing to the darkening sky. "I don't think either one of us can even hear our own music anymore," I said at last.

"No, I suppose not," Walter said with a sigh. "But there is one choice we are both still free to make. You will have children some-day, Betsy, and so will I. We can allow them to step to the beat of their own drummer."

I wrote Walter's words in my notebook that night so I would always remember them. Then I closed it and tucked it deep inside my dresser drawer. I was quite sure they were the last words I would ever write.

— CHAPTER EIGHT —

S hortly after my engagement to Frank Wyatt, Lydia fell sick with a terrible case of food poisoning. When she woke up vomiting in the chamber pot for the third morning in a row, I begged her to go see a doctor.

"No, I'll be all right," she said with a groan. "Now move. I have to go to work."

"I'll ride into town and tell them you're sick. Lydia, you'll never get well if you don't stay in bed."

"Horse feathers. I don't want to stay in bed." She pulled off her nightgown and began dressing. I followed her around the tiny room, pleading with her to stay home and rest and recover.

"What if it's influenza? You might spread it to all your customers!"

"Betsy...." she finally said, stopping so abruptly I bumped

into her, "it isn't food poisoning or the flu. It's something much, much worse."

"You're dying? No, Lydia, I won't let you die, I won't! You can't die!"

She smiled slightly at my histrionics, then took me by the shoulders and gave me a little shake. "I'm not dying, either. I'm . . . I'm in the family way."

I gaped at her, not comprehending. "But that's impossible! You aren't married!"

Tears sprang to her eyes. "Oh, my sweet, innocent Betsy. You don't have to be married to make a baby. I love Ted, and when you love someone . . . you'll do anything for them."

When I realized what she meant, I covered my face and wept. Lydia pulled me into her arms. "Please don't hate me, Betsy. If you turn your back on me now it will be the worst punishment of all."

"I could never hate you." I took her hand in mine and linked our pinkie fingers. "I'll stand by you no matter what. Just don't forget, you promised that I could be your maid of honor when you marry Ted, remember?"

"Ted doesn't know about the baby yet," she said. I could see that she was worried about telling him. "I'm meeting him tonight after work. That's why I have to go."

Lydia left without eating breakfast. When she hadn't come home by midnight, I was certain that she and Ted had eloped. What on earth would I tell Father? Neither of us had even met Ted Bartlett. Should I tell Father about the baby or not? I paced in the front hallway in the dark, rehearsing what I would say to Father, when the front door opened a crack and Lydia crept inside. I expected the hallway to light up with her beautiful smile, but her tear-streaked face was pale with shock and despair.

"Lydia, what's wrong? What happened?" The only thing I

could imagine was that there had been a terrible train wreck and Ted Bartlett was dead.

"It's Ted . . . he's . . . Oh, Betsy, what am I going to *do*?"

She fell into my arms, sobbing. "Is he dead?" I whispered.

"Worse—he's *married*!"

"Married! But he can't be! He—"

"He already has a wife and two children," she said between sobs. "He showed me their pictures. He's been lying to me all this time, Betsy. *Lying!* And now my life is over. I've ruined my life and I don't know what to do!"

I wrapped my arm around Lydia's waist and helped her up the stairs to our room so we wouldn't wake up Father. Lydia's problem was my problem. We had vowed to take care of each other, and I wracked my brain for a solution.

"Can't he get a divorce?" I asked.

"He refused. Ted's father-in-law owns the notions company he works for."

I would have cheerfully loaded Father's shotgun and murdered Ted Bartlett if I thought it would help.

"Listen," I said, seating Lydia beside me on the bed, "I just remembered something. When I was in school I heard about a girl who had . . . you know . . . the same problem. And later on I heard that she went to a special home to have the baby. I can find out where that home is and you can just go away for a while until your baby's born. Someone will adopt it, Lydia. When Nellie Bly investigated the baby-buying trade, she found out there are dozens of nice Christian families who are willing to legally adopt babies. Everything is going to be all right, I promise you."

Lydia didn't go to work for three days. She lay in bed crying, convinced that she had ruined her life. As soon as I could get away, I drove to the school and discreetly asked Mr. Herman if he knew about the special home for unwed mothers. When I returned, I told Lydia what I'd learned, hoping it would cheer her.

"No one will be able to tell that you're expecting for a while, so you'll only have to be away for four or five months. They'll let you live right there in the home and you can have your baby there, too. When you come back home we'll tell everyone you had rheumatic fever or that you went to stay with a dying aunt. No one will ever know the truth."

"But how can I give my own baby away and never see him again?" she asked, rubbing her still-flat tummy. "He's mine . . . mine and Ted's."

"You have to, Lydia. It's the only way. Trust me, the baby will grow up in a good Christian home, and you'll have a brand-new start in life. You'll meet someone else in no time at all. There will always be dozens of boys lining up to marry you."

"Not if I'm tarnished goods."

"I'll make sure they never know," I said, holding up my little finger. "I promise."

After that, Lydia seemed resigned to her fate. She went back to the dry goods store the next day but came straight home from work every night, too exhausted from her pregnancy to run around. She didn't even date on the weekends.

One night as we prepared for bed she asked me to read one of my poems to her. "It's been ages since you've read to me, Betsy, and I know you must have written dozens and dozens of new ones by now." I tried to avoid the truth by mumbling a faint excuse, but she suddenly gripped my arm. "I know! Will you write a new poem for me? A poem about my baby? I want to give it to him after he's born so he'll always know that I loved him even though I had to give him away."

I closed my eyes. "I can't . . . I don't write poems any more."

"What do you mean? What are you talking about?"

"That part of my life is over now that I'm marrying Frank.

He's made it very clear that he wants nothing to do with poems or books or writing of any kind . . . except for the Bible."

"Betsy, no! Don't listen to him!"

"He'll be my husband. I'll have to listen to him."

"It's none of Frank's business what you do when he's not there. You can write during your free time, can't you? While he's out running around his stupid orchard?"

"You don't understand. It's not a matter of Frank *letting* me write—I *can't* write. When I'm with Frank it's like . . . it's like I don't have any more poems inside me. They've all shriveled up, Lydia, like blossoms after a frost."

"But you're a writer! It's who you are."

"Not anymore. I'm not the same person I used to be. Frank makes me feel like someone else . . . someone he has created. I attend the Women's Missionary Guild now. I've even taken 'the pledge.' From now on I have to try to be the wife he wants me to be, the wife he expects me to be or . . ."

"Or what, Betsy?"

"Or he won't marry me."

Her velvety eyes searched mine as if trying to read my heart. "You don't love him, do you?"

"No," I said miserably. I didn't even have to think about it.

"Not even a tiny bit?"

"Not even a tiny bit." I sank onto the bed as I confessed my hopeless situation. "He hates books, Lydia. He won't allow any in his house. And he never laughs. I've never heard him, not even once, not after all this time together. I don't know how I'm ever going to stand it."

She knelt on the floor in front of me. "It's not too late to call the whole thing off. Tell him you want to cancel the engagement."

"I can't. Father will be furious. You know how badly he wants this partnership. He'll be so disappointed with me if I mess things up now, and I couldn't stand to disappoint him. He even made Frank promise to call it Wyatt & Fowler Orchards. If the deal falls through now, it will kill Father. It will absolutely kill him."

Lydia stared past me into the distance and a strange peace gradually came over her. She'd been desolate for the past few days, sunk deep in her own misery, and now, with a strength I'd never seen before, she made me dry my tears and gently nudged me into bed.

"Let's go to sleep, Betsy. Maybe things will look better for both of us in the morning." At the time I thought it was because we were both emotionally exhausted, but looking back, I realize that Lydia had made up her mind that night. She knew exactly what she needed to do. Drawing strength from her newfound tranquillity, I fell sound asleep.

———

Later, Lydia told me how easy it had been to follow through on her plan. Frank came for dinner on Sunday, and as he was taking the shortcut home through our orchard, Lydia slipped out of the house and ran after him.

"Frank . . . Frank, wait! We found a pocket knife on the sofa. Is it yours?"

He turned to her, rummaging through his pants pockets. "I don't think so. Mine is—"

Suddenly Lydia cried out as she tumbled to the ground. "Ow! Oh dear, how clumsy of me. I've turned my ankle."

Frank rushed to her side. "Lydia, are you all right? Here, let me help you." She allowed her hands to linger on his chest as he lifted her to her feet. "Is your ankle okay? Can you walk on it?"

"Yes . . . Ow! No . . . no, I don't think I can." She leaned against him. "Oh, I feel so silly! How will I get home?"

"I . . . I could carry you."

"Oh, would you?" Lydia's velvet eyes gazed up into his and Frank was a goner. Lifting her into his arms, feeling her slender arms around his neck, her body pressed close to his, merely sealed Frank's fate.

She smiled up at him as they neared the house. "Thank you so much, Frank. You can leave me here on our porch. I'm embarrassed to have Father know how clumsy I am."

We weren't expecting Frank the following night, but he dropped by to ask Father a question. Lydia just happened to be outside, returning from a mysterious errand in the barn as he was leaving. "Thank you so much for your kindness last night," she said, smiling.

"You're welcome. How's your ankle?"

"Oh, it's much better. Silly of me to twist it like that. I guess I'm just not used to walking on rugged terrain like you are. How do you do it all day?" She gazed up into his eyes.

"Well, I . . . I . . ."

"Whenever I see you riding on your wagon or out in your orchard, you look so tall and strong, like you could stand up against just about anything! You really love your work, don't you?"

"I . . . yes. Yes, I do."

"And your orchard is so beautiful, too! How do you get everything to grow the way you do? Wyatt Orchards is like the Garden of Eden! You must be very proud of all that you've built."

"Yes . . . I am."

She took his hand and pressed it briefly between both of hers. "Thank you again, Frank." She stood on tiptoe to plant a shy, quick kiss on his cheek. "Good night."

The next night, after concocting another lame excuse to see my father, Frank lingered in our yard, hoping Lydia would appear. She came out of the darkness as he neared the barn.

"Frank!" Before he knew what had hit him, she was in his arms. "I've never felt this way about a man before," she murmured as they clung to each other.

"Oh, Lydia . . . you're so beautiful!" He kissed her, clumsy with passion, his broad hands gripping her, pressing her close to himself. Suddenly, Lydia pulled away.

"We shouldn't . . ."

"Lydia . . . please don't go."

She twisted from his grasp and hurried into the house. Helpless, he watched her go, beside himself with longing.

Frank called on me the following two nights but he had really come to see Lydia. All the while Frank and I sat outside together on the front porch, he seemed sweaty and on edge, glancing around nervously. After I said good-night and went inside, he waited for Lydia by the barn, pacing. She didn't disappoint him.

Lydia teased him with stolen kisses and passionate embraces until the fire inside Frank Wyatt had been stoked red-hot. Then one night she led him into the barn, to the blanket she had waiting, spread out on the fresh, sweet hay. She became the downfall of this morally upright man as his ice-filled veins melted with years of stored-up desire.

They met in the barn every night for the next week, then one night Lydia didn't show up. By the time she reappeared a few nights later, Frank was half-crazed with yearning. He pulled her down beside him on the blanket in the barn.

"Where have you been, Lydia? I can't . . . I can't live without you!"

"There's something I need to tell you, Frank."

"Please don't say you can't see me anymore, Lydia! You're all I think about all day. I can't concentrate on anything, wondering if you'll be here, if I'll be able to hold you—"

"I'm going to have a baby."

It took a very long moment for the truth to sink in. Then Frank suddenly released her as if she were a live coal. "You can't be!"

"I can be, Frank, and I am. It's what happens when two people . . . do . . . what we did."

Shock extinguished the heat of Frank's passion. He shot to his feet. "What are you going to do?"

Lydia stood to face him, playing with the buttons on his shirt. "I think you mean, what are *we* going to do?"

"But . . . but I'm engaged to Betty. The wedding is next month."

Lydia laughed. "I'm sure she'll agree to cancel the engagement once she learns what her sister and her fiancé have been doing."

"But she can't call off the wedding. I mean . . . your father and I made a deal. He promised to deed all his land to me. And his pond! I can't lose everything now!"

Lydia saw the real Frank Wyatt and she hated him. He didn't care one bit about her or her feelings, only about annexing her father's land. With so much greed in his heart, there would never be any room for love. But even though she knew the truth, Lydia threw herself into his arms—a sacrifice, tossed into the flames to be wholly consumed.

"Marry *me*, Frank. Not Betty," she begged. "I can easily convince Father to deed the land to you once we're married. He won't refuse. He wants this deal as badly as you do. He won't care which daughter you marry as long as his grandson inherits Wyatt Orchards."

"Are you sure? I have plans, you know, and I need that pond for—"

"Trust me, Frank."

When Lydia didn't come home that night I was worried sick. She had been disappearing from the house for an hour or two every evening lately, but she wouldn't tell me where she'd been. "I just went for a little walk," she would say. Or, "I needed to do some thinking."

I suspected from her disheveled appearance each time she returned that she was meeting someone, but I was afraid to consider who it might be. I even thought about following her, but it terrified me to think where she might lead me. I would surely die if I found my sister with Walter Gibson.

On the morning after Lydia stayed out all night, I walked through the orchard with Walter's breakfast like a woman approaching the gallows. I fully expected to find my sister in his arms. But as I emerged into the clearing, it wasn't Lydia I saw with Walter but his driver and two porters. They had parked his carriage near the cottage and the servants were loading Walter's two chairs and all his books onto the back of a wagon.

My heart seemed to stop beating. Walter was leaving.

He stood near the bottom step, leaning on his cane as he peered down the path, watching for me. When he spotted me, his relief was visible. "Betsy! Thank heavens! I was so afraid I would have to leave before you came."

"You're leaving?" I asked numbly. "Why didn't you tell me?"

"Because I didn't know. The servants arrived early this morning with the news. It seems there is a business crisis of some sort, and my father has summoned me home immediately. I'm so sorry."

"Yes . . ." I murmured. "Yes, so am I."

I don't know why it hadn't occurred to me that Walter would leave one day soon. He had rented the cottage for a month and the time was nearly up. I hadn't allowed myself to think about it any more than I'd allowed myself to think about my approaching wedding. Walter was always going to be here in the little stone cottage to talk to me and laugh with me—except now he wasn't.

"Here, your breakfast is getting cold," I said. "And it's a long way to Chicago on an empty stomach." I set the tray on the tail-gate of the wagon. During the time we'd spent together I'd noticed that Walter's illness caused a weakness in his arms as well as in his legs. He couldn't lift anything heavier than a book.

Before Walter could reply, his driver emerged from the cottage and bowed slightly. "That's the last box, sir."

"Thank you, Peter. I'll be ready in a moment."

Walter motioned for me to follow him as he slowly hobbled across the grass toward the pond, out of his servants' earshot. I glanced over my shoulder as I walked and saw the driver move the breakfast tray to the table on the porch and slam the tailgate closed. One of the horses whinnied as if impatient to leave.

When Walter finally halted I knew that we didn't dare look at each other. Fighting tears, I bent to gather a handful of stones and began tossing them into the water. He gazed solemnly into the distance and sighed.

"We've talked of so many things this summer, Betsy. And now . . . now for the first time I'm at a loss for words."

"I know . . . I don't think there is an easy way to say good-bye."

"No, I suppose not. I think it was Emily Dickinson who wrote, 'Parting is all we know of heaven, and all we need of hell.' " He sighed again.

I threw my last rock into the water. The waves made a *shushing* sound as they gently lapped the shore, like a mother soothing her baby.

"Will we ever see each other again?" I asked, finally looking up at him. I had only a few more moments to memorize the contours of his face, the softness in his eyes. He turned to me at last and shook his head.

"I don't think so."

"I was afraid you'd say that." I could hardly speak past the terrible ache in my throat. "I'll never forget you, Walter."

"Nor I you. But 'Better by far you should forget and smile, than that you should remember and be sad.' "

"Elizabeth Barrett Browning?" I guessed.

"Close. Christina Rossetti." He took my hand in his. "I left a present for you in the cottage."

I looked up at him in dismay. "But I have nothing to give you."

"That's not true. I'm a wealthy man from all that you've given me these past weeks. The Bible would call them 'riches stored in hidden places.' " He lifted my hand to his lips and closed his eyes as he kissed it. I felt his warm breath on my skin. Then he let go and turned away.

I watched him through a haze of tears as he slowly limped across the grass to the carriage. The driver helped him climb aboard. Then Walter Gibson disappeared from my life, heading down the dusty road without looking back.

I don't know how long I stood there beside the pond. Eventually I stumbled up the porch steps and went inside the empty cottage. Walter's lemony scent lingered in the air and I wanted to close all the windows to hold it inside.

I found the present he'd left for me on the little table beside the window. It was one of his books. A leather-bound copy of *Pilgrim's Progress*.

When I finally returned home, I was relieved to find Lydia in the kitchen, sitting across the bare table from our father. But I knew right away from the tension in the air that I had walked into the middle of something. Father's face was as white as milk and he looked so deeply shaken that I feared he would suffer apoplexy.

"Father, what's wrong! Are you all right?" It occurred to me that he might have found out about Lydia's baby.

"Sit down," he grunted, then he frowned at my sister. "Tell her, Lydia."

As I lowered myself into a chair I saw that once again my sister possessed an unnatural tranquillity. I couldn't imagine its source, but she was as calm as my father was upset.

"I have wonderful news, Betsy," she said. "I'm married! Frank Wyatt and I eloped last night."

The enormity of Lydia's sacrifice stunned me. I knew exactly why she'd made it. But my first thought, my overwhelming thought was, *I'm free. Thank God, I'm free!* My relief was so profound, I closed my eyes and wept. Father misinterpreted my tears.

"Now look what you've done!" he bellowed at Lydia. "You've destroyed months of bargaining and planning in a single night and you have the gall to call that good news?"

"I already told you," Lydia said, "Frank still wants to merge his orchard with ours. He's willing to sign legal papers and everything, confirming the agreement you already made. But he's in love with me, not Betsy."

"Where in blazes is Frank?" he shouted. "Why didn't he come here to tell me this news himself?"

Because Frank Wyatt was a coward. Most bullies were. Lydia laid her hand on Father's arm.

"You need to calm down. All this shouting isn't good for your heart. I told you, Frank had to take care of his livestock. He's coming down with the wagon in a little while to move my things up to his house. You can talk to him then."

But Father wouldn't be calmed. "What about your sister? How could you do this to her? How is Betty supposed to hold her head up in church after sitting in the Wyatt pew for so many weeks? Don't you care about her feelings at all, you selfish hussy?"

I reached for Lydia's hand and our eyes met. Hers brimmed with love for me. She hadn't acted selfishly but selflessly. I wanted to explain the truth to my father but she silently pleaded for me not to. Still, I wanted him to know at least part of it.

"I'm not angry with Lydia at all," I said. "I don't love Frank."

"But what's to become of you now?" he asked hoarsely. "Nearly twenty-one years old and no marriage prospects. I won't always be around to take care of you, and then what?" He pushed his chair back and stood, wagging his finger in Lydia's face. "She's your responsibility now! Yours and Wyatt's! Since you're the one who's stolen her land and her future, it will be up to you to take care of her, you hear me?"

He slammed the kitchen door on his way out, rattling the dishes in the cupboards. I felt so emotionally drained, first from Walter leaving and now this, that I didn't think I could ever move from the chair. But Lydia still looked serene as she offered me a hand to help me up.

"Come upstairs and help me pack, okay, Betsy?"

As soon as I walked into the little room under the eaves that we'd shared all our lives, the enormity of Lydia's sacrifice struck me once again. "You shouldn't have done it," I wept as I helped pack her clothes. "We could have found another way if you didn't want to go to the home for unwed mothers."

"But I have everything I've ever wanted," she said with a smile. "A beautiful house, plenty of money . . . and I can still have my baby. I get to keep Ted's baby, and that's the best part of all."

I saw then that her serenity was merely a facade she had erected to keep her true feelings at bay. She still loved Ted Bartlett. But if she ever faced up to all that he'd taken from her she would start screaming and never be able to stop. He had stolen her trust, her virginity, her dream of a happily married life with him. But she wouldn't give up the only thing she had left—his baby. I wondered how long my sister could continue to avoid reality. And at what cost.

"You're married to *Frank*," I murmured, still finding it hard to comprehend.

"Yes. So what? You don't love him, Betsy, you told me you didn't."

"But you don't love him, either. You did this for me."

Lydia drew me into her arms. "We promised to take care of each other, remember? We made a pinkie-promise." Tears brimmed in her eyes as she held up her little finger.

"But this is too much," I cried as I hugged her tightly. "You paid much too great a price!"

Seven and a half months later, Matthew Fowler Wyatt was born.

PART III

Wyatt Orchards

Spring 1931

"For, lo, the winter is past, the rain is over and gone;

The flowers appear on the earth; the time of the singing

of birds is come, and the voice of the turtle is heard

in our land. . . ."

SONG OF SONGS 2:11-12

— CHAPTER NINE —

By the time Aunt Batty finished her tale, I felt numb. The boys had arrived home from school, and I could hear them on the back porch, thumping the snow off their boots. Becky had fallen asleep on the rug with both cats curled up beside her. I was about to get up and see about starting supper when Aunt Batty clamped her hand on my arm to stop me.

"Your children deserve their own dreams," she said quietly. "Don't ask them to live yours. Maybe they'll want this old orchard someday, maybe they won't. If it's your dream to make a home here, then good, fight to keep this place for yourself. But don't do it for them. You'll heap so much guilt on the poor little things they'll never be able to hear their own music. Let them follow the beat of their own drummer."

Later, when I was alone upstairs, I went into Becky's bedroom and looked at Aunt Batty's photograph again. She was right—

Walter Gibson did have kind eyes. But this time I also noticed the limpness in his slight body, the way he sat as if it required an enormous effort to hold himself together. No wonder Aunt Batty had to help him shave.

Funny, she hadn't mentioned shaving him in her story this afternoon.

All of a sudden I got that strange, tingling feeling again. If Aunt Batty shaved Gabe Harper like she'd wanted to do last week, maybe she would recognize him as Matthew Wyatt. It was worth a try. But first I would have to figure out a way to talk them both into it.

I waited until Aunt Batty brought Gabe his supper tray that night and followed her into his room. "I've been thinking," I said, leaning casually against the door frame. "Now that your hobo story is finished and all mailed off to Chicago there's really no need to be looking like a hobo anymore, is there?"

"Um . . . I suppose not." He scratched his chin self-consciously. "But I guess I've grown used to having a beard after all this time. It feels like part of me."

"Well, my kids get used to having dirt behind their ears, too, but I make them take a bath anyhow, whether they want one or not. Now, I'm thinking you're long overdue for one. You're finally well enough to wash yourself—so a shave and a haircut would finish up the job real nice. Don't you think so, Aunt Batty?"

"Sure thing, Toots. And as I said, I'm a real crackerjack at shaving people."

I could tell by the way Gabe ate with his head bent down, and by how quiet he'd become, that he wanted to be shaved about as much as Queen Esther and Arabella did. I would have to bully him into it.

"I once saw 'The Wild Man of Borneo' in a sideshow act," I

said, "and he wasn't half as woolly as you are. Can you cut hair, too, Aunt Batty?"

"Why, sure. Nothing to it—snip, snip!" She made scissoring motions with her fingers.

Gabe ran his hand through his hair protectively. "Um, listen—"

"Tonight would be a real good night for a bath, too, " I added. "The reservoir on the stove is full of hot water. Why not get all cleaned up?"

"Can we watch you shave him?" Jimmy asked. I was still leaning against the doorjamb and all three kids ducked beneath my outstretched arm like a game of "London Bridge."

I smiled sweetly. "You don't mind if they watch, do you, Gabe?"

He was trapped and he knew it. "I guess not."

Aunt Batty grabbed a hank of Jimmy's shaggy bangs and pretended to cut them with her fingers. "Maybe I should practice on you while Mr. Harper finishes his dinner."

"Naw. Mama says company should always go first," Jimmy said, wriggling out of her grasp.

"All right, then. Can one of you boys tell me where your daddy kept his razor and shaving soap?" she asked.

"I'll get you what you need," I said.

Sam's shaving things were still in the washstand in the kitchen where he'd left them. An age-cracked mirror in a painted wood frame hung above it. As I opened the drawer, I remembered how Sam would shave in front of that mirror every morning, and how the smell of his shaving soap would slowly drift through the kitchen. When the weather got warm he would move the washstand onto the back porch, picking it up like it weighed nothing at all, so he could clean up outside in the fresh air.

Sometimes Sam would put a dab of shaving cream on Jimmy's

face and hold him up to the mirror and let him shave it off with
a teaspoon. Jimmy and Luke loved to watch their daddy strop his
razor blade on the leather belt. One time little Luke said that the
sound of the blade slurping back and forth reminded him of a
thirsty horse lapping water, and Sam and I had laughed and
laughed.

The boys had never known how their grandfather had used a
leather strap just like that one to beat his two oldest sons when
they were boys. Sam had whispered the awful truth to me one
night in the darkness of our bedroom. He'd held me tightly and
told me how he'd hated the sight of that belt in his father's hand.
His older brother, Matthew, had always seemed to get the worst of
it. Big as he was, Sam had trembled as he'd remembered, and
he'd vowed never to use a belt on his sons that way.

I lifted the mug of shaving soap to my nose. It smelled like
Sam. I thought of Aunt Batty trying to keep Walter's lemony scent
in her little cottage after he'd gone, and I wished I had loved Sam
the way she had loved Walter. Instead, I had used Sam to get what
I'd wanted the same way Frank Wyatt had planned to use Aunt
Batty. I was no better than he was.

I gathered Sam's shaving things together, along with a towel
and a pair of scissors, and returned to Mr. Harper's room. He had
finished eating.

"Aunt Batty's barber shop is now open for business," she declared as we helped Gabe out of bed and onto a chair. He was still
pretty weak and shaky. She tied the towel around his neck and
trimmed his hair first, chattering a blue streak while she worked.
When she was ready to shave him, I fetched a basin of warm water
and set it on his lap, then stood nearby, ready to call a halt to the
proceedings if Aunt Batty began to butcher him. But she was surprisingly good at it, just as she'd said. She didn't draw a single
drop of blood. And she had done a good job on his hair, too. She

gave him a hand mirror and a hairbrush and let him comb it him-self.

"Thank you," he said as he stroked his bare chin. "I look like myself again."

The man who emerged from beneath all that hair proved to be the biggest surprise of all. I felt like I'd just watched a woolly caterpillar turn into a butterfly. Mr. Harper had a lean, oval-shaped face with a strong, square jaw—but without the deep cleft in his chin that all the Wyatt men had. He wasn't as old as I had imagined him to be, but surprisingly young, in his thirties—Mat-thew Wyatt's age. His wavy, dark brown hair might have come from Ted Bartlett; his high forehead and curved brows might have come from Lydia Fowler.

"What a handsome thing you are without all that fur!" Aunt Batty exclaimed. "Put on some decent clothes and you could pass for a gentleman."

"But first he needs a bath," I reminded her. "Instead of him climbing all those stairs to the bathroom, the boys can help me drag the old copper tub in here and fill it up. Then I want every-one to clear out and give him some privacy—and that means you, too," I said, shooing Winky and the two cats off his bed. "Think you can get in and out by yourself?" I asked him.

"I'll manage." It was much easier to see Gabriel Harper blush with his face shorn.

I could scarcely wait to get Aunt Batty out of his room to ask if she had recognized him. "You did a nice job shaving him," I said as we filled buckets with hot water from the reservoir for the boys to haul. We'd already moved the bathtub into his room. "Gabe sure does look different now, doesn't he?"

"Like a newly shorn sheep."

"Does he look at all familiar to you, Aunt Batty?" I held my breath as she thought for a moment.

"Well, now that you mention it, he reminds me of a young Robert E. Lee, the famous general. Lee was a handsome man, don't you think? Even if he was on the losing side?"

I exhaled in frustration. "What I mean is, do you see a . . . a *family* resemblance."

"Oh, I couldn't say, Toots. I never met Mr. Harper's family."

I would have to come right out and say it. "Take a good look at him, Aunt Batty. Is he Matthew Wyatt?"

"Matthew! Don't be silly, Toots! His name is Gabriel Harper. He's a writer. From Chicago." She pronounced the words slowly and carefully, as if I were senile. "Matthew went to fight in that awful war."

"That war has been over for more than ten years. Please . . . look at him *closely*. You said he looked familiar, remember?"

"Did I?"

"Yes! The first time you met him. Could he be Matthew, finally home after all these years? Look at him, Aunt Batty. He's about the same age Matthew would be."

She peered into his room as if she expected him to jump out of bed and beat her with a stick, then she shook her head. "Oh, no. He's not Matthew." She seemed certain. I didn't know whether to believe her or not. I was so frustrated I wanted to shake her.

"Are you *sure* he isn't Matthew?"

"Positive, Toots."

I wasn't convinced. I saw too many similarities between Aunt Batty's story and Gabe's story for them to be a mere coincidences. While Gabe splashed in the tub, I got out the photograph album again to study Matthew's pictures. When I happened upon one of Lydia, I suddenly realized why she looked familiar to me. I could swear she was the same woman I'd seen in Gabe's Bible—or was I imagining things? I wished I could get another peek at his picture and compare the two, but the Bible no longer lay beside his bed. He must have put it back inside his burlap bag.

When Gabe finished bathing he changed into a clean pair of Sam's long johns and crawled back into bed. He looked exhausted. I quickly bailed out the bath water and cleaned the tub, then returned to his room one last time to make sure his leg was all right. I had grown accustomed to having a shaggy old tramp in the house, but this new Gabe looked like such a different man that I felt like I was tending a stranger all over again. And Aunt Batty was right—he was a mighty fine-looking man.

"So tell me, Gabe," I said, without looking up from examining his leg, "do you have a wife and family waiting for you back home somewhere?"

"No."

I dabbed on some more iodine. "You've never been married or you're just not married at the moment?"

"I've never been married."

Good. Then if he was Matthew Wyatt I could get him to fall in love with me and marry me and we wouldn't lose our home. I'd won a man's heart once before so I knew I could do it again. But wasn't I already living with the guilt of what I'd done? I don't know why, but I couldn't look at Gabe. I also don't know why, but my heart started hammering like a woodpecker.

"I want to ask you something. The name 'Gabriel Harper' sounds sort of . . . phony. Is it your real name or a pen name?"

He didn't answer. I knew that trick and I figured I could wait him out without speaking. But he took so long that curiosity finally made me look up. He frowned at me.

"Why all the questions? What difference does it make?"

"In other words, Gabe isn't your real name."

He looked surprised and more than a little angry. "I didn't say that. Don't start putting words in my mouth."

"Well, why can't you just be honest with me and tell me flat out? Yes or no?"

"Who says I'm being dishonest? I've never lied to you."

Maybe not, but I was an expert at dodging the truth and I knew it was exactly what Gabe was doing.

"You didn't answer my question, either," I said, planting my hands on my hips. "I asked you if Gabe was your real name and you said it didn't matter. But it matters to me."

"Why?" He pierced me with his angry eyes. "Why should it matter to you?"

I couldn't answer without telling him too much. Until I was certain who he was, I didn't want him to find out that Matthew Wyatt owned everything. He'd cornered me just like I'd cornered him. Neither one of us was willing to bring our secrets out of their hidden places. I carefully pulled his pant leg back down and covered his foot with the sheet.

"Shall I turn off your light?" I asked as I stood to go, "or would you like it left on for a little while?"

"Please turn it off. Thank you."

"By the way," I said over my shoulder, "you smell a whole lot better than you did."

———

Now that she'd cleaned Gabe up, Aunt Batty took it upon herself to get him out of bed every day and walk him all around so he could rebuild his strength. One morning she hiked down to her cottage and brought back a beautiful ebony walking cane with a silver handle.

"I thought maybe you could use this," she said, presenting it to him like a trophy.

Gabe looked it over with wonder. "This is almost too fine to use, Aunt Batty. It looks like a family heirloom. Are you sure—?"

"Of course I'm sure. I have no use for it. And if the day ever comes that I do need a cane, I'm much too short to use that one."

I glanced at the handle—it was carved in the shape of a dog's head. "Was that Walter Gibson's cane?" I asked.

"Yes, it's beautiful, isn't it? He left it with me when he went away. I've always kept the handle polished so it would look nice. It's real silver, you know."

But that didn't match the story she'd told me the other day. She'd said Walter had walked away without turning back, and I got the impression that he couldn't walk without his cane. Walter had given her a book for a present, not this. And what about shaving him? Where did that fit in? Aunt Batty's stories had more holes than Swiss cheese.

I let her and Gabe hobble around together while I sat down in Frank Wyatt's office and made a list of everything that needed to be done in the orchard. I'd lived here ten years so I had a pretty good idea of the routine, if not all the particulars, and I knew that during the winter months Sam and Frank had always trimmed trees. Later the trees would have to be fertilized. Then sprayed. Frank had always moved the beehives into the orchard after he sprayed so the bees could pollinate the trees. Once the weeds started growing I would have to disk between the rows, then run through them with a drag to even it out again. The vegetable garden would have to be plowed and planted, and the asparagus picked. The animals would need hay and corn. I numbered the paper from one to ten and wrote all these things down, trying not to let them overwhelm me. I would worry about picking and selling the fruit when the time came.

On a beautiful, sunny winter morning I made up my mind to start trimming trees—after I figured out how, that is. I hoped Gabe or Aunt Batty could tell me because it would just about kill me to have to ask one of my neighbors, like Alvin Greer, for help.

I found Gabe and Aunt Batty down by the barn, leaning on the pasture fence while Becky swung back and forth on the gate.

"There's a branch on that big oak tree out front that would be the perfect place to hang a swing," I heard Gabe saying as I approached. "But first we'll have to find a sturdy board and some rope."

"Can it just be *my* swing and no one else's?" Becky asked.

"Oh, but you'll get twice the joy out of that swing if you share it," Aunt Batty said. "That's what the Bible teaches."

"Are there swings in the Bible?" Becky asked in amazement.

"I'm sure there must be one or two," Aunt Batty said. "Let me think. 'Swing low, sweet chariot'? No, that's a song. . . ."

Winky spotted me first and he trotted over to greet me. I angled toward him so he could find me. Then Becky saw me, too. "Mama, guess what! Mr. Harper said he would make me a swing!"

"That's very kind of him," I said, bending to pat Winky's head. "Listen, I was wondering if either of you knew anything about trimming fruit trees?"

"You do it in the wintertime," Aunt Batty said confidently, "while the trees are dormant. This is a bit late to be getting started, though. Good thing we had that last snowstorm to postpone spring a little longer."

"But do either of you know how to do it? Have you actually trimmed trees before?"

Gabe shook his head. "I can't honestly say I've done it, but I once interviewed a fruit grower for a newspaper article. I know the general theoretical principles behind it."

"Don't use fancy words, Gabe. Just tell me what needs to be done."

"The idea is to open up the center of the tree so the light can penetrate and the fruit will ripen better. You also want to get rid of the smaller, newer branches that take energy away from the fruit-bearing limbs."

"It's just like the story Jesus told in the Bible," Aunt Batty added. "The gardener prunes the branches so the tree will bear more fruit. And any branch that doesn't bear fruit is cut off and thrown into the fire. Then—"

I quickly jumped in to cut off her sermon. "If I drove you out to one of the trees, Gabe, do you think you could you coach me through it?"

His jaw dropped. "You're not thinking of tackling this job yourself!" I could read his expressions easily now that his beard was gone and his hair was out of his eyes, and I could clearly see that I'd shocked him. It was the same reaction that Frank or Sam might have had if I'd stepped forward and offered to do their work.

"If I don't tackle it, it won't get done," I said. "Now, can you show me how to do it or not?"

"I'll do it for you, ma'am. I believe I'm nearly well enough . . . if I take it slow."

"Good. You can help me. The work will go much faster with two of us."

Gabe's frown deepened to genuine displeasure. "But I really don't think you can do it. I mean . . . those trees are bigger around than you are."

"So?"

"So!" He grabbed my arm and wrapped his fingers around my wrist. It was so slender his fingers overlapped. "The branches you'll be cutting are bigger around than this."

"Now, children, don't fight," Aunt Batty said sweetly. "There's plenty of work for both of you."

I pried his fingers off my wrist with a smile of triumph. "And plenty of tools for both of us, too."

"What about my new swing?" Becky whined as she followed us into the tool shed. I turned in time to see the look Gabe gave her as he rested his hand on her curly red hair. It was so gentle and loving, so . . . *fatherly*, that it brought a lump to my throat.

"I'll get to it, honey," he said in a voice as soft as cats' paws. "I promise."

"And what about fixing Aunt Batty's roof?" My words came out harsher than I'd intended them to.

"That can wait, Toots," Aunt Batty said. "But trimming trees can't." She took Becky by the hand. "Brr. I'm getting chilly out here. Let's you and me go inside and bake a pie for dinner, all right?"

Neither Gabe nor I spoke as we sorted through the equipment. I itched to get started, but Gabe paused to carefully examine each of the saws and tree-trimmers first.

"Some of these blades look pretty dull," he said. "I think I'd better sharpen them." He carried them straight into the barn and went right inside Sam's workshop like he knew exactly where he was going. He sat down at the grindstone and started treading the pedals to make the wheel spin as if he'd been doing it all his life.

"Did you once write an article about sharpening tools, too?" I asked nastily.

He concentrated so hard on his task that several moments passed before he looked up. "What did you say?" It was a look of pure innocence—or perfect acting, I couldn't tell which.

"You seem to know your way around a grindstone," I said.

"Yes. Would you mind bringing me a little water to pour on this stone? Thanks." He picked up a file and began sharpening one of the saw blades with it.

As I went to fetch some water I remembered that Gabe had cleaned out the barn for me and spent a night in Sam's workshop. That would explain how he knew his way around. But as I watched him work, his hands seemed mighty skillful for a city boy's.

I caught him wincing when he finished and he bent to massage his injured leg.

"Is it hurting again?" I asked.

"It's not too bad."

I hurried out of the barn ahead of him and lugged two pickers' ladders over to the truck. Gabe limped up with the tools in time to help me shove everything into the back. I climbed behind the wheel and he hoisted himself into the passenger's seat. Snow still covered the ground so I drove slowly, not wishing to get the truck stuck in a drift. I stopped at the closest grove of trees, just beyond the barn. I could have walked there much faster, but Gabe couldn't have.

As I pulled to a stop, I glanced down and noticed the big space between us on the front seat. That got me thinking about Aunt Batty's story and how Lydia had advised her to make sure her thigh "accidentally" brushed against Frank's. I got such a funny picture in my head of tiny little Aunt Batty trying to cozy up to my stuffy old father-in-law that I laughed out loud.

"What's so amusing?" Gabe asked, smiling.

"Nothing . . . I . . ." but I couldn't get the picture out of my mind. I knew exactly how horrified Frank would have been if she'd actually done it, and I laughed until the tears came. Gabe waited. "I'm sorry," I said wiping my eyes. The story was much too complicated to explain, so I said, "My father-in-law must be rolling over in his grave. You have no idea how he babied these trees."

He nodded and climbed from the truck. When I walked around to his side he was already studying the nearest tree. "Your father-in-law's attention to detail will make our job simple," he said. "He has these trees shaped very nicely. See how easy it is to tell the fruit-bearing limbs from the new growth? These are what we have to trim back." He pointed to several slender branches growing every which-way from the trunk and the central limbs.

"Then I guess we'd better get started." I brushed past him and began hauling out one of the ladders. He stood watching me.

"Listen, Eliza . . ."

I knew by his tone of voice that he was about to tell me all over again how I was much too scrawny to trim trees. It reminded me so much of my daddy telling me what I could and couldn't do that I whirled around to face him with my hands on my hips.

"What, Gabe?"

He looked at me for a long moment, then shook his head. "Nothing. I just wanted to warn you that those blades are sharp."

It was hard work—dragging the ladder from tree to tree, climbing up and down dozens of times, reaching over my head and stretching and clipping and sawing. I kept wishing I had overalls on instead of an annoying old skirt that got in my way every five minutes. By lunchtime my toes had grown so numb from the cold that I couldn't feel them anymore.

The trees were unending—row after row of them, perfectly spaced in straight, even lines. I recalled Sam once telling me that his father planted a hundred trees to an acre—and there were acres and acres of them. By the end of the day my legs and shoulders and neck ached so bad I wanted to cry, but I still had more trees to trim tomorrow. I was willing to bet that Gabe was hurting pretty bad, too, but we were both much too stubborn to admit it.

On the third or fourth day of work Gabe brought along his army canteen. In spite of Aunt Batty's denials, I still suspected that he might be Matthew Wyatt, so when he sat down on the running board of the truck to take a drink, I decided to ask him about the war.

"I see you brought back a little souvenir from the army," I said. "Did you fight in the Great War?"

He took a long swallow and wiped his mouth before answering. "I got this canteen from a tramp named Loony Lou. He was a very sick man the night I met him. I suspected he had pneumonia from the way he coughed. So I hung around him for a couple of days, feeding him, keeping him warm, pounding him on the back good and hard whenever he needed it. He nearly died, but when he finally pulled through he insisted that I keep the canteen as his way of saying thanks. It was the only thing of any value that he owned." Gabe stood and held it out to me. "Want some?"

"No thanks." I was an expert at telling lies myself so I figured I should be able to spot one pretty easily. This story had a ring of truth to it.

Gabe had climbed all the way back up the ladder again before I realized that he had neatly avoided telling me whether or not he had fought in the war.

No matter how hard we worked, it seemed like more trees always stretched forever into the distance like a house of mirrors. As long as the weather wasn't too windy or cold, we worked at it every day during daylight hours. I fell into bed exhausted each night and dreamt about trees, with branches that reached out toward me like scrawny arms that tried to grab me and strangle me. I would wake up in a cold sweat, grateful that it was just a dream—until I remembered that I still had more trees to trim tomorrow.

"You don't have to work so hard, Gabe," I told him one afternoon. He had sunk down on the truck's running board for the third time to take a break. I thought he looked a little pale.

"I'm just trying to keep up with you," he said with a faint smile.

"You're not getting feverish again, are you?" I pulled off my glove and felt his forehead. His brow was cool. When I realized what I'd just done, I turned away in embarrassment. I gazed down the long rows of trees we'd already finished, with the piles of brush heaped beneath them, then looked at the long row we still had to trim. When I finally risked a glance at Gabe, he was staring at me with an odd look on his face—as if he'd never seen me before.

"What? Why are you looking at me like that?" I asked.

He blushed. "I . . . nothing. I admire you, that's all. You're an amazing woman." He lifted the canteen to his lips and took a swig. "How long have you been trying to run this orchard on your own?"

"Only a few months. Just since my father-in-law died last November."

"How did he die?"

"He dropped dead of a heart attack. The doctor said he was gone in a matter of minutes. At least he had the courtesy to wait until after the harvest was all in."

"And your husband?"

"He passed away a little over a year before his father."

"Listen, I know it's none of my business, but why don't you hire some help? There are plenty of men out there who are looking for work."

"I can't afford it. My father-in-law left some debts."

He swallowed another drink. "Do you think you can run this place all by yourself?" He might have lit a match to kerosene, my temper flared so hot and so fast.

"I can't tell you how sick I am of everybody asking me that! Every time I hear those words it just makes me all the more determined to hang on. This is my home! My kids' home! Nothing and nobody is ever going to force us out of here. I may not run things the way Frank Wyatt did, but this is the only home I've ever had and so help me God, I won't be homeless again!"

Gabe resembled a dog with his tail between his legs after my outburst. I flung him a quick apology. "Sorry. I didn't mean to yell."

"That's all right," he said quietly. "I know what it's like to be homeless, too."

My heart softened a bit. "Riding the rails, you mean?"

"Not only then." He fumbled with the lid to the canteen, trying to screw it back on straight. "I really don't have a place to call home. I lived in a boardinghouse in Chicago before I started my travels."

"Don't you have a family?"

"No."

My heart softened a bit more. I wanted to ask him what had become of his folks, but I knew that if he asked me the same question I wouldn't answer it. Besides, if he was Matthew Wyatt I already knew the answer. Gabe stood and stretched his arms and shoulders, swiveling his head in a circle to get the kinks out of his neck.

"I think I know just how achy you feel," I said quietly.

He gave me a slow, gentle smile. "Yes. I'm quite sure you do."

We both looked away at the same time as if realizing that we'd given away too much of ourselves.

"Well, I guess we'd better get back to work," I said, looking at the row ahead of us.

"What about all those piles of brush?" he asked, looking at the sections we had already finished.

"I don't know what to do with it all, but I know it can't stay there. I remember Sam telling me that dead wood attracts insects. He always used to run the hay rake down the rows to collect the brush at one end."

"Can't we use some of the bigger pieces for kindling?"

The way Gabe said *we* gave me a funny feeling. I wasn't sure if it was a contented feeling or an irksome one. "Yes, once it's dried out," I said. "Even so, there's way too much of it."

"I was wondering . . . you know how the hobos sometimes camp down by the railroad tracks? I think some of them might be willing to gather up the wood for us and haul it away if we let them use it for their bonfires."

He'd said it again—*we*.

"All right," I said after a moment. "But make sure you tell them to camp on my property, on this side of the tracks. The other side belongs to Alvin Greer, and he'll call the sheriff to run them off."

I let Gabe borrow the truck that evening. He filled the back of it with brush and drove the first load down to the railroad crossing for his friends to use. In the weeks that followed I would see people creeping through the orchard around dinnertime, gathering up armloads of branches—pitiful men and sometimes women, dressed in shapeless rags. One or two of them didn't look much older than my Jimmy. They were homeless, hungry, cold.

As I sat down each night to the meals Aunt Batty cooked, I prayed that my kids and I wouldn't end up like them.

CHAPTER TEN

T here are only a few more acres of trees left to trim," I told Gabe one morning as we loaded the truck. "Why don't you get started on Aunt Batty's roof today, and I'll finish trimming them myself." Gabe had already taken a good look at the damage and had given Aunt Batty a list of the supplies he would need from the lumberyard. I had no idea if she could afford them or how she would pay for them, but I had enough worries of my own as spring approached without taking on hers.

"Well, let's think about this a minute," Gabe said slowly. I could hear the hesitation in his voice.

"Is there something wrong with my idea?" I asked impatiently.

"I don't like you working all alone out there, so far away from the house. If something should happen—"

"Like what?"

"Well . . . you could fall off the ladder—"

"I haven't fallen yet, have I? Besides, you could fall off the ladder down at Aunt Batty's house, too. What's the difference?" I dared him to imply that I was a helpless woman, but he had sense enough not to. He carefully examined a saw blade before tossing it in with the others.

"How about if I keep working on the trees," he finally said, "and you can drive Aunt Batty into town for the supplies."

"I don't know one piece of lumber from the next," I said. "It would be easier if you drove her into town."

He wouldn't meet my gaze. "I'd rather not."

"Why?"

"It's not my truck. It's yours." He turned away a little too quickly. I couldn't see his face but I got the feeling there was another reason why he didn't want to go. After all, he'd driven my truck once before down to the hobo camp. Besides, he could always hitch the horses to a wagon instead of taking the truck. As I watched him limp over to close the door to the tool shed, still leaning on Walter Gibson's cane, I tried to work out what the real explanation might be. Far as I could tell, Gabe had no reason at all to avoid Deer Springs—unless he was afraid folks might recognize him as Matthew Wyatt. And if he *was* Matthew, the joke was on him because *he* owned the truck, not me!

"I wouldn't mind a lift out to that last section of trees before you head into town," he said when he'd hobbled back to the pickup.

I don't know which annoyed me more—the fact that Gabe was hiding something, or the fact that he'd been making all the decisions lately. Two weeks ago he had moved back out to the workshop to sleep, telling Aunt Batty she could have the spare room downstairs. Then he'd started getting the cold frames ready for planting and sharpening the plow blades without being asked. Last night I found him tinkering with the tractor. You would have thought he could hear my father-in-law's voice, plain as day, ordering him around like he used to order Sam: *"Son, it's time to do such-and-such . . . Son, you need to fix the thing-a-ma-jig."*

In the end, I drove Aunt Batty to the lumberyard. I had extra eggs and milk to sell, and I wanted to stop by Mr. Wakefield's office while I was in town and see if he'd had any luck tracking down Matthew. Judging by the sleepy, confused look on the old lawyer's face, he might have been sound asleep at his desk since the last time I was there.

"Sorry, Eliza. I haven't heard a thing about Matthew. Sorry . . . I wrote to Washington but these things take time. Sorry . . ."

"That's all right, Mr. Wakefield." He looked so pitiful I had the urge to pat him like a baby until he fell back to sleep.

Aunt Batty and Becky were sitting in the truck waiting for me by the time I walked back to the lumberyard. The wood, tar paper, and shingles were all loaded and ready to go. Lord knows how she paid for them.

For the next few weeks Gabe was everywhere at once, working like a house-a-fire. He would rise before dawn to do chores, then he'd work on Aunt Batty's roof for a while, then he'd putter around the barn or the orchard, getting everything ready for springtime. I almost never had to nag the boys to do chores as long as Gabe worked alongside them. But the very thing I'd feared—that they would grow attached to Gabe—was slowly happening, and I didn't know what to do about it. Try as I might, I couldn't keep my kids from sneaking out to the barn and hanging around him every time I turned my back. Luke, especially, had taken a shine to him, and it amazed me to hear the boy actually talking to Gabe—although they both spoke so softly I could never understand anything either of them said. Whatever they were discussing, Gabe seemed very patient with Luke's stuttering and all.

Gabe won Becky's heart when he made her the swing like he'd

promised. She danced in circles around Aunt Batty and me as we watched him hang it from a limb of the old oak tree in front of the house.

"Lydia's boys used to have a swing on this very same tree," Aunt Batty said. "In fact, they might have hung it from that very same branch."

"You're right, they did," Gabe said.

I looked up at him in surprise as he climbed out on the limb to tie the ropes. Had he just given himself away?

"How do you know where their swing was?" I asked him.

"I found some remnants of the old rope still embedded in the bark up here." He prodded at the wood with his finger, dusting us with bits of rotting hemp. "See? Twenty-year-old rope."

It was the same with everything he did—Gabe seemed so at home on my farm, it was as if he'd lived here his whole life. He plowed the field where we always had our vegetable garden and started slips in the cold frame. He fixed nesting boxes in the chicken coop so the hens would set and strung up new chicken wire so the hawks wouldn't take the baby chicks. He oiled and sharpened and repaired all the tools and equipment as if they belonged to him. And he kept the inside of the barn as neat as a pin, just the way Frank always insisted it be kept.

"You seem to know an awful lot about running a farm," I told him one day at lunchtime. "Did you grow up on one?"

"I spent a couple of summers on my aunt and uncle's farm." He didn't look up from his plate when he spoke. I could tell he hated answering my questions. If he had been a turtle he would have retreated inside his shell. I understood how he felt. I did the same thing whenever people started asking me about my past, but that didn't stop me from questioning Gabe.

"Where was their farm?"

"Out east."

"Really? Which state?"

"New York." He avoided my next question by turning to Aunt Batty. "If you don't mind, I'll need you to come down to the cottage tomorrow morning and tell me how you want a few things done."

"All right. How's my roof coming, by the way?" she asked.

"The work is going pretty well. All this rain we've had has slowed me down, though."

"I'm not in a hurry," she said. "And the rain is good for the apple trees."

It occurred to me that I wasn't in a hurry for Gabe to finish, either. Once he repaired the roof he would probably go home to Chicago. The thought of getting by without his help gave me a panicky feeling. I remembered Aunt Batty saying she'd been unprepared for the day Walter Gibson had left her, and I decided I'd better get used to the idea of Gabe leaving before it took me by surprise.

"You know, Gabe," I said as I refilled his coffee cup, "you've paid me back a dozen times over for doctoring your leg. You're free to leave whenever you need to go."

He didn't reply but I felt his eyes on me. When I finally looked at him he said, "A man's life is a very big debt to repay." He had dangerous eyes—mysterious and dark. I couldn't look into them for very long without feeling like I was falling off the edge of the world. Their softness pulled me toward him, yet the pain I saw in them pushed me away at the same time.

"What about your job with the newspaper?" I asked. "Shouldn't you be getting back to work one of these days?"

"I'm not sure I still have a job. I gave my editor this address when I sent in my story. I'm still waiting to hear from him."

I knew how good Gabe's hobo story was, and I wondered how much money the newspaper would pay him for it. Enough to settle Frank Wyatt's loan at the bank? When I looked at the calendar this morning I realized that half of the ninety days Mr. Preston had given me had already passed. I'd saved every cent I'd earned from selling our extra eggs and milk in town, but I knew that it wasn't going to be enough. Time was running out, and I still had no idea where the money would come from.

Alvin Greer must have realized the time had grown short, too, because he paid me a visit that very afternoon. I heard a car pull into my lane, and when I saw that it was Mr. Greer, I put on my coat and went out onto the back porch to talk to him. I knew it would be neighborly to invite him inside, but I didn't want him in my parlor again, eyeing everything like he couldn't wait to get his hands on all of it.

"Good afternoon, Mrs. Wyatt," he said, tipping his hat.

"Good afternoon." I folded my arms across my chest and waited. It didn't take him long to get the hint and come to the point.

"Are you aware that a gang of hobos has been camping on your property down by the tracks?"

"Yes, I know."

"Would you like me to run them off for you?"

"No, I told them they may camp there. They have no place else to go."

He gave me a stern look. "Do you think that's wise? I mean, you're here all alone with three small children."

"It's the Christian thing to do, isn't it, Mr. Greer? Doesn't the Good Book say whatever we do for one of the least of our brethren we do for the Lord?"

Mr. Greer was trying to hold back his temper as if he had an excited dog on a very short leash. "I didn't come here to discuss the Good Book—"

"Why did you come here?"

"Well, I got a letter a few weeks back from Mr. Wakefield, your attorney, saying you couldn't take me up on my offer to buy this place until he'd settled Frank Wyatt's estate. Now I know these things take time, so I wondered if you could use some help in the meantime?"

"No, thank you, Mr. Greer. I already have help."

He blinked in disbelief. "You do?"

It occurred to me that Alvin Greer might recognize Matthew Wyatt so I decided to introduce him to Gabe.

"Yes, sir. My husband's Aunt Betty has moved in with the children and me to help us out," I explained. "And I took on a manager to handle the orchard. He's working out in the barn if you'd like to meet him." I turned and led the way without waiting for Mr. Greer to reply. Gabe stepped through the door just as we arrived.

"There you are," I said. "I'd like you to meet my neighbor to the north. This is Mr. Alvin Greer." I purposely neglected to introduce Gabe by name, waiting to see how he would introduce himself. Gabe removed his glove and held his hand out to Greer.

"Gabe Harper. How do you do?"

I watched Greer's face, waiting for the moment of recognition. It never came. The men exchanged a few pleasantries, but it was quite clear that Greer was suddenly in a big hurry to leave. He had called on me today expecting to find a damsel in distress, and he'd cast himself in the role of my knight in shining armor. The fact that I didn't need his help, that he wasn't going to get his hands on Wyatt Orchards, had lit the fuse on his temper and he needed to leave before it exploded.

"What's wrong with him?" Gabe asked as Greer's car spun out of my driveway.

"I told him you were my manager."

"He has a problem with that?"

"He wants my orchard. He's just licking his chops, waiting for me to fail so he can take over."

"What right would he have to take over your orchard?" Gabe asked. He looked peeved as he watched Greer's car drive away.

"His wife used to be a Wyatt. He figures she's entitled to it as a blood relation and I'm not."

The very next day Dan Foster, the county sheriff, came to pay me a visit. He was a formidable-looking man in his late fifties and as burly and barrel-chested as a prize fighter. He wore a crisp brown uniform with a shiny brass badge pinned on it, and a pistol strapped on his hip. I'd always pitied any criminal who crossed Sheriff Foster's path. When I saw him climbing out of his car I thought maybe he'd brought news of Matthew, so I hurried outside to invite him in.

"No, thank you, Mrs. Wyatt," he said, tipping his hat. "It isn't you I've come to see. Alvin Greer tells me you've hired a manager and I'd like a word with him, if I may."

I stared at him dumbly. Then I recalled Aunt Batty saying that Sheriff Foster's wife was also a Wyatt and I knew they had ganged up on me.

"Why? What's this all about, Sheriff?"

"Alvin tells me the fellow's a stranger and I—"

"What business is it of yours if I hire a stranger? Don't you have anything better to do than run around to every farm in the county and check out their hired hands?" I thought he might get riled but he didn't.

"We're your neighbors, Eliza. We all understand how hard it must be with your menfolk gone. But why not ask your neighbors for help, first?" He spoke kindly and I was a little sorry for being so suspicious of him, but I just couldn't help it.

"I know you think it's your job to protect me from strangers, but I can take care of myself, Sheriff. It's none of your business who I hire. Besides, for all you know, the man is kin to me."

"Believe me, it would ease my mind a great deal if that were true." He watched me closely, waiting for me to confirm it, his hand resting casually on his gun. I didn't have the nerve to lie to him. He finally cleared his throat and said, "I've known Frank Wyatt all my life, and I can remember when your husband, Sam, stood only this high. It's for their sakes that I'm stopping by. I'm very concerned for you and the kids, ma'am. And it is my job as county sheriff to protect law-abiding citizens from dangerous vagrants and con artists."

"Thank you, but I can assure you that he's neither one."

"I'll still need to talk to him, ma'am." He reached inside his jacket and drew out an envelope. "This letter came from Chicago by registered mail for a Mr. Gabriel Harper, at this address. Bill White down at the post office asked me if I knew anything about it, and I said I'd deliver it to Mr. Harper myself since I'd planned on driving out anyway."

I don't know why I felt so protective of Gabe, but I did. He had secrets in his past that he didn't want me or anyone else to know about, but he couldn't possibly be a dangerous fugitive or anything, could he? Gabe was so gentle and soft-spoken I honestly didn't think he was capable of breaking the law. So why was I reluctant to hand Gabe over to him? Sheriff Foster might even recognize him as Matthew Wyatt—wasn't that what I wanted? I felt very confused.

"He's working down at Aunt Betty's house this morning," I finally said. "I'll be glad to go get him—"

"Thanks, but I know how to get to Betty Fowler's cottage." He climbed back into his car and drove off.

I wanted to go down there and hear what the sheriff and Gabe had to say to each other, but I would have to rely on Aunt Batty's report. I asked her about their meeting that afternoon as I mixed up a batch of bread dough. We seemed to be eating bread faster than I could bake it lately. Aunt Batty was in the kitchen with me, giving the pantry a good spring cleaning now that Queen Esther had finally rid it of mice.

"That Dan Foster was being downright nosy," she told me. She wrung out her cleaning rag as if it were the sheriff's neck. "He questioned poor Gabe as if he were wanted for murder, asking where he'd lived previously and where he'd worked—he even had the gall to ask him for a list of references. Dan can be a real bully when he wants to be—which is a good thing, I suppose, when you're dealing with criminals."

"What did Gabe say?"

"He may be a quiet man, but he wouldn't let Dan bully him. He said his name was Gabriel Harper, he lived in Chicago, and that any business he had with Wyatt Orchards was none of Dan's. I cheered him on. I said, 'Good for you, Gabe!' and that got Dan all worked up. He said this happens to be a private conversation and he asked me to leave, and I said this happens to be my house, maybe he ought to leave! Things went downhill fast after that."

I smiled as I turned the dough out of the mixing bowl and began kneading it. "I'm sorry I missed it," I said.

"Oh, it was great fun! Dan was mouthing threats by the time he pulled out of there. He vowed to check up on Gabe, and he swore that if he found out Gabe was taking advantage of a defenseless widow there would be 'you-know-what' to pay."

Aunt Batty disappeared into the pantry again and I heard her banging things around in there. I was a little disappointed that I hadn't learned anything new about Gabe, yet like Aunt Batty, I couldn't help but cheer him on.

"What about the letter the sheriff had for Gabe?" I asked, suddenly remembering it.

Aunt Batty stuck her fluffy head out of the pantry. She had a big grin spread across her face. "That was wonderful news! Gabe's story is going to be serialized in the Chicago newspaper!"

My hands froze on the dough. "So now he'll probably leave us."

"Oh, I don't think so, Toots. Gabe has a stubborn streak a mile long. I saw that for myself today. The sheriff tried to run him off and that just made Gabe dig in his heels all the more. You told folks he's your manager and by golly, from now on Gabe is going to manage Wyatt Orchards!"

I covered my face with floury hands and wept with relief. I hadn't realized how much I dreaded the thought of being on my own again. I had come to rely on Gabe more than I cared to admit. Aunt Batty laid down her cleaning rag and wrapped her arms tightly around me.

"You poor little thing," she soothed. "You've been carrying a mighty heavy burden, haven't you? But you don't have to worry anymore because God sent you a guardian angel to help you out for a little while."

I wiped my eyes and bent to rest my head on her shoulder. "I think He sent me two angels."

One cold, rainy morning I noticed one of our cows acting funny. My father-in-law had taken her to be bred last summer and I figured she must be about to calve. But unlike the other three cows who'd always known what to do when their time came, Myrtle was a first-time mother and I could see she was having trouble. Afraid to leave her for very long, I dashed back to the house through the rain to get help. Becky and Aunt Batty were in the kitchen getting a new batch of eggs ready to take into town to sell.

"Is Gabe still working down at your house?" I asked her.

"Yes, he's working on the inside today on account of the rain."

"Becky, I need you to run and get him," I said. "Put on Luke's old galoshes and take my umbrella. Tell him Myrtle's having trouble calving and I could use his help."

"Don't bother sending her for Gabe," Aunt Batty said, reaching out to hold Becky back. "He won't be any help. He hardly knows which end of the cow to point toward the feeding trough. I like Gabe a lot, but . . ." she lowered her voice to a whisper, "he doesn't know what he's doing."

"What do you mean? He does all kinds of things for me around the farm."

"Mind you, he's getting better at it every day," she said, wiping off another egg. "But when Gabe first started helping out with the chores, Jimmy could milk two cows in the time it took Gabe to milk one—and that was only after he got over his fear of being kicked."

I still wanted to believe Gabe was Matthew Wyatt. If so, he would have left home some time ago and might have forgotten a lot of things by now. "Maybe he's just out of practice," I said. "He lived in the city for a long time, you know."

"I would bet he's lived in the city all his life! That young man never grew up on any farm!" She dropped her voice to a whisper again and added, "He comes to me for advice."

"Advice about what?"

"Everything!" she said with a shrug. "When to start the hot bed, how to get the chickens to set, when to plow the garden, how the manure spreader works . . . The horses spooked him pretty badly at first. I suppose because they're so big. He said he'd never owned a horse in Chicago—just cars. I told him you have to let a horse know who's boss, and he laughed and said they already know they are! He's much better with them now and hardly ever gets their harnesses on backward anymore. But yesterday morning I told him that the raspberry canes Frank started last fall were ready to be clipped and he had no idea what I was talking about."

"Neither do I and I've lived here ten years. How long has Frank raised raspberries?"

"As far back as I can remember," she said, examining another egg. "Lydia knew how much I loved raspberries so she always let me pick my fill every year. I had to buy them after she died. They weren't nearly as good, you know. You have to eat raspberries the same day you pick them or all they'll be good for is jam and—"

"Listen, what should I do about the cow?" I hated interrupting her, but Aunt Batty's thoughts could take more twists and turns than a circus' rubber lady. Do you know anything about birthing calves?"

"Most of the cows I've owned managed fine on their own. Although I do remember a time or two when Father had to turn a calf. I would haul hot water for him and things like that, but I was always too small to be much help. It takes a man's strength."

"Will you come out to the barn and take a look at Myrtle for me?"

"Sure, Toots."

But after watching the cow closely all morning, it was clear to both of us that she was in trouble.

"I'm afraid you're going to have to help Myrtle out," Aunt Batty told Gabe when he walked up the hill for lunch. "We don't want to lose her or her calf."

"Sure," he said, blowing on his soup to cool it. "What do you want me to do?"

Aunt Batty winced. "I'd better let you finish your lunch before I spell out the unpleasant details." She laughed when he suddenly stopped eating, his spoon poised midair. "Have you ever watched the birthing process before?" she asked him.

"Um . . . my uncle's dog had puppies one summer," he said. "And it seems as though Arabella has a new 'kitten' or two every time I turn around." He looked at Becky and winked.

Don't do that, I wanted to shout at him. *Don't make my children love you, then walk out of their lives!* But it was already much too late for any warnings. I could tell by the way Becky took Gabe's hand as we walked out to the barn after lunch that she thought the world of him. He carried a bucket of hot water in the other hand. He still limped slightly, but he no longer needed the cane.

Poor Myrtle bellowed in misery. Aunt Batty took charge. "Let's get her into the smallest stall so she can't move around so much. Eliza and I will try to hold her still while you turn the calf. Soap up your arm, Gabe."

He looked horrified. "You don't mean . . ."

"I'm afraid so. You'll have to take your coat off. And make sure you wash clear past your elbow."

Gabe didn't move. I felt so sorry for him that I was about to swallow my pride and drive over to ask Alvin Greer for help. But suddenly Gabe sighed in resignation and shrugged off his coat.

"I wonder if the *Tribune* will be interested in an article about this?" he said as he lathered up.

"Now, Myrtle is not going to like this . . ." Aunt Batty warned when he was ready.

"I don't think I'm going to like it much, either," he mumbled.

"So mind she doesn't kick you. Watch her rear hooves."

"They won't be easy to dodge, considering where I'll be standing. But thanks for the warning." He took a couple of deep breaths, as if he were about to dive under water, then asked, "What am I looking for again?"

"The calf's head. Once you figure out which end is which, feel your way down from her head to her shoulder or her front leg and try to turn her around. My guess is, the calf is facing the wrong way."

"Why do I have the feeling that it sounds easier to describe it than to do it?" he joked. He stepped up to the cow and patted her rump gingerly, wary of her hind legs.

"Talk to Myrtle, Eliza," Aunt Batty coached. "Say soothing things to her."

I stood near the cow's head. I stroked her muzzle and talked to her the way I talked to the kids when they were sick, telling her everything would be fine. But thinking back on my own experiences with childbirth, I wouldn't have blamed Myrtle if she hauled off and kicked me, too.

Gabe had finally gotten up the nerve to do what he needed to do. But he wasn't inside more than twenty seconds before he let out a yell and his face contorted with pain.

"Oh, I'll bet she's having a labor pain," Aunt Batty said. "I forgot to mention those. She'll have one from time to time, and my father said they just about squeeze the life out of your arm."

"He wasn't joking!" Gabe groaned. He went limp for a moment when it finally ended but he didn't quit. He and Myrtle continued to struggle for what seemed like hours and hours. He found the calf's head, lost it, found it again, then began the slow, arduous task of turning it around—in between the cow's labor pains. I thought he would be cold without his coat on, but he worked so hard that sweat poured down his face and plastered his dark hair to his forehead. When he thought he finally had the calf in the right position, Aunt Batty told him to step back and let Myrtle finish.

Within minutes, she gave birth to a beautiful new calf. I saw pure joy on Gabe's face as we all witnessed the miracle of birth. Then tears rolled down my own face as I watched the newborn struggle to stand on wobbly legs for the first time. Aunt Batty and Becky held hands and danced in circles right there in the barn.

"Thank you! Thank you!" I wept as I hugged Gabe. We clung to each other tightly, overwhelmed with emotion. A moment later

I hugged Aunt Batty and Becky, too, but even as I did, I was keenly aware that it wasn't the same. I didn't have the same, powerful emotions flooding through me the way they had as I'd held Gabe—and that scared me.

"Myrtle's new calf needs a name," Gabe said as he lifted Becky into his arms.

"Angel," she said without hesitation. "Let's name her Angel."

"All right, Angel it is!"

That night as I tossed in bed, I couldn't erase the memory of Gabe's embrace from my heart. Was I falling under his spell like Becky Jean had? I'd never fallen in love before, so these sensations were all brand-new to me. Still, I could easily imagine it happening to Gabe and me in the same slow, sure way Aunt Batty had fallen in love with Walter Gibson.

A wiser part of me knew I had to prevent it from happening. Walter Gibson had returned to Chicago, and this very afternoon Gabe had talked about writing an article for his newspaper as if he planned to return to Chicago, too. He wouldn't stay on the farm—Aunt Batty insisted that he knew nothing about farming.

I couldn't risk falling in love with him. I couldn't.

But how did I stop it?

————

I worked awfully hard that spring, doing a man's labor every day. I had to learn how to do everything—and I'd be doing it for the rest of my life if I wanted to hang on to the orchard. I could tell that Gabe didn't much like me shoveling manure and slogging the team of horses through rain and mud, but it took the two of us working together just to get all the spring chores done. Now that the snow had melted it was time to start fertilizing the trees. Aunt Batty watched Becky for me and did all the cooking and other household chores while I worked outside. Those two had become thick as thieves.

In spite of what Aunt Batty said, I never saw one single sign that Gabe didn't know what he was doing. Was he putting on an act for her sake, so she wouldn't recognize him? Or for mine?

As time passed, I became more and more frightened by the easy familiarity that was developing between Gabe and me. Our closeness grew stronger as we worked side by side, discussing things and making decisions. I'd never had a relationship like that with anyone before, not even with my husband, Sam. He had worked with his father all day while I'd had my own household chores to do. But Gabe and I had gotten so we could anticipate what each other needed. We'd be ready to hand over a tool or turn the horses around before the other person even had a chance to ask. We worked like a pair of trapeze artists, performing smoothly together in perfect rhythm, one ready to catch the other at exactly the right moment. Like I said, it scared me to death.

When it was time to harvest the asparagus, I decided to have our whole family pick it instead of hiring help. That way all the money we made could go toward the mortgage. Jimmy and Luke were thrilled to miss a day or two of school—until they found out how hard they had to work.

I used the wagon and a team of horses to take the crop to the fruit exchange. It was slowgoing, but it saved me a little money on gasoline. I asked Gabe to come with me since I'd never sold anything at the fruit exchange before, and I was afraid they'd take advantage of me because I was a woman. I thought he might refuse since he'd always given me a pile of excuses why he couldn't go into town, but this time he didn't.

We had harvested a beautiful crop, and quiet, gentle Gabe stood his ground with all the buyers, arguing back and forth with them like a big-city lawyer until we got the best possible price. But when I counted everything up, I still didn't have nearly enough money to pay off the bank loan.

Afterward we went to the feed store. I had to spend some of my egg and milk money for onion sets and garden seeds and all the other things we needed for spring planting. When I told Becky to go pick out the feed sacks she wanted me to buy, Gabe looked so perplexed I knew he wasn't acting.

"Are you an authority on chicken feed, now?" he asked her, ruffling her red curls.

"No, silly. It's for my *clothes*," she said. "Mama always sews me new ones with the cloth. Which sack do you think is the prettiest?"

"Don't ask me!" he said, holding up his hands in protest. "High fashion has never been my area of expertise."

"Birthing calves wasn't either," I teased, "but you did just fine with that."

Gabe laughed as he backed away from us. "I'd sooner birth a whole herd of calves than help ladies shop for clothes, believe me! I'll wait for you outside."

In the end, Becky picked a yellow print with orange flowers that was so sunshiny-bright I wondered if Aunt Batty was having a bad influence on her taste. Aunt Batty had stayed home that day, but she'd smiled mischievously as she'd waved good-bye to us, saying, "Maybe I'll have a little surprise—or two—when you get back."

We'd hardly drawn the team to a halt beside the barn before Becky hopped down and ran up to Aunt Batty asking, "Where's the surprise? Can I see the surprise now?"

Aunt Batty led us all into the barn as if leading a parade down Main Street. There in the corner, rooting around in their pen, were two new baby piglets. Becky squealed with delight as she scrambled over the gate.

"You might have to bottle-feed them for a while until they get used to being without their mama," Aunt Batty told her. But my daughter was already cradling one of them in her arms like a baby and rocking it to sleep, so I knew the idea thrilled her. What worried me was where the piglets had come from, and how much they'd cost, and how I was going to pay for them. My father-in-law had always bought a few pigs to raise each spring, but I figured we would have to do without this year.

"How. . . ? Where. . . ?" I stammered. "I can't pay—"

"Don't you worry about any of that," Aunt Batty said with a smile. "We have to have ham and bacon, don't we?"

We had to have spray for the fruit trees, too, and I wished I didn't have to worry about how I would pay for that—but I did. I had studied my father-in-law's receipts and record books trying to figure out what to buy and how much I would need. Near as I could tell, he had always bought the spray ingredients on credit and paid it back when he sold the crop. But when I went into town to place my order at Peterson's store, Merle Peterson had changed his tune.

"I'm sorry, Mrs. Wyatt, but Frank had an established line of credit with us and you don't. I'll need to see some proof that your own credit is good before I can extend you a line."

"That's ridiculous! My credit record is exactly the same as his! We both own Wyatt Orchards." As soon as I'd said the words I remembered that they weren't true. I didn't own Wyatt Orchards; Matthew did. This was one lie that Mr. Peterson could sniff out very easily. I held my breath, waiting for him to demand proof.

"Even if the deed is in your name, ma'am, I would be extending credit based on your future crop—and since you have no farming experience, I have no way of knowing whether or not you'll be able to bring in a decent harvest all by yourself."

I forced myself not to cry—or lose my temper. "I'm not all by myself. I've hired a manager. Would you like to speak with him?"

"Sure. If he comes highly recommended from some other established orchard it would certainly count in your favor."

He'd cornered me again. It sounded like Merle had talked to Sheriff Foster. I had to find some way out of this. Maybe I could fake a letter of recommendation for Gabe. But if all my problems were God's punishment on me for lying, I would surely wind up in worse trouble if I kept on doing it. My sin had me up a tree and I couldn't figure out how to climb down.

"What if I promise you a share of my crop?" I asked.

"That's what a line of credit amounts to, ma'am." He was losing patience with me. He sifted through the litter of papers by his cash register as if he had important business to tend to and I was keeping him from it. I thought about my kids and decided to beg.

"Please, Mr. Peterson, I know my manager and I are going to bring in an excellent harvest this year, but even if we don't, you know how valuable Wyatt Orchard's assets are. You could take our cows or the horses or some of our equipment and easily pay yourself back if it comes to that."

"Not in these hard times, ma'am. Entire farms are selling for pennies an acre, and farm equipment is a dime a dozen."

He was right. Mr. Wakefield had warned me that I probably wouldn't get much if I auctioned off Frank's equipment. Besides, I needed that equipment to run the farm.

"Mr. Peterson, how long have you done business with Wyatt Orchards?" I asked.

"Years and years," he replied without looking up. "My father did business with your father-in-law before you and I were even born."

"Then if you've known our family all your life, isn't that recommendation enough? You attend the same church we do. You probably grew up with my Sam and his brother Matthew. Your kids go to school with mine. Doesn't any of that count toward my line of credit? Can't you please find it in your heart to help us out? I'll bet if you shook your family tree hard enough a Wyatt relation would fall to the ground."

He looked up in surprise, then an angry glare froze on his face. "I don't have to shake hard at all. My father and Frank were cousins. I don't know how he did it, but Frank cheated my father out of his rightful share!"

I'd played the wrong card and lost the hand.

I'd once heard a sermon in a Lutheran church in Ft. Wayne, Indiana, about how the sins of the fathers were visited upon their children for two or three generations. I was so afraid that my daddy's sins were going to drive up in a wagon some day and pay me an unwelcome visit that I asked Daddy about it as soon as he picked me up from church that day. He looked real uneasy when I told him what the pastor had said, but my daddy never was much good at answering any of my questions.

"Just do what the Good Book says, Eliza," he'd mumbled. "You can't go wrong if you do what the Good Book says." But for a long time afterward, I couldn't get the preacher's warning out of my head. I pictured it like a ghoulish family reunion in a cemetery somewhere, with all my daddy's ugly old sins coming by to pay me a visit like a bunch of long-lost relatives.

Now the exact same thing was happening with Frank Wyatt's sins and his long-lost relatives. Frank didn't have any children left, so the sins were all being visited on me and my kids. I'd noticed that my father-in-law didn't have any close friends and that people seemed to steer a wide path around him at church, but I'd never known why. Now Alvin Greer and Merle Peterson had told me the reason—Frank had cheated his relations out of their inheritance. If every Wyatt cousin felt as bitter about it as they did, there would be a long line of them waiting to bid on Wyatt Orchards if I had to auction it off. And they'd only bid a penny each.

I worried about what to do as I drove the team home from town. The spraying had to get done before the trees budded. If I didn't spray I wouldn't get any fruit. Terrible things would nibble away at it, like blight and coddling moth and brown rot and tree borers. But if I spent all my money on spray, how would I earn enough to pay off the mortgage in the forty-some days I had left? Should I ask Gabe for a loan? No, I should pay him for all the work he'd done already! Maybe I could find my daddy and beg him for money—if he had any, which I doubted.

I returned to Peterson's the next day and used my asparagus money to buy the stuff I needed to spray my trees. I would have many long hours to figure out how to beg, borrow, or steal more money to pay the bank as I rode up and down the orchard rows on the spray rig.

It took all four of us to spray—Aunt Batty and Becky driving the horses, Gabe and I operating the rig. The boys begged to cut school again and help us out but Gabe told them that their education was more important. I recalled what Aunt Batty had said about letting my kids dream their own dreams instead of forcing them to live mine, and I knew Gabe was right.

The spray surrounded us like a blue fog, sticking to our hair and turning our clothing stiff. The stench of sulfur was awful. "We smell like we've all taken a boat ride down the River Styx to Hades," Aunt Batty said. Surely this was punishment enough for my sins, wasn't it? I kept waiting for a miracle—for God to drop five hundred dollars out of the sky into my lap—but April turned to May and there was still no miracle in sight.

One rainy morning when we couldn't work outside, Aunt Batty and I chopped rhubarb and made a batch of preserves. I enjoyed having another woman to do my household chores with, even if Aunt Batty did drive me to distraction sometimes, singing hymns at the top of her voice.

"I need a miracle real bad, Aunt Batty," I told her as I pulled boiling hot jelly jars out of the kettle with a pair of tongs. She had been singing about what a friend she had in Jesus, so I thought maybe she could pull a few strings for me. "Next time you talk to God, could you ask Him real nice for me?"

"Why, sure, Toots. What kind of a miracle do you need?"

"He already knows. And tell Him I'm sorry about the lies and everything. I promise I won't do it anymore."

After we finished spraying, Gabe and I moved all the beehives back into the orchard. Aunt Batty said it was best to do it at night so the bees would all be home in their beds. I headed up to my own bed afterward, but when I happened to glance out my window once the lights were out, I noticed that Gabe's light in the barn was still burning. I started taking note of it after that, and no matter how late I turned in, Gabe's light always stayed on long after mine.

One night my curiosity got the best of me. I put my coat on over my nightgown and crept outside to see what he was up to. From outside Gabe's window I could clearly hear the *clackety-clack* of his typewriter keys.

I cried myself to sleep that night because the truth had finally sunk in—Gabe was a writer, not a farmer. Only a man who truly loved to write would stay up after a long, hard day of work to do it. Gabe was helping me because I had helped him, but that didn't change what he was. Mr. Wakefield was a lawyer and Reverend Dill was a minister and Gabe was a writer. Period. Even if he was Matthew Wyatt—and I was starting to doubt that he was—he would always want to write, not farm.

"I can't change what I am, Eliza," my daddy had once told me. I'd begged him to settle down somewhere so I could have a home to live in and a real family like all the other kids had. *"Look it up in the Good Book,"* he'd said. *"A leopard can't change his spots."* Gabe

could grow a beard like a hobo or put on a pair of farmer's overalls, but he couldn't change what he was any more than my daddy could.

Change was all around me this time of year. The robins had returned, the buds were swelling on the trees, and the orchard was about to bloom. I used to grow excited every spring, waiting for all the trees to bloom and the birds to start singing again. But I'd been through too many changes this past year to get excited this time. I lay awake worrying night after night, watching the light in Gabe's room burn until well after midnight, unable to sleep as I counted the days until the Deer Springs Savings and Loan would demand their money. Only one week left . . . then five days . . . then three.

Two days before the loan was due, I was pacing in my bedroom shortly before dawn when I thought I heard Winky barking outside. I peered out of my window and saw a ghostly figure dressed in white, fluttering through the cherry orchard. I ran to a different window for a better view, and I couldn't believe my eyes. Beneath lacy pink branches that had seemed to flower overnight, Aunt Batty danced in circles in her nightgown, with Winky barking and leaping for joy alongside her. As the sun slowly rose behind them, a chorus of birds burst into song. If fairies and wood sprites had crept out from behind the trees and joined the celebration, it wouldn't have surprised me in the least.

I ran downstairs and slipped into my coat and a pair of boots. As I grabbed Aunt Batty's coat off the hook and hurried outside with it, I told myself I was only going out there to keep the poor, silly woman from catching her death of pneumonia. But in my heart I knew something else drew me. The miracle of springtime had exploded all around her and I needed a miracle to descend upon me, as well. Aunt Batty had promised me an angel and God had sent me two. Maybe another wonder would drop out of the sky along with the cherry blossoms.

Aunt Batty grinned when she saw me hurrying toward her, then she lifted her arms in the air and twirled like a ballerina. I halted her in the middle of her spin and draped her coat over her shoulders.

"What are you doing out here in only your nightclothes?" I chided. "You'll catch your death!"

"Not death, Toots—life! Resurrection life! Eternal life!" She spread her arms wide and her coat slipped to the ground. "Walter told me to come out here and see God's promise for myself!"

I knew that a few more of her tent stakes must have slipped loose if she heard Walter talking to her after all these years. Winky must have suffered the same affliction. He was still leaping and twirling and barking as if he hadn't noticed that his dancing partner had stopped. I bent to pick up Aunt Batty's coat and slipped it around her again. She gripped my hands.

"Did you come out to dance with us?" she asked, twirling me around in a circle with her.

"No. I . . . I thought you might be cold."

"Come and join us, Gabe!" she suddenly called out. I turned around, mortified to see Gabe walking toward us. He had dressed hastily, with one strap of his bib overalls still undone and his coat unbuttoned. He had forgotten his shirt altogether.

"What's going on out here?" he asked, combing one hand through his tousled hair.

Aunt Batty dropped one of my hands and beckoned for him to join our little circle. "Come on, we're celebrating life!"

"Life?" He seemed as puzzled as I was. He halted a few feet away from us, his hands shoved safely in his pockets. I freed my other hand from her grasp and quickly pulled my coat closed over my nightgown.

"Yes, *life!*" Aunt Batty said, spreading her arms wide again.

"I've seen spring come to the orchard every year as far back as I can remember and I've never grown tired of it. Oh, the wonder of it! The outrageous beauty! God didn't have to give us cherry blossoms, you know. He didn't have to make apple trees and peach trees burst into flower and fragrance. But God just loves to splurge. He gives us all this magnificence and then, if that isn't enough, He provides *fruit* from such extravagance!"

Gabe and I exchanged uneasy glances. "You're barefoot, Aunt Batty," he said. "Maybe we ought to go inside and talk about this."

"Oh, but the promise of eternal life is out here, all around us! A week ago these trees were just dead sticks—now they're bursting with life! It's a message from God, just like Walter said."

"When did Walter tell you all this?" I asked warily.

"Oh, years ago!"

I frowned. Couldn't she see that her stories had more holes than her old moth-eaten yellow sweater? "You told me all about Walter Gibson, but you never said—"

"That's because I didn't get to finish Walter's story. Well, I guess it's my story, too."

"You mean there's more?"

"Much more! Jesus said that whoever believes in Him will never die! You and your kids will see Sam again, Gabe will see all his friends and loved ones again, I'll see mine. . . . Springtime is God's promise that someday we'll all share His resurrection life! Our weeping may endure for a night, but joy comes in the morning!"

PART IV

Aunt Batty's Story

Deer Springs, 1895

"Every blade of grass has its angel that bends over

it and whispers, 'Grow, grow!' "

THE TALMUD

— CHAPTER ELEVEN —

My father's house seemed very quiet after Lydia married Frank Wyatt and moved away. I missed her terribly. It was just Father and me in the long winter evenings—and he never was one to waste words. Frank hired a girl from town to help Lydia with the housework and the new baby, but Lydia was still much too busy to visit me very often. I wrote some halfhearted poems and stories, but without my sister's encouragement I lacked the confidence to send them away to be published. The year dragged slowly past.

The following spring I poured all my creative energies into planting a vegetable garden for Father and me. It cheered me out of my winter doldrums to plant the seeds, then tend them and nurture them and watch them grow. I had spent all morning in my garden one hot day in early July when Father called me inside around noontime.

"Betty, get in here. It's time to fix lunch."

I tried not to let his bossiness irritate me. That's just the way Father was. Besides, the sun was getting too hot to hoe weeds. I hung my straw hat on a hook by the door and waited a moment for my eyes to readjust from the bright sunlight. When they did, I couldn't believe what I saw. Father sat at the kitchen table counting money like a Wall Street banker. He had a huge stack of cash piled in front of him.

"Where did all that money come from?" I asked.

"We have boarders again."

"Boarders? You mean, someone rented the cottage?"

"Yes, that Gibson fellow came back. He paid for two months this time."

Surprise sucked the breath right out of me. I stared at my father, afraid to believe him, afraid to raise my hopes too high. "Really?" I finally managed.

It peeved Father that I would question him. "You think I'm making it up? The man came back, I'm telling you. He drove up in his fancy carriage while you were working outside, and he rented the cottage for the rest of the summer."

I had read about hearts soaring in novels, but I'd never known what it meant until then. I would have turned and run straight down to the cottage but my clothes were all sweaty and I had dirt beneath my fingernails.

"Does he want meals again?" I asked as I started pumping water into the sink to scrub up.

"He says there are two of them to feed this year. That's why he paid me all this money."

I suddenly knew what it meant to have your heart sink, also. Mine plummeted. "Two people? Who's with him, Father?"

"His wife, I suppose."

I took my time fixing lunch as I steeled myself to meet Walter's wife. She would be a very beautiful woman, of course, and very elegantly dressed in fine linen and silk—no feed sack aprons or muslin petticoats for Mrs. Walter Gibson. Her skin wouldn't be sun-browned and freckled like mine, either. Rich women always sat under parasols when they went out in the sun to preserve their delicate, porcelain complexions. And she would be thin—"slender as a reed," a novelist would describe her—and every bit as graceful as one. I considered strapping on my bust-perfecto corset, just so she wouldn't pity me, but I needed Lydia to help me man-handle the laces.

How could Walter bring his wife back to the place where we'd shared so many happy memories? I wondered as I finally carried the tray of food down to the cottage. Then I nearly turned around and ran home when I realized the truth. Of course! Walter didn't know I was here! He thought I married Frank and moved out of my father's house. He would expect my sister or someone else to bring his meals, not me. I slowed my steps, searching for a way to avoid seeing him. I couldn't think of one.

As I emerged from the trees into the clearing, I saw Walter sitting all alone in a cane chair facing the pond. I drew a deep breath, trying to will back my tears at the wonderful sight of him. I had believed I'd never see him again. Then the cottage door opened and our second boarder came out onto the porch. It was his servant, Peter.

I was so relieved, so overjoyed, I nearly dropped the lunch tray. "Walter!" I called out to him as I hurried across the grass.

He turned and saw me. "Betsy? What a wonderful surprise!" He tried to smile but he appeared shaken. "I didn't realize you and your husband lived nearby."

"We don't. I didn't . . . I mean, I never got married! The engagement was called off!"

A slow smile spread across his face and the faint dimple I'd missed so much finally appeared. "Really? And all this time I've been imagining you reading *Pilgrim's Progress* over and over again. I figured you must have memorized it by now."

I couldn't help laughing. "No, I've been free to read whatever I want . . . dozens and dozens of books. But what about you, Walter?"

"Me? I've read dozens of books, too."

I laughed again. "That's not what I meant and you know it! Are . . . are you married?"

"No. I'm afraid my poor health has prevented that."

"I'm sorry, Walter."

"I'm not." His eyes twinkled as the dimple in his cheek deepened. "And the young lady I was betrothed to certainly wasn't sorry, either. So it looks like we've both had a narrow escape from the bonds of matrimony. Was your father very disappointed?"

"No, he got what he wanted—my sister married my fiancé." I laughed at the shocked look on his face "It's a long story with a happy ending for everyone. Father's land is part of Wyatt Orchards now."

"That big establishment up on the hill?"

"Yes, and Father was finally able to retire. He lived to see the grandson who will inherit his land someday, so he's a contented man."

"And I guess in a way I could say the same thing about my father. Howard Knowles Gibson may not have his own son working beside him, but my sister has married well and her husband is being groomed to run the business in my place."

"So you're free to pursue your own dreams, Walter?"

"In a manner of speaking." He gestured to his chair and I noticed for the first time that it was a wheelchair. "This contraption makes it pretty difficult for me to be the captain of a whaling ship—although I suppose I could still be a Hindu snake charmer."

I felt awkward suddenly. I didn't know what to say. I remembered the tray in my hands. "Well, here's your lunch . . . and the food is getting colder by the minute. Would you like to have a picnic out here or shall I take it inside?"

"On a beautiful day like today, I think I'd like to eat out here. Bring the little folding table here, will you, Peter?"

I watched the servant fetch it, set it up, and arrange the food on it. I waited for Walter to invite me to stay and visit with him while he ate, like we always used to do, but he had grown very quiet. He looked down at the food, not at me. Peter pulled up a chair for himself but none for me. Neither man ate. They hadn't even unfolded their napkins. The silence grew uncomfortable.

"Listen, I should go and let you eat in peace," I said quickly. "Enjoy your meal."

Walter didn't argue with me. I ran back to the house to hide my tears.

I was still sitting at the kitchen table with my face in my hands an hour later when someone knocked on the back door. It was Peter, returning the lunch tray. I ducked my head so he wouldn't see my swollen eyes and red nose.

"Thank you, Peter. You didn't have to walk all the way back here with that. I would have come for it."

"If you have a few minutes, miss," he said quietly, "Master Walter would like to speak with you. But he said I should not interrupt you if you were busy."

"I'm not busy. I'll . . . I'll be down in a few minutes."

I soaked a towel in cold well water and pressed it over my eyes. A quick look in the mirror showed me that it hadn't helped one bit. Lydia used to put cucumbers on her eyes after a late night out but it was too early in July for cucumbers. Would pickles work just as well? I fetched a jar from the pantry, then quickly decided it would make matters worse to arrive smelling like dill and vinegar.

Suddenly I had a flash of inspiration—I would tell Walter I had been reading a sad book! I quickly considered the possibilities and decided on *Les Miserables*. That story would bring tears to anyone's eyes, even a "tough nut" like Father or Frank Wyatt. I wished I had a copy of the book to tuck under my arm for credibility but I didn't own one. Instead, I practiced smiling in the mirror a few times, then set off down the path to the cottage.

Peter sat on the front step, whittling a chunk of wood. He quickly stood, bowing slightly when he saw me. "Master Walter is inside, miss. Please go in."

Walter sat in his wheelchair, bending over a box of books. There were crates of books everywhere, as there had been last year, and a small daybed had been set up in the dining area for Peter.

Walter looked up when I entered. "I hope I'm not keeping you from your work," he said.

"Not at all. Father is napping and I was just reading Victor Hugo's *Les Miserables*. It's such a sad book, don't you think?"

He studied me for a moment, then shook his head. "You're not a very convincing liar, Betsy. I know I hurt your feelings earlier and I wanted to tell you how very sorry I am. Will you forgive me?" All I could do was nod. He smiled slightly, then looked away. "Thank you. I would love nothing more than to spend my meal-times talking with you like we did last summer, but it's awkward with Peter here. He's my dinner companion and I feel obliged to converse with him. I hope you understand."

I digested his words for a moment. "You're not a very convincing liar, either," I said. "I've never heard of a master dining with his servant before, much less feeling obliged to talk with him. Nor do I know many servants who would be comfortable sharing polite dinner conversation with their masters."

He laid down the book he'd been examining and looked up

at me in surprise. "Well, it just so happens," he said, smiling slightly, "that I have been reading *Les Miserables*, too. 'Down with the nobility!' 'Liberty and equality for the masses!' I thought I would try putting it into practice with Peter."

I began to laugh. And when I thought about what conclusions Walter might have reached if I'd arrived smelling of dill pickles, I laughed harder still. Without thinking, I threw my arms around his neck and hugged him.

"You make me so happy, Walter! Oh, how I've missed you!"

I pulled away again, suddenly shy. I looked at his beloved face, his soft gray eyes, and I saw the same love I felt for him reflected there. I knelt on the floor in front of him, and forgetting all caution, I spoke the words that I knew were true. "I love you, Walter."

He reached out to caress my cheek. His hand quivered with palsy as he lifted it. "Yes," he said. "Yes, I know. But we never should have fallen in love with each other. I never should have allowed it to happen." His hand dropped back into his lap.

"Why? Because you're rich and I'm poor? Because you've traveled all over the world and I've barely left Deer Springs? Or is it because you're handsome and charming and I'm plain and fat?"

He reached up again and brushed away my tears with unsteady fingers. "You're the most beautiful woman I've ever met, Betsy."

He meant it! I saw it in his eyes, and the truth stunned me. Walter had looked inside my heart and he saw me as beautiful. A moment passed before I could speak.

"Then why?"

"Because I'm going to die."

"No, you're not! Don't say such a terrible thing, don't even think it!"

"It's true, Betsy. My father has taken me to dozens of doctors, hired the finest specialists, sent me to all the best clinics here and abroad, and they've all said the same thing. The disease is progressing rapidly. All the other family members who've had these symptoms have died. There's no cure."

"Don't listen to them, Walter. I'll take care of you. I won't let you die."

"I've already accepted the truth," he said gently, taking my hand in his limp one. "I don't mind dying. I decided to come here to a secluded place to make it easier on my family. So they wouldn't have to watch me deteriorate. But now I'm hurting you. Now . . . I'll have to leave. And I'm so very sorry."

"Please don't leave me again," I whispered. "Please. Whatever time you have left, I want to spend it with you."

"I can't," he said, closing his eyes. "I can't. It hurts me too much . . . wanting to touch you, to kiss you, to hold you in my arms—and knowing that I can't do any of those things. And it's not fair to you."

"Why don't you let me decide what's fair? Leaving me isn't fair!"

Walter silently shook his head. The sharp planes of his thin face, the dark circles that rimmed his eyes seemed much more prominent in the shadowy room.

I longed to throw myself into his arms again, to press my face to his and feel the roughness of his whiskers, to feel his breath on my cheek, his fingers in my hair. I wanted Walter to be the first man I ever kissed, the only man. But he turned his face away from me and called for his servant.

"Peter, I'm tired," he said. "I need to lie down for a while." I heard the bone-deep weariness in his voice. "Please go home now, Betsy."

But I didn't go. I couldn't move. I watched Peter wheel Walter's chair the short distance to the bedroom and remove the blanket that covered his legs. Then Peter lifted him into his arms like a child and laid him on the bed. I understood why Walter hadn't allowed me to watch him eat. He could no longer feed himself. And I understood why he had allowed me to glimpse his helplessness now.

I waited until Peter wheeled the chair away, then I ran into the room and sat down on the bed beside him, bending to rest my head on his chest, my arms encircling his thin shoulders.

"My pain won't go away if you leave me," I wept. "You'll only be gone from my life that much sooner. Please give me whatever time you have left," I begged. "Please. That's all I ask."

He laid his hand on my hair. "Betsy . . . my love . . . don't you understand? The weakness that started in my legs has left them paralyzed. Now it's spreading to my arms and I can scarcely feed myself. Eventually it will affect all of my muscles. I'm already having trouble swallowing. But when the muscles that work my lungs become paralyzed, I'll stop breathing. I'll suffocate to death. I can't put you through that ordeal or all that work."

"It's not work when you love someone. Please let me be the one who takes care of you, not Peter. If you're really dying, then I want to stay beside you until you draw your very last breath."

"And what will I do for you in return?" he asked sadly. "I'm a helpless invalid. I have nothing to give you."

"Just give me yourself, your love. That's all I want—"

"No." He shook his head. "That's not a loving relationship. Taking care of me will keep you from accomplishing your own dreams."

I sat up so I could look into his eyes. "You're wrong. You can help me accomplish my dreams. I want to write books. You can read what I've written. You can coach me and encourage me when I'm stuck. I value your opinion—even when you're wrong." I managed to smile, and he smiled in return as we remembered all our spirited arguments about the novels we'd read. "I don't think I have the courage to write a book without you, Walter."

I watched a tear slowly slip from the corner of his eye and run down his temple. He was silent for a long time as he studied my face.

"There's a book of poetry over there on my dresser," he finally said. "Read me the sonnet where the marker is, would you? It's called 'The First Day' by Christina Rossetti."

I rose to retrieve the book, then sank down beside him again to read it aloud.

> I wish I could remember that first day,
> First hour, first moment of your meeting me,
> If dim or bright the season, it might be
> Summer or winter for aught I can say;
> So unrecorded did it slip away,
> So blind was I to see and to foresee,
> So dull to mark the budding of my tree
> That would not blossom yet for many a May.
> If only I could recollect it, such
> A day of days! I let it come and go
> As traceless as a thaw of bygone snow;
> It seemed to mean so little, meant so much;
> If only I could now recall that touch,
> First touch of hand in hand—did one but know!

" 'Did one but know . . .' " he repeated when I finished reading. "Will you do something else for me, Betsy?"

"Anything."

"Take your hairpins out and let your hair down, then take off your shoes and go barefoot."

"Why?"

"That's the way you looked 'the first day, first hour, first moment of your meeting me.' Miss Rossetti may not remember, but I'll never forget it because that's the day I fell in love with you."

"You didn't! I looked horrible that day!"

"No, you looked like an angel from a Da Vinci painting—a barefooted angel, quoting Henry David Thoreau, no less." He smiled as he watched me pull out my hairpins. I shook my head until my hair fell loose, then I unbuttoned my shoes and kicked them off along with my socks.

"Does this mean that I can stay?" I asked when I finished. "And that you won't leave me and go away again?"

"I'll agree to let you stay on one condition."

"I know—no 'hovering.' I'm not allowed to ask you how you're feeling every two minutes."

"Oh, that's right, 'no hovering.' I'll have to amend that to *two* conditions—'no hovering' is one, and the second is that you'll marry me." I stared at him, dumbfounded. "You see," he continued, "I'll be facing St. Peter at the pearly gates soon, and I don't want to have a lot of explaining to do about us living here together."

I still couldn't speak.

"Betsy?"

"Yes," I said in a tiny voice.

"Please kiss me."

On the happiest day of my life, I married Walter Gibson. A justice of the peace performed the simple ceremony out by our pond. I went barefoot and wore a crown of wild roses in my bushy hair. Peter served as our best man and ring bearer, having shopped the day before for our two wedding bands. Lydia was my matron of honor, holding baby Matthew in her arms instead of a bouquet, and it was a toss-up as to which of those two bawled the most. The only other person who attended was Father, and he stood around in muddled bewilderment, wondering why a wealthy, intelligent man like Walter would marry someone like me. We honeymooned in our cottage to the accompaniment of hammers and saws as a crew of hired workmen quickly built and plumbed a new kitchen and bathroom addition.

"Hire as many laborers as you need," Walter told the foreman, "but I want it finished in two weeks. Not one day longer. My bride and I need peace and quiet."

They finished in thirteen days. Peter moved into the farmhouse with my father. He walked down to the cottage two or three times a day to help me lift Walter in and out of his wheelchair and get him dressed. Walter also hired a live-in maid named Helen to cook and clean for Peter and my father, and it was a happy ending for everyone when Helen and Peter fell in love and were married, too.

Walter and I settled into a blissful union that few married couples ever attain, even after many years of marriage. He was a tough taskmaster, though, making sure that I spent part of each day writing, but afterward we would read to each other and talk and laugh and love. The workmen built a ramp off the front porch for Walter's wheelchair and we spent as much time outside as the weather allowed, watching the ducks and geese on the pond, the deer that came to the edge of the woods, the changing seasons in the orchard, and the panorama of stars in the night sky.

One warm summer night as we lay in bed, listening to the frogs and the crickets serenading each other down by the pond, Walter suddenly asked, "Did I ever tell you about my very first night in this cottage?"

"No, I don't think so," I said, nestling closer to him.

"I didn't sleep. Not one wink. That racket out by the pond! Oh! I'd never heard anything like it! I tore up a perfectly good linen handkerchief and tried stuffing little pieces of it in my ears, but I could still hear that confounded noise. When the frogs finally had mercy and called it quits, your fiendish rooster woke up and started cock-a-doodle-doing! If only I'd had a shotgun! Well, I made up my mind to leave that very next morning. I couldn't stand another night of all that infernal noise. Surely Henry David Thoreau was never kept awake the entire night at Walden Pond."

"What changed your mind?" I asked, laughing along with him.

"You did."

"Me?"

"You brought me my breakfast and you must have stayed up half the night yourself reading the book I'd loaned you because you could already discuss it as enthusiastically as if you had written it yourself. You looked so beautiful and fresh and alive, like a sweet, delicious peach picked right off the tree! I decided that I didn't care if the local fauna did keep me up all night, I was staying!"

"And I'll bet you don't even hear the frogs anymore, right?"

Walter laughed. "I wait until you're asleep before I stuff cotton in my ears."

"You know what, Walter?" I said with tears in my eyes. "No one in the whole world ever told me I was beautiful before."

He turned to kiss my hair. "Then the whole world must be as blind as a bat."

———

Peter turned out to be an able carpenter, and since he had little else to do to occupy his time, he began lining the walls of our cottage with book shelves. As fast as he finished a shelf, I would load it with books and Walter would write to Chicago and ask his servants to send more of his collection. One day I unpacked a tattered set of leather-bound journals. Walter had printed his name on the title page and filled the contents from cover to cover with his neat handwriting. I opened the diary to the first entry:

Tuesday, June 23, 1884—Aboard the *S. S. Hibernia*:

I was born to the sea! Everything about it from the salt in the air to the cry of the sea birds makes me feel more alive and invigorated than I've ever felt in my life! I longed to pitch in with the men and cast off the hawsers and weigh the anchors as the tugboats nudged us out of the harbor in New Jersey yesterday, but the captain knows that my father is a major shareholder in this steamship line and he was intractable. I argued that I had captained the crew team at Yale, winning the college championship for the Bulldogs two years straight (and sending those despised Harvard boys home in defeat), but he insisted that he would not allow me to do anything that would jeopardize my life or his job. I then warned him that I might one day run the company in my father's place and I vowed to demote him to cabin boy, but he remained unmoved. . . .

I laughed out loud and skipped ahead to the next entry:

Friday, June 27, 1884—aboard *The S. S.* (Satan's Ship) *Hibernia:*

I hate the sea! Everything about it from the relentless rocking to the savage swaying makes me feel more nauseated and ill than I've ever felt in my life! Little did I know when the tugboats nudged us from the safety of the harbor in New Jersey four days ago that they were sending us into twenty-foot swells and gale force winds and a watery grave at the bottom of the sea! I long to pitch myself overboard and end my misery quickly, but the captain still won't allow me to do anything that would jeopardize my life or his job. He handed me a bucket, threatened to lock me in my stateroom if I didn't stay below deck, and assured me that I would live to see the port of

Southampton, England, in two weeks' time. If I live to see Southampton, heaven knows I will surely die there because I will never step one foot aboard another ship. . . .

"How did you ever get home again?" I asked Walter when I could stop laughing.

"Here, let me see that," he said from across the room. I handed him the diary, then knelt by his feet as he looked it over. "Ah, this is only my first journal. By the time I survived a derailed train in Europe and a deranged camel in Egypt, the sea seemed tame in comparison."

"I didn't know you could write."

"I should hope so. I'm a Yale graduate, you know."

"No, I didn't know that, either. And you used to be the captain of a crew team? What else haven't you told me about yourself?"

"The truth is all here in these journals. It's the unvarnished record of the three years I spent running from the responsibilities of adulthood."

"This sounds like good stuff," I said, taking the journal from him again and paging through it. "Does it tell how you explored new worlds, tamed savage tribes, and rescued several foreign princesses from pirates?"

"Not that I recall, but your version sounds like it would make a great adventure novel. You should write it someday, Betsy. No, these diaries mostly tell how I was bitten by a variety of savage insects, ate a good deal of very bad food, and traveled by every imaginable conveyance from rickshaw to yak back."

"Let's read these together," I said, settling comfortably against his legs.

"What? And have you discover what a coward I really am? Not on your life!"

I thought of the unfaltering courage Walter showed every day in the face of a slow, certain death, and my eyes filled with tears. I turned away so he wouldn't see them. "You're the bravest man I've ever met, Walter. And we're going to read these journals cover to cover. You're going to take me with you to all these places because that's the only way I'll ever go there."

Walter was a gifted storyteller. As summer turned to fall, I joined him on his exotic adventures in the jungles of Africa, the rain forests of Brazil, the pyramids of Egypt, and the gold fields of Alaska. His journal entries triggered even more memories, and I quickly scribbled them down in my own brand of shorthand as he reminisced. When he sent for his collection of National Geographic magazines, I saw photographs of many of the places he'd described. I had once dreamed of traveling around the world like Nellie Bly—now I traveled the world with Walter in our little cottage by the pond.

———

I had been feeding Walter and shaving him ever since we were first married, but I'll never forget the cold October day when I realized he could no longer move his arms. I had just read him one of the chapters I'd written, and when he told me it was superb I ran to his wheelchair and hugged him in joy. He couldn't hug me in return.

"I'm sorry, Betsy," he whispered.

"It's all right. I know you love me. And I know you'd hug the stuffing out of me if you could."

His embraces had always been weak, but it was a small death just the same. I would miss his caresses and the warmth of his arms around me—and in the years to come I would miss him entirely. But I had already made up my mind I would never weep while Walter was alive. There would be time enough for tears all too soon.

I bought Walter a wooden music stand so he could prop up the books he wanted to read, and he learned to turn the pages by holding a rubber-tipped stick in his mouth. I would have gladly given up my novel-writing to spend every waking moment with him, but Walter refused to let me quit.

As the months passed, he eventually grew dissatisfied with the books on our shelves, new as well as old, and he asked for a Bible. He found such tremendous comfort in reading it that we began reading it and discussing it together, just as we had discussed so many other books. But I was angry with God for what He was doing to Walter, and I found no comfort at all in what I read. It took my husband's patient explanations, his quiet, steadfast faith, to help me see what he alone saw on those sacred pages.

"Listen to this, Walter. It says 'whatever you ask for in prayer, believe that you have received it, and it will be yours.' That means if we pray and believe that you'll get well—"

"No, Betsy. God isn't a genie inside a magic lamp whom you can pray to and get all your wishes. Jesus taught us to pray, 'Thy will be done on earth as it is in heaven.' That's because in heaven the angels do God's bidding without question. They rejoice to do His will, and we need to do the same."

"But what if I don't like His will? What if I don't agree with it?"

"Well, God gave us free choice. We don't *have* to serve Him." He leaned his head back against the chair and sighed. "You know, all my life I felt that way about working for my father. His will must be done, whether I agreed with it or not. I had to do his bidding without question. Our heavenly Father never forces us to serve Him . . . but do you know what? God really *does* know what's best for us. He created us. His perfect will is perfect for us, whether we can understand it with our limited minds or not. Even so, He allows each of us to decide: Will we choose our own way or maybe society's way—and end up settling for less than perfection? Or will we let God take us where He has chosen—and be amazed?"

I stood behind Walter's chair and rested my cheek against his hair. "I don't like where He's taking you."

"Do you know why we constantly fight the notion of death, Betsy? I just read about that in Genesis the other day. It's because God created us to live forever with Him in Eden. Death was not God's choice; it was man's. Death is unnatural, a punishment for sin. But God countered man's choice with another perfect plan— He redeemed us in Christ so we could live forever with Him."

I moved around to the front of his chair and held Walter's precious face in my hands. "And in the meantime? Here on earth?"

"We must pray, 'Thy will be done on earth, as it is in heaven.' Promise me that you'll always write, Betsy. Don't let your father or anyone else impose his will on you. And don't ever settle for any other life except the one for which God created you."

"What about His will for you?" I whispered. I couldn't speak any louder without weeping.

"The same thing," he said. "We'll pray for God's will to be done—whether it means that I live or I die. And we'll pray that He'll grant us the grace to accept it."

I kissed his forehead, his eyebrows, the knuckles of his hands. "Why did God have to make our lives so fragile and so short?"

Walter thought for a moment before answering. "Because life is very precious to Him. He treasures each life He created and He wants us to treasure it, too—like fine porcelain china. God knows what it's like to live and die in a frail human body like ours. His Son suffered physical death, Betsy, so that you and I can face it without ever being afraid."

Walter's paralysis inevitably spread, just as the doctors had warned it would. He lost weight as it became more and more difficult for him to swallow. It required an enormous effort for him to talk, and his speech became so slurred, I would soon be the only person who could understand him.

"I want you to write to Chicago and ask my father's lawyer to come," he told me one dark winter morning. "Then arrange for a local lawyer to meet with us at the same time. Do you know of any good lawyers in this area?"

"There's John Wakefield, here in Deer Springs. He took over his father's practice about ten years ago."

"Good. Ask him to come."

I knew that Walter wanted to prepare his will, but I couldn't bring myself to say the word out loud when I contacted the two lawyers. They met alone with Walter in our bedroom and it was one of the very few times I ever left his side. They talked together for about three hours, then John Wakefield emerged to ask Peter and me to come in and witness the signing. Of course Walter could no longer sign his name. I held back bitter tears as my once-vibrant husband held a pen between his teeth to draw an *X* on the appropriate line.

"Thank you, Betsy, for not leaving me alone to die," Walter said as I held him in my arms that night. "Thank you for demanding your own way. I don't know how I ever deserved your love . . . but I feel sorry for any man who has to die alone."

After the lawyers came and left, Walter no longer insisted that I work on my novel. It remained in the bedroom bureau drawer where I'd left it so that I could spend every last moment with him. As the snow piled in deep drifts outside our cottage windows one afternoon, he asked me to read the scenes from the Gospels that told of Christ's death and resurrection. When I got to the part where Jesus met the disciples on the road to Emmaus, Walter interrupted me.

"Do you know why they didn't recognize Him?" he asked.

"No, why?"

"Because Jesus' body wasn't 'revived' from the dead like Lazarus' body had been. He was resurrected. They didn't recognize Him because His resurrected body was as different from his physical body as an apple is from an apple seed. He was changed. That's what Paul meant in Corinthians when he wrote about the resurrection of the dead. The body that is sown in weakness will be raised in power; it's sown a natural body, but it's raised a spiritual body."

Walter must have known by my lack of response, my failure to even debate the Scriptures with him, that my faith and hope were as paralyzed as his limbs. I watched him struggle, with what little strength he had, to find a way to help me see.

"Look at those trees outside our window, Betsy. If you never saw spring before, you would lose hope, you would chop them all down, believing they're dead. But spring will come again. They will blossom again and bear fruit. I'm in the winter of my life, and you're looking at my dying body and seeing it like those trees, without hope. But in Christ, new life will come. Jesus said, 'Whoever lives and believes in me will never die.' This isn't the end. You and I will live for all eternity."

"That won't stop me from missing you," I said, battling my tears.

"I know. When I left you last summer and went back to Chicago, I couldn't see you but you were alive in my heart because I pictured you making your home in a new place, married and going on with your life. And even though you couldn't see me, you imagined me living in Chicago, going to work each day, riding home in my carriage every evening. It will be the same after I leave you this time, too. You can keep me alive in your heart because I'll still be alive in eternity. I'm simply making my home in a different place."

I lost the battle to hold back my tears. I lay down beside him on the bed and pressed my face tightly against his. "I'll never stop loving you!" I wept. "Never!"

"Nor I you, for all eternity. Watch the trees, Betsy. When you see the blossoms you'll know I'm with Christ . . . and that I'm alive forever. And some day these dry, dead limbs of mine will blossom with resurrection life."

———

A few short weeks later I knew the end was very near. Walter's breathing had become painfully labored. It made my own chest ache to hear him struggle, but he never complained. I held him in my arms and talked to him, read to him, sang to him, keeping my own panic at bay so he wouldn't suffer the terror of slow suffocation. The night before he died he strained to speak to me one last time.

"Go into the orchard every spring, Betsy. . . . Look at the flowers. . . . They're God's promise that we'll see each other again."

I was holding Walter in my arms when he drew his last breath. He held it for a moment, then simply exhaled, like a quiet sigh of relief. And he was gone.

———

The next morning I sent for John Wakefield. He told me that Walter had arranged with a local undertaker to ship his body home to his family. They buried him in Chicago. I didn't go to the funeral. I couldn't watch them put Walter in that box and lower it into the cold ground.

I'd like to say that I handled Walter's death well, that I was prepared for it and I didn't grieve as those who have no hope. But it isn't true. I sank into a dark place where no light could reach me. It was winter outside my window and winter deep in my soul. When my tears were gone I grieved without tears.

Lydia held me in her arms and tried to console me with her love, but it was as if she stood outside my shuttered cottage, peering through the windows in vain. I couldn't open the door to her or anyone else.

And then on a warm spring morning the cherry trees blossomed, just as Walter knew they would. One day the orchard appeared dead and lifeless, the next day I looked out my window and didn't recognize the view. The trees' beauty beckoned to me, whispered to me, until I found myself outside, standing beneath clusters of fragrant pink flowers. At that moment I knew two truths with absolute certainty. Walter was alive. And God was here, with me.

I met God in the orchard that morning—not in a tangible form you could see or hear, but I felt His presence comforting me the way I could once sense the comfort of Walter's presence when we sat in the same room, even with my back turned to him. God seemed to say, "When everything else is gone, I'm still here."

And I knew then that I wanted to do God's bidding—on earth as it is in heaven—because I would never find the peace that Walter had found unless I did. I wanted to live my life according to God's plan, not other people's plans—to become the person He created me to be. God changed my name that morning. People think a woman who isn't married, who lives with her father and writes books, and who wanders around in a cherry orchard talking to God must be crazy. Surely she has a few "bats in her belfry!" But I would be the woman God wanted me to be. And so He changed my name to Batty.

The first thing I did when I finally went back inside the cottage that morning was to open the bedroom drawer to retrieve my neglected manuscript. Except when I opened the drawer, it wasn't there. Instead, I found a note:

Dear Missus Gibson,

I didnt steel this book frum you. Master Walter tole me to write this note and explane that he sent it to a publishur. He sed to tell you its reddy but he nos you wood never send it your self so he axed his lawyer to do it.

Peter

PS - He sed to add I love you (frum him, not me) and to tell you to start writing another book.

About a month later, John Wakefield arrived at my door. I had closed up the cottage and moved back into the farmhouse with Father once Peter and his wife had returned home to Chicago.

"Good afternoon, Mrs. Gibson," John said, tipping his hat. "How are you today?"

"I'm fine, John. What's all that stuff in the back of your wagon? You aren't moving away from Deer Springs, are you?"

"No," he chuckled, "This is your furniture, not mine. Where would you like it delivered?"

"Mine? What is it? Where did it come from?" I walked over to the wagon and lifted the tarpaulin to peer beneath it. Mr. Wakefield followed me.

"According to the terms of your late husband's will, he wanted you to have the desk and chair he used when he worked for his father. And he asked that I also purchase a typewriting machine for you."

The desk was made of cherry wood, with brass drawer pulls and a polished top that gleamed like a mirror in the sunlight. "It's enormous!" I said.

"Yes, it's a beauty, all right. I wish I could afford a desk like that for my office."

The Remington typewriting machine looked incredibly complicated compared to a simple pen and paper. "Oh dear, John. I haven't the faintest idea how to use that thing."

He smiled as he rested his briefcase on the wagon wheel and pulled a sheaf of papers from it. "Mr. Gibson said to tell you, and I quote—'Learn how, Betsy. Your handwriting is atrocious'—end quote."

I laughed and wept at this message from Walter. It seemed to come from beyond the grave. "Were there any other orders from the boss?" I asked as I wiped a tear.

"Yes, he retained my services as your lawyer." Mr. Wakefield was trying to balance the briefcase and sift through the papers at the same time. I steered him to a chair on the front porch so his papers wouldn't end up scattered to the four winds.

"Mr. Gibson requested that I protect your interests," he continued, "especially once you start receiving book contracts. I am to examine all your contracts thoroughly before you sign any of them."

"You mean *if* I receive one."

"No, Mr. Gibson seemed quite confident that you would. That's why he paid me in advance." He dug into the briefcase at his feet and handed me a thick, closed folio. "You'll want to keep this in a safe place, Mrs. Gibson. It's the title and deed to your house."

"My house?"

"Yes, the little stone one down by the pond. Mr. Gibson arranged to purchase it from your father along with two acres of land. He intended to purchase the pond as well, but that belongs to Frank Wyatt and he refused to sell it—in spite of the very generous offer Mr. Gibson made him." Mr. Wakefield dug into the briefcase again and retrieved another packet of papers. He handed them to me.

"What's all this?"

"These papers explain the details of the trust fund your husband provided for your support. The principal will be held in a bank in Chicago, but a very generous monthly living allowance from the interest payments will be deposited to an account that he set up for you here at the Deer Springs Savings and Loan. There are no restrictions whatsoever on that account. You may spend as much as you like, for whatever you like."

Mr. Wakefield's eyes grew misty as he saw the tears rolling down my cheeks. He leaned over to take me in his arms and awkwardly patted my back. "He loved you a great deal, Betsy . . . and he left you very well-provided for."

Walter had a few more surprises for me. About six months after he died, I found a letter addressed to Betsy Gibson in my mailbox one morning from a New York publishing company. My hands trembled so badly as I slit it open that I nicked myself with the letter opener. I left bright red drops of blood on it as I read:

> *Dear Mrs. Gibson,*
>   *Congratulations. Your manuscript has been accepted for publication . . .*

When I finally stopped whooping and shouting and dancing long enough to read the rest of it, I realized that Walter must have dictated a cover letter to accompany my manuscript when he submitted it. I couldn't believe my eyes when I read the publisher's words: *We also like your idea for a series of books for young ladies and would like to contract you to write four more novels. . . .*

"A *series!*" I cried out loud. "What on earth were you thinking, Walter?"

Of course, the series of books I wrote under my married name was published and became very popular. Then about two years later, when Father had his last stroke and became bedridden, I decided to read Walter's travel journals aloud to him in the evenings. When I opened the first page, I was stunned to find another note from Walter, misspelled by Peter:

Dear Missus Gibson,

Master Walter sed to tell you that boys like exciting stories too and that you shud write sum. He sed he always wanted to be a brave hero and so plese make him a hansum one.

Peter

PS—He sed he loves you and dont forget that he rescues the princesses from the pie-rats.

The first adventure story I wrote for boys began aboard the *S. S. Hibernia* as it sailed the high seas in twenty-foot swells and gale-force winds. Unlike Walter, the intrepid hero did not require a bucket. My publisher loved the book, but he thought the series' author needed a masculine name. I chose "Herman Walters" in honor of my favorite teacher, Mr. Herman, and my real-life hero, my husband, Walter Gibson.

These books became every bit as popular as the girls' series, and I lived "happily ever after" as they say, caring for my aging father and writing books in my secret writing haven in the cottage by the pond. Few people in Deer Springs ever knew I was an author.

After Father died I continued living in the farmhouse and writing down in the cottage, often until after midnight. If I needed to research a scene in one of my adventure stories, I would sometimes put on one of Walter's old suits and tramp around in the woods by the pond to experience what it felt like for my hero to sneak around in the jungle in the dark. That's what I was doing the night my father's house burned down. I was on my way back to the farmhouse when I saw Frank Wyatt run out of my back door and hurry up the hill. A moment later I heard a big *whoosh* and flames shot out of my farmhouse windows.

Of course, there weren't any telephones or anything, so the house burned to the ground before the volunteer firefighters could do much about it. I knew why Frank had done it. My father had deeded the house and his last few acres of land to me, but if I died without an heir, it would become part of Wyatt Orchards. Lydia had already died by that time, so Frank burned the house, hoping I would die, too. But I shocked the socks off Frank when I emerged from the woods still wearing Walter's suit and stood beside him as the firemen doused the smoldering wreckage.

"Betty! You . . . you're alive!"

"Surprised, aren't you, Frank?"

"I . . . you . . . I thought . . ."

"I'm sure they'll never suspect that you were the arsonist."

Even in the dim light I saw his face turn pale. "W . . . what are you talking about?"

"I saw you do it, Frank. You were hoping to kill me, weren't you?"

"Kill you! You're mad as a hatter!"

"Fine. You can tell the whole world I'm your crazy spinster sister-in-law if that makes you happy. And you can have the last of my father's land, too. But I own the cottage and the two acres it sits on. They will never belong to you, Frank. Never. The deed is in my name."

Frank Wyatt never spoke a single word to me after that night.

PART V

Wyatt Orchards

Summer 1931

"The day is thine, the night also is thine:

thou has prepared the light and the sun.

Thou has set all the borders of the earth:

thou has made summer and winter."

PSALM 74:16-17

— CHAPTER TWELVE —

W hen Aunt Batty finished her story, I stared at her in won-
derment. "*You're* Betsy Gibson? *You* wrote all those books I
loved so much when I was a girl?" Gabe and I had coaxed her
inside the farmhouse to tell her tale around the kitchen table over
a pot of coffee.

"Yes, that's my real married name," Aunt Batty said. She always wore a thin gold chain around her neck, and now she pulled
it out from inside her nightgown. A gold wedding band dangled
from the end of it. "I like to wear Walter's ring close to my heart,"
she said.

"And you're Herman Walters, too?" Gabe said. He seemed
even more flabbergasted than I was.

"Yes . . . I hope you're not too disappointed to discover that
Herman Walters is a woman?"

"Not at all! I'm just amazed to finally meet him . . . or her . . .

I mean, *you!*" He sprang up from his chair and bent over tiny little Aunt Batty, hugging her like a long-lost relative. "Your stories saved my life when I was a boy," he said, his voice husky with emotion. "I really mean that! They were the only escape I had sometimes—from . . . everything."

"I'm glad I could help," she said, patting his back.

I suddenly had an idea how Aunt Batty might save my kids and me, too, but I was scared to death to ask. What if she took offense and stormed out of the house and abandoned us? But if I didn't ask, we might not have a house at all in another two days.

"Aunt Batty, what ever became of the trust fund Walter left you?" I finally got up the nerve to ask. "Did it survive the stock market crash?"

"I don't know and I don't care. Walter left me more money than I ever needed. Especially once my books started selling like hot cakes."

"Might some of it still be in Mr. Preston's bank?" I asked.

"Not on your life! I never trusted my money in that mule-headed man's bank—or anyone else's bank! The trust fund deposited it there every month and I withdrew it every month."

"That turned out to be a wise decision," Gabe said, "considering how many banks have failed this past year."

I pictured my kids and me living like hobos, and summoned all my courage to ask, "Aunt Batty, if you still have any of that money left . . . could I borrow five hundred dollars? I'll pay you back just as soon as we harvest this year's crops."

"Sure, Toots! Take all you want. What on earth do I need it for? How soon do you need it?"

"Right away. Today. Now."

She stood up, pulling her coat off the back of her chair, and slipped her arms into it. "Okay, let's go."

Gabe looked at me in surprise. "Shouldn't you let her get dressed, Eliza?"

I still wore my nightclothes, too, but I hadn't removed my coat. "No, please, I'm afraid if we don't go now . . ." I didn't want to say that sometimes Aunt Batty's memory failed her and that if we didn't go while her memories were fresh, I was afraid she would forget where she kept her money.

Gabe frowned as I handed Aunt Batty her shoes. He was still scowling as he followed us two nightgown-clad ladies down the hill to the cottage. I was excited, yet afraid to get my hopes up. The money might be in gold doubloons or even Confederate money for all Aunt Batty cared.

Everything in her cottage was still topsy-turvy, but I was relieved to see that her parlor and her enormous desk were miraculously undamaged over the winter. We had removed all the books from the lowest shelves and they were still packed away, but Aunt Batty started scanning the remaining books, perusing the titles.

"Look for stories about greed," she said. "That's where I keep the larger bills."

"Here's *Silas Marner*," Gabe said, pulling it from the top shelf. He handed it to her. "Will this do?"

"Yes, that's an excellent choice, Gabe."

She held the book upside down by its spine and ruffled the pages until the money that she'd hidden there fluttered to the floor. It was genuine! Aunt Batty scooped up three twenties, two fifties and a one-hundred dollar bill. My heart pounded with excitement as I turned back to the bookshelves. I'd never heard of half the books but I stopped when I found Charles Dickens' *A Christmas Carol*. "How about the Ebenezer Scrooge story?" I asked.

"Even better. Open it up and see, Eliza."

I turned it upside down and rifled through the pages as she had done.

"Merry Christmas! And God bless us, every one!" Aunt Batty cheered as three one-hundred dollar bills floated out. We had found more money than I needed in only two books!

"Well, would you look at that?" Aunt Batty said suddenly. Gabe had pulled *Treasure Island* off the shelf and a letter had fallen out of it.

"What is it?" I asked her.

"Remember that last letter from Matthew you asked me about? Here it is! I hid it in one of his favorite books."

The envelope she handed to me was limp and as thin as tissue paper. Matthew had written it on stationery from a hotel in France:

April 14, 1918
Dear Aunt Betty,

Thank you for writing and telling me the news about my mother. I've seen so much death over here that I suppose I should be used to it by now, but I'm not. I loved her. And she never stopped loving you and me, did she? Please take care of Sam for her sake, okay? And for my sake, too. Don't let his father destroy him like he destroyed everyone else.

Love now and always,
Matthew

But finding the letter wouldn't help me unravel the mystery of whether or not Gabe was Matthew Wyatt. Except for the signature, the letter was typed. I slid it back into the envelope and tucked it inside *Treasure Island* again.

"Here's your money, Toots," Aunt Batty said, pushing the bills into my hands. For a moment I was too overwhelmed to speak. I had enough for the mortgage! More than enough.

"I . . . I'll pay you back. I promise. . . ."

She waved me away. "Oh, I don't want it back."

"No, I can't take this unless you make it a loan. I intend to pay you back just as soon as I sell our fruit."

She walked away from Gabe and me and stood gazing through the front window as if deep in thought. "Tell you what, Toots," she finally said, facing us again. "I've always wanted to own Walter's Pond. Will you sell it to me for five hundred dollars?"

"Gladly," I said, wiping tears of relief. "You have a deal."

That's when I took a good look around for the first time and noticed that Gabe had finished the kitchen roof and cleaned up the mess. The wainscoting could have used a coat of paint, and Gabe's carpentry would never win first prize at the county fair, but Aunt Batty could use her kitchen again.

"How long ago did you finish here?" I asked Gabe.

He shrugged. "Month or so ago."

I stared at Aunt Batty in wonder. "Yet you didn't leave me? You stayed with me?" That seemed like an even bigger miracle to me than finding the money.

"You needed me, Toots," she said. "You and those wonderful kids of yours. How could I leave all of you?"

"But . . . but you've worked so hard for me all this time . . . and you didn't have to."

She pulled me into her arms. "It isn't work when you love someone."

On the day that the mortgage was due, I walked into Mr. Preston's bank and handed him the $528.79 Frank Wyatt owed him. Mr. Preston looked shocked. And a little disappointed.

"Well, Mrs. Wyatt, how about that? Frank Wyatt must have kept a few extra bills stuffed under his mattress, eh?"

I remembered finding the money amongst the pages of Ebenezer Scrooge's story and smiled. "That's really none of your business, Mr. Preston."

I drove home feeling happier than I had in a long time. But trouble was determined to hound me. Wouldn't you know that as soon as I overcame one crisis, the next one would rear its ugly head? This time the weather turned against me. Gabe had loaded Aunt Batty's radio onto the pickup truck and driven it up to my house for all of us to enjoy. That's how we heard the announcement—the weather bureau had issued a frost warning for our area that night.

"Uh-oh, that's bad news," Aunt Batty said, shaking her head. "A frost could kill the blossoms. And no blossoms means no fruit."

"Smudge pots!" I said, remembering. "My father-in-law used to set up smudge pots in the cherry and pear orchards if there was going to be a frost. He'd fill them full of oil, float a corn cob in each one for a wick, and let them burn all night."

Gabe was already on his feet. "I guess we'd better get started before the temperature drops."

All six of us bundled up and set to work. Becky and Aunt Batty gathered up corn cobs while the rest of us hauled hundreds of pots out of the attic of the apple barn and loaded them onto the back of the truck. But when we went to fill them from the big fuel oil tank we discovered that it was nearly empty. There was no place to buy more oil this time of night, either. I was so upset I couldn't think straight.

"Listen, it'll be all right," Gabe soothed. "We don't have to light them yet, and we don't have to fill them to the top. We'll just put a little oil in each one and I'll stay up and refill them when they start to burn out."

I remembered the story in the Bible about the widow and her

kids who were in as big of a fix as I was in. God told her to have faith and just keep filling all the jars she had with oil, and the jug didn't run out until she was all finished. I guess Aunt Batty's prayers must have helped us that night because that's exactly what happened with my oil barrel. Gabe kept filling smudge pots about half full, and even though I kept expecting the big drum to run dry any minute, it never did. We set out all the pots near the most vulnerable trees, then I sent Aunt Batty and the kids to bed. Gabe and I each had an extra gallon container full of oil and after lighting the pots sometime after midnight, we stayed up all night refilling them.

The hardest part was staying awake. By five o'clock in the morning I felt tuckered out. I topped off all the pots that needed it, then climbed into the pickup truck to rest for a minute and warm myself up. I had just leaned my head back and closed my eyes when Gabe opened the passenger door.

"May I join you?" he asked, rubbing his hands together to warm them.

"Sure, climb in." I started the engine and let the heater warm us both up. "You'd better talk to me," I said, closing my eyes again, "or I'm going to fall sound asleep."

"Why don't you go home and go to bed, Eliza? I can finish by myself. It's nearly dawn."

"No," I yawned. "We're really scraping the bottom of the barrel now, and it'll be a regular juggling act for you to keep all those fires burning by yourself."

Gabe chuckled. "There were times tonight when I felt like one of those guys in the circus who has to balance a dozen plates at a time and keep them all spinning."

"While riding a unicycle," I added, laughing with him, "and not letting any of them fall and break."

"But we did it," he said with a contented sigh. "We should

congratulate ourselves." He stuck out his hand, waiting for me to shake it. I hesitated, then stretched out my own hand and gave his a quick shake. Gabe's skin was rough and calloused, his grip rock-hard. We touched only briefly, but it sent a shiver through me that went all the way to my toes. I hoped he hadn't noticed how rattled I was.

"Are you warm enough?" I asked. When Gabe nodded I shut off the engine. The sudden silence rattled me even more so I started chattering, just like Becky does. "You know, all the time my father-in-law ran this place I never realized how demanding it all was. I had my own chores to do in the house while taking care of the kids, so I never gave much thought to what went on out here in the orchard. I know it took the two of them to get every-thing done, though. Frank had to hire help for a while after . . . when it was just him." I stopped as abruptly as I started.

"May I ask you a question?" Gabe said after a pause. He sounded so serious it scared me.

"You can ask, though I can't promise I'll answer."

"You never talk much about your husband," he said. "Your kids are starting to talk about him and I think it's helping them grieve for him. But I've noticed that you don't. You hardly even say his name. You avoided saying it just now when you were talk-ing."

"That isn't a question."

"I know. I guess the question is 'why not?' But that's really none of my business." He sighed. "I'm tired, so I'm wording this very poorly. What I really want to tell you is that if you ever need to talk . . . if you ever want to talk about Sam . . . I'd be very happy to listen."

"Thank you."

Gabe waited. The long silence became uncomfortable. I knew he expected me to pour out all the grief and sorrow I had stored up for so long, but I had nothing to say. He finally broke the silence first.

"I think one of the things that makes it so hard for your children is that their father is so completely gone. There aren't any pictures of him, no belongings of his lying around anywhere in the house, no sign that he ever existed except for these clothes you loaned me or maybe what they see of him in each other—like the color of his hair or his eyes."

"That was my father-in-law's doing. He did the same thing each time one of them died—he erased every trace of them. There aren't any pictures of his wife or other sons, either."

"But Frank Wyatt is dead now. You could bring Sam's memory back if you wanted to."

"I don't. I think it's better this way." I felt close to tears and I didn't know why. How could I admit to Gabe that the sadness I felt whenever I thought of Sam or mentioned his name was caused by guilt, not grief?

"Do Becky and Luke get their red hair from him?" he asked quietly.

"No. From my mother." As soon as I'd told him, I was sorry. If he started asking me about her, the dam would break for sure. Thankfully he didn't. He was still stuck on Sam.

"I can't help wondering what your husband was like. I have a fairly clear picture of what his father was like—but not him."

I realized that I didn't have a clear picture of Sam either, and I'd been married to him for nine years. The truth made me angry and it loosened my tongue because I knew that the fault wasn't mine or Sam's—it was his father's.

"Sam never had a chance to find out who he was," I said in a trembling voice. "He stuffed all his dreams and all his feelings down inside himself and lived his entire life trying to be the son his father wanted him to be, trying to please him. I say 'trying'

because you could never please Frank Wyatt. He never saw all the
things you did right, only the one tiny thing you did wrong. He
was like that man in the Bible who tries to take the speck of dust
out of someone's eye. I heard a preacher talk about that verse one
time. I happened to be near a logging area, and I had just seen
all those huge piles of logs everywhere. I could imagine that miserable man in the parable with one of those beams in his eye and
I knew that it must have hurt him a lot. A speck of dust in your
eye is bothersome enough.

"Then I met my father-in-law," I continued. "He had one of
those big old beams in each one of his eyes, and they blinded him.
He couldn't see Sam—he couldn't even see his grandchildren. All
he ever did was criticize, and he never showed them one ounce of
love or gratitude or approval. Even worse, those beams caused
Frank so much pain that he lashed out all the time, like a
wounded animal. I almost envied Sam when he died and he could
finally get away from his father. I've always hoped the Good Lord
himself was waiting for him on the other side and that Sam would
finally get to hear *someone* say, 'Well done, my good and faithful
servant.' "

Gabe was very still. The engine made a ticking sound as it
cooled. Then Gabe said quietly, "My father was the same type of
man." I didn't move, didn't say a word, afraid he wouldn't continue if I did. "The thing is—"

But then Gabe did stop. He shook his head, and his whole
body seemed to shiver as if he couldn't bring himself to talk about
the man. I understood. I couldn't talk out loud about my daddy,
either. We had both reached a wall we weren't willing to climb.

"Hey, the sun's coming up," he said suddenly. "Maybe we can
finally let these fires go out."

He climbed out of the truck and walked around to lean
against the front fender on my side, facing the sunrise. I climbed

out, too, and stood beside him, stretching.

"I'll run into town today and buy some more fuel oil," I said. "Then we can fill all the smudge pots to the top and let them burn on their own tonight."

Out of the corner of my eye I saw Gabe looking at me. He was biting his lip, trying not to smile.

"What's so funny?" I asked, facing him square on.

"Your face. It's covered with soot. You look like Al Jolson."

I couldn't help smiling. "So do you. We could start our own traveling minstrel show."

Gabe laughed as he pulled a bandana from his pocket. "Here, hold still. I'll wipe it off for you." He held the back of my head with one hand and began dabbing my face with the handkerchief. We stood just inches apart, closer than we'd ever stood before, and my heart began thumping foolishly. All of a sudden Gabe stopped wiping. I made the mistake of looking into his eyes the same moment that he gazed into mine. His were as soft and warm as melted chocolate. His hand still held my head and he pulled me gently toward himself, finally closing his eyes as our lips met.

That kiss was like the touch of a match to fuel oil. Gabe's other arm came around me as he crushed me to himself, and what began as a gentle kiss quickly blazed with intensity. My arms encircled him, clung to him, and I returned his kiss with a passion I'd never experienced before. The feelings that seared through me frightened me, the strength of them terrified me. I felt safe in his arms, protected, even as all the barriers I'd built to protect myself turned to ashes. I was in love with Gabe, plain and simple.

I don't know what might have become of us if it hadn't been for Winky. Aunt Batty must have let him out for his morning run, and he sneaked up on Gabe and me, sat down at our feet, and barked. The unexpected sound of it made me jump right out of Gabe's arms. Winky was just a silly, half-blind dog, and all Gabe

and I had done was kiss, but I felt as though I'd been caught by
my daddy, doing something I shouldn't do. I nearly tripped over
one of the oil containers as I quickly backed away from Gabe. He
reached out to steady me but I twisted away from his dangerous
touch. Once burnt, twice shy, as Aunt Peanut used to say. I started
to run.

"Eliza, wait!"

"No. Stay away from me."

"But why?"

I whirled around to face him and I began trembling from head
to foot as I realized the truth. "Because I don't even know who
you are."

Gabe couldn't have looked more stunned if I had whacked
him with a two-by-four. I turned and hurried away before he had
time to recover, but I could have sworn I heard him mumble,
"Neither do I. . . ."

———

After that morning I was afraid to get near Gabe again. It
wasn't that I didn't trust him; the truth was, I didn't trust myself.
I avoided being alone with him, and when all else failed and I had
to work beside him, I kept Winky between us as a reminder. Except for operating the spray rig, most of the jobs like running the
corn planter up and down the rows, could be done by one of us
alone. I made sure we stayed apart.

Between disking and dragging and spraying, I soon memorized every square inch of the orchard. I got in the habit of using
the big work horses instead of the tractor in order to save gasoline, and as time passed, I grew to enjoy their quiet company.
They reminded me of the beautiful Percheron horses I'd known
so well as a child.

As spring inched toward summer and the apple blossoms

faded and died, a gradual change took place in me until one morning, as I stood in the middle of the orchard, I realized that these weren't Frank Wyatt's trees anymore—they were mine. Mine! I had trimmed them and fertilized them and babied them through frost and protected them from insects. I had fallen in love with my land and I didn't care whose name appeared on the deed—I could no more hand the orchard over to Matthew Wyatt without a fight than I could hand over Jimmy or Luke or Becky Jean.

My lawyer had still heard nothing about Matthew, so I didn't have to hand over the orchard just yet, but as time went on, it seemed as though I was handing over my children to Gabe Harper. It worried me to death. Gabe had won Becky's heart by making the swing, and now he spent a good deal of his spare time teaching Jimmy and Luke all sorts of things, like how to play mumblety-peg with a pocket knife. But when Jimmy came into the kitchen one afternoon waving his daddy's fishing pole, it was the last straw.

"Mama! Look what we found in the tool shed! Mr. Harper said he'll take us fishing this Saturday like Dad used to do."

I grabbed the pole from Jimmy's hand and stormed outside to find Gabe. He was cleaning out the shed and hanging all the tools on nails the way Frank Wyatt used to do. Gabe gaped in surprise when I threw the fishing pole at his feet.

"Here! Put this thing back where you found it and don't you dare take my sons fishing!"

He looked bewildered as he bent to pick it up. "Why not?"

Because they'll fall in love with you and you'll break their hearts when you leave us, my heart screamed, but I couldn't say the words out loud.

"Because you never should have promised to take them fishing in the first place," I said instead. "You're not their father!"

"I know I'm not!" His knuckles turned so white as he gripped the fishing rod I was sure he would snap it in half. He took a step toward me. "Jimmy was helping me clean up in here and he found the pole. He asked me if I'd ever gone fishing when I was a kid, and when I said that I had, he begged me to take him. How could I tell him no, Eliza? How?"

I didn't answer. Gabe and I stared at each other for a long moment, then he finally said, "If you don't want me to take them fishing, then I won't. But you'll have to be the one to break the news to them, because I can't do it."

My eyes filled with tears. I was so angry I was shaking. "Don't you dare hurt my kids, Gabe Harper! Life has hurt them badly enough already!"

He threw down the pole and seized my shoulders. His face was angry, his grip hard, but when he spoke his voice was soft. "If I ever hurt any of you, I promise that it won't be intentional. It'll be because . . . because it's out of my control." Then he released me and stalked out of the shed.

Friday night after dark, Gabe and the boys dug in the garden for night crawlers, collecting them in an old tin can. Early Saturday morning the three of them drove the truck down to the river to go fishing. Jimmy and Luke each caught a couple of fish and they were in seventh heaven. Aunt Batty cleaned them and cooked them for dinner. But I had no appetite at all.

The fishing trip was just the beginning as they spent more and more time together. The boys begged Gabe to help them practice hitting and catching a ball so they wouldn't be the last ones to be picked for the baseball teams at school. On a lazy Sunday afternoon, Gabe and Aunt Batty set up bases under the clotheslines for a game of stickball. Luke held the bat, Gabe pitched, and Jimmy, Becky, and Aunt Batty covered the three bases. I stood at the kitchen door, watching.

"Eliza, come on out here and catch for us," Gabe called to me
from the pitcher's mound. "We need you."

"I . . . I don't know how. I've never played baseball."

"You've never played baseball?" Gabe said, scratching his
head. "What kind of a half-baked school did you go to?"

If he only knew, I thought.

"Come on, Mom," Jimmy begged. "We need you to be our
catcher."

"No . . . I really can't."

In just a few swift strides Gabe crossed the backyard and took
me by the arm, pulling me into the game before I could protest
further. "All you have to do is stand here behind home plate and
catch the ball if Luke misses it. But Luke isn't going to miss it, are
you, buddy? Just keep your eye on the ball and swing the bat like
I showed you."

They quickly drew me into the fun and laughter. Luke concentrated so hard as he waited for Gabe to throw the ball that the tip
of his tongue stuck out just like Winky's. But the look of pure joy
on Luke's face when he finally hit one clear over Gabe's head
brought tears to my eyes. Aunt Batty jumped up and down cheering as it sailed past her. Winky waddled around the outfield barking and looking bewildered as he tried to find it. Becky hugged
her brother as he passed her at first base.

We were a family, just like the one I used to dream about when
I was a kid—except that we weren't a family. Gabe wasn't the
daddy and Aunt Batty would eventually go home, and I would be
abandoned once more. I couldn't understand why God kept
taunting me, giving me what I longed for, then snatching it all
away again. My mama was right—love was just like cotton candy.
It disappeared the moment you got a taste of it in your mouth.

While the others cheered and patted Luke on the back, I hurried into the house to hide my tears. I was sitting at the kitchen

table with my hands over my face when I heard the screen door open and close behind me.

"Eliza?" Gabe said softly. "Are you all right?" He rested his hand on my shoulder but when he felt me tense up he quickly removed it again. I wiped my eyes with the heels of my hands.

"Yes . . . I'm fine."

"I hope I didn't do something to upset you."

"It isn't you, Gabe. I'll be okay."

He pulled out the kitchen chair next to mine and sat down, resting his arms on the table. "I worry, sometimes, that doing things together like this brings back too many memories . . . that it makes you miss Sam."

I looked up at him in surprise. "No, that's not it at all. Sam never had a chance to do things like this with me and the kids. It's just that—" I stopped, shaking my head. "Nevermind."

"Eliza, you can talk to me when something's bothering you. You can trust me—"

"Can I really?" I said angrily. "And then you'll return that trust and share all your secrets with me?"

Gabe stared at me and I knew he was waging an internal battle. I could see it in his eyes. There was pain in them and a loss that was crushing him. Sam had a similar look in his eyes when I first met him. But Gabe seemed to have even more anguish than Sam stuffed deep inside him. I was immediately sorry and I wanted to say so, but it was too late. Gabe quietly shoved back his chair and left.

———

A few days after the ball game, Luke came home from school as angry as a hornet. I saw him fighting with Jimmy as they came up the driveway, punching and tussling with each other—and they almost never did that.

"What's wrong with you two?" I called from where I was working with Gabe outside the barn. "Stop it before one of you gets hurt."

"He started it, Mom," Jimmy said. "He's been trying to pick a fight all the way home."

Luke took a swing at Jimmy and missed. "Sh-shut up!"

"Luke, come here a minute," I said.

He ignored me, slamming into the house without talking to me. Gabe and I were right in the middle of unhitching the horse from the cultivator, but I planned on getting to the bottom of it as soon as we finished. I'd no sooner walked through the kitchen door a few minutes later when Becky let out a wail and Luke pushed past me like a house-a-fire. All I could get out of Becky between sobs was that Luke had done something mean to make her cry. I left her in Aunt Batty's arms and followed Luke outside.

When I didn't see him anywhere, I went looking for him in the barn. I heard Gabe muttering to the horses as he gave them some feed, then I saw Luke's red hair as he ducked behind a pile of hay. He was sobbing. Gabe hurried around the side of the stall to see who was there.

"Hey, buddy, what's wrong?" Gabe asked. "No, wait a minute, Luke. Don't run away. Come here. We're friends, aren't we? Can't you tell me what's wrong?" Luke didn't answer, but he sniffled like he was still crying. Neither one of them saw me as I stood outside the door, listening.

"Something happened at school today, didn't it," Gabe said. He wasn't asking a question, it was as if he knew. "I'll bet I can guess what's wrong," he continued. "Give me three tries, okay? And if I guess your secret, I promise I'll tell you a secret about myself. Do we have a deal?" I didn't hear Luke's reply, but I could tell by what Gabe said next that he must have agreed. "Okay, let's see. I'm guessing that some ignorant loudmouths at school teased you about something—probably something you can't change, like having red hair or not having a father. And their teasing made you feel so angry and upset and confused that before you knew what was happening—boom! You came home and took out your feelings on everyone else. Am I right?"

"How d-did you know?" Luke asked in amazement.

"Well, that's where my little secret comes in. Promise you won't tell anyone?" Gabe spoke so softly I had to strain to listen. "When I was in school the other kids used to make fun of me all the time because I had a lot of trouble talking. I couldn't seem to make the words come out right. I knew what I wanted to say inside my head but my tongue would trip over the words as if it had a huge knot tied in it."

"You st-stuttered like I do?"

"All the time."

"Honest, Mr. Harper?"

"Cross my heart and hope to die. But my stuttering was much, much worse. I couldn't even finish a sentence. Now that I'm all grown up, I think I know why I had a hard time getting my words out."

Gabe paused for such a long time I wasn't sure if he was going to tell Luke or not. When he finally spoke his voice sounded different—softer, yet harder at the same time.

"I was afraid of my father when I was a kid. He talked so loudly when he was angry that he made the walls of the house shake— and my father was angry all the time, usually at me. He expected a lot from me because I was his firstborn son, but I couldn't seem to do anything right. Sometimes my insides would get all twisted up in knots until I thought I was going to be sick, and when he asked me a question the knot would spread to my tongue so I couldn't talk. The more my father hollered and yelled at me, the w . . . worse it got."

I heard the powerful emotions in Gabe's voice as he stumbled over the word, and I knew he wasn't just making the story up to help Luke feel better.

"P-promise y-you won't tell anyone?" Luke asked softly.

"I promise."

"I was s-scared of my g-grandpa."

Tears filled my eyes at his words. I remembered how Luke had tried to follow Grandpa Wyatt around after Sam died, so hungry for the love and attention Sam had given him, but the old man could never find it in his heart to show affection. The only emotion he knew how to show was anger. He'd been mean and hateful for so many years that all his feelings came out the same way. So if one of the boys worried him or frightened him, any concern he might have felt came out of his mouth as rage. If Frank had ever loved his children or his grandchildren, he'd never known how to tell them.

"Know what else?" Luke asked. His voice was so close to a whisper I had to stand stock still, careful not to rustle the straw or creak a floorboard, in order to hear him. "I was w-with Grandpa . . . when . . . he f-fell."

I caught my breath, unaware I was holding it until my lungs nearly burst. Gabe's voice was gentle. "The day he died, you mean?"

"Uh-huh. Grandpa fell over . . . and then he looked up at me. He said 'help' . . . but I r-ran away."

"Because you were scared, Luke?"

"No . . . I was m-mad. Grandpa wouldn't help Daddy when he got sick. So I w-wouldn't help Grandpa."

I covered my face and wept silent tears. God help me, I might have done the same thing if Frank Wyatt had asked me for help. But it nearly broke my heart to think that Luke had carried such a heavy burden all alone, all this time. I was about to give myself away, to run and gather Luke in my arms, when I heard Gabe say, "Come here, son."

I could tell by the shuffling sounds and by Luke's muffled sobs that Gabe had taken him in his arms. I think all three of us were crying, because when Gabe spoke again his voice was breaking.

"Listen, Luke . . . and I want you to really listen. Every single one of us has done things when we're angry that we're sorry for later."

I remembered the angry words I'd hurled at my daddy and I stifled a sob.

"But God knows if we're sorry in our hearts—and He forgives us. Then we need to forgive ourselves. But listen to me . . . are you listening, Luke? It wasn't your fault that your grandfather died. It *wasn't*. Even if you had gone for help as soon as your grandfather fell, it wouldn't have made any difference. Your mama told me he had a heart attack. And there's not a thing in the world anyone could've done about it. Do you understand? Not you, not the doctor . . . no one. You don't need to feel bad about it anymore."

Luke began to weep, great heartbreaking cries that I knew would heal him in the end. I quickly turned and ran from the barn so that I could mourn for all that Luke had lost. It wasn't until later, when I'd returned to the kitchen to help Aunt Batty make supper, that I remembered what Gabe had said—*I was my father's firstborn son.* Just like Matthew.

"Is Becky all right?" I asked Aunt Batty as I pulled a paring knife out of the drawer to help her peel potatoes.

"She's fine. We had a little talk. Did you get everything straightened out with poor little Luke?"

"Gabe is talking to him," I said. Then I had another thought. "Aunt Batty, did Matthew stutter when he was a boy?"

The potato she was peeling slipped out of her hand and rolled across the table. She quickly scooped it up, then patted my arm with her starchy hand. "Don't you worry about little Luke. He'll outgrow his stuttering one of these days."

"Like Matthew did?"

She didn't answer me, concentrating as she peeled the skin off in one long, dangling curl—a trick I had never mastered.

"Trouble plagued Matthew's life from the moment he was conceived," she finally said. "I often wondered if he would have had a happier life if Lydia had given him up for adoption like I wanted her to. Of course, then I would have been the one who'd had to endure Frank Wyatt all those years."

I didn't say anything to Gabe during supper, but after we'd eaten and I'd cleaned up the dishes, I went out to the barn to find him and thank him for talking to Luke. The light was on in the workshop where Gabe slept, so I knocked on the door. He didn't answer. I pushed it open and peeked inside.

"Gabe?"

The room was empty. Not two feet away, propped on an overturned apple crate, stood Gabe's typewriter. There was a sheet of paper in it with words typed on it. The paper stuck out as if he had walked away in the middle of writing something. My curiosity was too great to resist. I bent over to read it:

> *My father is everywhere. There are no pictures of him, no pipes or tobacco pouches or favorite chairs to remind me of his habits and gestures, but he's everywhere, just the same. He's in the wind that whistles through the open door of the barn and raises the dust I forgot to sweep. I hear his voice, feel his censure in the sagging fence post and in the tool I failed to return to its proper place.*
>
> *I came back to make amends with him. I came back because I missed the land and I longed for home all the years I was away. Every field and barn I marched past in France beckoned to me to stop and to turn a spade through the rich earth and to inhale the familiar fragrance of horse and hay. I was once reproved for breaking rank to stop*

*beside a pasture fence to stroke a mare, but I craved the familiar rough-
ness of her tawny coat. I offered a French farmer my weekly allotment
of cigarettes if he would simply allow me to come inside his barn and
milk his only cow.*

*I hated my father, but I loved the land. Eventually the love out-
weighed the hatred and it drew me home. I hungered for the changing
seasons in the orchard: the stark beauty of naked branches against the
winter sky; the lacy pink capes that clothed them in spring; the fruit
hanging heavy from them in summer like gaudy jewels; the leafy flames
that consumed them at the autumn sacrifice. I came home to make
amends, to say I was sorry for the bitter words we'd hurled at each
other when we parted. But it's too late. My father is gone.*

Yet he's everywhere, and I cannot stay.

*I'll keep my promise to bring in the harvest, but my father is here
and nothing I do pleases him. I can never be happy in a place where
I've known so much pain. . . .*

I slipped out of the workshop and returned to the house,
more certain than I'd ever been that Gabe was Matthew Wyatt. But
what should I do about it? I loved Wyatt Orchards, too, and I was
scared to death that I would lose it. And I was scared to death that
I was in love with Gabe and certain that I would lose him. Hadn't
he just written that he could never stay here? Everything seemed
so tangled up I feared I would never get it straightened out. I finally decided to wait a little longer and see what clues John Wakefield's letter to Washington would turn up.

It was time for the hay to be cut and mowed, then forked onto
the wagon and stored in the barn. It was hot, itchy work. Jimmy
and Luke helped us out. School had closed a few weeks early
when the district ran out of money to pay the teachers. We worked
from dawn until sunset, and at the end of each long, hot day Gabe
took the boys down to Aunt Batty's pond for a swim. I once saw
him pull off his shirt as they headed down the hill and I caught a

quick glimpse of that terrible, jagged scar above his heart.

"A few more weeks and it'll be time for the cherry pickers to start coming," Aunt Batty reminded me one morning when we'd finished the haying.

"You're right. We'd better clean up the pickers' quarters and wash the bedding before they get here." I had done it every year when Sam and Frank were still alive, so at least I would be doing a familiar job.

Aunt Batty and I were working together one morning, filling straw ticks with fresh hay when an ancient, sputtering Ford pulled into my driveway. I should have known such a relic of a car could only belong to Mr. Wakefield. He stepped out and greeted us with a bow and a tip of his hat.

"Good morning, Mrs. Wyatt. Mrs. Gibson. How are you ladies this morning?"

"I'm fine, John," Aunt Batty replied. "It's good to see you again." I could tell by her beaming face that if he'd given her a million dollars it wouldn't have been as great a gift as calling her by her married name.

"Would you like to come inside for a cup of coffee, Mr. Wakefield?" I asked. He had his briefcase with him and I wanted to be sitting down if he had any important news to share.

"Well, sure, if you don't mind. Though I hate to disturb you ladies. You look pretty busy. . . ."

"Go ahead, Toots," Aunt Batty said. "I can manage without you for a while."

I sat Mr. Wakefield down at my kitchen table and put a cup of coffee and a piece of Aunt Batty's rhubarb pie in front of him as he opened his briefcase.

"I have good news this time, Eliza," he said. "I finally received word from Washington. They've confirmed that Matthew Wyatt did *not* die during the war."

I sank onto a chair as my knees suddenly gave out. "So . . . he's alive?"

"Well, he was still alive as of December 1918. Matthew received an honorable discharge on the twelfth of that month in 1918. Here's a copy of the information listed on his discharge papers if you'd like to see it."

I scanned the document while Mr. Wakefield devoured his pie. Matthew had served in the infantry as part of the American Expeditionary Forces stationed in France. The papers listed the battles and campaigns he'd participated in—Cantigny, Belleau Wood, St. Mihiel—and the decorations and citations he'd received. His hair color was listed as brown, his eyes brown, and his height and weight seemed about the same as Gabe's, too.

"What does this mean?" I asked. "It says 'date of separation . . . destination . . . reason and authority for separation.' "

Mr. Wakefield swallowed a quick sip of coffee before setting down his cup to explain. "Evidently Matthew was hospitalized in France for shrapnel wounds he received at the Battle of St. Mihiel shortly before the war ended. They sent him home to the United States to recover—that's the 'separation' it mentions. They discharged him directly from the army hospital."

I recalled the scar above Gabe's heart and wondered what a shrapnel wound looked like. "What's the next step?" I asked. "We know he's alive, but how do we go about finding him?"

"I'm going to write to the army hospital that discharged him to ask if they have a forwarding address for him. Once again, getting an answer may take a while—and a lot of time has passed since he was discharged—but I'll let you know as soon as I hear anything."

He eagerly accepted a second piece of pie.

I rejoined Aunt Batty after Mr. Wakefield left. My face must have told her I was upset because the first thing she asked was, "More troubles, Toots?"

I nodded. "Mr. Wakefield came to tell me about Matthew Wyatt. It seems he didn't die in the war after all. Matthew might still be alive."

She stopped stuffing straw. She closed her eyes as joy and relief flooded her face. "Matthew's alive! Imagine! After all this time!"

"Yes, and I need to find him, Aunt Batty. The kids and I are in trouble."

"What kind of trouble could you sweet things be in?"

I took a deep breath and let it all out at once. "It seems that I don't own this house or the orchard after all. Frank Wyatt willed everything to Matthew."

"No! I don't believe it!" she exclaimed. "That has to be a mistake!"

I sat down beside her. "It's not a mistake. Mr. Wakefield showed me Frank's will."

Aunt Batty shook her head, insistent. "Frank would *never* give Wyatt Orchards to Matthew. Never in a million years! Not after he learned the truth."

I stared at her. "The truth? You mean Frank found out that Matthew wasn't his son?"

"Yes."

I suddenly recalled a line from Gabe's story: *The night I found out that he wasn't my real father I felt born again.* I shivered.

"Aunt Batty, did Matthew know that Frank wasn't his real father, too?"

"Yes. They both found out. And I happened to be there the day they did. . . ."

PART VI

Matthew's Story

1901

"And the Angel of the Lord . . . touched him, and said,

Arise and eat; because the journey is too great for thee."

1 KINGS 19 : 7

— CHAPTER THIRTEEN —

For my sister, Lydia, life with Frank Wyatt was very difficult—
and very lonely. Frank had no friends to speak of, and his
greed and ruthlessness drove away the last of his family members.
The only measure of joy Lydia found in life was in her three
sons—especially Matthew, her eldest. I purchased a Gramophone
around the time Samuel was born, and Lydia would bring her babies down to my house as often as she could sneak away. I recall
so clearly how she would lift little Matthew in her arms as if he
was her dancing partner and whirl him around my parlor as the
music played, and the two of them would laugh and laugh. But by
the time Matthew started school, Frank had crushed the last spark
of laughter out of the poor child as thoroughly as a cider press
squeezes juice from an apple.

I happened to be up at Lydia's house one night, helping her
nurse Samuel and little Willie through a bout of the measles,

when I saw for myself how Frank raised his sons. Seven-year-old Matthew had just recovered from the measles, too, and had done his chores that night for the first time in over a week. I don't know if the child was in a hurry or had simply forgotten, as children are apt to do, but Matthew failed to latch the door to the chicken coop for the night. When Frank discovered it, he stormed into the house, bellowing with rage.

"You worthless kid! What's the matter with you? Can't you do anything right? Get up!" He grabbed Matthew by the arm and hauled him out of the kitchen chair where he sat eating his cookies and milk before bed. Frank was such a tall, broad-shouldered man that my stomach lurched at the sight of him clutching his helpless, terrified son. "I'll teach you not to disobey me, you irresponsible whelp!"

"No, Frank! Listen, please!" Lydia cried, rushing to Matthew's defense.

"Get out of my way," he said, shoving her aside. "If I listened to you, my sons would all end up in hell."

"But he didn't do it on purpose," she pleaded. "He made a simple mistake!"

"You stay out of this!" he warned. "The Bible says, 'Foolishness is bound in the heart of a child; but the rod of correction shall drive it far from him.' "

He dragged Matthew toward the back door by his spindly arm. Frank paused only to remove his razor strop from its hook above the washstand. Tears sprang to my eyes when I glimpsed the thick, leather belt in Frank's work-hardened hand.

"Frank, don't!" I cried. "He's only a child!"

He turned on me with a look that froze my blood. "Get out of my house! This is none of your affair!" He turned the same withering gaze on Lydia and she backed away from him in fear.

Matthew whimpered pitifully. In his terror, he had wet himself.

But he didn't struggle against his father's grasp or scream for help. That's how I knew with horrifying certainty that this wasn't the first time he had been beaten. Only a child who had suffered an even harsher punishment for resisting would have learned not to.

The windows rattled as Frank slammed the kitchen door on his way out. It took me a moment to recover from my shock, then I started after Frank, determined to stop him.

"Betsy, no! Don't!" Lydia cried, holding me back.

"I can't just stand here and let him beat that child."

"Please, you have to . . . or it'll be much worse." She was trembling from head to toe, and I suddenly realized that I was, too.

"How long has this been going on?" I could barely get the words out. Lydia closed her eyes and turned her face away from me. I jerked her back. "Lydia, *how long?*"

"It won't happen again, I swear it won't. It was my fault because I was distracted with the other two being sick and I didn't make sure Matthew did everything perfectly. Frank only gets angry when they make a mistake, and I'll be more careful from now on. I'll make sure they don't make any mistakes."

"They?" I asked in horror. "Surely Frank hasn't . . . he wouldn't beat little Sammy? He's only a baby! What could a five-year-old possibly do that's worthy of a beating with a razor strop?" When she didn't answer me I grabbed her shoulders, shaking her slightly. "Lydia, answer me!"

"Frank says they have to learn to obey him immediately from the time they are very young. And they are learning, Betsy, honest they are. They both try hard now to do what he says right away. This time it was my fault—"

"Lydia, stop it! This is insane! Frank can't expect perfection from mere children—or even from you, for that matter. You're leaving him tonight, this very instant—and you're taking those poor babies with you."

"I can't! How are we supposed to live?"

"I have enough money to support all of us. Let me take care of you. Come home with me, please. For your own sake as well as for theirs."

Lydia gave a harsh laugh. "Do you really think Frank Wyatt will give up his sons that easily, without a fight? Oh, he'll let me leave him. He no longer needs me now that he has three heirs. But who's going to protect my boys from their father if I'm not here? Who's going to make sure they don't make a mistake?"

"But *he's* the one who's mistaken! What Frank is doing isn't right!"

"No? Well, who's going to stop him? Who's going to come be- tween a father and his right to raise his children in his own home as he sees fit? Frank is a pillar in this community, a pillar in his church. There's nothing I can do except stay here and try to pro- tect my sons as best I can."

"Don't you see what Frank's doing? It's his own sin and guilt that he's trying to purge out of them. Frank can never forgive himself for his 'great sin' with you, and so he's taking it out on you and his sons. You have to leave him, Lydia. You have to get out of here."

"No. I'm staying." Her tears and her trembling had stopped. She was calm suddenly, with that terrible serenity I had once mis- taken for inner strength. "This is the life I deserve," she said with eerie detachment. "Frank is the punishment for my sin."

"But it doesn't work that way. God doesn't punish us like that. He forgives us if—"

She laid her ice-cold hand on my arm. "The baby is crying, Betsy. I have to go to him. Frank doesn't like to hear him cry. You'd better leave before Frank comes back."

When I walked down the hill toward home, the night was fearfully still. As much as I'd dreaded hearing the sound of little Matthew being beaten, much worse was the silence of a seven-year-old child who'd already learned not to scream. I wept that night for a long, long time. I'd never felt more helpless in my life.

———

"I hate him! He's impossible to please!" Twelve-year-old Matthew threw himself into Walter's wine-colored leather chair with such fury I feared he would break the springs. I didn't say a word. The boy needed to vent his frustration, and my cottage was the only safe place in the world where he could do it. Matthew's stored-up rage had already caused him to start picking fights at school, and then he'd been doubly disciplined—by the principal and later at home. As a result, Matthew had quickly learned to stuff his anger deep inside. I tried to provide an outlet for him so it wouldn't build to volcanic proportions.

"Tell me all about it," I said, offering him a piece of spice cake and a glass of milk. He set them on the table beside the chair, too overwrought to eat.

"Why is my father so hard on me? I can't do anything right, and Willie—his precious Willie—never does anything wrong! I can't stand living there another minute! I'm running away, Aunt Betty. This time I'm leaving for good and I'm never coming back!"

"I know, Toots. I know how hard it is for you at home, and I don't blame you in the least for wanting to run. But you're only twelve years old. Your father will send the sheriff after you quick as a wink, and then he'll beat the tar out of you for disgracing him."

"What did I ever do to deserve this?" he moaned. "My father can't even stand to look at me. I see it in his eyes every day and I don't know why. He hates the sight of me."

I longed to tell Matthew the truth; that every time Frank looked at him he was reminded of his own sin. But I couldn't explain it to the poor child without exposing his mother's sin as well. I bent over his chair and drew him into my arms. He was stiff with resistance at first, but he eventually melted—as he always did—starved as he was for love.

"You know what, Toots?" I said as he clung to me. "I love you, and your mother loves you, and your heavenly Father loves you—now and always."

Matthew dried his tears on his sleeve, and after a while, he dug into his cake. "Did you make this just for me?" he asked.

"You bet I did. And I have another surprise for you, too. Guess what came in the mail today?"

"A new Herman Walters book?" He almost smiled.

"The latest one. It's called *Danger in the Jungle.* Sounds exciting, doesn't it?"

He was soon absorbed in the book, thousands of miles away from his father. I loved watching him read, slumped in Walter's chair with one of his lanky legs sprawled over the arm of it. I wrote nearly every book in that series for Matthew, so he would have an escape from his sorrowful life. If only for a few hours.

"Can I take this book home with me?" he asked when it was time for him to go do his chores.

"You'd better not. You know what'll happen if your father catches you with it."

"But why, Aunt Betty? What does he have against books?"

"I don't know the answer to that, Toots," I said, reaching up to smooth his dark hair off his forehead. He already stood several inches taller than me. "But you know you're welcome to come down here and read anytime you want."

In the years that followed, Samuel would also read every single book in the series. But he never did confide in me or accept my consolation the way Matthew did. Sam was as skittish as a wild rabbit, the result of growing up in constant fear. H. G. Wells once wrote a book called *The Invisible Man,* and that's the best way to describe poor Sam—he tried his best to be invisible, to disappear into the background where he could never get into trouble. He couldn't live up to his father's standards of perfection any better than the rest of us could, so his only defense was to slide through life as silently and invisibly as possible.

But what broke my heart more than anything else was the fact that no matter how many times Frank beat those boys, no matter how many times he withdrew his love and approval as punishment, his sons still strove with all their might to please him. Willie had somehow managed to earn his approbation—Matthew and Samuel saw the nods of acceptance he received, and it created false hopes in them that they might one day receive such looks as well. It also created in them an intense hatred for their father's favorite son.

Frank Wyatt claimed to know the Bible and quoted it all the time, but he had somehow overlooked the tragic story of Jacob's favoritism toward his son Joseph and the murderous jealousy that resulted in Joseph's brothers. What happened to little Willie was Frank's fault as surely as if he had drowned the child in the pond with his own two hands.

The image of Willie's blanched, lifeless body being dragged from the icy water is one that I have never been able to erase from my memory. Worse was the fact that Frank made Matthew and Samuel stand shivering in the muddy snow at the edge of the pond and watch the sheriff and his deputies haul the corpse into their boat. They saw their brother's frozen, staring eyes, his silenced scream. That's the only reason I stayed there on that dreadful day. Lord knows, no one else would offer those boys an ounce of comfort.

Willie's death changed everyone and became the great dividing line between the way things had always been and the way things would forever be. Matthew never forgave himself for allowing his brother to step out onto that ice. In the years that followed he endured unending verbal and physical abuse, but he accepted his father's beatings and wrath as the punishment he justly deserved. Sam blamed himself for disappearing and not being there to help either of his brothers. His self-imposed penalty was to stick close to Matthew from now on, enduring Frank's tirades along with him. If either of the boys had ever dreamed of leaving Wyatt Orchards to escape their father once they grew up, they no longer considered it an option. The orchard became their prison cell, Frank their jailer, a life sentence their punishment for murder.

Lydia never got over the loss of her youngest child, either. She withdrew almost completely from the reality of the world around her, battling bouts of deep depression. I understood her grief, having lost my beloved Walter, but while I accepted God's consolation and yielded to His will for my life, Lydia accepted her suffering as God's wrath. Frank Wyatt put that notion into her head.

No one could console Frank after the death of his favorite son, and he expressed his grief through the only emotion he knew how to show—anger. After the last of the mourners had gone home on the afternoon of Willie's funeral, he turned on Lydia with unimaginable rage. I had walked up to their farmhouse to tell Lydia that Matthew and Samuel were down at my cottage and to ask if the boys could spend the night with me. That's how I overheard Frank ranting.

"Now look what you've done, you slut! This is God's judgment for our sin! The son of David and Bathsheba died for their adultery and now my son has died for ours!"

I had silently entered through the kitchen door and heard Frank's shouts coming from the parlor. I hurried inside, terrified that he might beat my sister, yet knowing that I was helpless to stop him if he did. I heard the sound of glass shattering and froze in the doorway at the sight of Lydia huddled on the floor, while Frank pelted her with her favorite china knickknacks as if stoning her for adultery.

"God says, 'Vengeance is mine! I will repay!' " Frank yelled, "and I have paid dearly for my one moment of weakness with you! The devil used you to bring me down, Lydia! I should have seen your harlotry for what it was and rebuked you the first time you tempted me!"

He picked up a porcelain teacup I had bought for her, decorated with violets, her favorite flower, and he hurled it with such force it shattered into dust in front of her. Lydia's hands bled from tiny cuts as she tried to scoop the fragments of her treasures together again. Frank smashed the matching saucer next.

"The child of David and Bathsheba's sin is the one who died!" he shouted. "But that would be too small a price for us to pay! God demands justice, and my punishment is that the innocent son had to die! Now I'll have to look at our bastard every day for the rest of my life—to see the fruit of our sin, in the flesh!"

Frank scooped up a framed studio portrait of Lydia and the three boys, taken two or three years earlier, and flung it to the floor. He stomped it with the heel of his shoe until the frame, the glass, and the photograph were pulverized. I still hadn't moved from the doorway, paralyzed by Frank's violence. Frank never even saw me as he swept from the room, blinded by rage, and ran up the stairs, his shoes crunching on the broken glass that littered the carpet.

I crept into the room and whispered my sister's name.

"Lydia . . . Lydia, come with me, honey, I'm taking you home now."

She didn't move, didn't look up. Nor did she weep. Her beautiful, haunted eyes stared, unseeing, at the carpet. Only her hands had life in them as they idly fingered the broken shards of her keepsakes.

I crouched carefully in front of her, lifting her chin until she faced me. "Lydia? Honey, listen to me. Frank's wrong. Everything he said just now is wrong. God didn't take Willie's life in order to punish you. It was an accident . . . a terrible, tragic accident. That's all."

Lydia gave no sign that she had heard me. She stared as if looking straight through me. I wrapped my arms around her and tried hugging her, but she still didn't respond. Finally I stood and tried pulling her to her feet. She was a dead, lifeless weight.

"Lydia, please . . . come home with me. The boys are already there, and none of you will ever have to return to this horrible house again. You don't need to stay with Frank any longer. You've paid your debt, Lydia . . . you've more than paid it. Please let me help you."

Her lifeless eyes finally met mine. "You want to help me," she said in a flat, hoarse voice, "then go home. Leave me alone."

"I'm not leaving unless you come with me," I said, taking her bleeding hands gently in mine. She yanked them free.

"No. Go home and take care of my boys. That's how you can help me."

I felt torn. I wanted my sister out of this house, away from her monster of a husband, but I also didn't want to leave young Matthew alone for too long. He suffered under an even greater burden of guilt than Frank or Lydia did, believing that Willie's death was his fault, and I worried that he might try to harm himself. I pleaded with Lydia in vain until we both heard the sound of

Frank's footsteps upstairs. He had probably changed from his good suit into his work clothes and he would be thundering down the stairs again at any moment. Terror filled Lydia's eyes.

"Leave!" she begged. "Keep Matthew out of his sight!"

I did leave, but I watched from a distance until Frank also left the house and went out to the barn. I needed to be sure that he wouldn't harm my sister. I needn't have worried. She told me later that after they laid Willie in his grave Frank never touched her again—not even so much as the brush of his hand on hers. They occupied the same house, slept in the same room, the same bed, but lived thousands of miles apart.

When Lydia finally emerged from her shock, the depression lifted temporarily. She was still a beautiful woman, though deeply troubled. She was also starved for love and affection. About a year after Willie died she began traveling to the city by train on the pretense of seeing a doctor for "female troubles." But she later confided in me that she was having an illicit love affair—the first of many that followed. I watched helplessly as she tried to bury her pain by becoming the very thing Frank accused her of being. Yet how could I condemn her? Who knows what I might have become if I had been the unfortunate woman to have married Frank Wyatt?

To the outside world Wyatt Orchards must have seemed like the Garden of Eden. The trees flourished, the land prospered, and Frank became one of the wealthiest fruit growers in the county. He purchased the latest in modern farm machinery, experimented with new grafting procedures, hired extra farm laborers in addition to his two sturdy sons, and even employed domestic help for his wife. Proud of all he had built, he began the tradition of hosting an annual fall open house so that everyone in the county would see and envy his realm. And envy him they did.

One of the saddest ironies of the whole tragedy was that

Matthew was a natural-born farmer. Frank couldn't have asked for a more perfect son—one so in love with the land, so in tune with the rhythms of the seasons and with the animals and the trees under his care. Yet Frank remained totally blind to the great gift God had given him.

At twenty-one, Matthew had become a handsome man, pursued by nearly every eligible girl in Deer Springs. He'd inherited Lydia's haunting beauty in a masculine form, with her dark, hypnotic eyes and alluring smile. And if his natural father, Ted Bartlett, had possessed half the charm Matthew did, it was little wonder that Lydia had fallen so hard for him. All the girls in Deer Springs flocked to the open house in droves each fall, hoping to catch the eye of Wyatt Orchards' crown prince. With each passing year, Matthew's love for Wyatt Orchards grew stronger—and his hatred for his father grew stronger as well. The two rival emotions simply could not coexist in Matthew's heart indefinitely.

The open house of 1916 set the final disaster into motion. The day had been a huge success, with hundreds of people paying homage to Frank's accomplishments. Lydia had set up serving tables in the backyard for food and cider, and once the festivities ended and the last few stragglers had gone home, I helped her clean up. Suddenly we heard a terrible uproar coming from the barn, with Frank hollering and Matthew shouting. We couldn't imagine what had provoked such a clamor. We dropped everything and ran inside.

One of the Peterson girls cowered in a corner of the barn by a mound of hay, and Matthew stood with his back to her, protecting her and defending himself from his father at the same time. Frank had a buggy whip in his hand and threatened to lash out at both of them with it.

"Don't you dare stand there and deny it!" Frank roared. "I caught you in the act!"

"We weren't doing anything! Just kissing, nothing more!" Matthew stood his ground, holding his father at bay with his hands outstretched. When he signaled over his shoulder for the girl to escape, she ran from the barn, weeping with fright.

Frank took advantage of the distraction to charge forward, scourging Matthew with the whip. "I'll teach you not to carry on your lewd acts! Maybe this will drive the lust out of you!"

At first Matthew simply held his arms above his face, defending himself from the onslaught as he backed toward the hay mound. But as the whip cracked across his forearms, his hands, and his scalp, leaving savage welts, something inside Matthew finally snapped. Years of stored-up rage suddenly exploded. He lunged at his father and wrestled the whip from his hand, throwing it to the ground. Then Matthew turned on Frank with murder in his eyes.

"I swear before God that I'll kill you before you'll ever lay another hand on me!" He sank his fist into Frank's gut, and before the older man could recover, Matthew began pummeling him, raining blows on him until Frank staggered backward against the wall. Matthew kept after him, beating him relentlessly. Lydia and I watched helplessly, screaming in vain for him to stop, unable to get close enough to intervene without risking injury ourselves.

Frank tried fighting back at first, landing a few blows to Matthew's jaw, but the boy wrapped his hands around Frank's throat and wrestled him to the ground, choking the life from him. Frank's eyes bulged and his face turned red, then blue, as Matthew straddled him, pounding his head against the floor. I believe Matthew would have killed him then and there if Sam hadn't rushed into the barn just in time. He grabbed his brother from behind, breaking his grip, and pulled him off their father.

But rage still fueled Matthew's strength. He wouldn't quit. He tossed his brother backward into the hay, then scooped up the buggy whip and lashed Frank mercilessly with it, just as Frank had scourged him.

"You sorry excuse for a man!" Matthew shouted. "This is for all the years you tortured me with your cursed strap! How does it feel to be helpless? How does it feel? I was a child! I couldn't defend myself against you back then, but I swear you'll pay for everything you did to me all those years!"

The whip shredded Frank's shirt into rags and sliced his face and arms with bloody gashes as he tried to defend himself. Again, Sam came up from behind and seized his brother.

"Stop it, Matthew! Stop it! Don't kill him! He isn't worth hanging for!"

"I'd rather hang than grow up to be like him! I hate you!" he cried as he spit in Frank's face. Matthew wrestled to free himself from Sam's grip so he could finish Frank off. "I can't tell you how many times I've wanted to kill you! How many times I've wished to God you weren't my father!"

"He isn't!" Lydia screamed. "He isn't your real father, Matthew! You won't ever be like him because Frank isn't your real father!" She was desperate to stop Matthew from killing him.

Her words finally penetrated Matthew's murderous rage. He stopped struggling long enough for Sam to wrest the whip from him. Sam shoved him backward into the hay, away from Frank, then planted himself between the two men, pleading with Matthew as tears streamed down his face.

"Don't kill him, Matt," he begged. "I hate his guts as much as you do, but I don't want you to hang for giving him what he deserves."

Matthew turned to his mother, his chest heaving. His handsome face twisted with the force of his hatred. "Is it true? What you just said?"

"It's true," she wept. "I should have told you the truth years ago. Frank isn't your father. I deceived him because I was already pregnant with you and your real father was married to someone else."

"My *real* father?" he murmured. "You mean this worthless piece of . . . *dirt* is no relation to me?" He swung his boot at Frank, kicking straw and manure on top of him. Frank lay prone, breathless and bleeding, unable to raise himself with a broken wrist and three cracked ribs.

"He's no relation, Matthew," Lydia said soothingly. "Leave him be. You've paid him back enough, already."

Matthew looked like a man who has suddenly awakened to find that his long nightmare was simply a dream. He laughed out loud. "You mean—you mean there's not one drop of his stinking blood in my veins?"

"No, Matthew. Not one drop. You'll never be like him. You couldn't be."

But then his smile faded as the full meaning of what his mother had done also sank in. He shook his head in bewilderment, a wounded child who has been cruelly betrayed. "But . . . but if he isn't my father, then *why?* Why did you let him beat me all those years when he had no right to? I thought you loved me. . . ."

Lydia swayed when she realized what she had just done. "I do love you, Matthew . . . I do," she cried. "But a fatherless child would have nothing, he would be nothing. I wanted the very best for you. I wanted you to have all of this."

"So . . . so you let him beat me? You thought *that* was best for me?"

I saw what was happening and I quickly wrapped my arms around Lydia to hold her up. I was terrified for her—and for Matthew. She had confessed the truth to save her son, to prevent him from committing murder, but she had lost him all the same. I had to get Matthew away from both his parents so I could reason with him.

"Come with me, Matthew, come in the house with me," I said, releasing Lydia and gently taking his arm. "You're bleeding. I'll fix your cuts."

"Not my house!" Frank wheezed. My heart froze at the hatred in his voice. "That boy will never step one foot in my house again!" Frank winced in pain as he propped himself up with his uninjured arm. His eyes met Lydia's and stabbed through her. "What you did . . . lying to me all these years . . . is unforgivable! You thought you could steal my orchard from me? Well, your son will never own so much as a clod of dirt from my land! I'll see John Wakefield tomorrow morning and I'll write your bastard out of my will! Now get him out of my sight and off my land . . . tonight! I don't ever want to see his face again!"

I quickly hustled Matthew out of the barn while he was too numb to resist. Lydia followed and so did Sam, but I turned to Sam as we reached the door and stopped him. "Go back and help your father," I told him.

He shook his head. "No. I hate him, too!"

"I know, Sam. But you're all he has left. He'll treat you differently from now on, you'll see."

"I don't care! I want to go away with Matthew!"

"You can't, son," I said gently. "Your father needs you. Drive him into town now. Tell the doctor . . . tell him Frank got trampled by one of the horses . . . tell him the reins lashed him." Sam reluctantly did as he was told.

I built a fire as soon as Lydia, Matthew, and I reached my house. All three of us were shivering. I made a pot of coffee and urged Matthew to sit down and drink some, to let me wash his cuts, to eat something, but he paced the floor as shock and hatred pumped through his veins.

"Please don't hate me," Lydia begged. "Please, Matthew!" He wouldn't look at her.

"I'm leaving here," he said, raking his fingers through his hair. "I've got to get out of here tonight."

"Now wait a minute, Toots," I soothed. "You need to think this through. Don't go off half-cocked without any plans and no money in your pockets. You can stay here with me for a while."

"I do have plans. I'm going to enlist in the army. I've been thinking about it for a long time now."

"That's a terrible idea," I said. "It's only a matter of time before the United States gets pulled into that awful war that's going on over in Europe, and if you enlist now you'll be one of the first ones sent over there. You don't want to die that badly, do you?"

He didn't answer, but as I watched him pace, I wondered if maybe enlisting in the army was the best solution. Matthew had stored up a lifetime of rage, and maybe the battlefield was the best place to vent it. Maybe then he would come back to us emptied of hate.

"I need my clothes and things," he finally said, stopping in front of me. "Will you go get them for me, Aunt Betty?"

I sighed in resignation. "I'll go see if Sam and your fa—if Sam took Frank into town to see the doctor yet. Once they're gone you can gather your things yourself."

And that's what he did. Lydia and I cried as hard as we had at Willie's funeral as we watched him stuff his belongings into a worn satchel. His leaving was another death in our family, another loss. When he kissed us good-bye, we both wondered if we'd ever see him again.

"Promise you'll write to me, Toots," I said as I pushed a Bible and two twenty-dollar bills into his hand. "Let us know where you are and if you're all right."

"Please forgive me, Matthew," Lydia said as she clung to him for the last time. "I lied because I love you! I didn't want to lose you!"

He simply nodded, unable to speak. Then Matthew freed himself from her grasp and left us.

———

I tried to convince Lydia to divorce Frank. She refused. "I deserve whatever he does to me," she insisted. "I lied to him."

Surprisingly, Frank didn't publicly expose her shame and kick her out. At first I wondered why, but then I realized that Frank didn't want the outside world to know that his little kingdom had flaws. The scandal of a divorce would taint Wyatt Orchards' name and injure Frank's reputation. Much better to hide their dirty little secret and pretend that nothing was wrong inside the big white house on the hill. Matthew had simply gone off to do his patriotic duty, that's all.

More than a year passed before we heard a single word from Matthew. Then in early March of 1918, he sent a letter to Lydia in care of my address. He wrote from somewhere in France to say that he had forgiven his mother. The war had changed him, he said. It had shown him the destructive power of unchecked hatred. He was tired of killing. Tired of all the desolation. He wanted to feel the rich soil beneath his fingers again, to nurture life and tend things and watch them grow. He wanted to come home but he knew that he never could. Wyatt Orchards was no longer his home. It would belong to Sam someday—Frank Wyatt's real son.

"Did Frank have his will changed to Sam's name?" I asked Lydia after she showed me Matthew's letter.

"Of course," she replied. "As banged up and sore as he was, he rode into town to see his lawyer first thing in the morning. I found the old will crumpled up in the garbage the day after Matthew left."

An eerie stillness began creeping over Lydia then, like a killing frost. As she stared into space, my sister begin slipping away from me. I struggled to find a way to pull her back.

"Listen, Lydia, why don't we write a letter to Matthew right now. I have some money saved up and I'll be glad to loan it to him. He can buy his own farm and settle down somewhere—maybe he can even find a place nearby that's for sale, and we can visit him. I'll ask John Wakefield to keep his eye open for a nice piece of land, okay?"

Lydia nodded and finished her coffee, but she didn't write the letter. I watched her put on her coat and walk up the hill to her house, and I wondered if she'd even heard a word I'd said.

That night I was down in my cottage typing a manuscript when my front door suddenly opened and Lydia walked in. She wore no coat or boots even though a light dusting of snow covered the ground. She floated across the room toward me as if sleepwalking, her eyes wide open, staring at me, through me. Her hands looked darker than her arms, and I thought at first that she wore gloves. But as she handed me the letter she had received from Matthew that morning I saw crimson fingerprints on the envelope and realized that Lydia's hands were covered with blood. Dark streaks of it stained the front of her calico dress and apron.

"Lydia, what's wrong? You're bleeding! Where are you hurt?" I grabbed her hands, thinking she might have slit her wrists, but I couldn't find any wounds.

"Write to Matthew for me," she said. "Tell him he can come home now. Tell him I fixed everything for him."

"What do you mean? What are you talking about? Lydia, sit down and let me see where all this blood is coming from."

"It isn't mine," she said, smiling slightly. "It's his."

"Whose?" She didn't answer. I'd never seen her this far removed from reality before. I gripped her shoulders, terrified for her. "Lydia, tell me what you've done!"

"I killed Frank."

I released her, backing away. "No . . . Oh, please, no!"

I left her standing in the living room of my cottage and raced up the hill in the dark. As much as I hated Frank Wyatt, I didn't want my sister to hang for his murder.

"Frank!" I yelled as I banged their kitchen door open. "Frank, where are you?" I tore through the house, calling his name, until I found him curled in a pool of blood on the floor of his study. I knelt beside him. He turned his head and looked at me, his eyes filled with horror, his mouth working soundlessly. He was still alive!

A bloody butcher knife lay on the floor beside him. He clutched his gut with both hands as the blood poured out of him. I ran to the kitchen and grabbed some towels, then knelt beside him again and wadded them into the wound in his stomach. He moaned as I pressed hard to stem the bleeding. His eyes rolled back.

"No, don't black out on me, Frank! Stay awake! Stay with me!" I looked around the room for something to splash on his face to revive him, but the coffee cup on his desk was empty. I slapped his cheeks until his eyes opened again. "Where's Sam? Frank, I need Sam to go get help! Where is he?"

He mouthed the word "barn."

"Hold this tight against the wound Frank, and don't black out on me! I'll be right back!"

I found Sam in the barn with the horses. His eyes went wide when he saw the wild look on my face, the blood all over my hands and dress.

"Your father's been hurt. He needs a doctor. Get into town as fast as you can and bring Dr. Gilbert back with you!"

Sam leaped onto the horse's back without bothering to saddle him, and raced off into the night. By the time I heard the doctor's carriage outside I had a blanket over Frank and I'd managed to slow his bleeding. He was still conscious, though he hadn't spoken. His eyes followed my movements as I picked the bloody knife off the floor and hid it in his desk drawer. Moments later the doctor walked into the room, shrugging off his coat.

"What happened here, Betty? How is he?" I didn't answer as I moved aside to let Dr. Gilbert examine him. "You kept him from going into shock . . . that's good. This looks like a pretty nasty stab wound, though. What happened?"

"I don't know," I said calmly. "Lydia came down to my house and told me he'd had an accident. I sent Sam for help and tried to stop the bleeding."

"You had an accident, Frank?"

I saw him hesitate for just a moment, then nod.

"I could use some boiling water, Betty, and as many towels as you can spare. What happened, Frank?" I heard the doctor ask again as I left to fetch them. "Can you tell me what happened?" I didn't hear Frank's answer.

"Where's Lydia?" Dr. Gilbert asked when I returned to the study a few minutes later. "I need to find out what caused this wound so I know what I'm looking at."

I remembered Lydia's strange, disquieting state and I was suddenly afraid for her. "I . . . I don't know. I left her at my cottage. I'll go find her."

I raced down the hill again, wondering how I could have been so stupid. I'd left Lydia alone!

My cottage door stood open but Lydia was gone. I wandered around in the dark for several minutes, calling her name, shivering with cold and fear before I thought of grabbing a light and looking for her footprints in the fresh snow. I followed them across the yard toward the pond with dread clutching my heart.

Her trail led out onto the thin ice, out to the black, gaping hole Lydia had fallen through. Only her apron floated on the inky surface.

I sank down in the soft snow at the edge of the pond and wept.

PART VII

Wyatt Orchards

Fall 1931

"That I will give you the rain of your land in his due season, the

first rain and the latter rain, that thou mayest gather in thy corn,

and thy wine, and thine oil. And I will send grass in thy fields for

thy cattle, that thou mayest eat and be full."

DEUT. 11:14-15

— CHAPTER FOURTEEN —

O f course, Dr. Gilbert was nobody's fool," Aunt Batty said as she finished her story. "He insisted that it looked like an attempted murder and a suicide—and he was right. He and Frank had a terrible falling-out because of it. The editor of the *Deer Springs News* was about to print the doctor's speculations on the front page of the paper when Frank found out and threatened to sue him for libel. The paper had no proof to back up those accusations, Frank said. No murder weapon was ever found, no suicide note—and they had Frank's sworn testimony about what had really happened."

"So did he print the story?" I asked. Aunt Batty and I sat on one of the narrow wooden bunks in the pickers' quarters, with the clean straw still piled in the wheelbarrow in front of us. Neither of us had gotten any work done as she'd told the tragic tale.

"No, the newspaper backed down rather than face a lawsuit it couldn't win. The official story will always be that Frank Wyatt accidentally stabbed himself while sharpening an auger. When his distraught wife went for help she lost her bearings in the dark and fell through the thin ice and drowned in the pond."

I tried to figure out what all this meant for me and my kids, but I couldn't think clearly after learning the horrible secrets that were hidden in this family's past. The tiny picker cabin felt stifling, so I stood on the bunk and shoved one of the windows open to let in a little air.

"Do you think Lydia altered Frank's will before she tried to kill him?" I asked as I sat down beside Aunt Batty again.

"Well, if Frank's will gives everything to Matthew—then yes, I think she must have swapped the two. Lydia told me she'd found the old one in the garbage. That must have been what she meant when she said she'd fixed it so Matthew could come home again."

"But why didn't Frank ever notice the switch?"

Aunt Batty shrugged. "How often does anybody dig through his records and reread his own will? As far as Frank knew, the old one went into the trash and the new one went into effect. He thought Sam would inherit everything."

A faint breeze blew into the room, carrying the sweet smell of fresh straw. I saw a faint glimmer of hope for the first time since I'd learned about Frank's will from Mr. Wakefield.

"Aunt Batty, will you come into town with me and explain to Mr. Wakefield what really happened? Maybe he remembers drawing up the second will. Maybe he'll be able to see that the old one was all crinkled up and then ironed out or something."

"I wouldn't get your hopes up, Toots," she said, taking my hand between hers. "Frank worked very hard to bury the truth along with Lydia. No one will ever believe us because no one ever knew that Matthew wasn't Frank's real son. We're just Frank's crazy old sister-in-law and his scheming daughter-in-law. Besides, if that's the only official will that was ever found and it was all legally signed and attested to, then there's really nothing Mr. Wakefield can do but enforce it."

"So I have to wait until they find Matthew?"

"I think that would be the wisest thing."

"But what will Matthew do? The orchard is in his name—do you think he'll take it away from us?"

"I really don't know," she said with a sigh. "That depends on how much Matthew has changed in the past fourteen years, and what he's been doing with himself all this time. He once loved this place . . . but he loved Sam, too. Maybe he'll agree to let the two of you share the place."

She bent to lift the half-filled tick we'd abandoned and held the mouth of it open. I grabbed a big handful of straw and stuffed it inside. If only I knew for sure whether or not Gabe was really Matthew. If only I knew what to do.

———

All of a sudden it was midsummer, and things got so hectic at the orchard that I didn't have much time to worry about Matthew Wyatt. Frank's regular pickers came back to harvest the Montmorency cherries—and later the peaches and pears and apples—but there were so many other people out of work that year that I found men standing in line every morning, begging to pick cherries for me. Some of the city folks said they'd work for a quart of milk or a dozen eggs—anything, just so they could feed their families. I thanked the good Lord that my kids would always have enough to eat as long as we lived on a farm.

Gabe did a fine job of overseeing the work—teaching the newcomers how to pick and breaking up the squabbles that broke out between them and the regulars. He set up a table for me at the end of one of the rows and Aunt Batty showed me how to record each person's name and the number of buckets they picked so I could pay them at the end of the day. We dumped all the day's pickings into lugs and loaded them onto the wagon, then Gabe and I drove the horses to the open-air market early the next morning to sell our cherries.

I'd never been to the open-air market before. We watched what all the other growers did, then got in line and paid our quarter to get on the market ourselves. The buyers who came to look over our cherries seemed determined to pay rock bottom prices, blaming it on the economic depression. Gabe drove a hard bargain though, refusing to budge, and as more growers arrived with their fruit, they slowly bumped us down the line without making a sale. I started to get worried.

"Take their price, Gabe. It's the best we can do."

"No, I won't let you be cheated." Gabe looked as tough and unyielding as all the other farmers—a far cry from the soft-spoken Gabe I'd grown accustomed to. "This is top-quality fruit and they all know it. We could probably sell it at the fruit exchange for the price these crooks are offering. I think we should stand firm."

We were almost out of line and off the market when one of the buyers finally agreed on Gabe's price. Relief flooded through me as we drove to the buyer's stall and unloaded the lugs onto his platform. I felt drained, and this was only my first crop of cherries, my first day on the market. I still had the rest of the season's harvest to sell.

"I'm not sure my nerves can take all this bargaining," I told Gabe as we drove the empty wagon home again. "I'm not cut out to be a poker player."

Gabe laughed. "You'll get used to it. The secret is not to appear too anxious to sell. Act as though you could take it or leave it."

"Well, you were certainly a good actor." I kept my eyes on the road ahead of us, afraid to look at Gabe, aware of him watching me. "With all that ballyhoo you sounded more like a sideshow hawker than a writer."

"Sometimes a journalist has to use a bit of ballyhoo if he's a free-lancer like me. Editors can be a lot like fruit buyers—why pay top dollar for a story if you can get it for a little less?" Gabe shifted slightly on the seat beside me and I felt him brush against me.

"Well, you got us a real good price. I'm grateful. And I want you to take some of this money as your pay."

"No, keep it. I don't want any money. I'm still paying you back for saving my life."

I glanced at him, then quickly looked away. "Gabe, that debt has long-since been paid."

"Well, I don't feel that way. I'm still very much in your debt."

His stubbornness frustrated me. "Listen, it's not right that you work so hard all the time for nothing."

"I'd hardly call it nothing," he said, sounding huffy himself. "Don't forget, besides the fact that you saved my life, I've been getting free room and board all this time—while a lot of other men are out of work."

"Be reasonable, Gabe—"

"I am being reasonable! You're the one who's being unreasonable. You—" Gabe stopped. He shook his head, laughing softly.

"What's so funny?" I asked.

"When it comes to 'mule-headed stubbornness,' as you once called it, I'd say we're pretty evenly matched—you and I."

He spoke the last words very softly—you and I—like they were holy or something. I could tell by his voice that he was looking at me but I kept my head down, concentrating on the horses' hind-quarters in front of me. We sat side by side on the wagon seat, dangerously close, and I knew that if I looked into his eyes just then I'd want to kiss him again—and then I would be lost. Winky couldn't come to my rescue this time. How could I love someone so much and yet be so afraid of him at the same time?

"Why are you so afraid of me?" Gabe suddenly asked. He'd read my thoughts and that scared me even more. "Have you been that badly hurt by someone, Eliza?"

I realized that I was trapped alone with Gabe, the very thing I'd tried to avoid all summer. I didn't want to open my heart to him but I had no way to escape. We were still a good mile or so from home. I snapped the reins to speed the horses into a trot.

"No," I finally answered. "I already told you why . . . because I don't know anything about you."

"Fair enough. But I don't know very much about you, either." His voice had a hard edge to it all of a sudden, that I'd never heard before. My heart hammered with fear. "Shall we tell all there is to tell, Eliza? What would you like to know? Where I spent my childhood? Albany, New York. Now, where did you spend yours?"

I was afraid to answer, afraid not to. "No one place," I finally said, swallowing hard. "I traveled all over with my daddy . . . because of his work."

"Well. That explains why you don't know how to play baseball." His tone was so cold I had to fight back my tears. "What was your father's line of work?" he continued. "Some sort of traveling salesman? My father was an attorney. A very prominent attorney, in fact."

"Why are you acting this way?" I asked, trying not to cry.

"Because I care for you, Eliza, and I think you care for me. I want to know why you keep pushing me away. You say it's because you know nothing about me—but you know a lot about me. We've worked together for nearly six months, you've talked with me every day, you've seen how I treat you and your kids. What more do you need to know?"

"Is Gabe Harper your real name?" I blurted out.

My question took him by surprise. He hesitated just a moment too long.

"Yes."

I knew he was lying. I knew it.

I pulled the horses to a halt and tossed the reins to him, then stood to climb down. Gabe grabbed my arm to stop me. "What are you doing? Where are you going?"

"I'd like to walk for a while, if you don't mind."

He pulled roughly on my arm, jerking me back down onto the seat. "If anyone is going to walk, it'll be me," he said, pushing the reins into my hand. Before I could stop him, he jumped to the ground and strode down the road with his back to me. He had a slight limp in his step, just as I'd warned him he would.

I flicked the reins and signaled to the horses to giddap, passing Gabe a moment later and leaving him behind.

From then on I made Gabe go by himself to the open-air market or the fruit exchange. He didn't like my decision, but I insisted that one of us needed to stay home and oversee the pickers, and he finally agreed. Sometimes Jimmy and Luke rode along with him, but only if they'd finished pulling weeds in the vegetable garden for Aunt Batty. She had a real green thumb when it came to making things grow, and she had brought in a bumper crop of vegetables. Gabe took some of the produce into town to sell, but a lot of it Aunt Batty just gave away to folks. I didn't mind. We had much more than we could ever use.

Aunt Batty helped me with the canning that summer. I got so used to hearing her singing those hymns for all she was worth that I even joined in with her and Becky every once in a while. Aunt Batty had somehow convinced my daughter that cleaning strawberries, peeling tomatoes, and stuffing cucumbers into pickle jars was fun, so we had an extra pair of willing hands. One afternoon the three of us were giggling like schoolgirls as we canned peaches, and without even thinking I tossed four peaches into the air and did a little juggling act, just to see if I still remembered how. Becky stared at me, dumbfounded.

"Mama! How'd you do that?"

Aunt Batty looked up from her pot of boiling syrup and applauded. "My goodness, Eliza! We had no idea you were so talented!"

I quickly caught the four peaches and set them on the table, angry that I'd given away a secret part of myself like that.

"Do it again, Mama!"

I couldn't look at Becky. "Not now. We have work to do."

"Wait till I tell Jimmy and Luke and Mr. Harper what you can do!"

"No! You will not tell them a thing, Becky Jean! I won't do it again—for them or anybody else."

My words came out harsher than I'd intended. Becky's bottom lip quivered as she fought tears. "Why not, Mama?"

"Because . . . just because." I'd always hated it when my daddy gave me that answer, and now here I was saying the same thing. But there were some things I just couldn't explain to a four-year-old.

We canned about sixteen quarts of peaches that day and stored them on the shelves in my cellar. It always gave me a feeling of pride to see the rows of home-canned goods on those shelves—tomatoes, green beans, pickles, peaches, pears, and rows of colorful jams and jellies—food that would feed my family come wintertime.

Aunt Batty bribed Jimmy and Luke with Herman Walters' adventure books and got them to do all kinds of chores, like running the cultivator between the corn rows and cleaning out the root cellar. Pretty soon we would fill that root cellar with potatoes, onions, carrots, squash, beets, and turnips. The two pigs she bought had fattened up real nice, and the rich cream from Myrtle's milk had earned us extra cash from the creamery in town. The money helped us buy all the necessities we couldn't grow, like coffee, baking powder, flour, and sugar. A lot of people went hungry that year, but the good Lord had blessed us with abundance, and Aunt Batty made sure we all thanked Him every night when the six of us gathered around the table for dinner.

In August the new Sears, Roebuck & Co. catalog arrived. During more prosperous times, I always ordered new school clothes for the boys and let their last year's school clothes become play clothes. But this year money was too tight. The boys would have to make do with hand-me-downs and patched-up clothes come September. They certainly wouldn't be the only kids at school with their ankles showing below their britches. We needed to save our money to buy a load of coal to get us through the winter and to buy spray ingredients next spring at Peterson's store since Merle wouldn't let me buy on credit. Gabe had given me a list of farm supplies we just couldn't do without, and the only other thing I ordered from Sears that year were new shoes for Jimmy to replace the ones he'd outgrown.

I finished filling out the order form at the kitchen table one night and had tallied it all up when it occurred to me that Aunt Batty might have something she wanted to add. I went looking for her in the parlor where all three kids sat around the radio listening to *Amos 'n Andy*. She wasn't there.

"Where's Aunt Batty?" I had to practically shout before I got anyone's attention. "Hey there! Have you seen Aunt Batty?" It was like they were all hypnotized or something. I had to wonder whether listening to that radio was doing my kids any good.

"I think she's outside talking to Mr. Harper," Jimmy finally answered.

I saw no sign of her out in the yard. When I went inside the barn, I heard voices coming from the workshop where Gabe slept. He'd left the door open just a crack. I knew it was wrong to eavesdrop, but I couldn't resist. I wanted to hear what she and Gabe were talking about.

"No, don't spare my feelings, Aunt Batty," Gabe said. "I asked for your honest opinion. I want to hear what you really think of it."

"I think it's a very good story," she said. "And very safe."

"Safe? What do you mean?"

"Is this the kind of writing you do all the time? Newspaper articles like this?"

"Yes. Why?"

"Because this article is very well-written, very informative . . . but very dispassionate," Aunt Batty told him. "That's fine for newspaper articles; it's what's expected. But I've come to know you pretty well, Gabe, and you're a very sensitive, perceptive man, capable of great feeling. Why doesn't the true Gabe Harper come through in your writing? You're not a dispassionate person."

"You said it yourself, it's not what's expected in a good newspaper article. I don't write fiction or essays—"

"Why not?"

"Well . . . because . . . I just don't."

"Get angry, Gabe! Get excited, get passionate! All truly great writers are never afraid to put their feelings, their very selves, into their work. It's true of every profession, I think. It's why John Wakefield makes such a fine attorney . . . it's what Eliza had to learn in order to make this orchard work. Great writers don't hold back part of themselves. But I think you're holding back, Gabe."

"Why do you say that?"

"There's none of your own experiences in what you write, only your indifferent observations. You need to put yourself onto the page."

Silence filled the long pause. I wondered what they were both doing.

"That idea scares you to death for some reason, doesn't it?" Aunt Batty finally said. "I can see it in your eyes."

"Yes, I admit it scares me."

I remembered how good Gabe's hobo story was, yet I'd learned nothing about him from reading it. But the stories Gabe wrote about his father and about his younger brother falling through the ice—those had the kind of feeling I think Aunt Batty meant. He must not have let her read those stories—and I thought I knew why.

"Do you know why my books were so popular?" Aunt Batty asked. "It was because when I wrote my series for girls, I remembered my own girlish yearning to be like Nellie Bly and I tapped into my own soul. I wrote about the longing I had to be my own person, not just somebody's daughter or wife, my longing to make the right decisions and to be what God created me to be, my longing to make my mark on the world like Nellie Bly did. And when I wrote my series for boys, I wrote out of my deep love for Walter—each one of my heroes faced death and danger with the same courage and faith that he'd shown. But if I hadn't risked putting myself onto those pages, those books never would have sold. So the question is, why are you so afraid to put yourself onto the page?"

There was another long silence before Gabe replied, "I don't know why."

"What events in your life changed you the most, Gabe? Fighting in the war is one of them, I would imagine."

"Yes . . . but I can't write about the war. I've tried . . . and I just can't."

"None of us will ever be all that God wants us to be until we face our past, face the people and the events that God put in our lives that shaped us and made us who we are. But first we have to get over our anger at Him for allowing the bad things to happen. Jesus says if we ask our Father for bread, He won't give us a stone. We have to stop seeing the bad things in life as stones—they're really God's bread. They'll nourish us and help us grow if we accept them as food for our souls."

I heard shuffling sounds as Aunt Batty stood up. When she spoke again her voice came from just inside the door. I ducked down behind the grain bin, but I heard her say before she left, "Write your own story, Gabe. I guarantee it will not only be powerful, but it might help you accept your past."

———

I drove the wagon into town the next day to mail the Sears order and to sell our cream and extra eggs. I stopped by Mr. Wakefield's office, too, and it was all I could do to keep from galloping the horses home in the August heat to tell Aunt Batty the latest news. She was out in the yard, taking the laundry we had scrubbed that morning down from the clotheslines.

"Looks like you're about to burst," she said when she saw me. "You've got news, I take it—good or bad?"

"I'm not sure. I paid Mr. Wakefield a visit while I was in town. He had a court date over at the county seat so he wasn't there, but his secretary let it slip that they might have found out where Matthew is living. The address the army hospital gave Mr. Wakefield is for a boardinghouse in Chicago. The address is thirteen years old, of course, but at least they know where to start looking. Mr. Wakefield has people pursuing a few leads for him in Chicago and they think they're getting close to finding Matthew. They might have some news for us in just a couple more weeks."

"Oh, that's wonderful news!" Aunt Batty still held one end of a bed sheet that was attached to the clothesline with a pin. She got so excited that she twirled right around in a circle with it like she was dancing around a May pole. Gabe walked out of the barn just then to unhitch the wagon.

"You're dancing, Aunt Batty. What are we celebrating this time?" he asked.

"Matthew!" she said with a grin. "We might be close to finding Matthew!"

"Who?" Gabe asked. But I saw his face. He had turned as pale as the bed sheet in Aunt Batty's hand. He knew who Matthew was. Pretending he didn't know was a lie, an act. I knew it was.

"Matthew Wyatt is my sister Lydia's oldest son," Aunt Batty told him. "He went off to fight in the Great War and never came back."

All of a sudden I wanted to stop her. I didn't want her to tell Gabe the rest—that Matthew owned the farm, not me. I was desperate to interrupt her, to distract her.

"Here, let me finish folding these clothes for you," I said, taking the sheet from her hand. "It's too hot for you to be standing around out here in the sun." But Aunt Batty was too excited to stop. I listened helplessly as she blurted out the truth.

"We've been looking all over for Matthew because Frank Wyatt's will deeded the orchard and everything else to Matthew, not to Eliza. Now it looks like we might be close to finding him at last. He's in Chicago, of all places!"

Gabe appeared even more shaken than me. He leaned against the wagon as if he might fall over if something didn't hold him up. Aunt Batty might have noticed it, too, if she hadn't been so excited. But a moment later Gabe pulled himself together. In a few quick strides he stood so close to me I could smell the scent of his shaving soap on his face.

"Your father-in-law left everything to someone else?" he asked in a tight voice. "None of this belongs to you and the kids? He left you with *nothing*?"

"That's right," I answered, my voice barely above a whisper.

I could see Gabe's anger building, but he didn't seem to have anywhere to release it. His jaw tightened and his hands balled into fists.

"No wonder everyone hated Frank Wyatt," he said through clenched teeth. "I hope he's rotting in hell!"

"Oh, Gabe, no!" Aunt Batty said. "I wouldn't wish hell on anyone, not even Frank Wyatt. Besides, I don't know a single person who ever loved that man. To me, that's hell enough. Can you imagine going through this wonderful life here on earth without ever being loved?"

I took advantage of the distraction to escape from Gabe, backing away from him and lifting the wicker laundry basket to hold between us like a shield. Without another word, he turned and strode back to the wagon, leading the horses away into the barn.

Gabe didn't seem like the same person after that day. I would catch him deep in thought at odd moments, like the time he stood on a picking ladder with an apple in his hand, just staring off into the distance, or the time I found him sitting on a milking stool beside Myrtle, staring into the empty pail while she bellowed to be milked. Most times when you tried to talk to him you got the feeling his thoughts were far away from Wyatt Orchards. Even the kids couldn't interest him in playing ball or going fishing anymore. He stayed out in the barn in the evenings instead of listening to the radio with all of us, and even Aunt Batty couldn't coax him inside.

His strange behavior made me feel like I walked a tightrope. If he really was Matthew, why didn't he just step forward and admit it? Was he trying to make up his mind what to do now that he knew everything belonged to him? And if he wasn't Matthew—well, maybe he was just trying to distance himself from us while he figured out how to say good-bye. Either way, it seemed as though we'd already lost the Gabe we once knew.

———

August flew past, and by the time the boys headed back to school in September, the end of the long growing season was almost in sight. We'd worked hard and now our labor had finally paid off. The tree branches were heavy with apples. Once they were picked and sold and the corn was harvested, we would all get a much-deserved rest.

Aunt Batty and I worked in the vegetable garden one afternoon while Becky napped. We were picking the last of the green tomatoes to fry before the frost killed them when Sheriff Foster's car came up the driveway in a cloud of dust. A feeling of foreboding shivered through me, though I didn't know why.

"Uh-oh," Aunt Batty said, echoing my thoughts. "Here comes trouble."

I didn't move as the sheriff climbed from his car. He waved when he saw us, then walked across the yard to where we worked.

"I need to have a word with that so-called hired hand of yours, ma'am," he said, tipping his hat. "The one who calls himself Gabriel Harper."

"I don't care one bit for your tone of voice, Sheriff," I said, trying to sound braver than I felt. Something about his grim face and the shiny badge pinned to his uniform made my heart start to pound. "Mr. Harper has worked very hard for me. We're about to bring in the last of the harvest and I never would have been able to accomplish it all without his help."

"Well," he said with a heavy sigh, "I really don't like being the one to tell you this, but the man who calls himself Gabriel Harper has been lying to you. He's not who he claims to be . . . and both John Wakefield and I have reached the conclusion that Harper came here with the deliberate intention of cheating and defrauding you."

I felt my knees go weak. Gabe? Came here to defraud me? "I don't believe it," I murmured. But even as I said the words, doubt flickered in the back of my mind. I knew he had lied to me when he said that Gabe was his real name. And I knew he'd only pretended not to know who Matthew was. He'd kept a secret hidden from me since the time he'd arrived, but it couldn't possibly be because he was out to cheat me, could it? That's the part I couldn't believe.

"Well, ma'am, it's true," the sheriff said. He looked at me with pity. "I can see the man has won your affection and trust—and that makes his crime all the more reprehensible, in my judgment."

My words came out in a rush of anger. "I don't know what crime you think he has committed, but it hasn't been against me! He's done nothing wrong in all the time I've known him, nor has he tried to steal my affections." I nearly choked on the lie. Gabe *had* stolen my affections, as well as my kids' affections. Whether he'd done it deliberately or not, I didn't know.

"Listen," I continued, "all of Gabe's actions toward me have been completely honorable! He has worked harder than any hired hand should be expected to work, and he's taken absolutely nothing from me except his meals and a bed in my barn."

"Now, calm down, Eliza. Give me a chance to tell you what John Wakefield and I have found out."

"What does Mr. Wakefield have to do with this?"

"I'm getting to that. See, after I talked to Mr. Harper some months ago, I began making inquiries in Chicago to try and look into this fellow's background."

"Why? What right did you have? What reason?"

"Let me finish." He held out his hands to quiet me. "The folks at the *Chicago Tribune* told me that 'Gabriel Harper' is a pen name he uses. But when I looked into his real identity, I found out that he claims his real name is Matthew Wyatt—same as your brother-in-law."

Gabe really was Matthew! A tidal wave of emotions washed over me—relief, fear, joy, disbelief. I couldn't even think about what that meant as far as the kids' and my futures were concerned. All I knew was that I'd found the very man I'd been searching for and I was in love with him and I was pretty sure he loved me. But the sheriff still acted as though he wanted to throw Gabe in jail. He delivered the news to me as if announcing some great tragedy.

"Now, John Wakefield told me that he's been trying to trace your brother-in-law's whereabouts," the sheriff continued. "I understand Matthew has an inheritance coming to him from Frank's will, isn't that right? Anyhow, Mr. Wakefield's search and my inquiries led us to this same man—this so-called Gabriel Harper."

I finally found my voice. "Is it a crime to use a pen name? If Gabe really is my brother-in-law, then that's wonderful news. And it's not against the law for him to live here and work for me, is it?"

"Eliza—that man who's been working for you is *not* the Matthew Wyatt who grew up here in Deer Springs."

"How do you know he isn't? People change. He went through a war—"

"There's a real simple way to find out. Is the tip of his right index finger missing? Nail and all? The real Matthew had an accident with a hay mower blade when he was twelve or thirteen years old. Fingers don't grow back. John and I believe this man came here to defraud you and your children out of their rightful inheritance. You were alone, vulnerable, needing his help."

"But Gabe didn't even know about Frank's will. I never told him one word about it."

"Don't defend him, Mrs. Wyatt. We believe he did know. This impostor, this Gabe Harper or whoever he is, knows all about the real Matthew Wyatt. John Wakefield subpoenaed his work records at the newspaper to see if he was entitled to the inheritance and found out that Harper listed his parents as Frank and Lydia Wyatt, his birthplace as Deer Springs—he even used Matthew's real date of birth."

Gabe knew much, much more than that. He knew all kinds of personal things, such as what kind of a father Frank Wyatt had been and the secret of how Willie had drowned. And he knew that Matthew wasn't Frank's real son, too. I felt as shaken as a tent in a hurricane. The sheriff must have noticed because he rested his hand on my shoulder to steady me.

"As I said, the real Matthew Wyatt has part of a finger missing. Now, if you'll just tell me where Gabriel Harper is, you'll see the truth for yourself."

I already knew the truth. Gabe did not have any missing fingers. That must be how Aunt Batty knew he wasn't Matthew, too. I turned to her—but she had disappeared! She had stood right beside me a moment ago when the sheriff pulled up—and now she was gone, silent as a cat. I couldn't take it all in. I was so stunned to think that Gabe was a criminal who had come here to cheat me that I couldn't speak. I still couldn't believe it. The sheriff rested both hands on my shoulders as if he knew I was about to fall over.

"We know that the real Matthew Wyatt moved to Chicago after the army discharged him," he said. "The police in Chicago are very concerned because Matthew appears to be missing without a trace. Your Mr. Harper might well be connected to his disappearance. Don't protect him, Eliza. Tell me where he is."

I struggled to comprehend the sheriff's terrible words. I didn't want to believe them. Had I fallen in love with a criminal? Had I allowed my children to sit on a murderer's lap?

"Um . . . Gabe's in the apple barn," I finally said. "He's getting the apple grader ready to use."

I followed Sheriff Foster across the yard and into the apple barn like a woman in a dream. But when we went inside, there was no sign of Gabe. Instead, Aunt Batty stood leaning against the grader, smiling just as big as you please. Winky sat at her feet, his tongue lolling as usual.

"Where's Mr. Harper?" the sheriff asked her.

"He's not here, Dan," she said. "I'm afraid he's gone."

The sheriff pushed past her and ran out the open rear door.

I gaped at Aunt Batty in disbelief. "You warned him, didn't you?"

"Yes, Gabe asked me to. Remember when he was working down at my house, and Dan Foster threatened to check up on him? Gabe made me promise that if the sheriff ever came back looking for him I would come and tell him right away."

"But why? What secret is Gabe hiding?"

She shrugged. "I didn't ask him. I just warned him that Sheriff Foster was here, like I promised I would, and Gabe bolted."

The sheriff returned just then, puffing slightly. "I hope you believe me now, Mrs. Wyatt. Innocent men don't run from the law. May I borrow your telephone? I'm sending for the dogs."

"I don't have a telephone."

He huffed in frustration. "Who's your nearest neighbor? Does Alvin Greer have one?"

"You don't need to send for your dogs," Aunt Batty said. "My Winky is an excellent hunting dog. Just give him something of Gabe's and he'll be hot on his trail in no time." Winky barked in agreement.

The sheriff looked at the fat little dog and frowned skeptically. "Miss Fowler . . . I really don't think—"

"Try it, Sheriff. Look, here's Gabe's bandana." She held it close to Winky's nose. He sniffed the cloth as if his life depended on it. "Find Gabe, boy! Go get Gabe!" she coaxed.

I'd never seen the little dog get so excited before. He barked as if he wanted to tell us something important, and his stubby tail whirled in circles.

"Go get him!" Aunt Batty urged again. "Find Gabe!"

Winky put his nose to the ground and led the way, waddling out of the back door of the apple barn on his short, bowed legs. I knew he really had sniffed out Gabe's trail because he trotted toward the barn in a straight line, not in the usual drunken, zigzag pattern his blind eye always caused him to take. I wanted to stop him but I didn't know how—or why. If Gabe was really the criminal Sheriff Foster claimed he was, why did I still want to protect him?

Winky led us to the workshop where Gabe slept. He pushed the door open with his snout, then jumped up on Gabe's bed and barked.

"He's not here," the sheriff said in disgust.

"No, but I'll bet he was just here," Aunt Batty said. "This is where Gabe's been living, and see? His typewriter and all his other belongings are gone."

I couldn't understand what Aunt Batty was doing. Why would she warn Gabe one minute and betray him the next?

The sheriff pointed to the clothes that lay neatly folded on a chair. "Aren't these his clothes? He wouldn't have gone far without these."

"They belonged to Sam," I said. "I loaned them to Gabe because he didn't have much to wear. He left them here because he isn't a thief."

"But he wore them recently, so they'll still have Gabe's scent," Aunt Batty said helpfully. She held one of the shirts near Winky's snout and the little dog grew excited all over again. He barked, then jumped off the bed and followed Gabe's trail out the back door of the barn. He led us down the path the cows always took to get to the pasture, then ducked under the barbed-wire fence and into the woods. Aunt Batty and I easily climbed between the wires, but it took Sheriff Foster a little longer to maneuver through the barbed wire without ripping his pants. Winky came back and waited patiently for him on the other side.

"Didn't I tell you he was a fine hunting dog, Sheriff?" Aunt Batty said proudly.

Winky barked again and took off into the underbrush. He led us to a thicket of dense weeds and fallen branches deep in the woods.

"That looks like some sort of a nest, all right," the sheriff said, resting his hand on his holster. "And I'll bet he's hiding in there. Stand back everyone."

Suddenly Winky barked three times, then took off toward home faster than I'd ever seen him run. Aunt Batty clutched the sheriff's arm. "Wait a minute, Dan. I wouldn't go poking around in there if I were you, because—"

"I said stand back, Miss Fowler. Harper knows he's cornered and he might be dangerous."

"But I think you should know that Winky has made a dreadful mistake and—"

"I want both of you to step back and stop interfering with this arrest," he said firmly. He pointed back down the path to a large pine tree. "Go stand over there, out of my way."

"We'd better do what the man says," Aunt Batty said with a shrug.

"But is Gabe—?"

"Trust me, Toots." She pulled me back down the path and we stood beneath the pine tree, waiting. Sheriff Foster pulled out his gun.

"Come on out of there, Harper," he yelled. "I know you're in there. You can't escape." When nothing happened, he picked up a dead tree branch and poked it into the thicket. "Don't make this any harder on yourself by resisting arrest."

He poked again, deeper, and I heard a rustling in the thicket. From the safe distance where Aunt Batty had dragged me I saw movement. A thatch of dark hair emerged, then Sheriff Foster let out a yell. At the same instant that he yelled, the powerful stench of skunk overwhelmed all of us.

"Ugh! I tried to warn him," Aunt Batty said, shaking her head.

I did feel sorry for Sheriff Foster. The stink was so nauseating it took your breath away and made your eyes water—and the skunk had sprayed him at close range before running off into the woods. The sheriff couldn't stop coughing and gagging, and we had to lead him back to the house since his eyes stung so badly he couldn't see.

When we reached the back porch I gave him a basin of water to rinse out his eyes, but I had no intention of inviting him into my house, smelling like he did.

"We can drag out the copper bathtub for you," Aunt Batty offered. "I'll fix you a bath of tomato juice. That's guaranteed to take away the stench."

"No . . . no . . ." he said, still sputtering.

"Well, at least let me give you a change of clothes," I said. But he couldn't get into his car and drive away fast enough.

"He should have listened to me," Aunt Batty said as the sheriff roared out of the driveway. Then, before the dust even had a chance to settle she burst into laughter as if she'd held it inside for so long she either had to laugh or explode. I stared at her.

"You led him to that skunk on purpose, didn't you!"

"I didn't do anything," she said as innocently as a child. "Winky did it."

"But—"

She patted my arm. "Winky thought the world of Gabe, you know."

— CHAPTER FIFTEEN —

We saw no more of Sheriff Foster that day. I waited and watched all afternoon, hoping Gabe would come back and explain himself, but he'd disappeared. Didn't he trust us enough, after all this time, to tell us who he really was and why he was running? I guess not because he was gone for good. Once again, I felt all alone.

"Where did Mr. Harper go?" Becky asked as we sat around the dinner table that night. I think we were all painfully aware of Gabe's empty chair.

"He didn't tell anybody where he was going," I said. "Back to where he came from, I suppose."

"You mean to heaven? Was he really an angel?" Becky asked.

"No, he wasn't an angel—" I began, but Aunt Batty interrupted me.

"Well, he was in a way," she said. "Angels are messengers from

God, sent to give us some help whenever we need it. That's what Gabe did. He helped all of us out, didn't he? He worked in the orchard for your mama, and he fixed my roof as good as new, and he taught you boys how to play baseball and swim and catch fish, and he made Becky's swing. . . ."

"Then why did he leave us?" Jimmy asked.

"I guess his work here must have been all finished," Aunt Batty said. "Maybe God needed Gabe's help someplace else."

"But we still need him here!" Jimmy said. I heard the tears in his voice. This was exactly what I'd been so afraid of—that my kids would feel the awful pain of being abandoned when Gabe left. And I felt the pain every bit as much as they did.

"You're looking to the wrong person for help," Aunt Batty said. "God is the one who helped us. He sent His messenger into our lives because He wanted us to know that we can rely on Him. And God is still here helping us, even though Gabe is gone."

My kids didn't want to hear all this church talk, and neither did I. We were all hurting much too badly to take any comfort in God just then.

"Is Mr. Harper c-coming back?" Luke asked.

Aunt Batty seemed to realize that her fancy words about God weren't getting through. She wrapped her arms around Luke, who sat at the table beside her, and gave him a hug.

"Listen, Toots," she said. "Gabe loved all of us very much, and he loved living here. He wouldn't have left us like he did unless he had a very good reason. And if there's any way in the world he can come back to us someday, I believe he will."

The more I thought about the mystery of Gabriel Harper, the more unsettled I felt. I had believed he was Matthew for so long that I still found it hard to root out the idea, even though I now knew for a fact that he wasn't. But why would he impersonate Matthew? Had he planted all those stories about his father and his brother Willie in that burlap bag of his, hoping I'd find them? Did he want me to think he was my brother-in-law? And what about his injured leg? He had arrived at our door a very sick man—he might have died!—and that wasn't something he could fake.

But the thought that unnerved me the most, the thought that made me want to lock all the doors when I went to bed that night, was the question the sheriff had raised—what had happened to the real Matthew Wyatt? Gabe must know the answer if he took on Matthew's identity. Why would he run from the sheriff if he had nothing to hide? Could Gabe Harper really be capable of . . . murder?

After I'd tucked the kids into bed for the night, I went out to the workshop in the barn where Gabe used to sleep. I told myself I needed to gather up those clothes of Sam's that he'd left behind, but in my heart I think I hoped to find Gabe hiding out there somewhere. I wanted him to offer me a simple explanation for this whole mess. I wanted to joke about what a silly misunderstanding it all was. I wanted to hear him laugh as I told him how Winky had saved the day and helped him escape from the sheriff. I wanted Gabe back—the old Gabe who'd worked beside me trimming trees and filling smudge pots and spraying apple trees and helping Angel the calf come into the world—not the dangerous Gabe who the sheriff insisted had lied in order to steal my orchard and my heart.

As I sat on the edge of Gabe's cot, listening to the gentle rustlings of the cows and horses in their stalls, I knew one thing for certain—Gabe had indeed stolen my heart. He was gone and he'd taken my heart with him. He'd left behind a big, empty, hurting place where it once had been.

I stood to go, scooping up the clothes I had come for. I knew I would have to hide them away in a drawer again, so they wouldn't remind me of Gabe. As I turned to leave I noticed that the door to the pot-bellied stove stood open a crack. I gave it a quick push with my foot to close it, but it wouldn't shut. The stove should have been empty in the summertime, but it wasn't. Something was jammed in the way.

I laid the clothes on the bed and bent to see what it was. Inside lay one of Gabe's notebooks—the one he had just asked me to buy for him the last time I went to town, in fact. One of the corners was charred, and it looked as though Gabe had shoved it into the stove in a hurry, then lit a match to it. The fire must have gone out when the door didn't close. I brushed away the burnt wooden match and singed paper, then pulled the rest of the notebook out of the stove. Gabe had shoved it in upside down and only a few blank pages at the end of the book had burned. I could still read the ones filled with writing.

I carried Gabe's notebook back to the house, and after locking all the farmhouse doors for the first time in my life, I took the notebook upstairs to read in bed.

I started writing when I was ten because the words had begun to pile up inside me and I had no other way to release them. All my hoarded thoughts and feelings exploded onto the pages of my journals where I could finally liberate them, sort through them, make sense of them. Writing became my secret release valve when the pressure to express myself built up. And without ever mentioning my father or describing him, every word I wrote had to do with him, about coming to terms with who he was. And who I was.

My father was a sturdy, square-shouldered attorney who carried himself with the dignity of a prince and the belligerence of a prize fighter. People naturally stepped aside when they saw him coming. They had to—my father would step aside for no man. But he was no boor. Raised in wealth and privilege, he possessed impeccable manners, dressing for even the most casual occasions in a starched white shirt, dark suit, waistcoat, and tie. He began going bald while in his thirties, but his demeanor was such that people saw a broad, wise forehead, not a lack of hair. Beneath his plain, almost somber appearance lay a magnetic, charismatic personality that drew people to him. He was a man to be respected, feared, and hated.

I descended from a long line of such men. My grandfather had been a prominent state supreme court justice, also respected, feared, and hated. My father groomed me to carry on the family legacy, just as my grandfather had groomed him to assume the state leadership of his political party. They expected me to study law, to pattern myself in their mold, to become a partner in their prestigious law firm. One day I would take over the reins of power, making or breaking potential candidates, keeping the political machine well-oiled.

By the time I was ten, my mother was no longer allowed to be involved in my life. Raising a son was a father's job. My mother's life consisted of making my father look good, orchestrating the endless stream of social events his position required, and raising my three sisters to be proper ladies. She also took part in various social causes—carefully chosen by my father, of course. Woman's suffrage was not among them.

My father reminded me of his expectations with every glance, every gesture, every breath he took. He was a loud, angry man whose voice carried through the walls and doors of our house. He had little patience for fools—and I seemed to be chief among them. He never physically abused me, never resorted to slaps or thrashings no matter how badly I deserved them. Instead, he used words as his most potent weapons—the tools of his trade as a lawyer and political mastermind—and he wielded them with deadly accuracy to attack, destroy, and avenge. Whether in the echoing courtroom or in the smoky political meetings he held in his study, my father marshaled words like a general commanding troops, deploying them to annihilate his enemies. I couldn't defend myself against his arsenal.

It wasn't that I had nothing to say—words filled my head. But my tongue continually misfired like a bomb with a faulty detonator, leaving me defenseless against the intensity and range of his firepower. The problem began when I was in fifth grade.

"Why is your arithmetic score lower than all the others?" my father bellowed as he surveyed my report card.

"I . . . I d . . . don't—"

"Stop it! You sound like a blithering idiot!" Father stared at me with his courtroom glare and I didn't dare look away, didn't dare cry. He shoved the report card under my nose. "I asked you a question!"

The words were right there in my mind. I knew what I wanted to tell him. But the knots that twisted through my stomach like a nest of snakes had spread to my tongue, immobilizing it. "M . . . my t . . . teacher—"

"Spit it out! What's the matter with you? Do you want people to think you're a moron?"

The more he raged, the worse I stuttered, and the more I stuttered, the worse he raged. I grew so nervous that my speech problem soon spilled over from home to school and the other boys mimicked and mocked me. I reacted with my fists. The punishment I received at school couldn't compare with the punishment of facing my father that night. Winning his approval was the sole purpose of my life—to lose it meant to lose all meaning. I lived an arctic existence in the best of times, basking in the feeble warmth and dim rays of his benediction. To lose even that scant winter sunlight meant suffering a frigid darkness that was unbearable. I faced him in his study, shivering.

"I would expect the son of an ignorant immigrant to resort

to using his fists," he began. "Certainly not my son. I have properly educated my son to use his brains to dispose of his enemies, real or imagined. But perhaps a mistake has been made. Perhaps it wasn't my son after all, who involved himself in this . . . brouhaha?" He hadn't looked at me from the time I first entered the room, but his eyes finally met mine as he spoke the last word. He froze me with his gaze.

"No, s . . . sir."

"Speak up!" he bellowed.

"It w . . . was m . . . me, sir."

"Stop that! You know how I hate your moronic stammering!" I nodded. He seemed satisfied with that. "Now, would you care to enlighten me as to the cause of your degrading behavior?" He held the headmaster's letter, which fully explained the incident, in his manicured hand.

Words stampeded through my brain like an ill-disciplined army, knocking each other down as they jostled for position, piling up in confusion and disarray. Very few of them ever made it past my lips. "Th . . . they were m . . . mocking me."

"What? M . . . mocking you? Why would anyone m . . . mock you?"

My mouth opened. My lips moved. I willed my voice to speak, to explain, but nothing came out. I felt sick with self-hatred.

"Get out of my sight if you're going to act like an imbecile!" he growled.

I fled to the bathroom and vomited.

Later, the words behaved themselves as they paraded onto paper, marching in orderly sentences and phrases. I composed letters of apology to the boys I had attacked, to my teachers and headmaster, to my father. I cited examples from literature and history to demonstrate that I understood my folly. I humbly begged their forgiveness. Then I worked harder than I ever had in my life to make the long journey back to my father's good graces, secretly warming myself beside the small bonfires of contentment I found in writing.

I learned to talk no more than necessary in school. Some of my teachers sympathized, allowing me to stay within my safe shelter of silence—most didn't. Most of my teachers knew my father and my grandfather as prominent, powerful men who had also attended their private, exclusive boys' school and contributed generously to their alumni fund. To compensate for my paralyzed tongue I learned to write, and once I'd expressed myself on paper, I could read what I'd written without stuttering. Armed with a dictionary and a thesaurus, my arsenal was nearly as well-stocked as my father's, even if my delivery lacked his firepower.

The summer after I finished fifth grade was one of the hottest ones on record. My father sent me to my aunt and uncle's farm downstate to escape the feverish heat that blanketed the city. Aunt June, my mother's youngest sister, had "foolishly married beneath her" and lived on a farm with her husband and five children. But if Aunt June had made a mistake, I certainly saw no sign of it. The three summers I spent with their loving, contented family were the happiest days of my life. My stuttering stopped completely. I spent a good part of the time devouring Herman Walters' adventure books, and for a little while I could forget my own blundering incompetence and self-loathing as I fearlessly triumphed with Walters' heroes. His books took me to places far beyond my father's reach. Then, in a rare burst of self-confidence, I sat down on my aunt and uncle's shady front porch as the cicadas buzzed, and I wrote an adventure novel of my own.

The evening I returned to the city, my father summoned me to his study to give an accounting of my summer. I brought the notebook filled with words, hoping it would do the explaining for me.

"What did you do with yourself all summer?" he asked, not

unkindly. I showed him my notebook. "What's all this?"

"I w . . . wrote a story. It's about p . . . pirates and—"

But he was already reading it, scanning the first page, flipping to the next and the next. My father could read very rapidly. He digested *The New York Journal, The Boston Globe,* and *The New York Times* every morning before I finished my bacon and eggs.

"This is nothing but banal, sentimental *trash,*" he said, slapping my notebook closed a few moments later. "I might have known that fool you call your uncle would encourage something like this."

He rose majestically from his club chair and carried my adventure story into the kitchen. Cora, our cook, bustled around the room working up a sweat as she prepared our dinner on the huge cast-iron stove. My father grabbed one of the stove's chrome lifters in his beefy hand and opened a lid.

"This is what we do with rubbish."

I saw the flames licking inside and cried out, "No!"

But he casually tossed my notebook into the fire and slammed the lid shut again. I ran from the kitchen, knowing my father would scorn my tears. The sound of that cast-iron lid closing so irrevocably has echoed in my heart ever since. In the years that followed, I would often lay in bed in the morning and listen to Cora slamming those lids as she stoked the fires to cook our breakfast, and the tears would come. My writing was rubbish—banal, sentimental trash. I never wrote fiction again.

My father wasn't entirely tyrannical. At times he was a glorious, glittering, gregarious man who drew people to himself by cords of their own obligation and neediness. Important people such as the mayor, the governor, and various state senators and congressmen attended the lavish parties my father hosted, and their longing for his approval seemed as great as my own. We all craved his respect and admiration more than light and air, knowing that only then would our lives have meaning.

It was possible to win my father's favor, and I strove with all my heart to do just that. But he doled out his words of approval like a miser handing out pennies to urchins. A grunt conveyed acceptance; a faint, grudging nod gave his endorsement; a near-smile appeared when his furrowed brow would smooth for a moment and his grim mouth would form into a straight, hard line instead of its usual down-turned snarl. I learned to recognize these as expressions of praise, and I sought to earn them as diligently as a monk seeks purity.

Since my father's one passion outside of politics and the courtroom was baseball, I took up the sport in high school. *"Will you come to my game, sir?"* I practiced pronouncing the words again and again, longing to ask him, but in the end I knew I'd never get past *"w . . . will"* or *"y . . . you"* without stuttering. Instead, I left copies of our game schedules where he was sure to find them. The entire season passed, his law practice and his political maneuverings keeping him too busy to come.

Then one miraculous day he finally did come. It was our team's last regular game of the season and we were tied with our school rival for the championship. That rivalry, which dated back to my father's years at the school, drew him from his office.

I nearly collapsed in a state of nerves when I saw him in the bleachers, but I quickly recovered when I recognized my long-awaited opportunity to make him proud of me. I played harder and better that afternoon than I'd ever played in my life, diving to the grass as I stretched to catch a ground ball; making a mad, sliding dash to steal third base; hitting a crucial single to bring in the run that tied the score. But I wasn't the star. Our pitcher, Paul Abbott, was clearly the star.

"That pitcher of yours is quite a player!" my father said at the dinner table that night. It was the first comment he'd made about the game. I waited for more, unconsciously holding my breath while he cut a piece of beef, then chewed it thoughtfully. "I'd say you have a long way to go to be as good as he is."

Devastating words. I'd wanted to hear just one word of praise—"Good job, son" or "I'm proud of you," but my best efforts at baseball had fallen well short of the mark. I never tried out for the team again. I valued my father's opinion above all others, and if he pronounced me a failure, then I saw myself as one.

During my sophomore year, one of my English teachers persuaded me to write for the school newspaper. "You write so beautifully—so flawlessly!" he insisted, and I lapped up his praise like a desert wanderer gulps water. I wrote for the school newspaper—careful, clean reporting that risked nothing of myself. I served as editor during my junior and senior years—the youngest student in the history of the school to earn that honor. My father never knew. I was terrified to tell him, terrified that he would pronounce my efforts rubbish and rob me of the worthiness I felt every time I saw my work, my name, in print.

My father's hold over me grew steadily stronger as I grew older. By the time I graduated from prep school, my life revolved around his like a planet in orbit around the sun, held captive to his will by the relentless pull of his personality. I would say anything, do anything he wished. I would attend the college he'd attended, I would study to prepare for law school, I would one day pursue a career in politics. My father blithely ignored the fact that someone who stuttered as badly as I did couldn't possibly succeed in either law or politics. He believed that by the sheer force of his will he could transform my tongue—his will had prevailed in everything else.

Writing courses were my favorites in college, and once

again I secretly wrote for the school newspaper. My father never saw the journalism awards I won. Away from his influence, caught up in the excitement and challenge of campus life, I experienced my first faint stirrings of confidence in myself. I could write well. It gave me enormous pleasure to write. I wanted to spend the rest of my life doing it. I hated all the courses that would prepare me for law school. The prospect of taking speech class struck terror in me. And so I returned home at the end of each school year to a dreaded summer job in my father's law office, determined to explain to him just how much I hated the idea of practicing law, determined to tell him the truth—I wanted to change my major to journalism.

The words never came. Back in my familiar orbit I became miserable at the thought of disappointing him. I needed his approval so badly I would do anything, say anything in order to get it. I silently returned to college each fall and continued preparing for law school.

I graduated with honors. At the commencement ceremony, I accepted my father's nod of approval like a starving man accepts moldy bread—hungering for more but grateful for whatever crumbs I could get. I'd been accepted into the same law school that he and my grandfather had attended. I would start in the fall.

I worked in their law office again that summer, and with my father involved in an important upcoming election campaign, I often worked extra hours stuffing envelopes at party headquarters. My father had never invited me to observe the secret political maneuverings that took place behind closed doors, but shortly before I started law school, he ushered me into his smoke-filled conference room one night. The sight of so many important men seated around the table awed me, but the amazing words that flowed out of my father's mouth that night struck me speechless.

"My son has a talent for writing," he told the other men. "He was the youngest student to ever serve as editor of his prep school newspaper, and his articles have won journalism awards in college. I think he's the man to help us."

I had to lean against the table to keep from falling over. He knew! My father had known all along about my writing, and he wasn't angry. But when he said the words I'd waited all my life to hear, it took my breath away.

"Yes, I'm very proud of my son."

He was proud of me! It was the first time in my life my father had ever praised me, and he praised me to his peers. I flew so close to the sun, basking in the warmth of his adulation, that the brightness blinded me to the truth of what came next.

"We need your help with something, son. . . ."

For the next several hours, my father and his cronies fed me slanderous information about one of their political opponents and I wrote everything down, sharpening and honing my prose until it became a lethal weapon. I willingly became their hit man, hired to assassinate their enemy's character.

Two days later my article appeared in leaflets that mysteriously appeared all over the city. Of course, my father and his party members could truthfully swear that they hadn't written those damning words—I had. As lawyers, they'd been careful not to be libelous, but my work was a masterpiece of innuendo and gossip that cast enough doubt in people's minds to ruin the opponent's reputation. He would lose his good name as well as the election.

What I had done horrified me. I had used words the way my father and grandfather did—corrupting them to hurt and deceive and destroy people. I'd prostituted the rules of good journalism, altering and shading the truth for power. I hated myself. But worse still, I hated my father. I'd allowed him to seduce me—violate me.

When I left home the following day, my father thought I'd gone to law school ten days early to settle in. Instead, I ran off to enlist in the army. I didn't write to him until after I'd completed my basic training, until it was much too late for even my powerful father or grandfather to change anything. I wanted nothing to do with officer's training, in spite of my college education. I joined the infantry with farm boys and immigrants' sons, hoping to lose myself in the great rank and file of enlisted men.

Seven months into my enlistment, on April 6, 1917, America entered the Great War. The army sent my friends and me to France to serve in the American Expeditionary Forces under General Pershing. They paraded us through Paris on the Fourth of July, then dispatched us to training camps to learn the realities of sandbag dugouts and mud-filled trenches—conditions we would soon experience on the Western front.

They issued me a 0.3-caliber Springfield rifle to fight the enemy, but I had no weapons against the despair and destruction of warfare—no defense against the realities of headless corpses strewn like mangled dolls, of cities and forests reduced to rubble and charred stumps, of children starving. I endured the horror of watching individual lives—men I knew and loved—become nothing more than impersonal "forces" sacrificed for military objectives. I knew I could have wrestled these images into manageable proportions by writing about them, but I had committed murder with my words and now I had to suffer the full punishment for my crime. I would purge my sins at the Battle of Cantigny on May 28, 1918, at Belleau Wood from June 4 to June 26, and at St. Mihiel on September 12. That was where

That was where Gabe's tale ended. It made upsetting bedtime reading. Added to everything else that had happened that day, I didn't sleep one wink.

Early the next morning I tiptoed downstairs to the kitchen to make a pot of coffee. The fall air was chilly, perfect weather for putting a blush on my apples, but it made me shiver at the thought of the coming winter. I threw a few sticks of wood into the stove to make a fire, and as I lowered the cast-iron lid into place again I thought of Gabe's story.

He must have heard me banging those lids shut every morning as he lay sick in my spare room. And if the story I'd read last night was true, the sound must have brought back painful memories. I recalled how Gabe had wept for his father the night his fever raged and had begged him for forgiveness. Tears came to my own eyes as I sat at the kitchen table, remembering how I'd left my own daddy in anger, too.

The spare-room door opened just then, and Aunt Batty came out. She wore her canary yellow sweater over her nightgown, and her hair stuck up every whichway. I must have looked just as tousled and bleary-eyed as she did because she came and stood beside my chair to hug me, resting her cheek on my hair.

"I didn't sleep very well either, Toots," she said. "I spent the whole night praying for that poor boy, praying that whatever it is that he's wrestling with, God will help him do the right thing."

I realized that Aunt Batty still didn't know everything I knew about Gabe. I hadn't told her what Sheriff Foster had said. I couldn't bring myself to say the words out loud yesterday. But Gabe had stolen Aunt Batty's heart, too. She had a right to know the truth about him. "You'd better sit down, Aunt Batty. I need to tell you something."

She silently poured herself a cup of coffee, then sat down at the table across from me, stirring the sugar around and around with a teaspoon. I drew a deep breath, just like Gabe used to do when getting ready for me to doctor his leg. Saying the words out loud would probably rip my wounds wide open again, too.

"The sheriff told me that Gabe used Matthew's name and his identity when he lived in Chicago. It seems Gabe knew all about Matthew—his birthday and his parents' names and everything else. I thought for sure he really was Matthew."

"No, didn't I tell you he wasn't? Matthew lost the tip of his finger when he was a boy and it always looked so ugly. Gabe had very nice hands, didn't he?"

I stared down at the tabletop, trying in vain to erase the image of Gabe's hands from my mind.

"The police are suspicious, Aunt Batty. They want to know what happened to the real Matthew. He disappeared and they think Gabe had something to do with it. I snooped in Gabe's bag and read some of his stories while he was still sick, and the sheriff was right—he knew all about Matthew Wyatt. He wrote about how Willie fell through the ice and died. And he described Frank Wyatt to a T. He knew that Frank wasn't Matthew's real father, too."

Aunt Batty pondered that for a moment before saying, "Maybe he met Matthew somewhere. Maybe Matthew told Gabe all those things."

"But why would Gabe steal Matthew's name and his identity? Sheriff Foster and Mr. Wakefield think he came here to steal the orchard from me."

She shook her head. "I don't believe that. Gabe never pretended to be Matthew when he lived with us. He told us he was Gabriel Harper, a writer . . . and he really was a writer. He let me read some of his pieces. What on earth would a journalist from Chicago do with an orchard?"

"I found another one of his stories last night," I told her. "He tried to burn it up in the workshop stove but it didn't catch fire. He must have written it within the last two weeks because I just bought that notebook for him. This story said that his father was a big-city lawyer who wanted to make him into a lawyer, too. But Gabe wanted to be a writer so he ran away and enlisted. I don't know if he's telling the truth this time or not."

Aunt Batty sighed. "I once wrote about being captured by headhunters in the jungles of Africa and I've never stepped one foot in Africa—much less met anyone who was interested in hunting my head."

"I just wish I knew the truth, that's all. Couldn't Gabe at least have told us the truth?"

Aunt Batty studied me for a long moment, her hands encircling her coffee cup. "You're in love with Gabe, aren't you, Toots?"

"No . . . yes . . . I don't know!"

"He loves you, too."

"How do you know that?"

"The same way I know you love him—it's written all over both of your faces. I saw you both trying to fight it. But you can't fight a force as strong as love. Walter and I tried and we failed miserably. I know Gabe must have had an awfully good reason to force him to leave you like this."

"It sure would help if I knew what that reason was. I didn't want to love him, Aunt Batty, because I was so afraid this would happen. God keeps teasing me, giving me what I long for and then snatching it all away again. My mama was right. She said love was just like cotton candy. It promises so many things, but when you try and take your fill, there's nothing there at all. Only a sweet, lingering taste—if you're one of the lucky ones. But I guess I'm not one of the lucky ones because right now love tastes pretty bitter to me. I've been thinking about it all night, and I've come to the conclusion that God must be punishing me for lying."

Aunt Batty looked at me as if she didn't believe I was capable of lying. "What did you lie about, Toots?"

Her faith in me stung my conscience like a hive full of angry bees. I knew it was high time I started telling the truth.

"Everything! I've been lying ever since I got off the train in Deer Springs ten years ago. Sheriff Foster says Gabe lied to me in order to steal the orchard from me, and if that's true, then it serves me right because I did the very same thing. I made Sam think I loved him so I could have a home here. I never told him the truth about myself, either. I'm an impostor, just like Gabe. And now God is paying me back for everything I've done. . . ."

PART VIII

Eliza's Story

New Orleans, 1904

"We are all strangers in a strange land, longing for home, but not quite knowing what or where home is. We glimpse it sometimes in our dreams, or as we turn a corner, and suddenly there is a strange, sweet familiarity that vanishes almost as soon as it comes."

MADELEINE L'ENGLE

— CHAPTER SIXTEEN —

The clearest memory I have of my mama is the day she took me to the circus when I was the same age as my Becky Jean. We had never gone anywhere before that day—only to the corner store and back, or to the big church on the next block once in a while. That was because my mama was very sick. Most days I would play alone in our room or watch people walk by on the street below my window while Mama slept, and I'd wait for her to wake up and fix me something to eat. She couldn't eat much herself and she had grown very thin. She would sit propped up in bed sipping her medicine while she watched me eat, and sometimes a big silvery tear would roll down her cheek.

The week before we went to the circus Mama had started having nightmares. She woke up screaming that she saw snakes in our room and horrible creatures crawling up our walls, and she scared me so bad I started having nightmares, too. But the day we went to the circus she got out of bed much earlier than usual and poured herself a glass of medicine and said, "How would y'all like to go to the circus, Sugarbaby?" I never have forgotten the velvety sound of Mama's voice or her slow, easy drawl.

"What's a circus?" I asked.

Tears swam in her eyes as she held her palm against my cheek. "My poor, sweet Sugar. Y'all don't even know what a circus is." She turned away and lit a cigarette, then crossed the room to her old steamer trunk. I loved our afternoons together when she would open that trunk and take out all her beautiful, shimmering costumes. They were made of smooth, silky cloth and covered all over with sequins and glitter and feathers and such. In one of the drawers Mama kept a little silver tiara, like a miniature crown, that glittered with make-believe diamonds. Whenever I felt sad or scared, Mama would take out that crown and let me wear it. She took it out that morning, too, and put it on my head. "My little angel," she whispered.

One compartment in her trunk held sheet music, all yellowed and brittle with age. Mama's hand shook as she sifted through the drawer, searching for something. I brushed cigarette ashes away as they fell on the pages, afraid they would catch on fire. When Mama didn't find what she wanted in that drawer she tried the next one, pulling out a handful of faded programs.

"See here? That's me, Sugar. Yvette Dupre. The Singing Angel."

I stared for a long time at the picture of my mama in a long, sparkly dress. She wore her coppery hair piled high on her head with the little silver crown nestled on top. She had been very beautiful before she got sick.

Mama turned the page to show me more pictures—a smiling man with a top hat and a cane, a funny-looking man with a big wooden doll on his lap. "I used to sing in the Vaudeville circuit," she said. "That's how I met your daddy."

I nodded as if I understood, but I didn't. She exhaled smoke, then dug through the stack of programs until she found one with a group of men dressed in funny-looking clothes.

"That's Henri—your daddy—right there. Handsome Henri Gerard."

I squinted for a better look, but the picture was so tiny I couldn't make out his face. Mama took another gulp of her medicine, then stared straight ahead for the longest time, her eyes empty and dark, her lips very pale. There was no life in her face at all, and that scared me. Sometimes she didn't seem to remember who I was.

I touched her hand. "Mama?" Her fingers felt as cold as the bars of the radiator when our heat was turned off.

She finally gazed at me, then at the programs in front of her. She looked as if she just woke up and had no idea where she was or how she got here.

"Mama?" I said again, pulling on her sleeve.

"Hmm?"

"Is this the place we're going to today?" I pointed to one of the leaflets.

"No, Sugarbaby. We're going to the circus." She suddenly came to life again, remembering, and sorted through all the programs until she found the one she wanted. It had a fancy design around the edge and red letters that had faded to rusty pink. Mama pointed to the picture on the front. "See there? That's an elephant, Sugarbaby. I know y'all never saw an elephant before, but they're just the most enormous things! See how tiny that woman looks beside it?"

The elephant's head looked like a snake. I felt afraid. "Will it eat me?"

"Why no, Sugar. It'll make you laugh. And see these clowns?

They'll make y'all laugh, too. And you'll see men swinging from little bitty swings, way up high in the air like monkeys, and . . . I just know y'all will love it." She took two more swallows of her medicine, draining the glass. When she set it down and crushed out her cigarette, I snuggled up to her. Mama drew me very close, holding me tighter than I ever remembered her holding me before, as if something awful might happen to both of us if she let go.

"You know I love you, don't you, Sugar?" she whispered. "You know I want to be a better mama, but . . . y'all understand that I'm . . . I'm not well?"

"Yes, Mama." In fact, she sometimes got so weak and wobbly she could hardly walk to the corner store for food or more medicine. The week before, she'd fallen coming up the stairs to our room and the lady who ran the boardinghouse had yelled and yelled at her. Said she would have thrown Mama out in the gutter where she belonged a long time ago if it weren't for me. I tried real hard to get Mama on her feet again but I couldn't do it alone. Finally one of the other boarders, a friend of Mama's, came and helped her up to our room. I didn't like that man. He had a lot of dark, coarse hair and spoke in a strange language with Mama, and he smelled like fish. But he helped her into bed that day and she slept for a long, long time.

Yes, I knew my mama was very sick. The medicine would make her better, stronger, for a little while. She would laugh and sometimes even sing, just like an angel, but when the bottle of amber liquid was gone, Mama would be sleepy and weak and scarcely able to talk again.

"You know I love you, don't you, Sugarbaby?" she whispered again. "If I didn't love you so much I wouldn't be taking y'all to the circus this afternoon, now, would I?"

We both got dressed in our Sunday clothes, and Mama put the

little crown on my head, fastening it real tight to my golden curls with hairpins so it wouldn't fall off. I felt like a princess. Mama drank one last dose of medicine for strength, then poured the rest of it into the little silver flask that she carried in her purse. We walked hand-in-hand to the corner where the streetcar stopped, then rode on it for a long, long way. When we finally got off, we walked some more until I saw a huge striped tent up ahead and heard the warble of the calliope and the excited rumble of voices.

The next few hours were the most wonderful ones I'd ever spent with my mama. I'd rarely seen her so happy and full of life, laughing and pointing to all the strange sights along the midway and in the side shows. When she saw how the cotton candy fascinated me, she gave me a nickel to buy some. It was sticky and sweet on my lips, but just when I expected to feel cotton in my mouth, it disappeared. I cried, thinking I must have done something wrong.

"Where did it go, Mama?"

"Oh, Sugarbaby, I'm so sorry. I should have warned y'all. It's supposed to melt in your mouth. That's what cotton candy does." She knelt in front of me to wipe away my tears with her handkerchief. Her smile faded and she got that scary, faraway look in her eyes for a moment. "And when y'all get a little older, you'll find out that's what love is like, too—just like cotton candy. Your mouth will water for it, and it will promise so many things, but when you try and take your fill of love, there'll be nothing there at all. Only a sweet, lingering taste—if you're one of the lucky ones."

I remember that the circus amazed me that day, but I can't honestly recall the magic of it anymore. In later years I saw the reality behind the false front—the clowns' painted-on smiles, the thrills that weren't thrilling at all once you knew how they were done—and after that, everything about the circus seemed phony and cheap. Even the man-eating tiger, which had frightened me so badly on that first day, proved to be as harmless as Queen Esther and Arabella.

What I do remember about that first trip to the circus was that there was so much going on all at once in those three rings that I didn't know where to look first. I didn't want to miss anything so I kept asking, "What are you watching now, Mama? Which one are you looking at?"

I remember the brassy music and the relentless excitement and my mama's beautiful laughter. I remember how she gasped when it seemed that one of the aerialists might fall, and how we both covered our eyes, then peeked between our fingers to discover that he hadn't really fallen after all. But what remains most vivid in my mind is the eerie way my mama kept looking at me with her sad, gray eyes, and touching my hair or my cheek with her ice-cold hands and saying, "You know that I love you, don't you, Sugar?"

When the show ended we sat on the bleachers listening to the band play until the tent was nearly empty. Mama's bottle of medicine was empty, too. I had seen her tip the little silver flask up real high so she could get the very last drop of it. Then she pulled out her compact and a tube of lipstick and she painted her lips scarlet, blotting them on a square of toilet tissue from her purse.

"Here's a kiss for you to keep, Sugarbaby." I tucked the fragile square into my pocket and kept that imprint of her lips for a long, long time—until it finally fell apart.

As soon as the music stopped, the roustabouts streamed into the tent, causing a great ruckus as they began dismantling the bleachers and circus rings. Mama stood and took my hand in hers.

"Eliza Rose Gerard, it's time for y'all to meet your daddy."

We walked across the empty circus rings, and when we stepped outside I was surprised to see everything stripped down already.

The sideshow tents, the cotton candy booth, the tent with the animals, even the ticket booths had vanished leaving a bare, trampled field where all the magic had been. Mama led me around
the back of the Big Top to a smaller tent where a group of circus
performers talked and laughed as they changed out of their costumes into ordinary clothes.

Then Mama pointed to the man who was my daddy.

He had bright red hair that stuck out in all directions and a
bulbous red nose to match. He wore baggy plaid trousers with
polka dot suspenders and a pair of shoes that seemed a mile long.
He was a clown. A foolish buffoon with the Bennett Brothers Circus.

Daddy sat on a little stool in front of a mirror, talking quietly
to another man as he wiped the white makeup and exaggerated
smile off his face. But he stopped—froze is really the right word
for it—when he looked up and saw my mother.

"Hello, Henri," she said. Mama was the only person I've ever
heard pronounce Daddy's name the French way. Everyone else
called him Henry.

"Yvette?" He sounded astonished and not at all sure it was
really her. I remembered how different Mama had looked when
she was called the Singing Angel, before she got so sick and
needed bottles and bottles of medicine. No wonder Daddy didn't
recognize her, thin as she was now.

Mama poked at her hair as if she could push it around and
make it beautiful again, as if she wished she still wore it piled high
on her head like in the picture. "Don't you know your own wife,
Henri?" she said with a tiny laugh. "Or your baby daughter?"

Daddy glanced at the other man, then back at Mama before
looking away. His cheeks turned nearly as scarlet as his hair. The
other man quickly stuffed his costume into a trunk and disappeared like some kind of magic act. Daddy fumbled to pull off his

nose and wig, then wiped off the last of his makeup with a towel before finally looking up at me. He tried to smile.

"She . . . she's grown since I saw her last."

"I should think so. Y'all have been gone more than two years, Henri. She'll be five years old on her next birthday, won't you, Sugarbaby?"

I didn't answer. I simply stared and stared at this stranger who was my daddy. Now that he'd taken his makeup off, I thought he was the most handsome man I'd ever seen—so different from all the men who came to our boardinghouse to visit Mama and bring her medicine. He had shiny black hair that he wore slicked back beneath his wig, and his shoulders looked very wide, his torso ramrod straight and muscular beneath his outlandish outfit. He still hadn't moved from where he sat when we first approached.

"What do you want, Yvette?" he asked. "Didn't you get the money I sent?" For a reason I couldn't understand, he seemed afraid of us.

"Is there someplace we could go and talk, Henri? I could use a cigarette."

Daddy stood and stripped off his costume and funny shoes, stuffing everything into one of the wardrobe trunks. He wore an undershirt and a normal pair of trousers beneath it. He never said one word as he put on his jacket and street shoes and led us across the trampled grass to a long line of rail cars, parked on a sidetrack at the edge of the field. Night had fallen and it was way past my bedtime. I don't remember much that happened after that because I was so worn out from all the excitement of the circus that I curled up on Daddy's tousled bunk and fell sound asleep while Mama and Daddy smoked cigarettes and talked and shared a bottle of her medicine.

The tiny train compartment was dark when I awoke. I didn't know where I was. I cried out in fright and Mama came out of the darkness and scooped me up in her arms. "You know I love you more than anything in the whole wide world, don't you, Sugar-baby?" she whispered.

I nodded and laid my head on her bare shoulder. She wrapped a blanket around me, then laid me down on the little banquette seat by the fold-down table where she and Daddy had sat earlier. "Go back to sleep now, Sugar." Her breath smelled like medicine as she kissed me. I went back to sleep.

The scream of a train whistle woke me next. I sat up and looked around the moonlit room. Instead of the familiar, cracked-plaster walls of the boardinghouse I saw the dark, wood-paneled walls of the train compartment. An overflowing ashtray and an empty bottle of Mama's medicine sat on the table alongside two sticky glasses. My daddy's jacket hung on a hook on the back of the door, but the rest of his clothes lay in a heap on the floor. The rail car lurched suddenly, then slowly began to move.

I looked around for my mother, but only my daddy lay sprawled on the rumpled bed. His head and one out-flung arm were all that showed above the sheet. The bottle and glasses on the table began to clink and rattle, then the entire room began rocking from side to side as the train gathered speed.

"Mama? Mama, where are you?" I called. Whenever I would wake up alone in our room at the boardinghouse, Mama always came running from somewhere down the hall as soon as I called her. This time she didn't come. The whistle shrieked again, a lone-some, mournful sound.

"Mama!" I wailed.

My daddy groaned and slowly sat up. He looked around grog-gily, then stared in disbelief when he saw me. "What the—! What are you doing here? Where's Yvette? Yvette!"

But it was useless for either one of us to call her. Mama had no place to hide in the tiny cubicle. I saw fear in Daddy's eyes, like

I had seen the night before. He tried to climb out of bed, winding the sheet around himself, but the movement of the train, racing at full speed now, made him unsteady on his feet. He fell back onto the bed again.

"Oh, God . . ." he moaned. "Yvette, how could you?"

"Where's my mama?" I cried.

Daddy scrubbed his face with his hands, then slowly lifted his head. "She left us. She's gone."

I was too young to understand death at the time, but a year or so later when Carlo fell off the high wire and died, and I heard his wife Bianca moaning and weeping, "He's gone . . . he's gone . . . how could he leave me," and crying out to God just like my daddy had that first morning, I finally understood that my mama had died of her terrible illness. She had vanished, never to be seen again, just like Carlo. The circus train had moved on to the next town leaving no trace of either of them.

Later still, when I learned all about heaven in a Lutheran church in Lima, Ohio, I knew that Jesus held my mama safe in His arms. I felt relieved that she would never be sick or wobbly-legged again. But on that first terrible morning as my daddy sat with his face in his hands, weeping for her, all I could do was cry along with him and hold on tight to Mama's silver tiara, which had fallen from my head during the night.

———

Daddy had no idea what to do with me. For the first three days he barely looked at me, let alone held me or consoled me. "Here . . . eat this," he would say, and he'd slide a plate of food across the table to me, pushing it with one finger. He took his own plate outside to eat on the rail car step with his back to me. I slept on the banquette seat as the train rattled and swayed through the night, then knelt on that same seat and watched out the window as farms and woods and towns streamed past in the early dawn light. I didn't leave the car for three days, still wearing the clothes Mama had dressed me in.

When the train stopped I would watch the city of tents go up in a vacant lot somewhere or in a farmer's field. "Stay here," Daddy said in his mad voice each morning as he left for clown alley to put on his costume and makeup. I knew there were probably tigers outside and elephants with heads that looked like snakes and I was too terrified to leave the car. Thank goodness Aunt Peanut finally took pity on me, or I don't know what might have become of me. She happened to walk by and see me looking out the window just as Daddy was leaving one morning.

"For crying out loud, Henry!" she said in her squeaky, midget voice. "You can't keep the kid cooped up in here for the rest of her life! She's a living, breathing human being! And your own flesh-and-blood, to boot!"

"You've got to help me, Peanut," Daddy begged. "I don't know what to do with her . . . or what she needs."

"Well, first of all she needs a little lovin' now and then, just like we all do." Aunt Peanut climbed up on the seat beside me and gathered me into her stubby arms. She was not much bigger than I was, a tiny creature with a woman's body and lipstick and rouge on her face. Such a grotesque stranger would have frightened me if I hadn't been so lonely for my mama. Longing for comfort, I hugged Peanut tightly and wept.

"See, Henry?" she said. "See? That's all the kid needs . . . just a little lovin'."

"Her mother's gone, Peanut, and I don't know what to do with her. Will you take her for me?"

"Take her? She's your daughter!"

"I know she's my daughter," Daddy said angrily, "but there's no room for her here, no place for her in my life."

"There's more room in here with you than there is in my sleeping car. You want her crowded in there with no light or air and bunks full of women stacked clear to the ceiling?"

"I don't want her here at all," he said, pacing in the tiny space. "A circus is no place to raise a child."

"Lazlo and Sylvia have children, and so do—"

"That's not what I mean. I know there are children here, but they'll all grow up to perform in the circus—they'll marry other performers. I don't want her to have a life like her mother's or mine. I want a real life for her, not one spent on the road ten months a year, living out of a steamer trunk."

Aunt Peanut stroked my hair. "That kind of life isn't going to fall out of the sky, Henry. You have to give it to her."

"I can't! *This* is what I do! I'm a circus clown, not a shop-keeper or a clerk in a bank. I had no intention of becoming a father. It happened by accident . . . so I married Yvette, and now she's gone and—"

"And you're a father," she said sharply. "And unless you're planning on leaving your kid in an orphanage somewhere, you're going to have to be a father to her, Henry."

"I don't know how!" he shouted. The sound made my skin prickle. It was one of only half a dozen times in my life that I ever recall my daddy shouting. Aunt Peanut released me and hopped off the banquette to go to him, laying her hand on his arm to soothe him.

"Didn't you have a father of your own?" she asked gently.

"He died when I was eight." Daddy snatched his derby off the table and jammed it onto his head. "I don't have time for this, Peanut. I'm going to be late for the parade, and I'm not even in costume yet." He yanked the door open.

"Just be the daddy you always wished you'd had, Henry."

Daddy froze in the doorway, then slowly turned to stare at her.

He looked as though he'd been slapped. "What did you say?"

"That's really all there is to it. If you wished your daddy had tucked you into bed at night, then tuck her in. If you wished your daddy had taken you on his knee and told you stories, then tell her stories."

He took his hat off, raked his fingers through his glossy hair a few times, then jammed it back on his head again. He seemed unable to speak.

"Teach her right from wrong, Henry. The Ten Commandments, the Golden Rule. You *have* heard of those, haven't you?"

"Yes . . . my mother was a good Christian woman." He spoke so softly I barely heard him. "She raised us by the Good Book. That's why I married Yvette after . . . when I found out she was in a family way."

"Then you'll do just fine," Aunt Peanut said, patting his arm. "Go on now, before you miss your wagon. I can probably skip the parade for once. I'll take the kid around with me today."

"No! Not to the freak show—"

"Why not?" She was suddenly angry. "If the circus is going to be her home, then she needs to learn that freaks like me are people, too. Or are you ashamed to have her meet your 'family,' Henry?"

"I'm sorry . . . I didn't mean—"

"Get out of here before I lose my temper."

She pointed her stubby finger at the door. Daddy left. Aunt Peanut packed an awful lot of explosive for a tiny little woman. But she also had a heart that was twice as big as most other people's. She reached for my hand.

"What's your name, honey?"

"Eliza Rose."

"Mmm. Your name is as pretty as you are. Come on, I'll show you around your new hometown."

I soon saw that it *was* like a town—a self-contained city of tents that magically moved from place to place during the night. There was the cookhouse where the chefs prepared all our meals; two dining tents, one for the performers and the other for the laborers; a wardrobe tent; a barbershop and laundry; tents for the elephants and other livestock; and a huge, elongated tent called the pad room, which had the men's and women's changing rooms on opposite ends and a stable for the performing horses in the middle.

These were the private areas of our tent city, but there were also public areas—the tents that were part of the show, such as the Big Top and the Midway. The marquee was the main entrance to the Big Top and the menagerie tent, where ticket holders could view all the exotic animals. The Midway had the sideshow tents on the left, the concession stands and ticket wagons on the right.

"My main job is here at the sideshow," Aunt Peanut explained that first day. She pointed to the bannerline that advertised the attractions inside the tent, and the huge picture of Peanut looked taller than she was. "I'm Queen Lily," she said with a humorless chuckle, "the world's tiniest woman and Queen of the Lilliputians. Then I change costumes for one of the clown routines with your father where I'm called 'Peanut'—but that comes later in the show."

She boosted me up on a little stage near the entrance to the tent. "Now you're on the bally platform," she said. "They'll stand one or two of us freaks out here to give the people a free look. That always makes them want to spend their money to come inside."

Aunt Peanut lifted me off the platform with a grunt and reached for my hand, but when I saw where she was about to lead me I stopped short. Mama had taken me inside the sideshow tent a few days ago and my first glimpse had frightened me so badly

I'd buried my head in her shoulder and refused to look.

"What's the matter, honey, you scared?" Aunt Peanut asked. "You don't need to be. The Abominable Snowman is really a dead stuffed Alaskan bear that's so old and moldy we have to keep pasting his fur back on." She took both my hands in hers and dragged me inside against my will, talking the whole time in her squeaky voice. "The two-headed calf was real once upon a time, but see? It's dead and stuffed, too."

"Is the snake real?" I whispered, hardly daring to look. A huge boa constrictor lay coiled in a glass box on the stage beside the calf, miles and miles of the scaly creature, as big around as a man's arm.

"Yeah, but it won't hurt you. Sylvia keeps it so well fed it just sleeps all the time. She drapes it all around herself for the show and the thing's as sluggish as the Mississippi. Let's go around to the back and I'll introduce you to the others."

I was glad to get out of that tent, but the little group of people standing in back, talking and smoking cigarettes, looked every bit as scary as the creatures inside.

"Hey, everybody, this is Henry Gerard's daughter," Aunt Peanut said. "Her name is Eliza Rose and she's going to be traveling with us for a while."

They all smiled at me and greeted me with, "Welcome, Eliza," and "Nice to have you, honey," but my heart pounded with fright as I tried to hide behind Aunt Peanut's skirts. Sylvia the snake woman was covered from head to toe with tattoos. Gloria the fat lady was the most enormous person I'd ever seen, with legs the size of tree trunks and a dress that could fit an elephant. One of the men in the group was so grotesque I hid my face. He had pure white hair on his pink scalp, and bulbous pink eyes, and skin that was nearly transparent. The bannerline claimed he came from a rare tribe of underground people, descendants from a marooned

spaceship from Mars, but I learned when I grew older that Albert
was really an albino. The only ordinary-looking person in the
whole group was the rubber lady—a contortionist who looked fine
standing still, but as soon as the sideshow started she would twist
her body into knots like a pretzel.

I longed to run back to the safety of my daddy's train compartment, but I didn't know my way through the maze of tents.
My new home and new family were so strangely bizarre they overwhelmed me. I'd never ventured more than a few blocks from the
boardinghouse with Mama, and up until she started having nightmares, my limited world had remained very safe. Now it seemed
as though I'd stepped inside one of Mama's nightmares.

"Goodness, you're shaking like a leaf!" Aunt Peanut said as
she tried to pry my fingers off her skirts. "I guess you can't stay
here with me, after all. If I went up on stage with you clinging to
me like this, they'd have to bill us as Siamese twins!"

I heard them all talking about me in low voices, asking Aunt
Peanut about my mama and trying to figure out who could take
care of me once the sideshow opened for business. They couldn't
seem to decide what should be done with me, and they argued for
such a long time that pretty soon we all heard the parade heading
back to the circus grounds.

"I guess I'd better take you back to your father," Aunt Peanut
finally said.

Daddy sat high atop a fancy parade wagon, pulled by a team
of four Percheron horses. I recognized him by the red nose and
wig and the gigantic shoes. He and the other clowns started climbing down as soon as the wagon came to a stop beside the pad
room. Daddy seemed startled when Aunt Peanut marched right
up to him with me in tow, as if he'd forgotten all about me.

"You were right, Henry," she said. "The sideshow scared her.
She'd better stay with you."

He looked as though he wanted to run away. His clown face was smiling but his real face wasn't. "Listen, I don't know—"

"And don't you dare lock her away in your compartment again!"

Aunt Peanut hoisted me up with a grunt and flung me at my father so suddenly that he had no choice but to catch me in his arms. Peanut turned to go.

"No, wait!" Daddy said. "What am I supposed to do with her?"

"Hold her, Henry," she called over her shoulder as she toddled away. "Just hold her!"

At first my daddy's arms were as cold and stiff as the stuffed Alaskan bear's in the sideshow, but as I buried my face against his chest and cried for my mama I felt his body slowly relax.

"I know... I know..." he murmured, and soon he wasn't simply holding me but hugging me, patting my back and gently rocking me to soothe my tears. He smelled of greasepaint and cigarettes and the Macassar oil he always used to slick back his real hair.

"Everything's going to be all right," he promised. "You don't need to cry. . . ."

— CHAPTER SEVENTEEN —

B ut I did cry. For days and days. It's a wonder Daddy's clown suit didn't sprout mildew. I clung to his baggy trousers so tightly he had no choice but to take me with him wherever he went. He hid me by his feet on the floor of the clown wagon during the parade, then seated me in a special chair beside the bandstand during the afternoon and evening performances. I watched the Bennett Brothers Circus perform over and over again until I knew every act and musical selection by heart.

Eventually the memories of my mother began to fade and my life slipped into its new routine. Early every morning the train would come to a halt and I would wake up in a new town to the shouts and whistles of the razorbacks as they unloaded the flatcars in a vacant field. They unloaded the cookhouse and wardrobe wagons first so that the performers could eat breakfast and get dressed for the parade. I'd go down to clown alley with Daddy after breakfast and watch him put on his clown suit, wig, and makeup. He drew big white circles around his eyes and mouth, then outlined them in black. By the time he'd painted on his smiling red lips and attached his buffoon nose, he no longer looked like my handsome daddy.

Meanwhile, the roustabouts and canvasmen would set up the tent city. I later heard a sermon in an Episcopalian church in Milwaukee about how Ezekiel spoke and the dead bones came to life and rose up and lived, and I thought it must have looked just like the bones of those tents coming together—first the skeleton, then a covering of canvas skin, then they were filled with music and wonder and life.

The first event in every town was always the parade. This gave the townsfolk a taste of what the circus had to offer and lured them to buy tickets to the Big Top. In most of the places we visited, the circus was the only entertainment people had all year and the town would pretty much shut down as if it were a holiday when we arrived. Where else could farmers who were tied to their land and their animals year-round see lions and elephants and dancing bears and giant snakes?

The big Percheron horses that had labored to unload the rail cars were quickly decked out in fancy plumes and glittering harnesses to pull the circus wagons in the parade. The bandmaster split his band in two, and half the musicians rode in the lead bandwagon while the other half rode in one of the tableau wagons in the middle of the line-up. These tableau wagons were covered all over with fancy carvings, brightly colored paint, and gold leaf to depict various fairy tales. When I grew older, Aunt Peanut dressed me up as Cinderella and I rode on one of the wagons, holding a glass slipper in one hand and waving to the crowd with the other. I had a lot of fun until Daddy put a stop to it. He said the cheers might go to my head and give me a taste for show business, which was the last thing in the world he wanted for me.

The clowns marched in the middle of the parade, pulling pranks and making everybody laugh. Sometimes Daddy walked down the street on a towering pair of stilts that made him look ten feet tall. The lions and tigers rolled by in their cage wagons, pulled by more horses, but Gunther only uncovered one or two of the cages for a peek so folks would be sure to come to the circus to see more. The elephants paraded near the end because they were the attraction that everyone was dying to see. The Gambrini family, who trained our elephants, dressed their three children in sparkling costumes and perched them on the elephants' backs to wave to all the people.

Last of all came the steam calliope, rolling down the street with a warble of organ pipes and the clash of drums, cymbals, xylophones, and bells. People would fall into step behind the calliope and follow us back to the circus grounds to see the show. They would have time to view Aunt Peanut's sideshow, to visit the menagerie tent, and to buy cotton candy and Cracker Jack before the afternoon performance began.

Daddy would take a short break to catch his breath after the parade and we would grab some lunch at the dining tent. But then the clowns would have to reassemble in the Big Top to entertain the children while the audience filed in for the shows. When the performance finally began, Daddy marched on his stilts again in the Grand Entry parade with the entire circus ensemble, then he came back four or five times throughout the show to perform his comic routines with the other clowns. It was their job to entertain the crowd while the workers cleaned up after the elephants and moved equipment in and out for the various acts. Daddy was also an expert stunt rider and he performed a clown routine with one of the show horses. He pretended that the horse had run wild with him hanging on for dear life, and he scared me half to death the first few times I saw him—riding backward, "falling" beneath the horse's belly, doing handstands on its back.

The circus performed two shows in most of the towns we visited, one in the afternoon and one in the evening. My daddy wouldn't get to sit down and take off his floppy shoes and makeup until the last audience had finally left the tent.

During the final performance, the roustabouts would take our tent city apart again and reload the train, saving the Big Top and pad room for last. They'd put everything on the train in the order we would need it in the next town, and as soon as they'd pulled the last tent stake everyone would board the train. We slept through the night as the locomotive hauled the five stock cars, ten flat cars, and four coaches to the next town, then we woke up the next morning and repeated the whole cycle all over again. When I heard a Sunday school teacher describe how the people in the Bible moved from place to place with their tents and their livestock, I thought for sure that Abraham, Isaac, and Jacob had traveled with the circus.

I slept on the banquette seat in my daddy's tiny compartment. Single men like Daddy usually bunked in the sleeping car with the other bachelors, rather than in a private compartment—the circus usually reserved those for their star performers and family acts. But the Bennett brothers regarded Daddy very highly, putting him in charge of all the other clowns, and he'd convinced them he needed space to plan out all the clowns' routines and to come up with new gags and acts. When I grew too big to sleep on the banquette seat, one of the carpenters built a fold-down bunk above Daddy's bed for me to sleep on.

After the last show my daddy needed time to unwind, so he usually went down to the pie car for a while every night to talk and relax and play a game of cards with the other performers. But he always listened to me say my prayers first, then tucked the covers tightly around me and said, "May the Lord keep His angels 'round about you."

By the time my first season with the Bennett Brothers' Circus ended and we returned to our winter home in Macon, Georgia, I no longer clung to my daddy day and night. To be honest, I'd grown sick to death of watching the same show over and over twice a day, and I'd begged him to let me stay outside in the "backyard" behind the Big Top instead. The other performers cheerfully shuttled me from tent to tent while Daddy worked, and there was always a willing pair of arms to hold me. They might belong to a clown or to an acrobat or a bareback rider, but some-one always watched out for me.

Eventually I felt at home everywhere, and everyone knew me and gave me little jobs to do. Gunther taught me how to water his lions and tigers without being afraid. Mr. Gambrini always took me along with his own three kids when his elephants went down to the river to cool off. He taught me how to swim and to ride on the elephants' backs. Lazlo taught me how to juggle, starting with two balls and working my way up to four. He taught me how to skip rope, too, only Lazlo could do it on a slack wire while I had to stay on the ground. Charlie the clown taught me how to ride a bicycle. He had a chimpanzee named Zippy who rode the bike as part of his act and Charlie sometimes paid me to "monkey-sit." The hardest part of monkey-sitting was keeping Zippy from smok-ing. He'd gotten hooked by watching the other performers smoke, and he picked up the cigarettes they tossed aside when their turn came to enter the Big Top. That chimpanzee could even blow smoke rings!

"Don't let him get his hands on any butts, Eliza," Charlie would warn when he left me in charge. "He's starting to get a smoker's cough." But Zippy was fast as lightning, and if I didn't get to the stubs first and crush them out, Zippy would snatch them right up and start puffing up a storm and there was no way on earth you could get the butts away from him after that.

Daddy taught me how to read when I grew older, then sent me to "school" with the other circus children for three hours every day. There were never more than a dozen or so of us, with our parents taking turns as teachers. Everyone except me had a part in his parents' acts and had to perform in two shows a day, so our education was pretty hit-and-miss. Once Daddy enrolled me in a regular school during the months our circus spent in Georgia. I hated it! I was so different from all the other kids that it was impossible for me to fit in and be accepted. I cried and stomped and fussed until Daddy finally gave up the idea. I went back to taking lessons with the other circus kids, in between training sessions as their families practiced their new acts for the coming season.

I longed to be part of my daddy's act—or any other act, for that matter. The Gambrini children wore spangled costumes and got to ride on the elephants' backs, grinning and spreading their arms gracefully as they showed off their skills. One elephant would lift little Angela Gambrini right up in the air on his trunk while she waved to the cheering crowd. Another family act trained the dogs and ponies, and their two young sons had learned how to put the animals through all their paces before they'd even learned how to read. The horseback riders balanced their kids high on their shoulders as they stood on the horse's back and galloped around the ring for the finale.

But Daddy absolutely refused to let me be part of the circus. When he caught Gina teaching me how to shinny up the rope she performed on, he chewed her out something awful, then wouldn't speak to her for a whole month. I offered to ride in the elephant act when the Gambrini kids caught the chicken pox and couldn't perform, but Daddy said, "Absolutely not!" But he was angriest of all the time I talked Charlie the clown into painting my face to look just like my father's. Daddy was furious with both of us.

"You're fired, Charlie!" he bellowed, "And you! You're washing that stuff off right *now!*" He dragged me to the washhouse by the scruff of the neck. I'd never seen him so angry.

"Why won't you let me be a clown?" I sobbed as he scrubbed my face clean. It's a wonder he didn't take off all my skin, too.

"You're grounded for a week!" he replied.

"So what? I'm grounded all the time, anyway! I have nothing to do all day, Daddy. Everyone's part of the show but me. Where do I fit in?"

"You don't. You're not part of this circus, and as long as I have anything to say about it, you never will be part of it!"

"But why?"

He finally stopped his merciless scrubbing and tossed me a towel. "Listen, I'm raising you here because I don't have a choice. But someday I want you to make a better life for yourself, away from this place."

I looked up at his scowling face and angry eyes, and I began to tremble. "You don't want me, do you, Daddy?"

"Of course I want you, but—"

"No, you don't. You've been wishing I'd go away ever since Mama died. She always told me how much she loved me, but you never do. You don't love me at all! The only person you care about is yourself!"

My words stunned him. The anger in his eyes turned to pain. "Eliza, if I didn't love you so much, I wouldn't be willing to let you go."

"That doesn't even make sense!"

"Yes, it does. Listen . . ." He fumbled for words, raking his fingers through his jet black hair. "If . . . if all I cared about was myself, then I'd be trying to make you over into my image. I'd want you to carry on in my footsteps and build some kind of a clown dynasty for me. But that's wrong. You're not me, you're your own unique person." He crouched in front of me, gently taking my shoulders. "There's a whole other world out there beyond the circus, Eliza. I don't want you to be a clown like me. I want you to be what you were meant to be."

"But . . . what was I meant to be, Daddy?"

He took the towel from my hands and carefully dried my tears with it. "I don't know, Eliza. That's something you'll have to find out for yourself."

———

I thought about my Daddy's words a lot after that, but I clearly recall the day everything changed forever for me, the day I no longer wanted to work in the circus. I was twelve years old and helping out in the concession booth outside the marquee when a young family came up to purchase some cotton candy. The mother had on a pretty blue-and-white dress and the father had on his Sunday shirt and trousers. He called her "dear" in a quiet, loving way as they bought cotton candy for their two children, a boy and a girl. The mother crouched beside the children and patiently helped them get the hang of eating it, smiling and laughing with them. But the father wasn't watching his children. Instead, he watched his wife's face, and the tenderness I saw in his eyes transformed his plain, rugged features.

When they went inside the menagerie tent, I left my post at the cotton candy booth to follow them. The father bought a bag of peanuts so his son could feed the elephants, but the boy was afraid to so the father lifted him up in his arms. The mother held the little girl's hand tightly as they looked at the tigers.

I had to hurry back to my booth, but when the show started I went inside the Big Top and searched the bleachers for that family. I didn't find them. Instead, I saw hundreds of families just like them—mothers and fathers and grandparents and children, all laughing and enjoying the circus together. The pain I felt was so excruciating I might as well have fallen from the high wire. It knocked the wind right out of me. For the first time in my life I knew I was missing something—a family—and I ached for one with all my heart.

When the show ended I stood by the main exit as the people streamed out, and I finally saw the little family again. The father carried his sleepy daughter in his arms while the mother held the little boy's hand. They would go home to the house they shared together, with a cozy kitchen, quilt-covered beds, and a warm stove in the parlor. They would wake up tomorrow and every morning in the same house, in the same small town where everyone knew their names.

I wandered out to my "backyard." The roustabouts had the city of tents almost completely dismantled and loaded onto the rail cars already. I saw Daddy in his goofy clown suit and floppy shoes and Aunt Peanut who was tiny enough for me to carry in my arms, and I hated them. For the first time in my life I longed for a real family, not the strange collection of circus people I'd grown up with.

That longing never went away. As the circus train traveled through the night, I would see warm lights glowing inside the homes we passed and I would grieve because I didn't live in one of those houses. The wail of the train whistle was a lonely sound that never failed to bring tears to my eyes. It meant moving on to another town, another state, where I'd be just a stranger passing through. Worse, I was part of a rowdy band of circus freaks, looked upon with suspicion and distrust wherever we went. The community locked all its doors whenever the circus came to town.

Day after day I watched the families who brought their children to the shows and I envied them—mothers and little girls in pretty dresses, fathers who bought Cracker Jack and cotton candy for their sons. And every chance I got, I begged my father to leave the circus so we could be a real family, too, and live in a real house instead of a train compartment.

But Daddy always sighed and said, "This is my job, Eliza. This is what I love to do." And the razorbacks would set the ramps in place behind the flatcars, and the colorful wagons would roll onto the train again, and the circus would move to the next town. And I would move with it.

———

Daddy wouldn't let me learn any circus tricks, but he did make sure that I learned some of the skills I would need in the outside world. I learned how to cook from the chefs at the cookhouse, and it's a good thing my husband had a big appetite because I'd learned to make everything in huge proportions. I learned how to sew from the wardrobe ladies, and when I became a teenager, Gina and Luisa taught me to use makeup and fix my hair. Charlie and the other clowns taught me to laugh at myself and at life. I'd handled a chimpanzee and elephants and even a trained bear, so I was never afraid of pigs and cows and chickens.

The sideshow people who once scared me so badly taught me not to look down on people who were different. "It's the heart that matters," Aunt Peanut taught me, "not what people look like on the outside. Some of the handsomest people in the world have hearts that stink worse than elephant manure."

I learned what it meant to stay flexible and roll with the punches as the circus weathered all sorts of crises—band members who suddenly quit between shows, roustabouts who got drunk and missed the train, horses with broken legs, and windstorms that blew rain into the wardrobe tent, soaking all the costumes. Even seasoned performers sometimes fell and injured themselves, or a catch might go wrong in the trapeze act and result in broken teeth and bruised jaws. When our star bareback rider broke her ankle, her brother put on a wig and dressed in drag to ride in her place. We coped with mud-mired fields and weeks of rain-canceled performances and paychecks that arrived late. We never had a train wreck, but we'd heard horror stories of other circuses that had, so the fear was always there.

My religious training was a patchwork quilt of beliefs, pieced together from a variety of denominations and sermons in churches scattered across America. We usually had Sunday off, and Daddy always made sure I went to church if he could find one nearby. I remember sitting on his lap in a rear pew when I was little, listening to the beautiful music and gentle prayers and wondering about this heavenly Father everyone always talked about. Surely He didn't wear a clown wig and floppy shoes. And the ministers all said He lived in a house with many rooms in a place called heaven, not in a train compartment.

One Sunday I came out of an Orthodox church after hearing a sermon about Adam and Eve, and I was madder than a hornet. I confronted my daddy with what I'd learned as he walked me back to the circus grounds.

"You're always telling me I have to do what the Good Book says, Daddy, but you don't do it! The Bible says it's not good for a man to live alone. That's why God made a helpmeet for Adam." I stomped my feet on the sidewalk for emphasis as I walked. The fact that I was all riled up seemed to amuse Daddy.

"I don't live alone," he chuckled, "I live with you—not to mention three or four dozen other performers."

"That's not what the Bible means and you know it! You need a wife, Daddy."

His smile faded. "I had a wife—your mother—and that didn't work out so good."

"Well, Mama is dead, and I think it's high time you got married again. I need a mother and you need a helpmeet. Why can't you marry Aunt Peanut—for real, this time?"

Daddy and Aunt Peanut got "married" during every performance. He walked around on stilts, and because he was so tall and she was so tiny it was impossible for him to kiss his new "bride." After Daddy would try three or four hilarious schemes that didn't work, the acrobats would finally come out and help the newlyweds by standing on each other's shoulders and lifting Peanut higher and higher until she and Daddy finally kissed and the audience cheered.

"You're joking, right?" Daddy asked. "You want me to marry *Peanut?*"

"Don't laugh! I love Aunt Peanut . . . and she loves you." He glanced at me with a worried look. "It's true, Daddy. She's always been crazy about you. If you weren't so busy flirting with Gina and Luisa and all the other pretty girls, you'd see how much she loves you."

"Well, I'm sorry," he sighed, "but I just don't feel the same way about her. She's a good friend, that's all. And besides, my love life is really no concern of yours."

We'd reached an intersection and I was so worked up I stepped out in the busy street without looking, right into the path of a rushing streetcar. Daddy stuck his arm out just in time and pulled me back.

"Hey! Watch out, Eliza!" The close call shook him. He crouched in front of me, gripping my shoulders. "Are you okay?" We were eye-to-eye and my usually cocky father looked pale.

"I'm fine." The near-miss barely fazed me. I wanted answers. "How come you didn't live with Mama when I was little?" I blurted out.

He stood again, shaking his head. We then continued walking, and I didn't think he would answer me, so it surprised me when he did.

"That marriage was a disaster right from the start," he said. "We met on the Vaudeville circuit, where your mother was the star singer, and Charlie and I did a comedy routine. Yvette claimed she loved me, but she always hated what I did, hated that I covered up my face with greasepaint and wore stupid clothes. She kept trying to change me, you know? Make me look for a different line of work. Then when she took to the bottle so bad, I kept trying to change her. That never works. You either accept each other the way you are or it's over. For us, it was over. I got a job with the Bennett Brothers and went on the road. She stayed in New Orleans with you. She said she didn't want to travel anymore."

As we approached another intersection Daddy reached for my hand. I guess the close call with the streetcar had scared him because it was one of the very few times that he ever did that.

"I'm telling you all this," he continued, "because I don't want you to mess up like your mother and I did. The Good Book is right—people shouldn't live alone. But you need to marry someone who's going to work together with you, Eliza, like a team, not someone who tries to change you. Watch how the Flying Falangas work together in their trapeze act sometime. They trust each other. They put their lives in each other's hands every day. And they're always there to catch the other person before they fall. That's what a husband and wife should have—teamwork and trust."

When I became a teenager Aunt Peanut decided I needed the company of other women to help guide me, so I moved out of Daddy's train compartment and into the women's sleeping car. The old Pullman car had been retired from passenger service and converted for use by the circus. There was nothing beautiful about those living quarters at all. The car was cramped and hot, with a narrow aisle down the center and bunks stacked two high and two across. Each berth had a pair of liver-colored curtains on rings that you could close for "privacy," but they didn't block out everyone's snores and giggles and tears. Or their secrets. I knew who was feuding, who was in love, and who was thinking of "blowing the show."

I felt all grown-up living on my own, and like the other women I bunked with, I began to take an interest in the opposite sex. I kissed a boy, one of the stable grooms, for the very first time one night when he walked me home to the women's sleeping car after the evening performance. I didn't think my daddy knew what I was up to any more now that I no longer lived with him, but I learned how wrong I was that night! We barely had time to duck behind the rail car for one little smooch before Daddy came charging around the corner with fire in his eyes. The poor boy took off running and I don't think he slowed down until he crossed the state line.

Meanwhile, my father dragged me off to his train compartment, corralling poor Aunt Peanut along the way. He was furious and I was scared. I had no idea what I had done wrong. I sat huddled beside Peanut on the banquette seat while Daddy paced the tiny room like one of Gunther's lions. He roared like one, too.

"What in blazes did you think you were doing? Guys like him are after only one thing, Eliza!"

He glared at me as if I should know exactly what that one thing was, but I was terribly naïve—and quite mystified. "What, Daddy? I don't have anything."

I was even more mystified when Daddy began to blush. "Tell her, Peanut," he mumbled.

"Oh no, you don't! That's your job, Henry." She hopped off

the banquette and headed for the door as fast as her tiny legs could go.

Daddy blocked her path. "Well, I'm asking you to help me."

"No way! I'm out of here!" Her voice squeaked even higher than usual.

They went back and forth like this until I felt ready to scream. "Tell me *what*!" I yelled, pounding my fist on the table.

Aunt Peanut finally relented. She booted Daddy out of the car and told me the facts of life. She finished her explanation by saying, "You see? Most boys won't bother to buy the cow if they're already getting the milk for free. Wait for a wedding ring, honey. Wait for Mr. Right."

I was disgusted with boys, my daddy, Aunt Peanut, and the world in general for several weeks.

———

Not long after my eighteenth birthday the circus played in New Orleans. I'd found out from Charlie that he and Daddy had grown up in New Orleans and that I used to live there with my mother. The last performance of a two-day run was about to start when Charlie came racing up to me at the concession booth where I worked. He was all out of breath.

"Where's your father, Eliza? Have you seen him?"

"No, not since lunchtime. Why?"

"The show's about to start! He already missed the preshow, and he's supposed to be lining up for the grand-entry parade right now!"

I couldn't believe it. "Daddy's . . . missing?"

"Yes! I've searched everywhere and I can't find him!"

I was suddenly very frightened. It wasn't like my daddy to be late for a show, much less miss one altogether. "I'll help you look for him," I said. I turned off the cotton candy machine, handed the cash box to the ticket-booth cashier, and took off at a run for the back lot, praying that something awful hadn't happened to him.

He wasn't in clown alley. He wasn't in the pad room either, and the horse he always rode in his stunt act was still tethered inside. The rail cars had been parked clear across the field from the Big Top, but I sprinted all the way over there when I ran out of other places to look. I bounded up to Daddy's compartment and flung open the door without even knocking, then stopped dead in my tracks in shock.

Daddy was there all right, sitting at the little table. And right beside him sat my mama. She wasn't dead at all! She looked just as thin and ill as she had the day she left me, thirteen years ago, but she was very much alive!

"Eliza? Sugar, is that you?" Mama asked. "Why, you're a beautiful young lady, Sugarbaby! Isn't she beautiful, Henri?"

Even if I hadn't recognized Mama's face I would have known her by that velvety drawl—and by the bottle of amber "medicine" on the table in front of her. I was almost too stunned to speak.

"Mama? You . . . you're *alive?*"

"Well, I think so, Sugar," she said with a little laugh. "At least I was the last time I looked."

I couldn't take it all in! If Mama was alive, then why had she gone away and left me here with Daddy? And why had my daddy lied to me all these years, making me think my mama was dead if she wasn't? I looked from one of them to the other, and the anger and betrayal grew inside me until my rage finally exploded.

"You lied to me, Daddy!"

"I didn't lie. I never said—"

"Yes, you did! You knew I thought Mama was dead, and you just kept on letting me think it was true!"

"Eliza, let me explain. . . ."

"No! Why should I believe a word you say? All this time you and Mama could have lived together and made a home for me so I would have a mother and a father like everyone else, but you were both too selfish!"

"That's not true—"

"You never wanted me! Neither one of you! Mama abandoned me on the doorstep because she didn't want me—"

"No, sugar, I loved you so much that—"

"And you didn't want me either, Daddy! You've been trying to get rid of me all these years, telling me to leave the circus and go out on my own. Well, you'll both get your wish! You'll never see me again!" I turned to run out the door and bumped smack into Charlie.

"There you are, Henry!" he cried. "What in blazes are you still doing here? Come on!"

Daddy bolted to his feet. "Holy smokes! What time is it?"

"You already missed the grand entry and it's almost time for your bareback routine. And look at you! Where's your face?"

Daddy's face was bare. His wig and red nose lay on his bunk beside the stained towel he'd used to wipe off all his greasepaint. He looked from Charlie to me, then to Mama, and I could see he felt torn.

"Fill in for me, Charlie," he begged. "I'm in the middle of something—"

"Are you crazy? I can't do that bareback routine, none of us can. We'll kill ourselves." He snatched up Daddy's wig and clown nose and shoved them into his hands. "Come on!"

"Eliza, please wait here for me," Daddy begged on his way out the door. "Give me a chance to explain. Talk to your mother for a while. I'll be back in half an hour, tops." He took off with Charlie, running across the field toward the Big Top.

I waited until they were out of earshot. "Good-bye, Mama," I said quietly.

"No, Sugar, wait!" She tried to stand but she was too wobbly—too drunk—to chase me.

I calmly walked back to the women's sleeping car, packed up everything I owned that wasn't already in the baggage car, and gathered all the money I'd saved from working at the concession stand. Then I left the Bennett Brothers' Circus for good.

The circus train was parked in a freight yard, so I had to walk almost a mile up the track through the rail yard to get to the passenger station. It was a huge, cavernous building, with so much space up by the ceiling that they could have had three or four trapeze acts and a couple of high-wire walkers up there at the same time. After living in cramped rail cars and tents all my life, I couldn't understand the waste of such a building. It made me feel very tiny, the way poor Aunt Peanut must feel all the time, living in a big person's world.

The station was a busy place, all lit up and bustling with people. Porters hauled huge carts of luggage to and fro, uniformed soldiers milled around looking lost, and exhausted families sat waiting on crowded benches, their babies wailing. I surveyed it all, wondering what to do, until I saw the window labeled "ticket sales," and a knot of people lined up in front of it. My feet made a sharp tapping sound that echoed on the marble floor as I walked over to the window.

"When does the next train leave?" I asked when it was finally my turn. The harried-looking agent behind the little window seemed distracted.

"Uh . . . the next train to where, miss?"

"Anywhere! I don't care. I just want the very next train."

He looked up at me for the first time and stroked his walrus mustache. "Listen, you look like a nice young lady. If you're thinking of running away from home, I'm sure that your family—"

The word *family* made me cold with fury. "I don't have a family," I said. "I'm not a child, I'm eighteen. Now please do your job and tell me when the next train leaves."

I realized after I had kids of my own that the man was just trying to keep me from making a big mistake, but at the time he seemed like a busybody. He took his time answering my question, stroking his mustache like he was petting a dog.

"Well, the train sitting on track five leaves in ten minutes," he said slowly. "It's northbound for Memphis, Louisville, Indianapolis, and points north."

I laid some of my money on the counter. "Kindly give me a ticket for as far as this will take me."

The ticket agent did not look happy. He kept glancing up at me as if memorizing the details of what I looked like and how I was dressed in case someone sent the police after me. But I knew my daddy wouldn't do that. The circus train would probably be in Arkansas before he even figured out I was missing.

"Do you have any baggage to check, miss?" the agent asked.

"I'd like to keep my suitcase with me, thank you."

I had already decided that I would watch out the window until I saw a town I liked and then just step off the train when it stopped there. It might be any one of the thousands of towns I'd traveled through over the years, towns I'd begged Daddy to settle down in. My dream house would be in a quiet little village where all my neighbors knew me and greeted me by name.

As soon as the agent handed me my ticket, I hurried down to track five and climbed aboard. I found my seat in the coach section and set my suitcase down by my feet, glad to see an empty seat beside mine. Five minutes later the train lurched forward, then slowly rolled out of the station. We passed The Bennett Brothers' Circus train on a sidetrack a few minutes later and quickly left it far behind.

━ CHAPTER EIGHTEEN ━

I think deep down I'd always known the truth—that my mother hadn't died, but had abandoned me like a litter of unwanted kittens along a country road. I hadn't wanted to face the truth. To admit what I was finally forced to face would have meant facing the why of it—why had she abandoned me? What was wrong with me that had made her turn her back and walk away from me when I was only four years old?

As I stared out of the train window that long, lonely afternoon, I was determined to put the past behind me forever. I would begin a new life and never look back. I convinced myself that I was just like the brave heroines in Betsy Gibson's books. They were often orphaned and stepping out in the world on their own, but I had a big advantage over them because I had "been around the block," as they say, having traveled with the circus. It didn't scare me one bit to travel by train across an unknown land. And I couldn't get homesick for a home I never had, could I? I didn't know the name of the town I was searching for, but I was sure I would recognize it as soon as I saw it.

I searched all that first afternoon with no luck, then slept on the train that night, the motion rocking me to sleep as it had for most of my life. I kept watching out the window all the next day, too. Then late in the afternoon on the third day, we finally began passing through little villages like the one I had dreamt of for years. In between these towns were farmland and fruit orchards and fenced pastures with dairy cows. I saw trees for my children to climb someday and country lanes to stroll down with the man I loved on Sunday afternoons.

When the train rolled into Deer Springs, I grabbed my suitcase and stepped off. I later learned that the passenger train only stopped there twice a week, on Tuesdays and Thursdays, so it was really my lucky day to be on one of the very few trains that stopped. The little town looked perfect, even before I saw the "help wanted" sign in the window of the diner across from the railroad station.

I didn't waste any time at all crossing the street and heading into that diner. I walked right up to Ethel Peterson, who sat at the cash register, and said, "I see by the sign in the window that you're looking for help."

Ethel was nearly as large as Gloria the fat lady had been, so I was counting on her to be just as jolly. But she eyed me suspiciously. "Well, that depends," she said. "Who might you be?"

"My name is Eliza Rose Gerard, ma'am, and I just moved to town. I'm looking for work."

"You have kinfolk here in Deer Springs?"

That's when all the lying began. I knew that if I told the truth about growing up in the circus, I would be branded a wild woman with loose morals, because that's the reputation circus people had. If I told them my daddy was a clown and my mama was a drunk, I would never have a chance for the respectable life I dreamed of having. I made up my mind to lie—and once you start lying, you can never stop, of course.

"I don't have kinfolk anywhere," I said, in a pitiful sort of voice. "My mama, daddy, and two sisters all died in the influenza epidemic last fall. In fact, I pretty nearly died myself. I decided to move somewhere and start a new life because the memories were just too painful to bear. I could really use the work, ma'am, if you're still looking for somebody."

I knew I had to change the subject fast before she had a chance to ask where my home had been. Fortunately it was close to suppertime and the restaurant started getting a little busy just then, so Ethel didn't have a lot of time to question me.

"How're you at figuring?" She handed me a pencil and one of the waitress's receipts to add up. I had always been good at arithmetic, thanks to my daddy, so there was nothing to it.

"It comes to one dollar and thirty cents," I told her, adding it in my head.

She opened the cash drawer and pointed. "Suppose a customer gave you two dollars. Can you make change?"

This was easy, seeing as I had sold cotton candy and peanuts from time to time. I made change so quickly and confidently that Ethel was impressed.

"Do you know how to wait tables?" she asked.

"Oh yes, ma'am," I lied. "Of course I do."

"See that fellow in the suit, sitting at the counter? Go on over and take his order. I'll be watching to see how you do."

A dapper-looking man in his late twenties sat all alone at the counter, drumming his fingers and staring down at the menu like he was trying to make up his mind. He was dressed like a city-slicker in a plaid double-breasted suit, and he looked out of place among the plainer folks in the diner. I noticed a large square sample-case by his feet and guessed that he was a traveling salesman.

It's all an act, I told myself as I took the order pad from Ethel and walked over to him. That's what Aunt Peanut had told me often enough. *"Make people laugh even when you're sad, act entertaining even when your heart is breaking. The show must go on."* I would simply play the part of a waitress.

"Hi, there," I said with a smile. "What can I get for you today, sir?"

My smile was wasted on him. He had his nose stuck in the menu and didn't even notice that I wore the same skirt and blouse I'd worn for three days instead of a pink-and-white uniform like all the other waitresses. He didn't seem to notice me at all, in fact.

"How's the special tonight?" he asked without looking up.

My confidence teetered and swayed like a dizzy aerialist. I didn't know what a "special" was. I took a deep breath and smiled to push back my tears, then spoke softly so Ethel wouldn't hear me.

"Listen, mister. I don't know anything at all about tonight's special. I'm not even sure I know what you're talking about. I'm new in town and I need a job. That lady over there told me to wait on you and if I do a good job I think she might hire me. Could you please help me out and pick something easy? It would mean a lot to me."

His head jerked up as I spoke and I hoped that Ethel couldn't see the astonished look on his face. It took a moment for him to digest all that I'd said, but when he'd finally sorted it all out he gave me a great big smile.

"Sure thing, doll face," he said. "I'll have the meat loaf dinner with mashed potatoes. Just write number two on the order slip, then take it over to the window behind you and stick it on one of those spikes. The chef will dish it up fast because the meat and potatoes are already cooked. In the meantime," he continued, turning his coffee cup over, "you can pour me a cup of coffee from that pot right over there, and pass me the cream pitcher and the catsup bottle."

"How can I ever thank you?" I said when I returned to fill his cup, my hands shaking.

"Whoa, take it easy, doll face. Pour slowly so you don't spill any. There you go. You're doing just great."

I set the coffeepot back on the hot plate and fetched him the catsup bottle and the cream pitcher, just like he told me to. "Do you think she can tell I'm nervous?" I asked.

"Naw, you've got such a pretty smile on your face . . . and people don't usually smile if they're nervous. By the way, my name is Harry Porterfield. What's yours?"

"Eliza Rose Gerard."

"That's a real pretty name, just like your smile. All right, Eliza, turn around like you're watching for my food and you'll see the cook set my plate up there in another minute or two."

I glanced casually over my shoulder just in time to see the sweating, red-faced cook set a plate in the little window between the counter and the kitchen. It had meat loaf, mashed potatoes, and green beans on it. I picked it up with two hands and carefully carried it over to my new friend.

"Now how did you know it would be there?" I asked as I set it in front of him. He laughed.

"I eat here every time I come to Deer Springs on my sales route. Hey, don't look now, doll face, but here comes Ethel. Good luck to you."

She waddled over to me on legs the size of an elephant's. Her shoes looked much too small for her swollen feet. "The job is yours if you want it," she wheezed. "You can start with the break-fast shift tomorrow morning. Be here at five A.M. sharp."

I felt so happy I floated out of the diner on wings, then stood outside for a moment gazing at my new hometown. All kinds of people walked up and down the sidewalks, hurrying in and out of stores, driving past me in wagons and cars—but still, Deer Springs seemed quiet and peaceful compared to the noisy hullabaloo of the circus. When I spotted a bench in front of the train station, I crossed the street to sit down on it. I felt so happy to be "home," I would have been content to sleep right out there on the bench in front of the train station all night.

I was still sitting there, happy as pie, when Harry Porterfield crossed the street and sat down on the bench beside me. "Congratulations, doll face. I heard Ethel say you got the job."

"I'm very grateful for your help, Mr. Porterfield."

"Hey, call me Harry. And she would have hired you even without my help. A pretty new face like yours will be good for business, don't you know?" I felt myself blushing. "Say, doll face, you going to sit right here until the diner opens tomorrow morning?"

"I might have to unless there's a hotel nearby that doesn't cost too much."

"Why didn't you tell me you needed a place to stay? There aren't any hotels in Deer Springs, but Miss Hansen down on Willow Avenue lets out rooms. That's where I always bunk. Come on, I'll show you."

He picked up his sample case and valise in one hand and my suitcase in the other, then motioned with a tilt of his head for me to follow him.

Miss Hansen was a tall, stringy woman with an unpleasant frown. "I don't want any hanky-panky in my establishment, Mr. Porterfield," she said when she saw the two of us. "I appreciate your business, as always, but I won't be a party to any hanky-panky."

"Why, Miss Hansen! I'm hurt that you would think such a

thing of me—let alone think it of this fine young woman here."

She snorted just like the horse Daddy used to ride in his act. "Humph! What kind of a respectable young woman runs around with a traveling salesman?"

"But I just met Mr. Porterfield in the diner a few minutes ago," I said in my own defense. "I asked him if he knew of a place to stay."

Apparently my answer made matters worse. Miss Hansen snorted again. "What kind of a respectable young woman travels all alone without a chaperone?"

They both looked at me, expecting an answer. All I had to do was mention the circus and any doubt about my respectability would fly right out the door—with my suitcase and me flying right out behind it.

"I'm an orphan, ma'am," I said, looking sad. "My family died in the influenza epidemic and I've been living with my maiden aunt ever since. But when she died in a fire a few weeks ago, I just couldn't bear all the painful memories back home and so I came here to start a new life. I just got a job at the diner. I start tomorrow morning and—"

"That's true, Miss Hansen," Harry said. "I ate dinner there tonight and I heard Ethel say the job was hers."

Miss Hansen reluctantly showed me to my room. I gasped in astonishment when I saw it. "Oh, it's beautiful! And it's so big!"

I'd been squeezed like a sardine into a tiny train compartment with my daddy for most of my life, and I'd had even less elbow room in the women's sleeping car. I couldn't get over all the wide open space between the bed and the bureau, between the bureau and the door, between the bed and the wall. There was even a pretty little dressing table with a ruffled skirt and a big square mirror that I'd have all to myself. Miss Hansen eyed me very curiously as I gazed around the room as if it were a palace.

"It's not a big room," she said. "I have much bigger ones— for couples, you know."

"This is beautiful. Thank you so much, Miss Hansen."

She put Harry in a room upstairs and me in a bedroom right next door to her own. I think she stayed awake all night, listening for hanky-panky. My bed was huge and comfortable, but I barely slept. Except for the winter months, this was one of the few times in my life I hadn't slept on a moving train and I couldn't get used to the stillness. I missed the comforting clatter of the wheels on the rails, the gentle rocking from side to side. I refused to cry over my treasonous parents, but I did weep for Aunt Peanut—and for Sylvia and Lazlo, and for the Gambrini family, and for Charlie and Zippy, and all the other people in my circus family. But when it was time to get dressed and go to work at the diner the next morning, I dried my eyes and began the first day of my new life in Deer Springs.

Harry showed up for breakfast around seven-thirty and gave me a boost of confidence right when I needed it. "You're doing great, doll face . . . and you look like a million dollars in that uniform."

"I never knew there were so many different ways to cook an egg," I told him. "Seems like everyone I've waited on this morning has wanted theirs a different way." I started to say that the circus cooks only knew how to make scrambled eggs, but I caught myself just in time.

"May I treat you to dinner tonight?" Harry asked when I brought him his check. He was a nice-looking man and smartly dressed, but he seemed a bit flabby compared to the well-muscled acrobats and aerialists I'd grown up with. Even the roustabouts and razorbacks had more going for them than poor, pasty-skinned Harry did.

"Thanks, Harry, but I don't think—"

"Please? I know you don't know a soul in this town and I hate the thought of you eating all alone."

I finally agreed, mainly because I didn't know how to refuse. We ate at the diner of course, since it was the only decent place in town. I could tell that Harry was already getting sweet on me when he tried to hold my hand as we walked back to the rooming house. I shook my head and stuck my hands in my pockets. When we reached the front porch he asked me to sit down with him for a few minutes.

"I have to leave on the train tomorrow," he said, "but I'll be back in town in a few weeks. I'd like to see you again, Eliza."

I pondered what to say as I watched a cat run across the street. A little boy sped past on his bicycle. "Let me ask you a question, Harry," I finally said. "Do you like being a traveling salesman?"

"I sure do. It's a great way to travel around and see the country, meet new people. . . . I grew up in a cramped little town like this one, so I was chomping at the bit to get away. This sales job was my golden opportunity. Why do you ask, doll face?"

"Because all I've ever wanted was to have a home and a family and to settle down in a nice little town like Deer Springs."

"You're kidding! I'd die of claustrophobia here!"

"Then I guess we don't have a whole lot in common, do we?" I rose to my feet. "Good night, Harry. And thanks again for dinner."

———

Getting off that train all alone in Deer Springs was about the bravest thing I've ever done. It shows you how badly I wanted that kind of a life. I'd learned how to put on a show and tell lies in the circus, where the man-eating tiger was a pussycat, the Abominable Snowman was a moldy old bear, and the clowns painted on their smiles, so I just faked everything I did. After handling a chainsmoking chimpanzee, unruly customers didn't bother me much. Lazlo had taught me to juggle four balls by the time I was ten years old, so getting the hang of waiting on a half-dozen tables seemed easy after that. Charlie the clown had his heart broken when Veronica ran off with an acrobat, but he still made the audience laugh. And Bianca's nerves went all to pieces after Carlo had his accident on the high wire, but the show still went on. That's how I nerved myself for everything I did—getting off the train, walking into the diner and asking for a job—and taking up with Sam Wyatt.

Sam came into the diner all the time, usually for breakfast, sometimes for supper, and once in a while for all three meals. He always sat hunched in a booth by himself with an invisible cloud of sadness all around him that looked as though it might rain all over you if you got too close. He was about three or four years older than me, and I guessed by his bib overalls, his muscular build, and his deeply tanned skin that he was probably a hired hand on one of the neighboring farms—except it was a mystery to me how a farmhand could afford to eat in a diner all the time.

Sam was so handsome it was all I could do to keep from staring at him whenever he came in. His solemn face and square jaw had a lot of character, and he had the fairest hair and bluest eyes I'd ever seen. I smiled and tried to be friendly whenever I waited on him, but he held me at arm's length without ever moving a muscle. He rarely looked up, and when he did he never made eye contact. In fact, he never spoke one word more than he had to in order to get his food and pay his check. He acted as though he didn't want anyone to notice him, like he wanted to blend into the booth and disappear.

"Who is he?" I finally asked another waitress named Debbie. "I've noticed he comes in here a lot."

Debbie pulled me aside into the kitchen as if it were dangerous to be caught talking about him out loud. "That's Sam Wyatt," she whispered. "He went to school here in Deer Springs with my older brothers. They always said he was a little . . . strange. All the Wyatts are."

"Strange? How so?"

"You know, kind of quiet . . . mysterious. Sam never used to hang around much with the other kids, only with his older brother, Matthew."

"Doesn't he have a wife or a mother to feed him?"

"Sam's not married!" Debbie reacted as if the idea was outrageous. "He runs Wyatt Orchards with his father. There's just the two of them there now, since his mother died. His two brothers are both gone, too. I don't know who's feeding his father, but Sam comes in here every couple of days to get a decent meal."

"Where did you say he lives?"

Debbie's eyebrows went up in surprise. "You haven't heard of Wyatt Orchards? It's the biggest spread in the county. If you take Spruce Road straight out of town for about two or three miles, you can't miss it."

I went for a walk down Spruce Road the following Sunday afternoon on my day off, determined to find out where the mysterious Sam Wyatt lived. Debbie was right—you couldn't miss the huge sign painted on the side of the barn: *Wyatt Orchards—Frank Wyatt & Sons, Proprietors.* I didn't care a fig about the orchard, but I took one look at that beautiful house with the wide front porch and the dark green shutters and the big oak trees all around it and I knew that I'd found the home I'd longed for all my life. I had to live there. I would live there. All I needed to do was win Sam Wyatt's heart.

With only three churches in town, it wasn't hard to find out which one he attended. I went up to him after the service the following Sunday morning, acting like his long-lost friend.

"Well, hey there . . . remember me? I wait on you at the diner sometimes. My name's Eliza Rose. What's yours?"

"Sam," he said, staring at the floor. "Sam Wyatt."

"Nice to finally meet you, Sam." I stuck out my hand and he had no choice but to shake it. He turned as red as my daddy's nose, then excused himself and hurried away the first chance he got.

Breaking through all the barriers Sam had built up was one of the hardest things I'd ever done. It took me more than six months to do it, too. I felt like I was walking the high wire, trying to keep my balance between being too friendly and not friendly enough, and I knew that one little mistake might send me tumbling. But I just kept a picture of that beautiful house in my mind and thought about it every time Sam brushed me aside. I kept working on him, kept smiling and acting friendly in the diner and throwing myself in his path at church. It was like taming a skittish animal, first getting him used to me, then winning his trust and confidence, until finally he was eating out of my hand.

When Sam came into the diner for supper one Friday night I gathered up all my nerve to take the next step. "Hey, Sam, how come I never see you at the picture show?" I leaned on his table so our faces were real close. "Don't you ever go?"

He glanced up at me, then looked away. "Um . . . no."

"Oh, you should go sometime! There's a real exciting Tarzan serial playing right now, in fact. And I'll bet you'd like Lillian Gish's movies, too. All the fellows like Lillian Gish. I'm going to the seven-thirty show tonight. Why don't you meet me there and find out what you're missing?"

He was silent for such a long time I thought sure he'd refuse, but he finally looked up and said, "All right."

I was surprised, but very pleased. We met outside the Ritz, and we each bought our own tickets and popcorn that first time. But afterward Sam said he'd enjoyed the picture show very much and that he'd like to go again sometime. That gave me the courage to take the next step.

"Say, Sam, would you mind walking me home? I get spooked sometimes, walking all alone in the dark. It's not far. I'm staying at Miss Hansen's rooming house over on Willow."

He agreed, and it seemed to me that he stood up a little bit taller at the idea of protecting me. I took advantage of our time together to get him talking about his orchard.

"What kind of work do you do, Sam?"

"I run an orchard with my father."

"Do you like it?" I asked.

"I've never thought about it," he said with a shrug. "Farming is all I know. What else would I do?"

At first, talking to Sam was like trying to pump a dry well. But as slowly as the changing seasons, Sam finally started loosening up. Pretty soon he was watching me in the diner instead of gazing down at the tabletop. Then I noticed him staring across the aisle at me in church instead of at his hymnal. He had that moonstruck look about him, and I could feel his eyes on me like two beams of light. One night I kissed him in the dark in the movie theater. Rudolf Valentino was kissing his leading lady, so I just turned to Sam, took his freshly-shaven face in my hands, and kissed him. Sam must have liked it a lot because he didn't wait for me to make the first move after that.

But I wasn't the only one who'd noticed Sam's growing interest in me. Frank Wyatt descended on Sam and me as we stood talking together after church one day and it was just like the plague of darkness the Bible always talks about. One minute Sam and I were laughing and the next minute Frank seemed to blot out the sun.

From the very first time I met Sam's father he scared me to

death. He seemed like such a cold, heartless man—and my opinion of him didn't change once I got to know him, either. On the
very first Sunday he met me he started giving me the third de-
gree—who was I, and where did I come from, and what was I
doing in Deer Springs? I knew I could never tell him the truth.

"My family died in the influenza epidemic, Mr. Wyatt."

"You say your name's 'Gerard'? What kind of a name is that?"

"French, I think. My daddy was born in New Orleans."

"New Orleans! What kind of work did your father do there?"

I pictured my daddy in whiteface with his red wig and bulbous
nose and gigantic shoes, and tears sprang to my eyes. I told myself
I was crying because I was scared of Frank, not because I missed
my daddy. Sam saw my tears and mistook my reaction for grief.

"It's still hard for Eliza to talk about her family," he told his
father. He pulled a bandana handkerchief from his pocket and
handed it to me as he steered me away from Frank. "I'm sorry
about my father," he whispered.

"I don't think he likes me."

"He doesn't like anybody, Eliza. He acts that way with everyone."

I knew Frank Wyatt wasn't satisfied with the way I'd answered
his questions, so I began embroidering my lies, thinking up a respectable profession for my daddy and rehearsing all the details
about where Daddy was educated and where we used to live so I'd
be ready the next time Frank questioned me. I didn't want to ruin
my chances to live in that beautiful house by the orchard.

By this time Sam was calling on me regularly at the rooming
house. He told me later that he was drawn to me because I was so
mysterious and exotic, and I seemed to have a knowledge of the
world that he didn't have. I liked Sam, but I never really got to
know him very well. Every time I looked into his blue eyes I saw a
lot of sorrow and pain in them. Even after all the time we spent

together, I still had no idea who he really was or what caused the sadness. In many ways, Sam remained a stranger to me, and since I was lying through my teeth about who I was, I guess I was a stranger to him, too.

After we went out together regularly for about three months and kissed all the time in the movie theater, I decided to take our courtship to the next stage. But just like that first kiss, I knew I'd have to make the first move.

"I think I'm falling in love with you," I said one night as we cuddled on Miss Hansen's porch swing. Even in the dark I saw the surprise in his eyes.

"You love . . . me?"

"Yes," I lied. "Why does that surprise you so much?"

"You're pretty as a picture, Eliza. I never thought I'd be lucky enough to have such a pretty girl fall for me."

"Well. . . ? Do you love me, too, Sam Wyatt?"

He looked me right in the eyes and I saw the truth even before he said it. "Yes," he whispered. "Yes, I do. More than I know how to say."

I can't tell you how guilty his confession made me feel. I'd coaxed him and tamed him and wormed my way into his life over the last several months until he'd lost his heart completely to me. I was probably the only person who had ever told Sam they loved him and it was all an act on my part. I liked Sam, I felt sorry for him, but I wasn't in love with him. Still, I pushed the guilt aside and said, "You know what, Sam? I'd marry you in a heartbeat if you asked me to."

He appeared stunned. "My father would never give us his permission."

I nuzzled his ear. "Aren't you old enough to make up your own mind?"

"Yes, but . . ."

"Well, I don't mind eloping. What could your father do about it after the fact?"

"I don't know." He released me and his arms fell to his lap as he leaned back against the swing. "I don't know," he repeated.

Sam was terrified of his father. I could see it, plain as day. I would have to do something to take his mind off his fear. I gave him a few days to think about the idea of marriage because I'd learned that Sam liked to think things through before he acted. Then, as we cuddled on the porch a week later, I tried again.

"I love you, Sam," I whispered. "If we were married we wouldn't have to say good-night when Miss Hansen turns off the porch lights. We could keep right on kissing all night, just like this . . ." I took his face in my hands and gave him the steamiest kiss he'd ever had in his life. After that, all thoughts of his father went up in smoke.

Eloping with me was the only act of rebellion in Sam's entire life. We honeymooned in a hotel room across the state line, and I don't think he worried about his father even once that night. But the next day. . . !

The next day Sam was shaking in his boots when he took me home. He was a big man, every bit as big and as strong as his father, but we both had jelly knees as we walked into the farmhouse kitchen that morning.

"Where have you been all night?" Frank demanded. If looks could kill, the sheriff would have arrested Frank for murdering us both.

"Eliza and I drove over the state line to see a justice of the peace last night," Sam said shakily. "We're married."

"You're *married*? To this . . . this *tramp*?"

"I love her."

"Oh, I'm sure you do!" His voice dripped with sarcasm. "Nevertheless, you're going straight to John Wakefield, and we'll just see about having this foolish little blunder annulled. I won't have her in my house."

"No," Sam said quietly. "No, I won't have our marriage annulled." He wrapped his brawny arm around my waist and pulled me close. "Eliza is my wife and I love her. If you can't accept that . . . then we'll both have to leave."

Sam and Frank stared at each other for a long, long time. I didn't realize until after I'd lived with Frank Wyatt for a few years what an incredibly brave thing Sam had done. When he took a stand against his father that morning, he risked losing everything he had—for my sake. I also didn't realize at the time what a rare thing it was for Frank to back down and give in to his son. But he did.

"All right, but I promise you this," Frank said, waving his finger in Sam's face. "I'll be counting carefully for the next nine months, and if she produces a baby one day before that time, I'll toss both her and the kid out in the gutter where they belong."

Thankfully, Jimmy was born one week after our first anniversary.

Except for the hateful stares of my father-in-law, I was very content in my marriage. I had the home I'd always longed for—even if it did include Frank Wyatt. From the very first time I stepped foot in Sam's house, I knew I never wanted to live anywhere else. It's not that everything was fancy and new—it wasn't. The wallpaper was faded, and there were worn spots in the carpet, and the wooden stairs creaked when you climbed them, but that was exactly what I loved about it. All my life I'd lacked a history and permanence, but I saw both of those things in every object in the house. I made up stories about all the people who'd lived here before me and the history of the furnishings they'd left behind. I didn't want to change a single thing. Every night as I would lay in Sam's arms and hear the train whistle in the distance beyond the orchard, I'd remember the loneliness and longing I'd felt all my life and I'd wonder if the people on that train were gazing at my farmhouse and wishing they were me.

The first winter Sam and I were married I sent a note to Aunt Peanut at the circus' winter address in Georgia.

Dear Aunt Peanut,

I just wanted to let you know I'm alive and well and very happy. I'm married to a really nice man and I live in a beautiful house in the country. Tell Charlie and the Gambrini family and everyone else I said "Hi."

Love,

Eliza

I didn't put a return address on it, and I mailed it from a town ten miles away from Deer Springs when I went there to see the doctor. I'd learned I was expecting Jimmy, and for some unknown reason Frank Wyatt had forbidden me to see Dr. Gilbert in Deer Springs.

Sam looked scared half to death when I told him he was going to be a father. "What's the matter, Sam? Don't you want kids?" I asked.

"No . . . I don't know. I guess I never thought . . . No."

"But why not? What are you afraid of?"

He didn't answer. The pain in Sam's eyes was so sharp I ached for him. I wished that I loved him the way he loved me because maybe then I could take away all the sorrow he had stored up inside himself. Sam finally walked out of our bedroom and out into the night, and he was gone for a long, long time. He was real tender with me while I was pregnant, though, like he thought he might hurt the baby if he hugged me too hard.

When my time came, Frank made Sam drive all the way to the neighboring town in the middle of the night to fetch a doctor. Through all my long hours of labor I kept thinking about my own mama, about how she had abandoned me, and I realized that I was as scared about having this baby as Sam was. When the doctor finally laid little Jimmy in my arms I cried, overwhelmed by the measureless love I felt for him. Yet at the same time I shuddered in fear at the thought that I might hurt him, lie to him, maybe even abandon him like my mama had abandoned me. It was terrifying to love someone so very much.

"What's the matter?" Sam asked when he saw me weeping over Jimmy that first night.

"I guess I'm scared, too," I admitted. "Being a mother is hard for me because I grew up without one."

Sam sat down on the bed beside me, a puzzled look on his face. "But I thought you said your whole family died in the influenza epidemic?"

He'd caught me in a lie! I panicked. "Um . . . no . . . that was my step-mother," I said quickly. "And she was never much of a mother to me." I needed to change the subject, fast. I lifted Jimmy and handed him to Sam before he could protest. "Here . . . you hold him."

Jimmy squirmed, then settled into his father's strong arms. He was awake, and he looked up at Sam as if memorizing his face. Sam's eyes filled with tears. "My goodness . . . my goodness . . ." he whispered. "He's so small. And I don't know how to be a good father. I'm so afraid I'll . . ."

I'd lived with Frank Wyatt long enough by then to understand why Sam was so scared. I thought of the advice Aunt Peanut had once given my father.

"You don't have to be scared, Sam," I told him. "Just be the daddy you always wished you'd had. If you wished your daddy had tucked you into bed at night, then tuck little Jimmy in. If you wished your daddy had taken you fishing, then take him fishing. That's all you have to do."

"Really?" he whispered.

"Yes. That's all there is to it."

From the day the children were born, Sam loved each of them with his whole heart. He never said the words out loud, probably because he'd never heard them from his own father and didn't know how, but I could see how much he loved them. If he lost patience with one of them he'd quietly walk away rather than lose his temper, and I admired him for that. He never once laid a hand on any of them in anger. When Becky Jean was born he just stared and stared at her with tears rolling down his cheeks. "A girl . . . a beautiful little girl!" he murmured. "She doesn't look real, Eliza. She looks like . . . like a little angel laying there!"

I felt the same love and fear that Sam did. I would go into my kids' rooms at night and watch them sleep, marveling at the fact that my children were part of me, yet they weren't. It terrified me to know how much they needed me, depended on me. I was so afraid that I'd disappoint them, maybe even fail them. Sometimes I'd remember how my daddy used to look at me with fear in his eyes and I wondered if it was for that very same reason.

Once, I came real close to telling Sam the truth about my past. Jimmy had just turned four and Luke was two when I learned that a competitor's circus was coming to the county fairgrounds. I was so excited to think that Sam and I could sit in the bleachers together watching the circus with our two boys—just like all the families I used to envy. I'd planned to wait until I was curled up beside Sam in bed at night, then tell him how this would all be a dream come true for me. But before I had a chance to confess, an advance man for the circus came through Deer Springs and knocked on our kitchen door just as we sat down to lunch.

"Good afternoon, folks. I'm with the Gentry Brothers' Circus and we'll be performing over at the county fairgrounds next month. I'd like to offer some free passes for your entire family if you'll let us post a bill on your barn out there."

Frank flew into a terrible rage, bellowing about how circus performers strutted around with hardly any clothes on, how they all lived such immoral lifestyles, and how disgraceful it was for Christian people to even consider attending a circus. He yelled so loud he made little Luke cry. I watched my father-in-law toss that poor man out on his ear and I knew that I could never breathe one word about growing up in the circus. Nor would my children ever get the chance to see one as long as their grandfather was alive.

———

My husband worked his entire life to please his father—an impossible task since Frank Wyatt was impossible to please. Sam never really did feel his father's love or approval, even as he lay dying. And he never should have gotten sick in the first place.

It started out as just a simple cut on his foot—a nail or something that had poked through the worn-out sole of his boot and sliced into him. His foot hurt him, but he kept right on working, limping around the barn as he shoveled out manure and milked the cows.

"Guess I need a new pair of boots," he said that night, showing me the hole in his sole. I doctored the cut on his foot but neither one of us thought much about it. It was September, a busy time of year in the orchard, and Sam kept on limping around, wearing those same boots because there wasn't any time to run into Deer Springs for a new pair.

A few days later he woke up with a low-grade fever. He complained of a stiff jaw and sore neck, and said he ached all over. We both thought he had the flu. I could tell Sam felt miserable, but

LYNN AUSTIN

he dragged himself outside to do a full day's work, fever or no fever, because his father expected him to. He got worse and worse.

One night Sam's moaning woke me up. His fever wasn't all that high but he was sweating so much he'd soaked all the bed sheets. His heart raced a mile a minute.

"Sam, what's the matter? What's wrong?"

He couldn't answer. The muscles in his neck and jaw went into such a horrible spasm that it distorted his face and froze his jaw. I leaped out of bed and began to dress. "I'm going for the doctor."

"No . . ." he moaned.

"Why not? Sam, I'm scared! What if. . . ?" It terrified me to think that it might be lockjaw, but I didn't want to say it out loud and upset Sam. "Listen, if I go get Dr. Gilbert in Deer Springs I can be back in half an hour."

"My father . . . won't allow . . ." he finally managed to say.

I didn't know what to do. All my instincts urged me to go get help but every time I mentioned going for the doctor it seemed to upset Sam even more.

He was no better in the morning. As soon as I heard my father-in-law stirring I ran downstairs to confront him.

"Where's my breakfast?" Frank asked when he saw me. "And where's Sam?"

"He can't get out of bed." My voice shook with fear. "He's sick—terribly, horribly sick. He needs a doctor."

"Sick! The cows have to be milked! And I need him in the orchard!" He glared at me as if Sam's illness was all my fault.

"He can't work. Go upstairs and see for yourself."

Frank grunted in disgust as if I was a silly, hysterical woman, then turned away. "He's a strong boy. He'll be fine in a day or two."

"He's not fine!" I yelled. "Go look at him! You have to send for a doctor!"

Frank's eyes flashed in anger as he whirled around, wagging his finger in my face. "Don't you *ever* tell me what to do!" He slammed the kitchen door on his way out.

I had my own chores to finish and meals to fix and kids to tend to, but every time I checked on Sam that day his condition was worse. The muscle spasms spread to his abdomen and legs and back, and they were so violent and so painful that his body went stiff as a board and his back arched clear off the bed. Sam was awake and alert—and in agony.

I watched for my father-in-law all afternoon, planning to confront him again the moment I saw him, but he stayed out in the orchard all day and didn't come back to the house until suppertime. I would have loaded up the kids and gone for help long before I did but Frank had the team of horses with him, and I didn't know how to drive the truck.

I waited until Frank said grace at supper time, then told him as calmly as I could, "Sam needs a doctor. I . . . I think he has lockjaw."

Frank reached for the mashed potatoes without even looking up at me. "I suppose you're a medical expert now?"

"No . . . but it doesn't take an expert to see how sick he is." I'd promised myself I wouldn't cry but I couldn't stop my tears. "Please, Mr. Wyatt, he's in so much pain. I can't stand to watch him suffering."

Frank continued to eat in silence.

"Please," I begged. "Please let me drive into town and fetch the doctor."

He raised his head and his voice. "You will not touch my truck or my horses! My son does not need a doctor!"

I knew then what I had to do. As soon as I'd tucked my kids in bed that night, I quietly left the house through the front door and ran all the way into Deer Springs. I was so distraught, shaking from head to toe with exhaustion and rage and fear, that it took me several minutes to convince Dr. Gilbert that I wasn't the one who needed medical care.

"No, please, Dr. Gilbert. It's my husband, Sam, who needs your help, not me."

"Sam Wyatt?"

"Yes. I think he has lockjaw. I think he's dying. *Please* come."

He asked me to describe Sam's symptoms and I knew by the grim look on his face as I told him, that I had cause for concern. He opened his cupboard and began packing things into his medical bag as he questioned me.

"Does Frank Wyatt know you're here?" he asked me when he'd finished.

"No. He refused to let me get help. I had to walk all the way here. He wouldn't even go upstairs and see how sick Sam was."

Dr. Gilbert shook his head. His clamped lips and angry eyes told me that he was furious. "Frank may not let me through the door, you know."

"You have to try, Dr. Gilbert. Please don't let Sam die!" I was nearly hysterical.

He gripped my shoulders, and his firm hold reassured me. "I'll do my best, Mrs. Wyatt. Listen, perhaps you should have some brandy before we go."

"I'll be fine. Just hurry."

It took no time at all to drive there in Dr. Gilbert's car. I convinced him to park on the road so my father-in-law wouldn't hear us, and we walked up the driveway in the dark. Frank's bedroom was right off the kitchen, so I sneaked Dr. Gilbert in through the front door and hurried him up the stairs.

Sam looked even worse than when I'd left him. He turned to us as we came into the bedroom and I saw the panic in his eyes, then his back arched horribly. "Help me!" he slurred as his jaw locked in a grimace of pain.

Dr. Gilbert examined him gently, but the slightest touch sent Sam's muscles into violent spasms. I stood beside the bed, wringing my hands, then nearly jumped out of my skin when I suddenly heard Frank's booming voice behind me.

"What are you doing in my house, Gilbert?"

Dr. Gilbert slowly turned to face him. "I'm treating your son—"

"No, you're not! We don't need you here! Get out!"

"Frank, your son has tetanus," he said quietly. "He's very ill. I'm going to give him an injection of antitoxin and—"

My scream interrupted him. Sam had started going into convulsions. His skin turned a horrible bluish gray as he struggled to breathe.

"He's having a seizure," Dr. Gilbert said. "It's cutting off his oxygen." He grasped Sam's shoulders to hold him down.

I'd never felt so scared or so helpless in my life. When the seizure finally ended, Dr. Gilbert quickly prepared a hypodermic needle.

"I'm going to give you some tetanus antitoxin, Sam. Then something to help relax your muscles."

I glanced over my shoulder, worried that Frank would try to stop him, but my father-in-law had left the room.

Dr. Gilbert did everything he could for Sam that night. He even showed me how to make a poultice and apply it to the cut on Sam's foot. But I could tell by the way the doctor gripped my shoulders again to steady me when it was time for him to leave, that he was just as worried about Sam as I was.

"I have to be honest with you, Mrs. Wyatt, and tell you that your husband is a very sick man. Tetanus antitoxin is most effective when it's given as soon as the symptoms appear, but . . . well, that decision was taken out of our hands." He sighed, then picked up his medical bag. "I'll be back first thing in the morning."

My husband's illness was too far gone for the antitoxin to work. Dr. Gilbert couldn't do a thing for him and neither could I. Sam died a horrible, painful death as the seizures finally became so violent he stopped breathing. Yet he was awake and aware of everything that was happening to him until the very end. The last words he heard me say were, "I love you, Sam."

The day he died I was so distraught I raged at my father-in-law in front of my kids. "It's all your fault!" I screamed. "Sam died because you wouldn't go for help! You killed your own son! If you had gone for a doctor sooner and Sam had gotten the antitoxin, he never would have died!"

Frank didn't respond to my outburst. He stared right through me with haunted eyes, and I had to wonder if he'd even heard a word I'd said. The hateful, manipulative Frank Wyatt I'd lived with these past years died with his son, leaving a broken, embittered old man in his place. What good was his orchard and everything he'd built without a son to inherit it? Still, I didn't feel one shred of pity for Frank. He'd reaped what he'd sown.

My father-in-law had hardly seemed to notice my kids before Sam died. I always figured he hated them because he hated me. But as he stood beside the graves of his wife and two sons he slowly looked up and saw Jimmy and Luke clinging to me, their faces pale with grief. He looked at his grandsons, really looked at them, for the very first time and I think he suddenly realized they were all he had left.

"Oh, dear God . . ." he whispered.

Frank seemed different after Sam died—not any kinder, and certainly not any warmer or more loving toward me or the kids. But he was a broken man, and he and I both knew it. We lived together like strangers in a boardinghouse, rarely talking, seeing each other only at mealtimes.

Then one cold November day a year later, Jimmy found his grandfather sprawled on the floor of the barn. I hurried outside when I heard my son's frantic yells, but the moment I looked into the cold, vacant eyes of the man I'd hated, I knew he was dead. I didn't feel one bit sorry. In fact, I found myself wishing he had suffered twice as much as poor Sam had suffered. I was about to turn my back on him when I noticed that Frank's hands were empty. They lay open, palms up, and there was nothing in them. He had grasped and controlled and manipulated with those hands all his life to get his own way, and now they were empty. Frank Wyatt's orchard and everything he had worked for had been left behind for someone else.

PART IX

Wyatt Orchards

Winter 1931-1932

"While the earth remaineth, seedtime and harvest,

and cold and heat, and summer and winter, and day and night

shall not cease."

GENESIS 8:22

— CHAPTER NINETEEN —

Aunt Batty and I sat at the kitchen table as the sun rose that morning. The cows needed to be milked, the horses had to be fed and watered, and the boys had to eat breakfast and get ready for school. But I felt too weary to move. Telling my story after all those years left me feeling empty and drained. My mama had left me and Sam had left me, and now Gabe had gone off and left me, too. What was wrong with me that made everybody turn their back and walk away from me?

"You were very blessed to have had parents who loved you so much," Aunt Batty said quietly.

"Are you crazy?" I asked. "Weren't you listening to me? Daddy never once told me he loved me, and Mama said it all the time and then she abandoned me!"

"You're standing too close to see it, Toots. Your father showed you how much he loved you in a hundred different ways."

"How? Name one!"

"He guided your decisions, raised you by the Good Book, took you to church. He made sure you didn't grow up to become a circus oddity, but instead a warm, loving woman who could become the person God intended you to be. Most of all, he let you go when the time came. He did everything a good parent should do. That's why you're such a wonderful parent yourself. You learned how to love from your daddy."

"But he lied to me about my mama!"

"Are you sure that's the way it was?" she asked gently.

When I thought about it, I had to admit that Daddy had never exactly said Mama was dead. I slowly pulled myself to my feet and opened one of the stove lids to put another stick of wood on the fire. "Well, I'm sure that my mother abandoned me," I said, closing the lid again.

Aunt Batty stood, too, and opened the dish cupboard, talking to me as she set the table for breakfast. "It looks to me like your mama knew she couldn't take proper care of you, and she loved you enough to give you to someone who could. My sister gave up her own chance at happiness for her child's sake, too. You know all about that kind of mother-love, don't you, Eliza? Just look at how hard you've been working to hang on to this orchard and provide for your kids. Your mother didn't abandon you, Toots. She made the greatest sacrifice a mother could make."

I watched Aunt Batty putting plates around the table and saw that she had taken out one too many. She started placing it where Gabe always sat, then caught herself.

"Gabe abandoned me," I said, fighting tears.

"Well, it looks that way right now," she said. "But Gabe loved all of us. Maybe he had a good reason for what he did. Maybe he made a sacrifice for the people he loved, too."

"Ha! I doubt that! From what Sheriff Foster said, it looks to

me like Gabe was trying to save his own skin and keep from getting arrested."

Aunt Batty didn't reply. She put silverware by all the places
and poured milk in the kids' glasses while I got out the frying pan
and started cracking eggs into a bowl to scramble them. When I
realized that I'd added enough eggs for Gabe, miscounting just
like Aunt Batty had, I covered my face.

"What am I going to do without him?" I wept.

Aunt Batty took me in her arms. "You've been depending on
Gabe's help," she said gently, "instead of on God's. But He knows
all about how you feel. Jesus suffered the pain of being abandoned when He hung on the cross for us. He cried out, 'My God,
my God, why have you forsaken me?' He made that sacrifice so
that He could say to His children, 'I will never leave you or forsake
you.' When everyone else is gone, Eliza, God is still here."

She led me back to a chair and sat me down, then took over
cooking the eggs. "God knew when it was time for Gabe to leave,"
she continued, "just like He knew when it was time for Walter to
go. God did it so that you and I would both turn to Him for
strength and discover the strength He's been trying to build inside us all this time. Look back on your life, Toots, and think
about all the experiences God gave you—the good ones and the
bad ones—and you'll see how they've shaped you into the woman
you are today. Accept those experiences as His daily bread. Thank
Him for them. Then be the person He created you to be. Growing
up without a home has given you the will and the determination
you'll need to run this place. . . . And your juggling skills will
come in handy, too."

Aunt Batty smiled as she tried to juggle the broken eggshells,
and I had to laugh as they all fell to the tabletop. She giggled
along with me.

"Will you teach me how to do that sometime, Toots?" she asked.

"Sure, Aunt Batty."

She gave the eggs in the frying pan a quick stir, then took a loaf of bread out of the bread box and began slicing it for toast. "Listen," she said, "all these troubles you've been having aren't a punishment from God. He wants to use them to draw you closer to himself—just like your mama's illness, which was a terrible tragedy, forced you to draw closer to your daddy."

I dried my eyes and stood up to help her. "I guess I haven't thought much about God these past few years," I said. "The way my father-in-law talked about God made Him seem like somebody I didn't really want to know."

"That's because Frank read the Bible and went to church, but he didn't know God. He just had religion. Eliza, it's good that you know about the Bible and that your daddy took you to church, but you need to get to know God."

"How do I do that?"

"Ask Him for help when you need it. Talk things over with Him the same way you used to talk with your Aunt Peanut or with Gabe. You have to learn to trust God to catch you when you feel like you're going to fall, just like those acrobats trusted each other. God may be big and strong, but He'll never crush you. Everything God does in our lives is perfect, even if doesn't always look that way on the outside. Your friends in the sideshow taught you that."

"I miss them all so much," I said. "They were my family, and I haven't been able to talk about any of them for ten years."

"You'll miss Gabe, too," she said, laying her hand on my shoulder. "We all will. But even if Gabe was still here, he couldn't meet all of your needs. Only God can do that. Gabe could help you work in the orchard, but only God can make the apples grow."

Later that morning I took a walk out in the orchard. I knew it was high time I talked to God. I told Him all the things I was sorry for, all the things I was afraid of, and I asked Him to help me keep this orchard going. When I opened my eyes and looked around, I saw that Aunt Batty was right—God was right there beside me. The tree branches were His hands, reaching out to me—and He held the gift of an apple in every single one of them.

———

One cool, fall morning the apple pickers began to arrive. At first I felt nervous about trying to manage the harvest all by myself, but then I started thinking about how smoothly the Bennett Brothers' Circus had run. I realized that no one person had tried to run that huge operation all alone, but everyone had worked together like a team, each person doing the job he did best. Some of my apple pickers had been coming to Wyatt Orchards for years and years and probably knew a lot more about it than I did, so I divvied up the work and paid the experienced ones a little bit extra to be my foremen. They thought of things I would have forgotten all about and kept me from making a lot of mistakes.

When it came time to take the apples to the open-air market, I thought about the fast-talking ballyhoo of the sideshow hawker with his *"Hurry, hurry . . . don't miss your chance,"* and when I realized that those fast-talking apple buyers were putting on an act just like that hawker, I wasn't afraid of them anymore. Aunt Peanut and Gloria the fat lady and Albert the albino had faced all those gawking people with strength and dignity, knowing they were just as good as the next fellow, so I stood tall and proud, too, when those buyers started gawking at me, a woman selling apples. I got the price I wanted and made enough money to pay my workers and buy the coal and other supplies my family would need for the winter. We didn't have any extras, but thank God we had enough.

Once I'd sold the apples, I swallowed my pride and went over to talk to Alvin Greer and some of my other neighbors about working together to slaughter the pigs and pick the corn. I let my neighbors borrow some of Frank's fancy equipment, and asked them for their advice about running things in return. Frank Wyatt had lived alone, worked alone, and died alone, and I made up my mind I would never be like him.

All through the harvest, Aunt Batty worked like a trooper right alongside me. The kids and I had all grown to love her, and since she'd retired from writing books, I begged her to stay with us and live with us and be our adopted grandmother. My daddy had never been very good at telling me he loved me, but I remembered how I'd longed to hear him say it, and I started telling my kids I loved them—all the time. I told Aunt Batty, too.

Gradually, the pain I felt over losing Gabe began to heal—just as my grief had healed after Sam died. I still got an empty feeling whenever I went into the workshop where Gabe used to sleep, or whenever I saw Myrtle and her calf, or when I watched the boys push Becky on her swing. But I only thought about Gabe once or twice a day now, instead of once or twice every hour, so I knew that my grief was slowly easing. Maybe one of these days I wouldn't think about him at all.

Around Thanksgiving time, the strangest letter came in the mail one day from the United States Army in Washington, D.C. It was addressed to Frank Wyatt, but I tore it open and quickly scanned it to get the gist of it.

It said the government was very sorry to inform Frank, but his son Matthew Wyatt had died in the war after all, in the Battle of St. Mihiel. Some new information had come to light after all this time, which revealed that a mistake had been made. The army now had evidence to prove that Matthew Wyatt's remains had been erroneously identified as another man's and were laid to rest in a cemetery in France under the wrong name. The army regretted the mistake and any unnecessary grief this news might cause.

I said a little prayer before I showed the letter to Aunt Batty, knowing how much she had loved Matthew, and knowing she might take this news kind of hard. She looked up at me with tears in her eyes after she'd read it and said, "I think you'd better show this to John Wakefield right away, Toots. I think this is the answer to your prayers."

As I drove into town, I couldn't help but wonder if Gabe had something to do with this strange turn of events. I quickly pushed the thought from my mind, though. I'd learned over the past few months to push all thoughts of Gabe aside as quickly as they came. The less I thought about him, the better off I was.

I found Mr. Wakefield working behind his desk in his cluttered office. "You look happier than I've seen you looking in a long time, Mrs. Wyatt," he said as he welcomed me in. "Are you bringing good news?"

"Well, I think so . . . in a way." I handed him the letter, then sat down to wait while he read it. He removed his spectacles when he finished and shook his head.

"What a pity. So often in my line of work I find that good news comes all wrapped up in the same package with tragic news . . . and that's true in this case, too, isn't it? Poor Matthew."

"I know. Aunt Batty told me so much about him that I almost feel as if I knew him . . . even though I never met him."

"Your husband's family has seen a great deal of tragedy, Mrs. Wyatt. Let's hope that it's all behind you now." His mournful, hound-dog face brightened a bit. "Because now that we have this letter, I'll finally be able to settle Frank's estate. The orchard is all yours, Eliza. Free and clear."

I jumped out of my chair and gave John Wakefield a big old hug.

———

"I've found our Christmas tree," Aunt Batty announced a few days before Christmas. She'd been out tramping around in the snow-covered woods near Walter's Pond for the past couple of days, searching for one. "It's going to take all five of us to haul it home, though," she said, "so everybody dress warm. And Luke, we'll need to borrow your sled."

"Maybe Winky could pull it for us," Becky said, "like a reindeer!" Everyone laughed—except Winky.

There were six inches of snow on the ground, so the kids piled onto Luke's sled and rode it to the bottom of the hill, whooping and squealing all the way down. They waited beside the frozen pond for Aunt Batty and me to catch up with them.

"Oh, aren't the woods beautiful?" I said as we followed her into the grove of trees. The snow looked fresh and clean and white, and it sparkled in the sunlight like sequins on a circus costume. Winky picked up a trail of some kind and wandered into the bushes with his nose to the ground.

"I hope he's not going to rouse another skunk," Aunt Batty said. Against my will, I thought of Gabe and felt a wave of sadness.

"Hey, look! What kind of animal tracks are these?" Luke asked as he crouched beside the path.

"I have a book at home with pictures of all kinds of animal prints," Aunt Batty told him. "You boys study those carefully and remember what they look like so you can look them up when we get home."

"You sound just like a schoolmarm," I teased. "And you thought you'd never be one."

"Well, who would have ever thought!" She laughed, shaking her head.

We had walked a little further when Jimmy suddenly stopped. "Whoa, these are man-size footprints!" he said. We all huddled around to see. Jimmy was right—the trail of prints that led off into the bushes where Winky had disappeared were much too large to have been made by Aunt Batty's feet. I heard Winky barking in the distance.

"Probably another hobo," I said, "looking for firewood and a warm place to camp." Then I quickly changed the subject before someone mentioned Gabe. "This is a pretty little clearing, isn't it?" I asked. "We should come down here for a picnic next summer. So how much farther to this tree of yours, Aunt Batty?" The path was growing narrower, making it hard for Luke to pull his sled.

"That's our Christmas tree right there," she said, pointing. "Think you boys can chop it down for us?"

She let Jimmy and Luke take turns chopping, and by the time we'd all heaved and shoved that snow-covered pine tree onto the sled and up the hill to the house, we were all sticky with pitch and soaking wet from the snow that coated the branches. Aunt Batty made hot apple cider to warm us up. We set up the tree in the parlor and decorated it that night after supper using a box of ornaments I'd found in the attic.

"These decorations belonged to Lydia—your grandmother," Aunt Batty explained to the kids as they unwrapped the shining glass balls from their tissue paper wrappings. "Your grandma was a beautiful woman and she loved beautiful things." Aunt Batty sat on the sofa, stringing popcorn. Every time she dropped a piece, Winky gobbled it up.

"Oh, look, an angel," I said, pulling it from the carton. "This should go on the very top, don't you think? Come here, Becky, and I'll boost you up."

"We had a real angel come and stay with us and help us once, didn't we?" she said as I lifted her in my arms. I thought about the night she'd poked Gabe in the hand with her fork to see if he was real and I smiled, even though my eyes filled with tears.

"Yes, we sure did. Like Aunt Batty said, God sends us His messengers to let us know that He cares about us."

When we'd finished decorating the tree, the kids gathered around Aunt Batty as she read the Christmas story from the Bible. I sat in my rocking chair with fat old Queen Esther purring away on my lap and looked at my beautiful, crazy family. I'd had the idea that a family should be perfect, with a pretty mama and a handsome daddy and kids that were all sugary-sweet and dressed up real nice. A family couldn't possibly have a chain-smoking chimpanzee, a clown for a daddy, and a midget for a mama. But as I looked at my three ragamuffin kids in their hand-me-downs, at funny old Aunt Batty with her nutty ways, at our one-eyed hunting dog and two overweight cats with mittens for kittens, I was sure of two things—what I had with Daddy and Aunt Peanut was a family, and so was this. I loved every one of them. Wyatt Orchards wasn't my home, this house wasn't even my home. Home is where your family is—the people you love and who love you. And even if I lost everything I owned tomorrow, I'd still have riches beyond measure.

My thoughts made me so teary-eyed that I decided to take the scuttle full of cinders outside to empty it before someone noticed that I was crying. I needed to fetch one last pail of coal before heading up to bed, anyway.

My mind was a hundred miles away as I walked out onto the back porch, so when the large shape of a man suddenly emerged from the shadows it scared me half to death! I dropped the coal scuttle down the steps as I cried out.

"I'm sorry, Eliza!" a soft, familiar voice said. "I didn't mean to startle you."

"Gabe?"

It was him! The next moment I was in his arms, kissing him like I had on that frosty spring morning in the orchard more than six months ago. I thought I must be dreaming, but I felt the grip of his strong arms around me, felt the passion and warmth of his kiss, and I knew that Gabe was real. I also knew that my heart hadn't changed in the months he had been gone. I still loved him, plain and simple.

Gabe pulled away first and looked into my eyes. "I need to explain why I left, Eliza. I want to tell you everything this time. No more lies. My real name isn't Gabriel Harper. It's Matthew—"

"No! Stop right there!"

I freed myself from his arms. The joy I'd felt only seconds before turned to anger. I wouldn't let him deceive me a second time.

"I know very well you're not Matthew Wyatt," I said, seizing his right hand. "The real Matthew had part of his finger missing! The real Matthew Wyatt is dead!"

"I know he's dead," Gabe said softly. "He was my best friend . . . and he died saving my life. My name is Matthew Willis. My father is Edmund Willis, an attorney and political boss in Albany, New York. That's where I grew up."

He sounded sincere, but I was still wary of trusting him. I studied him as my eyes adjusted to the darkness. His hair needed to be trimmed again, and his chin had a day's growth of beard on it. He looked tired—and worried.

"The sheriff said you tried to steal my brother-in-law's name and his identity," I said. "Is that true?"

"Yes, it's true. I did 'steal' it, as you say. And I'd like to explain to you how and why that happened. . . . But can we go inside first, where it's warm? I've been standing out here for a couple of hours now, trying to get up the courage to knock on your door." Gabe stood with his shoulders all hunched up and I could see him shivering, but I still hesitated.

"No. I don't want you to come inside yet, Gabe. I don't want my kids to know you're here. You hurt them awfully bad when you left us like you did, without a word of apology or explanation."

"But I want to explain it to them now—"

"No. You'll have to explain it to me, first. Go build a fire in the workshop, and I'll come out and hear your story after they're in bed."

It was hard not to let my excitement—or my fear—show as I went through the nightly routine of tucking my kids into bed. I could still feel Gabe's lips on mine, his arms holding me tightly, and my heart wanted to soar like the Flying Falangas on their trapezes. But I warned my heart not to even shinny up that rope again until I'd heard Gabe's story.

I tried to be real quiet as I put on my coat and boots to go back outside, but Winky waddled out to the kitchen and gave me away when he started barking. A moment later, Aunt Batty stuck her fluffy head out of her bedroom door. She looked at me curiously, and before I even had a chance to come up with an excuse for why I was going outside, she broke into a huge grin.

"Gabe's back, isn't he!" she said. I nodded sheepishly. "Oh, I just knew it! I could tell by the way Winky was barking this afternoon that those footprints belonged to someone he knew!" She gave me a quick hug, then said, "Well, don't just stand there—go to him!"

I brought Winky with me. It wasn't so much my choice as his. As soon as Winky saw Gabe sitting on the cot in the workshop he jumped into his arms and started licking him all over, his stubby tail whirling in happy circles. Gabe laughed—that deep, rumbling laugh that I loved so much—and at that moment he could have told me he was Al Capone or "Baby Face" Nelson and I wouldn't have cared. But I had a feeling that I would hear the truth this time. I sat down on the chair across from him.

"I found your notebook in the stove," I told him. "It didn't burn up. Was that the true story of why you left home?"

"Yes. I enlisted in the army because I was ashamed of what I'd done to my father's political opponent. I met Matthew Wyatt in basic training—we were bunkmates. People mixed us up all the time because we were about the same age and height, we both had dark hair and eyes, and we were both named Matthew. Even our last names, Wyatt and Willis, were similar. Of course, your brother-in-law was a lot stronger and more muscular than I was, since I was a city boy and he'd grown up on a farm. And he had lost part of his index finger.

"We spent a lot of time together," Gabe continued, scratching Winky's ears, "and we found out we had a lot more in common than our first names. Our fathers may have lived in different places and worked in different professions, but in many ways they were the same man. And your brother-in-law and I had both enlisted to escape from our fathers—and to try to figure out who we really were.

"Matthew and I spent nearly two years together. We sailed to France on the same ship, spent several months in the same training camp, fought in the same battalion. The war changed both of us. I don't think anybody can ever be the same after an experience like that. Matthew found out how homesick he was. He'd seen the world and he didn't care for it. All he wanted in life was to go home and live on a farm again. He used to stop and gaze at the cows and horses as we marched past them, and he didn't care if he got into trouble for it or not.

"I was glad that he'd figured out what he wanted to do after the war. I still had no idea what I would do. But then one day Matthew confided in me that he was illegitimate and that his father had disinherited him when he'd found out. Matthew knew that Wyatt Orchards would never be his. I was with him when he got Aunt Batty's letter, telling him that his mother had died. I was with him in Paris when he typed the letter back to her. He wasn't the same after that. He kept saying he had no reason to go back to Deer Springs, no mother or father and no home to return to. His mother's death made him very depressed.

"But we were right in the thick of the war just then, and we were all depressed. We couldn't imagine that we'd ever have a life again, that there was still a world of beauty and hope beyond all the horror and killing and death. I was just as depressed about my own future as Matthew was. I wanted to be a writer, but I didn't think I deserved to be one after what I'd done to my father's political opponent. I couldn't return home any more than Matthew could. I knew the influence my father had over me, and I knew that if I went anywhere near Albany, I would never have a life of my own. Matthew and I talked about our futures a lot, but we decided nothing mattered because we were both certain we would die in France. If a bullet didn't get us, then one of the diseases in the trenches surely would."

Gabe paused for a moment. "But we did live, through several major battles—Cantigny, Belleau Wood, and finally St. Mihiel. Too many men we knew did die in those battles, though . . . friends we'd lived with since boot camp. At St. Mihiel our bunker took a direct hit. There were six of us in there together, and four of our buddies died instantly. They were . . . well, one look and I knew they were all dead. I took a shrapnel hit in the chest—the scar you saw—and another hit in the gut. A falling sandbag had broken my leg.

"Matthew was wounded, too, but when he saw that I was still alive and couldn't walk, he made up his mind to get me to an aid station. Bombs and artillery shells and bullets were flying thick over our heads, but he carried me in his arms about a half mile back from the front lines. Everyone always called me 'Willis,' but that day Matthew kept calling me 'Willie.'

" 'Hang on, Willie . . .' he kept saying. 'You're not going to die, Willie. I'm not going to let you die.' I believe I would have died, too, if it hadn't been for him.

"Just before we reached the aid station, Matthew did a strange thing. He stopped and laid me down on the ground for a moment, and I saw him fumbling inside his uniform for something. Then he ripped open my shirt and I felt his hands near my chest wound. I didn't know what he was doing. I screamed for him not to touch the shrapnel sticking out. I was in so much pain that I was starting to go into shock. I felt him put something around my neck and I vaguely remember him saying that now I could start all over again. 'No one will care what happens to me, Willie. My mother is dead and no one else cares if I live or die.'

"He picked me up again and ran a few more yards. He told me he could see the aid station ahead and the medics running toward us with stretchers. Then he collapsed to the ground. He landed on top of me and I passed out from the pain. When I awoke, a doctor told me I had survived the field surgery, and that they were shipping me by train to a French hospital.

" 'What about my friend?' I asked. 'The one who saved my life?' "

" 'I'm very sorry,' he told me. 'Your friend had internal injuries—a ruptured spleen, massive bleeding . . . He died during surgery.' "

"For the next few weeks I was extremely ill. The wound in my gut had punctured my intestine, and peritonitis set in. When I recovered enough to be sent home to the States, they asked me to sign my separation papers. That's when I saw the name they'd written on all my documents—Matthew Wyatt. I was going to correct their error, but then suddenly the memory came back to me of Matthew laying me on the ground, pulling something out from inside his shirt, slipping something around my neck. He had swapped dog tags with me.

"I knew why he'd done it. I didn't want to return home to my father, and Matthew's father would never welcome him home. I also realized that by this time my family had already received word that I was dead. I was still so angry with my father that I decided to play along with Matthew's idea. Let my father mourn his only son's death. It served him right. I would begin a new life with a new identity. I could be a writer now, and no one would ever know or care.

"They discharged me from the army hospital as Matthew Wyatt, born in Deer Springs to Lydia and Frank Wyatt. Whenever I published a story I used the pen name Gabriel Harper.

"At first I felt liberated by my new identity, but as time passed, I reached a point where I didn't know who I was anymore. The loneliness of not having a family ate away at me, and I longed to see my mother and younger sisters again, my aunt June and my uncle and cousins on the farm, the many friends I'd left behind in Albany. I was afraid to fall in love because I would have to be married under a false name, and then I didn't know if the marriage would even be legal. And what would my children's names be?

"My new friends in Chicago knew nothing at all about the real me, only the multitude of lies I'd told about myself. I saw what a mess I'd made, but I couldn't see a way out. Finally, in order to escape the guilt of living a lie, I left my new life behind, too, and rode the rails as a hobo.

"I knew exactly where I was going the night I came to Wyatt Orchards. I wanted to meet Frank and Sam Wyatt and see the place where Matthew had grown up. I'd started writing his story as if it were my own, and I was so confused about who I was and who he was that I thought maybe if I came here I could figure it all out. Besides, I told myself I owed it to Matthew to make sure his brother Sam was okay.

"But you know the rest, Eliza. Frank and Sam are both dead, and when I found out how badly you needed my help, I decided to stay. I needed to pay you back for saving my life—and to pay Matthew back, as well. And somewhere along the way I fell in love with you. I woke up delirious and the most incredible woman I'd ever met was holding me and crying with me. Becky and Luke kept calling me an angel, but I thought I'd died and you were the angel.

"When Sheriff Foster confronted me down at Aunt Batty's cottage and threatened to check up on me, I knew the masquerade was over. It was time to run. It was only a matter of time before the sheriff discovered my false identity. But I couldn't leave you, Eliza.

"The worst moment of all came the day I learned that my lies had prevented you and your kids from inheriting this place. Matthew was so sure his father had changed his will. Believe me, the last thing in the world I wanted to do was take this orchard away from you and your kids. But that's what my lies had done.

"I wanted to explain all this to you but I didn't know how you would react. I decided to go to Washington and set the record straight, but first we had a crop to bring in. I kept hoping the sheriff wouldn't track me down until after the harvest, but it didn't work out that way. He came back to arrest me. After Aunt Batty warned me, I used the money I'd earned from my hobo story to go to Washington and turn myself in. I didn't know what the consequences would be, if I'd go to jail for impersonating Matthew Wyatt all this time or not, so I decided not to write to you or contact you until I'd cleared my name. I'd messed up your life enough with my lies. I couldn't involve you further.

"When I'd finally straightened out the mess in Washington, I went home to New York to see my family. They'd already received a letter from the army explaining the mistake, so they'd had time to get used to the idea of me returning from the grave. My father reacted pretty much the way I'd expected him to—he was furious that I'd deceived him. I couldn't make him understand why I'd done it. If he was happy to learn that his only son was alive after all these years, he never showed it. But it surprised me to discover that I no longer hated him. The months that I'd spent here with you and Aunt Batty changed me. I hadn't been able to tell you who I was, but I was finally figuring it out for myself.

"I'd always pictured God like my father, controlling and manipulating everyone. I thought I needed to earn His approval, and that I would never be quite good enough. But the day I hung up that swing for Becky, Aunt Batty pointed to it and said, 'That's just what our heavenly Father is like. He loves doing things to delight His children.' She and I talked while I worked on her cottage and she showed me how to find His forgiveness. That's why I could forgive my father . . . and myself."

Gabe leaned forward, kneading his strong hands together as he spoke. "I spent the happiest months of my life here, and I never wanted to leave. But I was afraid to come back, Eliza. I didn't know if you could ever forgive me or not after I deserted you like I did. I love you, and I love your kids and Aunt Batty, and I'm so sorry that I hurt all of you. I wouldn't blame you if you couldn't forgive me, but—"

Gabe never had a chance to finish his sentence. I was in his arms, kissing him, telling him the best way I knew how that I loved him and that I forgave him.

The most wonderful Christmas present the kids and I could ever wish for had come home to live with us, for good.

— EPILOGUE —

Spring 1932

We all got out of bed early that fine spring morning—probably because we were all too excited to sleep—and we hurried to finish our chores so we could get an early start on our trip. I cooked breakfast and Aunt Batty packed us a picnic lunch and Becky was feeding Winky, Queen Esther, and Arabella when she made an amazing discovery.

"Mama! Daddy! Come look! Arabella has kittens!" Gabe had just come in from the barn with the boys and didn't even have his coat off yet. Becky called him "Daddy" so easily—all the kids did—ever since the day Gabe and I were married, four months ago. Aunt Batty and I still called him "Gabe" out of habit, but he said he liked that name best of all because it was his writing name. Batty lived in the farmhouse with us all the time now, and she let Gabe use her cottage to write his books.

"Don't tell me," Gabe said as he hung up his coat, "Have you and Aunt Batty been knitting again?"

"No, Daddy, they're *real* kitties! Come look!"

We all dropped what we were doing and went to look at Arabella's nest behind the stove. Sure enough, curled up beside the cat and all the mitten-kittens Aunt Batty had knit, were two tiny newborn kittens with orange and white stripes. They looked just like Arabella.

Aunt Batty's eyes were as huge as saucers. "Where on earth did *they* come from?" she exclaimed.

"Yeah, where did those kittens come from, Mama?" Luke asked.

Gabe and I looked at each other and smiled. We would have to explain a few things to them, especially since they'd be having a new baby brother or sister next fall. But we didn't have time for long explanations that morning.

"They came from God," I said simply. "That's where every good gift comes from. Now, come on, let's eat up. We'll have to get a move on if we're going to make it to the circus on time."

This day my dream would finally come true. We would have to drive more than fifty miles to where the Bennett Brothers' Circus was performing, but the trip would be worth every mile. I'd told Gabe and the kids all about Daddy and Aunt Peanut and Charlie and Zippy and the Gambrini family, and they could hardly wait to meet them all.

When we arrived at the fairgrounds later that afternoon, I felt like I'd come home. Everything was wonderfully familiar, from the patched-up sideshow tent to the warble of the calliope and the smell of cotton candy. By the time we'd parked the truck, the first performance was about to begin, so we quickly bought tickets and went straight inside the Big Top. Gabe held Becky on his lap, and he let the boys gorge themselves on cotton candy and Cracker Jack.

"They'll have a tummy ache for sure," I warned him.

"Aw, it's only once a year," Gabe said.

The kids were amazed when they saw the towering clown on stilts—and even more amazed when I proudly told them, "That's your granddaddy!" Tears filled my eyes as I watched my daddy perform. I'd watched him perform hundreds of times before, of course, but that day I saw for the very first time how good he was at making people laugh, how much he loved the work he did, and how much the audience loved him.

When the show ended, I led everybody inside the sideshow tent. I felt a little nervous about how my daddy would react after all this time, but I knew Aunt Peanut would welcome me home with open arms—and she did. In fact, everybody in the whole sideshow had gathered around me to hug me and meet my family, and the ticket hawker had to stop letting paying customers inside. Nobody wanted to pay to see a midget, an albino, a tattooed snake woman, and a rubber lady all bawling their eyes out. The only ones who stayed dry-eyed were the two-headed calf and the Abominable Snowman.

I finally got up my courage to ask Aunt Peanut about my father. "How's Daddy? Is he mad at me for leaving him like I did? Do . . . do you think he'll want to see me?"

"*Mad* at you! Want to *see* you. . . !" she sputtered. "Oh, honey, this is the answer to all his prayers! Come on." She took me by the hand and dragged me out the rear door.

"Your father cried like a baby the night you left," Aunt Peanut said as we crossed the grass to the pad room. "When he ran back to his rail car after the performance and your mama told him you were gone, he put his face in his hands and sobbed. The only other time I ever saw Henry cry like that was when I showed him the letter you sent to me in Georgia. He wouldn't give that letter back to me, you know. He still carries it around with him."

The tent flap was open and I saw Daddy in his baggy trousers and floppy shoes, talking to Charlie. Charlie saw me first, and when his jaw dropped open in astonishment, Daddy whirled around to see why. I think he expected to see Gunther's tigers on the loose from the stunned look on Charlie's face. When he saw me instead, he looked every bit as stunned as Charlie.

"Eliza?" Daddy staggered to one side, like his legs were about to give out. I ran to him.

"Daddy!"

We clung to each other as if neither one of us wanted to let go. I inhaled his wonderfully familiar scent, a mixture of greasepaint and the Macassar oil he still used on his hair.

"Daddy, this is my family," I said when I could talk again. "This is my husband, Gabe, and this is Jimmy, Luke, and Becky Jean . . . and this is our Aunt Batty."

Daddy smiled as he shook Gabe's hand. He pulled a quarter out of each of the kids' ears and ruffled their hair. "These two have Yvette's hair," he murmured when he got to Luke and Becky.

"Yes, but Luke has your smile—don't you think so, Daddy?"

"Just as long as none of them inherits my nose!" he said, honking his phony red one.

We had a lot of catching up to do. Charlie couldn't wait to take Gabe and the kids to meet Zippy, and Aunt Batty and Aunt Peanut hit it off from the start, chattering away like two long-lost friends. Daddy and I finally had a moment alone.

"I've missed you, Eliza," he said. I could see the love in his eyes, even though he would never be able to find the words to say it.

"I've missed you, too, Daddy."

"Are you remembering to go to church every Sunday?" he asked gruffly. "Are you living by the Good Book?"

"Yes, I'm trying to. Aunt Batty is teaching me how."

Daddy's eyes filled with tears as he took both of my hands in his. "You look happy, Eliza. You know, that's all I ever wanted for you. That's all I ever dreamed of for you—that you would be happy."

Tears streaked his white makeup as they spilled down his face, and I realized that I didn't want his greasepaint to wash off. I loved my father's silly, smiling clown face most of all.

When I thought about happiness it wasn't the orchard or the big white house with the green shutters that I pictured—or any of the other things that had once seemed so important to me. I thought of my family—my circus family and my new family—and I smiled through my tears.

"Yes, Daddy. I'm very, very happy."

Their Eyes Were Opened to the World for the First Time

Becoming a Woman of Grace in a Time of Turmoil

Living in 1960s Atlanta, Mary Swan Middleton has it all until an unexpected tragedy strikes and Mary's eyes are opened to the world around her. Suddenly, the turmoil of a country coming to terms with segregation, the pain of the victims of prejudice, and the struggle of becoming a woman in the Sixties are thrust upon her. With no mother left to guide her, can Mary find her own way through this tumultuous time?

The Swan House by Elizabeth Musser

Page-turning Fiction From Kristen Heitzmann

Driven by hope and vengeance, Carina Maria DiGratia sets out for a new life in Crystal, Colorado. But she soon finds that the town nicknamed the Diamond of the Rockies is anything but luxurious. Realizing she can no longer depend on her family's reputation, she is forced to rely on the help of others. Two men vie for her trust, but both hide a secret. Will Carina learn the truth—and confront the secrets hidden in her heart—in time to prevent tragedy?

The Rose Legacy by Kristen Heitzmann